MURDER GONE COLD

NEW YORK TIMES **BESTSELLING AUTHOR**
B.J. DANIELS

Harlequin®
BESTSELLING
AUTHOR
COLLECTION

Recycling programs
for this product may
not exist in your area.

ISBN-13: 978-1-335-47486-5

Murder Gone Cold
First published in 2022. This edition published in 2025.
Copyright © 2022 by Barbara Heinlein

Cold Case Kidnapping
First published in 2023. This edition published in 2025.
Copyright © 2023 by Nicole Helm

Harlequin Enterprises ULC
22 Adelaide St. West, 41st Floor
Toronto, Ontario M5H 4E3, Canada
www.Harlequin.com

Printed in U.S.A.

CONTENTS

Also by B.J. Daniels

Harlequin Intrigue

Renegade Wife

Silver Stars of Montana

Big Sky Deception
Missing: Baby Doe

A Colt Brothers Investigation

Murder Gone Cold
Sticking to Her Guns
Christmas Ransom
Set Up in the City
Her Brand of Justice
Dead Man's Hand

Canary Street Press

Powder River

Dark Side of the River
River Strong
River Justice

Visit the Author Profile page
at Harlequin.com for more titles.

MURDER GONE COLD

B.J. Daniels

This new Intrigue series is dedicated to all my fans who have followed my books from Cardwell Ranch to Whitehorse and back again. I hope you like these wild Colt brothers and Lonesome, Montana.

PROLOGUE

BILLY SHERMAN LAY in his bed trembling with fear as the thunderstorm raged outside. At a loud crack of thunder, he closed his eyes tight. His mother had warned him about the coming storm. She'd suggested he might want to stay in her room now that his father lived somewhere else.

"Mom, I'm seven," he'd told her. It was bad enough that he still slept with a night-light. "I'll be fine." But just in case, he'd pulled out his lucky pajamas even though they were getting too small.

Now he wished he could run down the hall to her room and crawl into her bed. But he couldn't. He wouldn't. He had to face his fears. That's what his dad said.

Lightning lit up the room for an instant. His eyes flew open to find complete blackness. His night-light had gone out. So had the little red light on his alarm clock. The storm must have knocked out the electricity.

He jumped out of bed to stand at his window. Even the streetlamps were out. He could barely see the house across the street through the pouring rain. He tried to swallow the lump in his throat. Maybe he should run down the hall and tell his mother about the power going off. He knew she would make him stay in her room if he did.

Billy hated being afraid. He dreamed of being strong and invincible. He dreamed of being a spy who traveled the world, solved mysteries and caught bad guys.

His battery-operated two-way radio squawked, making him jump. Todd, his best friend. "Are you asleep?" Todd's voice sounded funny. Billy had never confided even to his best friend about his fear of the dark and storms and whatever might be hiding in his closet. But maybe Todd was scared sometimes too.

He picked up the headset and stepped to the window to look out at the street. "I'm awake." A bolt of lightning blinded him for a moment and he almost shrieked as it illuminated a dark figure, walking head down on the edge of the road in the rain. Who was that and...? He felt his heart leap to his throat. What was it the person was carrying?

Suddenly, he knew what he had to do. He wasn't hiding in his room being scared. He would be strong and invincible. He had a mystery to solve. "I have to go," he said into the headset. "I saw someone. I'm going to follow whoever it is."

"No, it's storming. Don't go out. Billy, don't. Billy?"

He grabbed his extra coat his mother kept on the hook by his door and pulled on his snow-boots. At the window, he almost lost his nerve. He could barely see the figure. If he didn't go now he would never know. He would lose his nerve. He would always be afraid.

He picked up the headset again. "The person is headed down your street. Watch for me. I'll see you in a minute." Opening his window, he was driven back for a moment by the rain and darkness. Then he was through the window, dropping into the shrubbery outside as he'd done so many other times when he and Todd were playing their game. Only the other times, it hadn't been storming or dark.

He told himself that spies didn't worry about a thunderstorm. Spies were brave. But he couldn't wait until he reached Todd's house. Putting his head down he ran through the rain, slowing only when he spotted the figure just ahead.

He'd been breathing hard, his boots slapping the pavement, splashing through the puddles. But because of the storm the person hadn't heard him, wouldn't know anyone was following. That's what always made the game so much fun, spying on people and they didn't even know it.

Billy realized that he wasn't scared. His father had been right, though he didn't understand why his mother had gotten so angry with his dad for telling him to face his fears and quit being such a baby. Billy was facing down the storm, facing down the darkness, facing down all of his fears tonight. He couldn't wait to tell Todd.

He was smiling to himself, proud, when the figure ahead of him suddenly stopped and looked back. In a flash of lightning Billy saw the face under the hooded jacket—and what the person was carrying and screamed.

Nine years later

CHAPTER ONE

CORA BROOKS STOPPED washing the few dinner dishes she'd dirtied while making her meal, dried her hands and picked up her binoculars. Through her kitchen window, she'd caught movement across the ravine at the old Colt place. As she watched, a pickup pulled in through the pines and stopped next to the burned-out trailer. She hoped it wasn't "them druggies" who'd been renting the place from Jimmy D's girlfriend—before their homemade meth-making lab blew it up.

The pickup door swung open. All she saw at first was the driver's Stetson as he climbed out and limped over to the burned shell of the double-wide. It wasn't until he took off his hat to rake a hand through his too-long dark hair that she recognized him. One of the Colt brothers, the second oldest, she thought. James Dean Colt or Jimmy D as everyone called him.

She watched him through the binoculars as he hobbled around the trailer's remains, stooping at one point to pick up something before angrily hurling it back into the heap of charred debris.

"Must have gotten hurt with that rodeoin' of his agin," she said, pursing her lips in disapproval as she took in his limp. "Them boys." They'd been wild youngins who'd grown into wilder young men set on killing themselves by riding anything put in front of them. The things she'd seen over the years!

She watched him stand there for a moment as if not knowing what to do now, before he ambled back to his pickup and drove off. Putting down her binoculars, she chuckled to herself. "If he's upset about his trailer, wait until he catches up to his girlfriend."

Cora smiled and went back to washing her dishes. At her age, with all her aches and pains, the only pleasure she got anymore was from other people's misfortunes. She'd watched the Colt clan for years over there on their land. Hadn't she said no good would ever come of that family? So far her predictions had been exceeded.

Too bad about the trailer blowing up though. In recent years, the brothers had only used the double-wide as a place to drop their gear until the next rodeo. It wasn't like any of them stayed more than a few weeks before they were off again.

So where was James Dean Colt headed now? Probably into town to find his girlfriend since she'd been staying in his trailer when he'd left for the rodeo circuit. At least she had been—until she'd rented the place out, pocketed the cash and moved back in with her mother. More than likely he was headed to Melody's mother's right now.

What Cora wouldn't have given to see *that* reunion, she thought with a hearty cackle.

Just to see his face when Melody gave him the news after him being gone on the road all these months.

Welcome home, Jimmy D.

JAMES HIGHTAILED IT into the small Western town of Lonesome, Montana. When he'd seen the trailer in nothing but ashes, he'd had one terrifying thought. Had Melody been in it when the place went up in flames? He quickly assured himself that if that had happened, he would have heard about it.

So…why hadn't he heard about the fire? Why hadn't Melody let him know? They'd started dating only a week before he'd left. What they'd had was fun, but definitely not serious for either of them.

He swore under his breath, recalling the messages from her that he hadn't bothered with. All of them were along the line of, "We need to talk. Jimmy D, this is serious. Call me." No man jumped to answer a message like that.

Still, you would think that she could have simply texted him. "About your trailer?" Or "Almost died escaping your place."

At the edge of the small mountain town, he turned down a side street, driving back into the older part of town. Melody's mother owned the local beauty shop, Gladys's Beauty Emporium. Melody worked there doing nails. Gladys had been widowed as long as James could remember. It was one reason Melody always ended up back at her mother's between boyfriends.

He was relieved to see her old Pontiac parked out front of the two-story rambling farmhouse. A spindly stick of a woman with a wild head of bleached curly platinum hair, Gladys Simpson opened the door at his knock. She had a cigarette in one hand and a beer in the other. She took one look at him, turned and yelled, "Mel… Someone here to see you."

Someone? Lonesome was small enough that he could easily say that Gladys had known him his whole life. He waited on the porch since he hadn't been invited in, which was fine with him. He'd been toying with the idea that Melody was probably mad at him. He could think of any number of reasons.

But mad enough to burn down the double-wide out of spite? He'd known some women who could get that angry, but Melody wasn't one of them. He'd seen little passion in her before he'd left. He'd gotten the impression she wasn't that interested in him. If he'd had to guess, he'd say she'd been using him that week to make someone else jealous.

Which was another reason he'd known their so-called relationship wasn't going anywhere. In retrospect though, leaving her to take care of the place had been a mistake. It hadn't been his idea. She'd needed a place to stay. The double-wide was sitting out there empty so she'd suggested watching it for him while he was gone.

Even at the time, he'd worried that it would give her the wrong idea. The wrong idea being that their relationship was more serious than it was. He'd half hoped all the way home that she'd moved back in with her mom or a friend. That the trailer would be empty.

He just never imagined that there would be no place to come home to.

"Jimmy D?"

From the edge of the porch, he turned at the sound of her voice. She stood behind the door, peering around it as if half-afraid of him. "Melody, I was just out at the place. I was worried that you might have gotten caught in the fire."

She shook her head. "I wasn't living there anymore when it happened."

"That's good." But even as he said it, he knew there was more story coming. She was still half hiding behind the door, as if needing a barrier between them. "I'm not angry with you, if that's what you're worried about. I'm just glad you're okay."

He watched her swallow before she said, "I'd rented your trailer to some guys." He took that news without reacting badly. He figured she must have needed the money and he *had* left her in charge of the place, kind of.

"Turned out they were cooking meth," she said. "I didn't know until they blew the place up."

James swallowed back the first few words that leaped to his tongue. When he did find his voice, he said, "You didn't know."

She shook her head. "I didn't." She sounded close to tears. "But that's not all I have to tell you."

He held his breath already fearing that the news wasn't going to get better. Before his grandmother died, she'd explained karma to him. He had a feeling karma was about to kick his butt.

Then Mel stepped around the edge of the door, leading with her belly, which protruded out a good seven months.

The air rushed out of him on a swear word. A million thoughts galloped through his mind at breakneck speed before she said, "It's not yours."

He felt equal parts relief and shock. It was that instant of denial followed by acceptance followed by regret that surprised him the most. For just a second he'd seen himself holding a two-year-old little girl with his dark hair and blue eyes. They'd been on the back of the horse he'd bought her.

When he blinked, the image was gone as quickly as it had come to him.

"Who?" The word came out strangled. He wasn't quite over the shock.

"Tyler Grange," she said, placing her palms on the stretchy top snug over her belly. "He and I broke up just before you and I…" She shrugged and he noticed the tiny diamond glinting on her ring finger.

"You're getting married. When?"

"Soon," she said. "It would be nice to get hitched before the baby comes."

He swallowed, still tangled up in that battle of emotions. Relief was winning by a horse length though. "Congratulations. Or is it best wishes? I never can remember."

"Thanks," she said shyly. "Sorry 'bout your trailer. I'd give you the money I got from the renters, but—"

"It's all right." He took a step toward the porch stairs. After all these years in the rodeo game, he'd learned to cut his losses. This one felt like a win. He swore on his lucky boots that he was going to change his wild ways.

From inside the house, he could hear Gladys laughing with someone. He caught the smell of permanent solution.

"Mama's doing the neighbor's hair," Melody said. He nodded and took a step off the porch. "Any idea where you're going to go?"

Until that moment, he hadn't really thought about it. It wasn't like he didn't have options. He had friends he could bunk with until he either bought another trailer to put on the property or built something more substantial. He and his brothers, also on the rodeo circuit, used the trailer only to stay in the few times they came home to crash for a while—usually to heal up.

Not that he was planning on staying that long. Once

he was all healed up from his last rodeo ride, he'd be going back. He'd left his horse trailer, horse and gear at a friend's.

"I'm going to stay at the office," he said, nodding to himself. It seemed the perfect solution under the circumstances.

"Uptown?" she asked, sounding surprised. The word hardly described downtown Lonesome, Montana. But the office *was* at the heart of town—right on a corner of Main Street.

"Don't worry about me," he said. "You just take care of yourself and give my regards to Tyler." He tipped his hat and headed to his pickup.

As he drove away, he realized his heart was still pounding. He'd dodged a bullet. So why couldn't he get that image of him holding his baby daughter out of his head? Worse was how that image made him feel— happy.

The emotion surprised him. For just that split second, he'd had to deal with the thought of settling down, of having a family, of being a father. He'd felt it to his soul and now he missed it.

James shook his head, telling himself that he was just tired, injured and emotionally drained after his homecoming. All that together would make any man have strange thoughts.

CHAPTER TWO

JAMES REACHED HIGH on the edge of the transom over the door for the key, half-surprised it was still there. He blew the dust off and, opening the door, hit the light switch and froze. The smell alone reminded him of his father and the hours he'd spent in this office as a child after his mother had died.

Later he'd hung around, earning money by helping any way he could at the office. He'd liked hanging out here with his old man. He chuckled, remembering how he'd thought he might grow up and he and Del would work together. Father and son detective agency. Unfortunately, his father's death had changed all that.

He hadn't been here since the funeral, he realized as he took in his father's large oak desk and high-backed leather office chair. More emotions assaulted him, ones he'd kept at bay for the past nine years.

This was a bad idea. He wasn't ready to face it. He might never be ready, he thought. He missed his father and nine years hadn't changed that. Everything about this room brought back the pain from the Native American rugs on the floor and the two leather club chairs that faced his dad's desk and seat.

He realized he wasn't strong enough for this—maybe especially after being hurt during his last ride and then coming home to find his home was gone. He took one final look and started to close the door. He'd get a motel room for the night rather than show up at a friend's house.

But before he could close the door, his gaze fell on an old Hollywood movie poster on the wall across the room. He felt himself smile, drawn into the office by the cowboy on the horse with a face so much like his own.

He hadn't known his great-grandfather Ransom Del Colt. But he'd grown up on the stories. Ransom had been a famous movie star back in the forties and early fifties when Westerns had been so popular. His grandfather RD Colt Jr. had followed in Ransom's footprints for a while before starting his own Wild West show. RD had traveled the world ropin' and ridin' until late in life.

He moved around the room, looking at all the photographs and posters as if seeing them for the first time. The Colts had a rich history, one to be proud of, his father said. Del Colt, James's father, had broken the mold after being a rodeo cowboy until he was injured so badly that he had to quit.

Del, who'd loved Westerns and mystery movies, had gotten his PI license and opened Colt Investigations. He'd taught his sons to ride before they could walk. He'd never stopped loving rodeo and he'd passed that love on to his sons as if it was embedded deep in their genes.

James limped around the room looking at all the other posters and framed photographs of his rodeo family. He felt a sense of pride in the men who'd gone before him. And a sense of failure on his own part. He was pushing thirty-six and he had little to show for it except for a lot of broken bones.

Right now, he hurt all over. The bronc he'd ridden two days ago had put him into the fence, reinjuring his leg and cracking some of his ribs. But he'd stayed on the eight seconds and taken home the purse.

Right now he wondered if it was worth it. Still, as he stood in this room, he rebelled at the thought of quitting. He'd made a living doing what he loved. He would heal and go back. Just as he'd always done.

In the meantime, he was dog tired. Too tired to go look for a motel room for the night. At the back of the office he found the bunk where his father would stay on those nights he worked late. There were clean sheets and quilts and a bathroom with a shower and towels. This would work at least for tonight. Tomorrow he'd look for something else.

LORELEI WILKINS PULLED into her space in the alley behind her sandwich shop and stared at the pickup parked in the space next to it. It had been years since she'd seen anyone in the building adjoining hers. She'd almost forgotten why she'd driven down here tonight. Often, she came down and worked late to get things ready for the next day.

Tonight, she had brought down a basketful of freshly washed aprons. She could have waited until morning, but she'd been restless and it was a nice night. Who was she kidding? She never put things off for tomorrow.

Getting out, she started to unload the basket when she recognized the truck and felt a start. There were rodeo stickers plastered all over the back window of the cab, but the dead giveaway was the LETRBUCK personalized license plate.

Jimmy D was back in town? But why would he… She recalled hearing something about a fire out on his land. Surely, he wasn't planning to stay here in his father's old office. The narrow two-story building, almost identical to her own, had been empty since Del Colt's death nine years ago. Before that the structure had housed Colt Investigations on the top floor with the ground floor office rented to a party shop that went broke, the owners skipping town.

Lorelei had made an offer on the property, thinking she would try to get a small business in there or expand her sandwich shop. Anything was better than having an empty building next door. Worse, the owners of the party-planning store had left in a hurry, not even bothering to clean up the place, so it was an eyesore.

But the family lawyer had said no one in the family was interested in selling.

As she hauled out her basket of aprons, she could see a light in the second-story window and a shadow moving around up there. Whatever James was doing back in town, he wouldn't be staying long—he never did. Not that she ever saw him. She'd just heard the stories.

Shaking her head, she tucked the basket under one arm, unlocked the door and stepped in. It didn't take long to put the aprons away properly. Basket in hand, she locked up and headed for her SUV.

She couldn't help herself. She glanced up. Was she hoping to see the infamous Jimmy D? Their paths hadn't crossed in years.

The upstairs light was out. She shook her head at her own foolishness.

"Some women always go for the bad boy," her stepmother had joked years ago when they'd been uptown shopping for her senior year of high school. They'd passed Jimmy D in the small mall at the edge of town. He'd winked at Lorelei, making her blush to the roots of her hair. She'd felt Karen's frowning gaze on her. "I just never took you for one of those."

Lorelei had still been protesting on the way home. "I can't stand the sight of Jimmy D," she'd said, only to have her stepmother laugh. "He's arrogant and thinks he's much cuter than he is."

"Don't feel bad. We've all fallen for the wrong man. And he *is* cute and he likes you."

Lorelei had choked on that. "He doesn't like me. He just enjoys making me uncomfortable. He's just plain awful."

"Then I guess it's a good thing you aren't going to the prom with him," Karen said. "Your friend Alfred is obviously the better choice."

Alfred was her geek friend who she competed with for grades.

"Jimmy D isn't going to the prom," she said. "He's too cool for proms. Not that I would go with him if he asked me."

Lorelei still cringed at the memory. Protest too much? Her stepmother had seen right through it. She told herself that all that aside, this might be the perfect opportunity to get him to sell the building to her. But it would mean approaching Jimmy D with an offer knowing he would probably turn her down flat. She groaned. From what she'd heard, he hadn't changed since high school. The only thing the man took seriously was rodeo. And chasing women.

FORMER SHERIFF OTIS OSTERMAN pulled his pickup to the side of the street to stare up at the building. Lorelei Wilkins wasn't the only one surprised to see a light on in the old Colt Investigations building.

For just a moment, he'd thought that Del was still alive, working late as he often did. While making his rounds, Otis had seen him moving around up there working on one of his cases.

The light in that office gave him an eerie feeling as if he'd been transported back in time. That he could re-write history. But Otis knew that wasn't possible. One look in the rearview mirror at his white hair and wrinkled face and he could see that there was no going back, no changing anything. But it was only when he looked deep into his own eyes—eyes that had seen too much—that he felt the weight of those years and the questionable actions he'd taken.

But like Del Colt, they were buried. He just wanted them to stay that way. Blessedly, he hadn't been reminded of Del for some time now. He'd gone to the funeral nine years ago, stood in the hot sun and watched as the gravedigger covered the man's casket and laid sod on top. He told himself that had been the end of a rivalry he and Del had fought since middle school.

He watched the movement up there in Del's office. It had to be one of Del's sons back from the rodeo. Small towns, he thought. Everyone didn't just know each other. Half the damned town was related.

Otis drove down the block, turning into the alley and cruising slowly past the pickup parked behind Del's narrow two-story office building.

He recognized the truck and swore softly under his breath. Del Colt had left behind a passel of sons who all resembled him, but Jimmy D was the most like Del. Apparently, he was back for a while.

The former sheriff told himself that it didn't necessarily spell trouble as he shifted his truck into gear.

As he drove home though, he couldn't shake the bad feeling that the past had been reawakened and it was coming for him.

CHAPTER THREE

JAMES WOKE TO the sun. It streamed in the window of his father's office as he rose and headed for the shower. Being here reminded him of the mornings on his way to school that he would stop by. He often found his father at his desk, already up and working. Del Colt's cases weren't the kind that should have kept his father from sleep, he thought as he got dressed.

They were often small personal problems that people hoped he could help with. But his father treated each as if it was more important than world peace. James had once questioned him about it.

They may seem trivial to you, but believe me, they aren't to the people who are suffering and need answers, Del had said.

Now, showered and dressed, James stepped from the small room at the back and into his father's office. He hesitated for a moment before he pulled out his father's chair and sat down. Leaning back, he surveyed the room and the dusty window that overlooked Main Street.

He found himself smiling, recalling sitting in this chair and wanting to be just like his dad. He felt such a sense of pride for the man Del had been. His father had raised them all after their mother's death. James knew that a lot of people would have said that Del had let them run wild.

Laughing, he thought that had been somewhat true. His father gave them free rein to learn by their mistakes. So, they made a lot of them.

Everything was just as his father had left it, he realized as he looked around. A file from the case his father had been working on was still lying open on his desk. Next to it were his pen and a yellow lined notepad with Del's neat printing. A coffee cup, the inside stained dark brown, sat next to the notepad.

A name jumped out at him. Billy Sherman. That kid who'd been killed in a hit-and-run nine years ago. *That was the case his father had been working on.*

He felt a chill. The hit-and-run had never been solved.

A knock at the door startled him. He quickly closed the case file, feeling as if he'd been caught getting into things that were none of his business. Private things.

He quickly rose, sending the chair scooting backward. "Yes?"

"Jimmy D?" A woman's voice. Not one he recognized. He hadn't told anyone he was coming back to town. He'd returned unannounced and under the cover of darkness. But clearly someone knew he wasn't just back—but that he was here in Del's office.

He moved to the door and opened it, still feeling as if he were trespassing. The light in the hallway was dim. He'd noticed last night that the bulb had burned out sometime during the past nine years. But enough sunlight streamed in through the dusty window at the end of the hall to cast a little light on the pretty young woman standing before him.

"I hope I didn't catch you at a bad time," she said, glancing past him before settling her gaze on him again.

Her eyes were honey brown with dark lashes. Her long chestnut brown hair had been pulled up into a no-nonsense knot that went with the serious expression on her face. She wore slacks, a modest blouse and sensible shoes. She had a briefcase in one hand, her purse in the other. She looked like a woman on a mission and he feared he was the assignment.

LORELEI LOOKED FOR recognition in the cowboy's eyes and seeing none quickly said, "I'm sorry, you probably don't remember me. I'm Lorelei Wilkins. I own the sandwich shop next door." When he still hadn't spoken, she added, "We went to school together?" She realized this was a mistake.

He was still staring at her unnervingly. When he finally spoke, the soft timber of his low voice surprised her. She remembered the unruly classmate who'd sat next to her in English, always cracking jokes and acting up when he wasn't winking at her in the hall between classes. She realized that she'd been expecting the teenaged boy—not the man standing before her.

"Oh, I remember you, Lori," he drawled. "Hall monitor, teacher's assistant, senior class president, valedictorian." He grinned. "Didn't you also read the lunch menu over the intercom?"

She felt her cheeks warm. Yes, she'd done all of that—not that she'd have thought he'd noticed. "It's *Lorelei*," she said, her voice coming out thin. She knew her reputation as the most uptight, serious, not-fun girl in the class.

"I remember that too," he said, his grin broadening.

She cleared her throat and quickly pressed on. "Look, Jimmy D. I saw your light on last night and I—"

"It's James."

"James…?" she repeated. She suddenly felt tongue-tied here facing this rodeo cowboy. Why had she thought talking directly to him was a good idea? She wished she'd tried his family lawyer again instead. Not that that approach had done her any good.

She took a breath and let it out, watching him wince as he shifted his weight onto his obviously injured leg. Seeing that he wasn't in any shape to be making real estate deals, she chickened out. "I just wanted to welcome you to the neighborhood."

"I'm not staying, in case that's what you're worrying about. I mean, not living here, exactly. It's just temporary."

She suspected that most everything about his life was temporary from what she'd heard. She was angry at herself for not saying what she'd really come to say. But from the look on his bruised face and the way he'd winced when he'd shifted weight on his left leg, she'd realized that this wasn't the right time to make an offer on the building. He looked as if he would say no to her without even giving it a second thought.

From her briefcase, she awkwardly withdrew a ten percent off coupon for her sandwich shop.

He took it without looking at it. Instead, his intense scrutiny was on her, making her squirm.

"It's a coupon for ten percent off a sandwich at my shop," she said.

He raised a brow. "Who makes the sandwiches?"

The question was so unexpected that it took her a moment to respond. "I do."

"Huh," he said and folded the coupon in half to stuff it into the pocket of his Western shirt.

What had made her think she could have a professional conversation with this…cowboy? She snapped her briefcase closed and turned to leave.

"Thanks," he called after her.

Just like in high school she could feel his gaze boring into her backside. She ground her teeth as her face flushed hot. Maybe she'd been wrong. Maybe some things never changed no matter how much time had gone by.

JAMES SMILED TO himself as he watched Lorelei disappear down the hall. He hadn't seen her in years. As small as Lonesome was, he'd have thought that their paths would have crossed again before this. But she didn't hang out at Wade's Broken Spur bar or the engine repair shop or the truck stop cafe—all places on the edge of town that he frequented when home. Truth was, he never had reason to venture into downtown Lonesome because he usually stayed only a few days, a week at most.

Seeing Lorelei had made him feel seventeen again. The woman had always terrified him. She was damned intimidating and always had been. He'd liked that about her. She'd always been so smart, so capable, so impressive. In high school she hadn't seemed to realize just how sexy she was. She'd tried to hide it unlike a lot of the girls. But some things you can't cover up with clothing.

What surprised him as he closed the door behind her was that she still seemed to be unaware of what she did to a man. Especially this man.

He sighed, wondering what Lorelei had really stopped by for. Not to welcome him to the neighborhood or give him a sandwich coupon. It didn't matter. He knew that once he found a place to stay, he'd probably not see her again.

Something bright and shiny caught his eye lying on the floor next to his father's desk. He moved toward it as if under a spell. He felt a jolt as he recognized what it was. Picking up the silver dollar money clip, he stared down, heart pounding. Why hadn't his father had this on him when he was killed? He always carried it. *Always*.

James opened it and let the bills fall to the desktop. Two twenties, a five and three ones. As he started to pick them back up, he noticed that wasn't all that had fallen from the money clip.

He lifted the folded yellow lined notepad paper from the desk. Unfolding it he saw his father's neat printing and a list of names. As was his father's habit, he'd checked off those he had interviewed. But there were six others without checks.

James stared at the list, realizing they were from Del's last case, seven-year-old Billy Sherman's hit-and-run. His father had stuck the list in his money clip? Had his father been on his way to talk to someone on that list? Why had he left the clip behind? He'd always had so many questions about his father's death. Too many. Ultimately, after what the sheriff had told him, he'd been afraid of the answers.

Moving behind the desk, he sat down again and opened the case file. His father's notes were neatly stacked inside. He checked the notes against the list. Everyone Del had interviewed was there, each name checked off the list.

But the list had stopped with a name that made his jaw drop. Karen Wilkins? Lorelei's stepmother? Why had his father wanted to talk to her? She lived a half dozen blocks from where the hit-and-run had happened.

CHAPTER FOUR

JAMES GLANCED AT the time. Almost one in the afternoon. He'd lost track of time reading his father's file on the hit-and-run. Finding Karen Wilkins name on the list had scared him. He couldn't imagine why Del wanted to talk to her.

He'd gone through everything several times, including all of his father's neatly handwritten notes. Del didn't even use a typewriter—let alone a computer. He was old-school through and through.

James realized that after everything he'd gone through, he still had no idea why Karen's name was on the list or why it might be important.

His stomach growled. He thought of the coupon Lori had given him. Pulling it from his pocket, he reached for his Stetson. It was a short walk next door.

As James entered the sandwich shop, a bell jangled over the front door. From the back, he saw Lori look up, her expression one of surprise, then something he couldn't quite read.

He walked up to the sign that said Order Here and scanned the chalkboard menu. His stomach rumbled again. He couldn't remember when he'd eaten—sometime yesterday at a fast-food place on the road. He'd been anxious to get home only to find he no longer had a home.

Lori appeared in front of him. "See anything you'd like?"

He glanced at her. "Definitely." Then he winked and looked up at the board again. He heard her make a low guttural sound under her breath. "I'll take the special."

She mugged a face. "It comes with jalapeño peppers and a chipotle mayonnaise that you might find too…spicy."

He smiled. "I'm tougher than I look."

She glanced at the leg he was babying and cocked a brow at that.

"It was a really big bronco that put me into the fence. For your information, it didn't knock me off. I held on for the eight seconds and came home with the money."

"Then it was obviously worth it," she said sarcastically. "Let me get you that sandwich. Is this to go?"

"No, I think I'll stay."

She nodded, though he thought reluctantly. When she'd given him the coupon, he could tell that she'd never expected he would actually use it. "If you'd like to have a seat. Want something to drink with that?"

"Sure, whatever's cold." He turned and did his best not to limp as he walked to a table and chair by the front window. This time of the day, the place was empty. He wondered how her business was doing. He wondered also if he'd made a mistake with what he'd ordered and if it would be too spicy to eat. He'd eat it. Even if it killed him.

What was it about her that he couldn't help flirting with her when he was around her? There'd always been something about her… He couldn't imagine how they could be more different. Maybe that's why she'd always made it clear that she wasn't in the least interested in him.

Fortunately, other girls and then women had been, he thought. But as he caught glimpses of her working back in the kitchen, he knew she'd always been an enigma, a puzzle that he couldn't figure out. Flirting with her sure hadn't worked. But, like his father, he'd always loved a good mystery and seldom backed down from a challenge.

Was that why he couldn't let this go? He needed to find out why her stepmother was on Del's list. Why the list was tucked in Del's money clip and why he hadn't had it on him that night. James knew he might never get those answers. Just as he might never know how his father ended up on the train tracks that night. So, what was the point in digging into Del's old unsolved case?

Wouldn't hurt to ask a few questions, he told himself. He wasn't going anywhere for a while until he healed. He had time on his hands with nothing to do—nothing but seeing about getting the wreckage from his burned trailer hauled away and replacing it with a place to live. He told himself he'd get on that tomorrow.

Lori brought out his sandwich and a tall glass of iced lemonade along with plastic cutlery and napkin roll. She placed the meal in front of him and started to step away. He grabbed her hand. She flinched.

"Sorry," he said quickly as he let go. "I was hoping since you aren't busy with customers that maybe you could sit down for a minute. Join me?"

"I guess I could spare a moment." She hesitated before reluctantly slipping into a chair across from him.

He smiled over at her. "I feel like you and I got off on the wrong foot somehow." He waited for her to say something and realized he could wait all day and that wasn't going to happen. She wasn't going to help him out. He took a sip of the lemonade. "Delicious. Let's start with the truth. What did you really come by for earlier? It wasn't to welcome me to the neighborhood."

She shook her head. "This isn't the time or the place." He raised a brow at that, making her groan. "You never change. Are you like this with every woman?" She raised a hand. "Don't answer that. I already know." She started to get up, but he stopped her.

"Seriously, you can tell me."

She studied him for a long moment before she asked, "Has your family lawyer mentioned that I've made several inquiries about buying your father's building?"

"Family lawyer?"

"Hank Richardson."

"Oh, him." James frowned. "He's our family lawyer? I guess I didn't realize that." She sighed deeply. "Why do you want to buy the building?"

"No one is using it. The place is an eyesore. I might want to expand into it at some point."

He nodded. "Huh. I'll have to give that some thought."

"You do that." She started to rise.

"Wait, I'm serious. I'll think about it. Now can I ask you something else?" She looked both wary and suspicious. "I was going through an old case file of my father's earlier. It was the one he was working on when he died. You might remember the case. Billy Sherman. Killed by a hit-and-run driver. So, I'm looking into it and—"

Her eyes widened. "What are you doing?"

He couldn't help but look confused. "Having lunch?"

"You're not a licensed private investigator."

"No, I'm not pretending to be. I just found the case interesting and since I have some time on my hands..."

She shook her head. "Just like that?" She sighed. "Are you living next door now?"

"For the moment. It's not that bad."

"Like your latest injury isn't that bad?" she asked, clearly upset with him.

"I'll heal, but if you must know my cracked ribs still hurt like hell." He took a tiny bite of his sandwich and felt the heat even though he'd mostly gotten bread. He knew instantly what she'd done. "This is good."

She was watching him as he took another bite. "I make my own bread."

"Really?" The heat of the peppers was so intense that they felt as if they would blow the top of his head off.

"You don't have to sound so surprised."

"Don't take this wrong, but back in high school, I never thought about you in the kitchen baking bread."

"Doubt you thought about me at all," she said and slipped out of her chair.

But as she started past, he said, "I thought about you all the time. But I was smart enough to know you were out of my league."

She'd stopped next to his table and now looked down at him. Her expression softened. "You don't have to eat that. I can make you something else."

He shook his head, picked up his sandwich and took another big bite. He'd eat every ounce even if it killed him, which he thought it might. The intense heat made its way down his throat to his chest. It felt as if his entire body was on fire. He sucked in his breath. Somehow, he managed to get the words out. "This isn't too spicy."

She shook her head. At least she was smiling this time as she walked away.

CHAPTER FIVE

JAMES HAD A lot of time to think since his spicy lunch had kept him up most of the night. It was a small price to pay, he told himself. He wasn't sure exactly what he'd done to Lori in high school or since that had her so upset with him. He'd been the high school jock and goof-off who'd gotten by on his charm. She'd been the studious, hardworking serious student who'd had to work for her grades. Why wouldn't she resent him?

But he suspected there was more to it than even his awkward attempts at flirting with her. He felt as if he'd done something that had made her dislike him. That could be any number of things. It wasn't like he went around worrying about who might have been hurt by his antics back then. Or even now, he admitted honestly.

He kept going over the conversation at lunch though. She'd tried to pass off her anger as something from high school. But he wasn't buying it. She hadn't been a fan of his for apparently some time, but when she'd gotten upset was when he'd said he was looking into his father's last case, Billy Sherman's hit-and-run.

Add to that, her stepmother's name was on his father's list. Del Colt had been meticulous in his investigations. He'd actually been really good at being a PI. Karen Wilkins wouldn't have been on that list unless his father thought she knew something about the case.

James was convinced by morning that he needed to talk to Karen. He knew Lori wasn't going to like it. Best that he hadn't brought it up at lunch.

But first, he wanted to talk to the person who'd hired his father to look into the hit-and-run after the police had given up.

ALICE SHERMAN GASPED, her hand over her heart, her eyes wide as she stared at James. It seemed to take her a moment to realize she wasn't looking at a ghost. "For a moment I thought… You look so much like your father."

James smiled, nodding. "It's a family curse."

She shook her head as she recovered. "Yes, being that handsome must be a terrible burden for you, especially with the ladies."

"I'm James Colt," he said, introducing himself and shaking her hand. "I don't think we've ever met." Alice worked at the local laundry. "I was hoping to ask you a few questions."

She narrowed her eyes at him. "About what?" She seemed really not to know.

"I hate to bring it back up and cause you more pain, but you hired my father to look into Billy's death. He died before he finished the investigation."

"You're mistaken," she said, fiddling with the collar of her blouse. "I didn't hire your father. My ex did."

That caught him flat-footed. He'd seen several checks from Alice Sherman in his father's file and Alice had been the first on Del's list of names. He said as much to her.

Her expression soured. "When my ex's checks bounced, I paid Del for his time. But what does that have to do with you?"

"I'm looking into the case."

Alice stared at him. "After all these years? Why would you do that? You...? You're a private investigator?"

"No. It was my father's last case. I'm just looking into it."

"Well, I'm not interested in paying any more money." She started to close the door.

"Please, Mrs. Sherman," he said quickly. "I don't mean to remind you of your loss. I just want to know more about your son."

She managed a sad smile. "Billy is *always* on my mind. The pain never goes away." She opened the door wider. "I suppose I have time for a few questions."

As James took the chair she offered him, she walked to the mantel over the fireplace and took down a framed photograph of her son.

"This is my favorite snapshot of him." She turned and handed it to him. It was of a freckle-faced boy with his two front teeth missing smiling broadly at the camera. "Billy was seven," she said as she took a seat on the edge of the couch facing him. "Just a boy. He was named after my father who died in the war."

"You've had a lot of loss," James said as she brushed a lock of her hair from her face. After the accident, it was as if she'd aged overnight. According to his father's file, Alice would now be forty-five. Her hair was almost entirely gray and there were deep lines around her eyes and mouth. "I'm so sorry. I don't want to make it worse."

"Have you found new information on the case?" she asked, her gaze intent on him. He realized that he might have given her the wrong impression.

"No, not yet. I'm not sure where my father had left

the case. Had he talked to you about his investigation before his death?"

"He called me that afternoon, asked if I was going to be home. He thought he might be getting close to finding the hit-and-run driver," she said. "I waited for him but he never showed up. I found out the next day about his pickup being hit by the train."

"He said he thought he might be close to solving the case?" He felt hope at this news. Maybe he wasn't playing at this. Maybe there was something he could find after all. "Did he tell you anything else?"

She shook her head. "Unfortunately, that's all he said."

This news had his heart hammering. He'd always wondered if his father's so-called accident had anything to do with the case. If he was that close to finding the hit-and-run driver... Sheriff Otis Osterman's investigation had ruled Del's death an accident due to human error on his father's part. Either Del hadn't been paying attention and not seen the train coming at the uncontrolled railroad crossing or he'd tried to outrun the train.

Neither had sounded like his father.

The autopsy found alcohol in his father's system and there had been an empty bottle of whiskey found on the floor of his pickup.

James had never accepted that his father had been drunk and hadn't seen the train coming. If he was close to solving the Billy Sherman case, there is no way he would have been drinking at all.

Alice had gotten up and now brought over more photographs of her son. He'd been small and thin. A shy boy, not an adventurous one. There'd been two theories of how Billy ended up outside on the street that night.

The obvious one was that he'd sneaked out for some reason. The other was that he'd been abducted.

"Is there any reason Billy might have left the house that night after you put him to bed?" James asked cautiously.

"No, never. Billy would have never gotten up in the middle of the night and gone out for any reason. He was afraid of the dark. He hated admitting it, but he still slept with a night-light. He was also terrified of storms. There was a terrible storm that night. The wind was howling. Between it and the pouring rain you could hardly see across the street." She shook her head, her gaze unfocused for a moment as if she were reliving it. "He *wouldn't* have gone out on his own under *any* circumstances."

"So, you're still convinced that someone abducted him?"

"His bedroom window was wide open." Her voice broke. "The wind had blown the rain in. His floor and bedding were soaked when I went in the next morning to wake him up and found him gone." All of this he'd already read in his father's file. He could see it was a story she'd told over and over, to the sheriff, to Del, to herself. "I started to call the sheriff when Otis drove up and told me that Billy had been found a few blocks from here lying in the ditch dead." She made angry swipes at her tears. He could see that she was fighting hard not to cry.

"The sheriff said he didn't find any signs of a forced entry," James said. "According to my father's notes, you said you locked the window before tucking Billy in at nine. Maybe you forgot that night—"

"No, I remember locking it because I could see the

storm coming. I even closed the blinds. It's no mystery. The only way Billy would leave the house was if his father came to his window that night. Sean Sherman. Not that he'll tell you the truth, but I know he took my boy. Have you talked to him?"

"Not yet." He was still working on the angle that Billy, like every red-blooded, American boy, had sneaked out a time or two. Having been a seven-year-old at one time, he asked, "Did Billy have his own cell phone?" She shook her head. "What about a walkie-talkie?"

"Yes, but—"

"Who had the other two-way radio handset?"

He watched her swallow before she said, "Todd. Todd Crane. But he swore he hadn't talked to Billy that night."

"I'm just covering my bets," James said quickly. He gathered that his father hadn't asked her this. "Did the sheriff talk to Todd?"

"I don't know. I think your father asked me about Billy's friends, but my son wouldn't have left the house that night even for his best friend, Todd."

James rose to lay a hand over hers as she gripped the stack of framed photos of her son. "Do you mind if I see his room?" Even before she led him down the hall, he knew Billy's room would be exactly like he'd left it even after nine years.

It was a classic boy's room painted a pale blue with a Spiderman bedspread and action figures lined up on the bookshelf.

Moving to the window, James examined the lock. It was an old house, the lock on the window old as well. Maybe Billy *had* been abducted and the sheriff had missed something. But wouldn't there have been footprints in the wet earth outside Billy's window? Unless he'd been taken before the storm hit and the prints had been washed away.

James left, promising to let Alice Sherman know if he discovered anything helpful. The look in her eyes was a stark reminder of what he'd set in motion. He'd gotten her hopes up and the truth was, he had no idea what he was doing.

KAREN WILKINS WASN'T HOME. Her car wasn't parked in front of her freshly painted and landscaped split-level. Nor was it in the garage.

Todd Crane, who would now be around sixteen, hadn't been on his father's list. But Del had talked to Todd's stepmother, Shelby Crane.

Since it was a Saturday, James figured the boy wouldn't be in school. He swung by the house only a few blocks from Alice Sherman's. The woman who answered the door was considerably younger-looking than Alice. Shelby Crane was a slim blonde with hard brown eyes.

"Yes?" The way she was holding the door open only a crack told him that Alice might have already called her.

"I'm James Colt and—"

"I know who you are. What do you want?"

"I'm guessing that you spoke with Alice," he said. "I'd like to talk to your son."

"No." She started to close the door, but he stopped her with his palm.

"Your son might know why Billy Sherman was outside that night," he said, his voice growing harder with each word.

"Well, he doesn't."

"If that's true, then I can't see why he can't tell me that himself."

"He doesn't know. He didn't know nine years ago. He doesn't know now." Again, she started to close the door and again he put a hand on it to stop her.

"Did he and Billy talk on walkie-talkies back then?"

"My son had nothing to do with what happened to that boy. You need to go. Don't make me call the sheriff." She closed the door and this time he let her.

As he started to turn and leave, he saw a boy's face peering out one of the upstairs windows. Then the curtain fell back, and the boy was gone. He wondered why Shelby was so afraid of him talking to her son.

His phone rang as he was getting into his pickup. Melody? He picked up.

"I just got a call from the sheriff's department," she said without preamble. "Carl said you have to get a permit to remove the burned trailer from your land."

"Why would he call you?"

Silence, then a guilty, "I might have tried to hire someone to haul it away before you got back."

James shook his head. Did she not realize he would have noticed anyway? The missing double-wide and the burned area around it would have been a dead giveaway. "No problem. I'll swing by and pick up a permit. Thanks for letting me know."

He was still mentally shaking his head when he walked into the sheriff's department.

Sheriff Carl Osterman, younger brother of the former sheriff Otis Osterman, was standing outside his office with a large mug of coffee and the family sour expression on his face. A short stocky man in his late fifties, Carl believed in guilty until proven innocent. Word was that he'd arrest his own grandmother for jaywalking, which could explain why he was divorced and not speaking with his mother or grandmother, James had heard.

"Wondered when I'd be seeing you," the sheriff drawled. "Suppose you heard what happened out at your place."

"It was fairly noticeable."

Carl took a long moment to assess him over the rim of his mug as he slurped his coffee. "You know those meth dealers?"

"Nope. I was on the road. I didn't even know Melody had rented the place."

The sheriff nodded. "You need a permit to haul that mess off."

"That's why I'm here."

"What are you planning to do out there?" Carl asked.

James shook his head. "I don't have any plans at the moment."

"Heard you were staying in your father's old office."

News traveled fast in Lonesome. "My family still owns the building."

Carl nodded again, still eyeballing him with suspicion. "Margaret will give you a form to fill out. Could take a few days, maybe even a week."

"I'm in no hurry."

"That mean you're planning to stay for a while?"

James studied the man. "Why the interest in my itinerary, Carl?"

"There's a rumor circulating that you've reopened your father's office and that you're working one of his cases. Last I heard you weren't a licensed private investigator."

He hid his surprise, realizing that Shelby Crane had probably called. "No law against asking a few questions, but now that you mention it, I worked for my father during high school and when I was home from college and the rodeo so I have some experience."

"You need a year and a half's worth before you can apply for a license under state law."

He pretended he always knew that. "Yep, I know. Got it covered. Application is in the mail." It wasn't. But damn, he just might apply now.

The sheriff put down his coffee cup with a curse. "Why would you do that unless you planned to stay in town?"

James smiled. He *wasn't* planning to. "Just covering my options, sheriff."

"The state runs a criminal background check, you know."

He laughed. "Why would that concern me?"

"If you have a felony on your record—"

"I don't," he said with more force than he'd intended.

"Good thing they don't check finances or your mental health."

James laughed. "Not worried about either." With a shake of his head, he turned and walked over to Margaret's desk. Without a word, she handed him the permit application.

"You'll need to pay twenty-five dollars when you return that permit," Carl called after him.

OTIS HAD JUST gotten through mowing the small lawn in front of his house. The summer air smelled of cut grass and sunshine. He turned on the sprinklers and, hot, sweaty and tired, went inside. He'd only just opened a can of beer and sat down when Carl called.

"You know what that damned Colt boy has gone and done now?" his brother demanded. James Colt was far from a boy, but Carl didn't give him a chance to reply. "He's been going all over town asking questions about his father's last case. He thinks he's a private eye."

He didn't have to ask what case. Otis was the first one on the scene after getting the call about the boy's body that was found in the ditch next to a house under construction in the new subdivision near where the Shermans lived. The memory still kept him awake some nights. He'd been a month away from retiring. Carl had been his undersheriff. The two of them had worked the case.

"Legally, James can't—"

"He's applied for a state license!" Carl was breathing hard, clearly worked up. "He says his experience working with his father should be enough. It probably is. It's so damned easy to get a PI license in this state, he'll get it and then—"

"And then *nothing*," Otis said. "He's a rodeo cowboy. I heard he's hurt. Once he feels better, he'll be back in the saddle, having put all of this behind him. Even if that isn't the case—which it is—he's inexperienced, the Sherman case is ice cold and we all know how hard those are to solve. And let's face it, he's not his father. I'll bet you five bucks that he quits before the week is out."

Carl sighed. Otis could imagine him pacing the floor of his office. "You think?"

"You know I don't throw money around."

His brother laughed. "No, not Otis Osterman." He sighed again. "I just thought this was behind us."

"It is," he said even though he knew it might never be true. Billy Sherman's death was unsolved, justice hadn't been meted out and what happened that night remained a mystery. There were always those who couldn't live with that.

Unfortunately, Del Colt had been one of them. Him and his damned digging. He'd gotten into things that had been better off left alone.

But Otis had five dollars that said James Colt was nothing like his father. For the young rodeo cowboy's sake, he certainly hoped not.

CHAPTER SIX

AFTER LEAVING THE sheriff's office, James drove aimlessly around town for a while. He knew he should quit right now before he made things any worse. What had he hoped to accomplish with all this, anyway? Was he so arrogant that he thought he could pick up where his father had left off on the case and solve it just like that?

So far all he'd done was stir up a wasp's nest that was more than likely going to get him stung. If he hadn't left Melody in his trailer, if she hadn't rented it, if the renters hadn't blown it up, if he'd gone to a motel and never gone to his father's office...

He reminded himself that getting involved with Melody was all on him. He thought of one of his father's lectures he and his brothers had been forced to endure growing up.

Life is about consequences, Del would say. *Whatever you do, there will be a repercussion. It's the law of nature. Cause and effect.*

What are you trying to say? one of his brothers would demand, usually himself most likely. *'Cause the effect I'm getting is a headache.*

His father would give him a reprimand before adding, *Don't blame someone else when things go wrong because of something stupid you did. Take responsibility and move on. It's called growing up.*

He and his brothers had made fun of that particular lecture, but it had never seemed more appropriate than right now.

His stomach growled. He looked at the time. Two in the afternoon. He hadn't had breakfast or lunch. He drove downtown. There was a spot in front of the sandwich shop. He took that as a sign.

"Tell me you aren't going to make a habit of this," Lori said when he walked in, but she smiled when she said it.

He smiled back at her. Distractedly he studied the chalkboard. The special today was a turkey club. He shifted his gaze to her. "I'll take the special and an iced tea."

"Do you want that on white, wheat or rye?"

"White." He hadn't been *that* distracted that he hadn't noticed her. Today she was dressed in a coral blouse and black slacks. The blouse was V-necked exposing some of the freckled skin of her throat and a small silver heart-shaped locket that played peekaboo when she moved. Her hair was pulled up again, making him wonder if it would fall past her shoulders if he let it down. "With mayo."

"It will be just a few minutes," she said, straightening her blouse collar self-consciously before hurrying into the back.

He took his usual seat. His leg was better today but his ribs still hurt. He kept thinking about his father's case, wishing he hadn't opened up this can of worms. Now that he had, what choice did he have?

Which meant he would have to talk to Karen Wilkins. Her stepdaughter wouldn't like it. Of that, he was certain. He just hoped that neither was involved. He liked Lorelei. He always had. Her stepmother owned a workout studio in town. Widowed, Karen was active in the community and had been as long as James could remember. He used to think "stepmother like stepdaughter." So why did Del have Karen on his list?

Deep in thought, he started when Lorelei set down the plate with his sandwich in front of him. She gently placed the glass of iced tea, giving him a worried look.

"You all right?" she asked. "You seem a little skittish."

He smiled at that. "I've been better."

"Is it true?"

"That's a wide-open question if I've ever heard one."

"Are you really applying for a private investigator's license?"

He chuckled. Thanks to the sheriff, he was. Probably also thanks to the sheriff everyone in town now knew. "Yep. How do you feel about that?"

She seemed surprised by the question. "It has nothing to do with me."

He nodded, hoping it was true. "Still, you seemed to have an opinion yesterday."

Lori looked away for a moment, licked her lips with the quick dart of her tongue, and said, "I was going to apologize for that."

"Really?" he said as he picked up his sandwich and took a bite. He chewed and swallowed before he said, "And I thought you were going to apologize for trying to kill me with that sandwich you made me yesterday."

Her cheeks flushed. "You didn't have to eat it," she said defensively.

He held her gaze. "Yes, I did."

The bell over the front door jangled. She looked almost relieved as she went to help the couple that came in.

CHAPTER SEVEN

AFTER JAMES FINISHED his sandwich and iced tea, he wrote a note on the bill Lori had dropped by on her way past his table. The shop had gotten busy. He could see her through the small window into the kitchen. She was making sandwiches in her all-business way. It made him smile. Whatever she did, she did it with so much purpose.

He wondered what would happen if she ever let her guard down. He wished he could be there when she did.

As he left, he pulled out the list of names. It was time to talk to Karen Wilkins and relieve his mind. She couldn't be involved. He had to find out why she was on the list.

James was surprised how young Karen looked as she opened the door. A small woman with chin-length blond hair and large luminous brown eyes, the aerobics instructor was clearly in great shape. In her late forties, Karen and her stepdaughter could have almost passed for sisters rather than stepmother and stepdaughter.

From the expression on her face though, she wasn't glad to see him. He wondered if it had anything to do with him taking over his father's old case. Or if it was more about his reputation. Would he ever live down his misspent youth?

"I hope I haven't caught you at a bad time," he said.

She was dressed in leggings, a T-shirt and sneakers as if on her way to her exercise studio. "Do you have a few minutes? I'd like to ask you a few questions."

The woman chuckled, reminding him of Lorelei for a moment. "Whatever you're selling Jimmy D—"

He raised his hands. "Not selling anything. I've taken over my father's old private investigative business temporarily. I'm looking into the last case he was working on before he died."

She raised an eyebrow and he saw her expression turn both serious—and wary.

"I'm here about Billy Sherman's hit-and-run."

Her eyes widened. "Wasn't that almost ten years ago?"

"It was. Please, I promise not to keep you long."

She didn't move. "Why would you think I would know anything about that?"

"Because you were on my father's list of people he wanted to interview."

Her face paled and he saw the fear. She quickly looked away. "I can't imagine how I could possibly help even if I didn't have a class in a few minutes." Her gaze shifted back to his but only for a second. "I was just leaving. I'm sorry. This really isn't a good time." With that, she closed the door.

He stood for a moment feeling shaken to his core. He knew from experience what guilt looked like. Fear too. Turning, he walked out to his pickup and had just slipped behind the wheel when Karen Wilkins's garage door gaped open, and her car came flying out. She barely missed the front bumper of his pickup before she sped away.

She seemed to be in an awful hurry to get to her class, he thought as he gave it a moment before he followed her.

"WHAT'S WRONG?" LORELEI FELT panicked at the fear she heard in her stepmother's voice the moment she'd answered her phone.

"It's...nothing, I'm sorry."

"It's not nothing. I can hear it in your voice. Mom—" Lorelei's mother died when she was three. Both her parents had been young—her mother twenty-two when she died, her father twenty-four. She barely remembered her mother. After her mother died, her father went for ten years before even dating.

It had been a shock when he'd come home from an insurance conference with Karen who had looked like a teenager at twenty-five. Lorelei had been thirteen, Karen only twelve years older. People said they could be sisters. At the time, the comment had made her sick to her stomach. How could her father do this to her?

Lorelei hadn't accepted the woman into their lives for a long time, refusing to call her mom. But at some point, her stepmother had won her over and she'd begun calling her mom since she'd never really had a mother before Karen.

The only time she called her Karen had been when she was angry at her like for grounding her or mentioning that she had a boyfriend when her father had said she was too young to have one. Most of the time though, she and Karen had been as close as biological mother and daughter.

"I'm just being silly," Karen said now. "I had a little

bit of a scare, for no good reason really. Let's forget it. Tell me how you are doing."

Lorelei looked to the ceiling of her shop kitchen. "I'm doing fine. Had a busy lunch crowd and now I'm prepping for tomorrow." Just like she did every day. "Mom, tell me what's wrong. You never call me at work."

"I shouldn't. I know how busy you are."

"I'm not busy right now. Talk to me."

Silence, then finally, "James Colt is back in town. Apparently, he's taking over his father's investigations business?"

"I don't know. Maybe. Mom, why—"

"That boy is trouble. He always has been. I just don't like the idea of him being in the same building as you."

"He's not in the same building," she said, unable to understand why her stepmother was so upset over this. "He's staying next door in his father's office."

"So, you've seen him?"

"He's stopped by for sandwiches a couple of times." She realized that her stepmother was calling from her car. "Are you in your car? Where are you going?"

"Nowhere. I mean...to the store. I'm out of milk."

Her stepmother didn't drink milk. Nor did she hardly eat anything but fruit and vegetables. Her stepdaughter owned a sandwich shop and her stepmother didn't eat even gluten-free bread. "Are you sure you're all right?"

"Sometimes I just need to hear my daughter's voice. I didn't mean to scare you."

Scare her? Lorelei realized that was exactly what she'd done. Scare her. This wasn't like Karen. Whatever had upset her... She realized that it seemed to be James Colt and his plan to take over his father's PI business. It had upset her too, but Lorelei had her reasons going all the way back to middle school. She couldn't imagine first how her stepmother had heard and second why that would upset her unless…

"Mom," she said as a bad feeling settled in her stomach. "Did James come by to see you?"

"I'm at the store about to check out," her stepmother said. "I have to go. Talk to you later." She disconnected.

Lorelei held the phone feeling a wave of shock wash over her. Her stepmother had just lied to her. She wasn't in the store checkout. Karen had still been in her car driving. She'd heard the crunch of tires on gravel. Where had her stepmother gone? Not the store with its paved parking lot.

She quickly called her back. But got voice mail straight away. She didn't leave a message.

AT FIRST KAREN WILKINS seemed to be driving aimlessly around town. James had finally pulled over on a side street with a view of Main Street near her exercise studio and waited. She pulled in front of the studio and he'd thought she was going to get out.

But a few minutes later, she took off again without getting out of the car. If she'd had a class, someone else was now teaching it apparently. This time, she headed out of town. James waited until another car got behind Karen Wilkins's car before he pulled out and followed.

A few miles out of town, he saw her brake lights come on ahead of him right before she turned down a gravel road and disappeared into the pines. He caught up, turned and followed the dust trail she'd made, wondering if she was finally going to park somewhere.

He didn't have to wonder long. Around a curve in the road, he saw her car stop in front of a large house set back in the pines. Pulling over, he watched her exit her car and hurry up the steps. As she rang the doorbell, she looked around nervously, before the door opened a few moments later.

The man in the doorway quickly pulled Karen Wilkins into his arms, holding her for a moment before he wiped her tears and then kissed her passionately. As he drew her inside, he glanced around—giving James a clear view of his face—before he quickly closed the door.

James felt as if he'd touched a live wire. He let out a low curse. He'd been hoping that he was wrong about Lorelei's stepmother. He'd hoped there was a simple explanation for her being on his father's list. James still didn't want to believe it, but there was no doubt that he'd upset Karen Wilkins on his visit to her house. Since then she'd been running scared.

And look where she'd run. Straight into the arms of Senator Fred Bayard.

CHAPTER EIGHT

JAMES DROVE BACK into town, stopping in at the local hardware store that his friend Ryan owned. He found him in the back office doing paperwork. "What is Senator Bayard doing in Lonesome?"

His friend looked up and laughed. "You don't get out much, do you? Fred had a summer home built here about ten years ago. He's one of my best customers, always building something out there on his property."

James didn't follow politics. The only reason he'd recognized the man was because his face had been in so many television ads before the last election. "Why here?"

Ryan leaned forward, his elbows on his desk. "His family's from here. It isn't that unusual. What has got you so worked up? I didn't know you were back in town, let alone that you cared about politics."

"Wait, the senator's from Lonesome?" That couldn't have been something he'd missed.

"His mother was Claudia Hanson, the postmistress. Fred grew up here. He was your father's age. Claudia moved them to Helena at some point when she married Charles Bayard, also a senator, and Bayard adopted Fred."

"I never knew that."

"His great-grandfather started the original sawmill

here in Lonesome about the time the railroad was coming through. Heard he made a bundle making and selling railroad ties to the Great Northern. Did you pay any attention at all during Montana history class?"

"Apparently not." He vaguely remembered this, but it had been out of context back then. "You've met him then?"

"Fred? He's a good old boy. Like I said, he stops in when he's in town, which isn't often. Most of the time he's in DC. The rest of the time, he's building corrals or barns or adding onto the summer house, even though he spends so little time here during the year."

James sank into the chair across from Ryan's desk, thinking about what he'd just seen. Karen in the man's arms. "Doesn't he have a wife?"

"Mary? I don't think I've ever seen her. She doesn't spend much time here. They have a big place outside of Helena. I think she stays there most of the time doing her own thing. Why the interest?"

He shook his head. "Have you ever seen him with another woman?"

Ryan looked surprised. He leaned back in his chair. "I'm guessing you have. Someone I know?"

"I'm probably mistaken." He quickly changed the subject. "I'm back for a while. I supposed you heard about Melody and my trailer." His friend nodded. "I'm staying at my dad's old office for the time being." He chewed at his cheek for a moment. "I'm thinking about getting my PI license."

"Seriously?"

"I need to heal up before I go back on the rodeo circuit. I thought it would give me something to do."

Ryan narrowed his gaze. "If I didn't know you so well, I might believe that. What's really going on?"

He sighed. "I'm kind of working Del's last case, Billy Sherman's hit-and-run death. It's never been solved."

"Like a tribute to your old man?"

"Maybe."

"And you think Senator Bayard is involved?"

He shook his head. "I was following a lead that made me aware of Bayard. You said he had his summer home built about ten years ago? So, he might have been here at the time of Billy Sherman's accident."

Ryan gave him a wary look. "Where are you going with this?"

James pulled off his Stetson and raked a hand through his hair. "I have no idea. I'm probably just chasing my own tail."

His friend laughed. "I'd be careful if I were you. Bayard carries a lot of weight in this state. Talk is that he might run for governor."

"Don't worry. I'm just following a few leads. I hate that Del didn't get to finish the case." He thought about mentioning what Alice had told him. That Del said he was close to solving it—and was killed that very night.

But he knew what it would sound like and Ryan knew him too well. Conspiracy theory aside, he had his own reasons for fearing what he might find if he dug into his father's death. His father had been acting strangely in those weeks—or was it months—before his death. Something more than the case had been bothering him.

"How's things with you?"

Ryan motioned to the paperwork stacked up on the desk. "Busy as usual. More people are finding Lonesome. I bought the lumberyard a few years ago. Quite a few new houses coming up, so that's good. You thinking about building out there on your place?"

"I'll see what my brothers want to do when they get back after the rodeo season."

"You can't see yourself staying long-term?"

A fleeting image of Lorelei popped into his head, followed by the little girl on the horse. He shook his head. "Nope, can't see myself staying."

LORELEI CLOSED THE shop right after her last customer left. She usually stayed open until six, but tonight she was anxious to leave. She'd tried to call her stepmother numerous times, but each call had gone to voice mail. After how frantic Karen had sounded earlier…

She parked out front. No sign of her stepmother's car. As she started toward the front door, she checked the garage and felt a surge of relief. Her car was parked inside. At the front door she knocked. Normally she just walked right in. But nothing about earlier had felt normal.

"Lorelei?" Her stepmother seemed not just surprised to see her but startled. True, Lorelei hadn't stopped over to the house for a while. She'd been so busy with the sandwich shop. "Is something wrong?"

"How can you ask that?" Lorelei demanded. "You called me earlier clearly upset and when I tried to call you back, my call went straight to voice mail. I've been worried about you all afternoon."

"I'm so sorry. I guess I turned my phone off. Come in." She moved out of the doorway.

As she stepped in, she tried to breathe, admitting to herself just how scared she'd been and how relieved.

Her stepmother seemed okay. But Karen wasn't easily rattled. Instead, she'd always taken things in her stride. In fact, she'd seemed really happy for a long while now. Except for the way she'd sounded on the phone earlier.

She turned to study her stepmother and saw something she hadn't before. How had she not noticed the change in her? Karen Wilkins was practically glowing. She was always slim and trim because she often led classes at her studio. But she appeared healthier and happier looking.

"You look so…good," she said, unable to put her finger on what exactly was different about her stepmother.

Karen laughed, brown eyes twinkling, clearly pleased. "Why, thank you."

"Has something changed?"

Her stepmother's smile quickly disappeared, replaced by a frown. "Why would you ask that?"

"I don't know. You just seem…different."

Brushing that off, Karen headed for the kitchen cupboard, saying over her shoulder, "I made some granola. I was going to call you and see if you—"

"Mom. Stop. Why were you so upset earlier when you called me?"

Her stepmother froze for a moment before turning to face her. "I feel so foolish. I got worked up over nothing." Lorelei put her hands on her hips, waiting.

Finally, Karen sighed and said, "James Colt paid me a visit."

Which explained her stepmother's reaction to him staying in the building next to the sandwich shop. "He came here? Why would he—"

"He's taking over one of his father's old cases apparently and was asking questions about something that happened years ago."

Lorelei noticed that her stepmother was twisting the life out of the plastic bag with the granola in it. "What case?"

"That hit-and-run... The boy, Billy Sherman."

"Why would he ask *you* about that?" But she was thinking, why would that upset her stepmother so much?

Her stepmother turned back to the cupboard. Lorelei watched her busy herself with fixing a bag to send home with her. "I have no idea. He's probably asking a lot of people in the neighborhood."

Lorelei frowned. The accident had happened probably a half mile from her stepmother's house. "I'm sure that's all it was," she said, even though her pulse was spiking. She knew her stepmother. Something was definitely wrong. "It still doesn't explain why you were so upset."

Karen sighed. "I was just sorry to find out that he's back in town and in the office next to you given the crush you had on him in high school."

"I didn't have a crush on him in high school!" she protested, no doubt too much.

"Lorelei, I was there. I saw your reaction to that boy. You're doing so well with your business. I'm just afraid you're going to get mixed up with him."

"I'm not getting mixed up with him. He's come over to the shop a couple of times. I don't know where you got the idea I had a crush on him."

Her stepmother merely looked at her impatiently before she said, "Here, take this home." Karen thrust the bag of granola into her hands and looked at her watch. "I'm sorry I have a class I'm teaching this evening. I wish you could stay and we could watch an old movie." She was steering her toward the door. Giving her the bum's rush, as her father would have said.

She wanted to dig her heels in, demand to know why she was acting so strangely. Was it really because she was worried about Lorelei and James Colt, her new neighbor, the cowboy impersonating a PI?

That was ridiculous.

JAMES HAD BEEN at his father's desk, head in his hands, when the pounding at his door made him jump. What the— "Hold your horses!" he called as he rose to go to the door. "What's the big—" He stopped when he saw Lori standing there.

Her face was flushed, her brown eyes wide, her breathing rapid as if she'd run up the stairs. She was still wearing what she'd had on earlier.

"Is there a fire?" A shake of her head. "Are you being chased by zombies?" A dirty look. "Then I give up." He leaned against the doorjamb to survey her, giving her time to catch her breath. He had a pretty good idea what had her upset, but he wasn't going to bring it up unless she did.

"Why are you questioning my stepmother about the hit-and-run accident?" she demanded.

"Why don't you step in and we can discuss this like—"

"Do you have any idea how much you upset her?"

He nodded slowly. "Actually, I do. Which makes me wonder why, and now why you're even more upset."

Lori took a breath then another one. Her gaze swung away from him for a moment. He watched her regain control of her emotions. She swallowed before she looked at him again. "Why did you question her?" Her voice almost sounded in the normal range.

He moved aside and motioned her into the office. With obvious reluctance, she stepped in, stopping in the middle of the room.

"I love what you've done with the place," she said derisively.

James glanced around, seeing things through her eyes. "I've been meaning to buy a few things to make it more…homey. I've been busy."

"Yes," she said turning to glare at him. "Intimidating my stepmother."

"Is that what she told you?"

A muscle jumped in her jaw. "I will ask you again. Why my stepmother?"

"She was on my father's list."

Lorelei stared at him. "What list?"

He stepped around behind the desk, but didn't sit down. "My father had a method that worked for him. Did you know he solved all of his cases? He was methodical. I wish I was more like him." He could see her growing more impatient. "He would write down a list of names of people connected to the case that he wanted to talk to. He'd check off the ones as he went. Your stepmother was on the list. He hadn't gotten around to questioning her before he was killed. I decided to take up where he left off and ask her myself."

"And?"

"And nothing—she got upset, said she had a class and threw me out."

"Maybe she did have a class."

He gave her a you-really-believe-that look? He watched all the anger seep from her. She looked close to tears, her back no longer ramrod straight, her facial muscles no longer rigid.

"Why would she know anything about Billy Sherman?" she asked quietly.

He shrugged and stepped around the desk to dust off one of the leather club chairs. She moved to it as if sleepwalking and carefully lowered herself down. Behind the desk again, he opened the bottom drawer, took out the bottle of brandy his father kept there and two of the paper cups.

After pouring them each a couple of fingers' worth, he handed her a cup as he took the matching leather chair next to her. He noticed her hand trembled as she took the drink. She was scared. He was afraid she had good reason to be.

He waited until she'd taken a sip of the brandy before he asked, "Can you think of any reason your stepmother would be so upset about talking to me about the case?"

She shook her head, took a gulp and looked over at him. "You can't really think that she is somehow involved." When he didn't speak instantly, she snapped, "James, my stepmother wouldn't hit a child and keep going."

"I'm not saying she did. But she might know who did."

Lori shook her head, drained her paper cup and set it on the edge of his desk as she rose. "You really think she would keep a secret like that?"

"People keep secrets from those they love all the time," he said.

She glared at him. "What is that supposed to mean?"

"Just that she might be covering for someone."

Her eyes flared. "If you tell me that you think she's covering for me—"

He rose, raising both hands in surrender as he did. "I'm not accusing you. I'm just saying…" He met her gaze, surprised at how hard this was. He and Lori had gone through school together and hardly said two words the entire time. It wasn't like that much had changed over the past few days, he told himself even as he knew it had. He liked her. Always had.

"I think your stepmother knows something and that's why she got so upset." He said the words quickly.

Her reaction was just as quick. "My stepmother wouldn't cover for *anyone*. Not for such a horrible crime. You're wrong. She doesn't keep secrets." She started toward the door.

"You might not know your stepmother as well as you think you do." All his instincts told him she didn't.

She reached the door and spun around to face him, anger firing those brown eyes again. "What are you trying to say?"

"That your stepmother might have secrets. Maybe especially from you."

She scoffed at that, and hands on her hips demanded to know what he was talking about.

"After I questioned her about Billy Sherman's death, your stepmother headed for her studio, saying she had to teach a class. But instead of teaching, she drove out of town and into the arms of Senator Fred Bayard."

He saw the answer as the color drained from her face. She hadn't known. "I'm sorry." He mentally kicked himself for the pain in her eyes before she threw open the door and stormed out.

He swore as he heard her leave. How did his father do this? He had no idea, but he suspected Del was a hell of a lot better at it than he'd been so far.

CHAPTER NINE

FOR THE NEXT few days, James avoided the sandwich shop and Lori. He felt guilty for exposing her step-mother. But he'd hoped that Karen Wilkins might be honest with her stepdaughter. He needed to know what the woman was hiding—other than the senator.

He'd called out-of-town body shops and left messages for them to call if they had a front end–damaged car from hitting something like a deer after the date of Billy Sherman's death. He didn't have much hope, given how much time had passed. He also assumed his father had done the same thing nine years ago without much success.

While he waited to hear back, he mulled over the case as he cleaned up the office and back bedroom. He bought a few things to make the place more comfortable by adding a couch, a couple of end tables, a coffee table, a large rug and some bookshelves for more storage.

For the bedroom, he'd bought a new rug for the hardwood floor and all new towels, rug and shower cur-tain for the bathroom. He'd even replaced his father's old vacuum with a new one and dusted and washed the windows. By the time he was through with all the haul-ing and cleaning his leg hurt and his ribs ached worse.

But when he looked around the place, he felt better. He'd also sent in his application for his private investigator license and dropped off his permit at the sheriff's office to have the burned-out trailer removed from the property. Margaret had suggested a company that did that kind of work. After a call to them, he was told the work would be done this week.

James had to admit he was pretty impressed with what he'd accomplished. But he was no closer to finding Billy Sherman's killer. Also, he realized that he missed Lori's sandwiches and the time he spent with her. He'd been hitting the local In-N-Out, but had pretty much gone through the fried food menu over the past few days. He found himself craving the smell of fresh-baked bread—and the sweet scent of Lori.

He just wasn't sure what kind of reception he would get so he decided to do some real work first. After pulling out the list of names, he grabbed his Stetson and headed for the door.

Maybe he'd get a sandwich to go, he thought as he locked and closed the office door behind him. He'd worried about Lori since he'd dropped the bombshell. All she could do was throw him out if she really couldn't stand the sight of him, right?

LORELEI HAD DRIVEN straight to her stepmother's house the evening after James had told her about her stepmother's relationship. She'd seen a light on and movement behind the kitchen curtains. Her stepmother's car was in the driveway, which was odd. She'd slowed and was about to pull in when she saw a second shadow behind the kitchen curtains.

She'd quickly pulled away, feeling like a coward. Why hadn't she confronted her stepmother and whoever was in the house with her? She told herself she needed to be calm before she did. That it would be better if she spoke about this with her stepmother when she was alone.

When she'd run out of excuses, she'd driven home and looked up Senator Bayard online. There were publicity photos of him and his wife, Mary, and their three daughters—all adults, but all younger than Lorelei.

James had to be wrong. He'd misunderstood. Although she couldn't imagine what had made him think that her stepmother would have an affair with a married man—let alone keep it from her only stepdaughter.

She knew that was the part that hurt. She and Karen had been close, hadn't they? And yet, the other night when she'd driven by, her stepmother hadn't been alone. Could have been a neighbor over, but Lorelei knew it wasn't true. The shadows had been close, then moved together as if one before breaking apart and disappearing from view. Her stepmother did have secrets.

The bell over the front door of the sandwich shop jangled and she looked up to see James Colt come in. He was the last person she wanted to see right now. Or ever. Emotions came at her like a squad of fighter jets. Mad, angry, embarrassed, upset, worried, resigned and at the same time her heart beat a little faster at the sight of him.

"Any chance of getting a sandwich to go?" he asked almost sheepishly.

"I suppose," she said, still battling her conflicting emotions.

He glanced from her to the chalkboard. She studied him while he studied it. He was wearing a blue paisley-patterned Western shirt that matched his eyes. She wondered if he'd bought it or if it was purchased by a girlfriend. It was tucked into the waist of his perfectly fitting jeans. One of his prizewinning rodeo buckles rounded out his attire. He shifted on his feet, taking her gaze down his long legs to his boots. New boots? She'd heard him hauling stuff in and out the past few days and knew he'd been shopping.

"I'll take the special on a roll," he said.

After all that, he'd chosen the special? "Iced tea?"

"How about a cola?"

"Fine. Have a seat. I'll bring it to you."

He nodded and met her gaze. "Lori—"

Whatever he planned to say, she didn't want to hear it. Turning on her heel, she hurried into the kitchen to make his sandwich and try to calm her pounding heart. What was it about the man that had her hands shaking? He just made her so…so…so not her usual controlled self.

Lori. No one had ever called her anything but Lorelei. Leave it to James to give her a nickname. Leave it to James to say it in a way that made her feel all soft inside.

JAMES COULDN'T GET a handle on Lorelei's mood. He hated to think what she was putting in his sandwich. Maybe coming here hadn't been his best idea. But he was hungry, and at least for a few minutes he got to breathe in the smell of freshly baked bread and stretch out his legs.

He didn't have to wait long. When he saw her coming, he started to get up but she waved him back down.

"I thought you'd prefer I take it to go."

She shook her head. "Barbecued pork is hard to eat in your pickup, though I'm sure you've managed it before," she said as she sat down in a chair opposite him.

He wasn't sure the last was a compliment so he simply unwrapped his sandwich and carefully lifted the top piece of bun to see what was inside.

"It's just pulled pork, my fresh coleslaw and house special barbecue sauce," she said, sounding indignant.

"It's your special sauce that I'm worried about," he said.

"It's not too spicy. A tough cowboy like you should be able to handle it." Her gaze challenged him to argue.

He put the sandwich back together and took a bite. "Delicious." He took another bite. He really was starved.

"Do you have to keep sounding surprised that I can make a decent sandwich?" she demanded.

"Sorry, it's just that you're so…so…" He waved a hand in the air, wishing he hadn't opened his mouth.

"So? So what? Uptight? Too good to do simple things?"

He took a bite, chewed and swallowed, stalling. "You're so…sexy." He held up a hand as if expecting a blow. "I know it's a cliché that a sexy woman can't cook. Still…"

"Sexy?" She shook her head and let out an exasperated sigh, but she didn't leave his table. He continued eating. He could see her working through a few things. But when she finally spoke, her words took him by surprise. "I need to know why my stepmother is on your father's list."

He wiped his mouth with a napkin and took a drink of the cola. "I don't know. That's why I went to talk to her."

He could see she was struggling with the next question and decided to help her out. "After she got so upset I followed her. She drove all over town, at one point made a couple of phone calls and then drove out of town. I didn't even know the senator had a house here until he opened the front door."

"Just because she went to his house— Isn't it possible they're just good friends?"

He shook his head. "He took her in his arms and kissed her. It was passionate and she kissed him back. They both seemed nervous, worried that someone was watching and hurriedly closed the door."

"Someone *was* watching," she said under her breath. She looked sick to her stomach.

"I'm sorry to be the one to tell you. I was surprised to see her name on the list. I went there hoping she'd tell me why. It was a shot in the dark. But then when she got so upset before I even had a chance to ask her..."

She nodded. "Refill?" she asked, pointing at his cola.

He shook his head. "You haven't talked to her?"

"I haven't wanted to believe it. I was hoping you were wrong." Her gaze came up to meet his. "I suppose if anyone knows a passionate kiss when he sees one, it would be you though."

He laughed, leaning his elbows on the table to close the distance between them. "You give me a lot more credit than I'm due." She harrumphed at that. "Why do I get the feeling that I did something to you back in grade school or high school or this week and that's why you're so angry with me?"

"You didn't. It's just that I know what kind of man you are."

"Do you?" he asked seriously before shaking his head. "I thought you were smarter than to believe everything you hear. Especially about me." He dropped his voice. "I've kissed a few women. But I'm still waiting to kiss the one who rattles me clear down to the toes of my boots."

She raised a brow. "You've been in town for a few days. I'm sure you have one in your sights already."

"Oh, I do," he said, realizing it was true. He just wondered if he'd ever get the chance to kiss her.

LORELEI CALLED HER stepmother after James left. "I was thinking we could have dinner together tonight if you don't have any plans. I could pick up—" She was going to suggest something vegan for her stepmother, when Karen interrupted her.

"You don't have to pick up anything. I can make us a nice salad for dinner."

She felt off balance. She'd been half expecting her stepmother to make an excuse because she was seeing her…lover again tonight? "Sure, that would be great."

"Good, then I'll see you about six thirty," Karen said.

"See you then."

She disconnected, telling herself that James was wrong. That what she'd seen last night might not even have been the senator. That her stepmother's name being on Del Colt's list meant nothing.

When she arrived at the house a little after six, her stepmother answered the door smiling and seeming excited to see her. She ushered her into the kitchen where she'd made a pitcher of lemonade. "I thought we could eat out on the patio. It's such a beautiful evening."

Lorelei had planned to question her after they ate, but she realized she couldn't sit through chitchat for an hour first. She watched her stepmother start to pour them each a glass of lemonade over ice.

"Are you having an affair with Senator Bayard?"

Her stepmother's arm jerked, lemonade spilling over the breakfast bar. Without looking at her, Karen slowly set down the pitcher, then reached for a dishcloth to clean up the mess. Without a word, she'd already admitted the truth.

"I can't believe this," Lorelei cried. "When did this happen? *How* did this happen? He's *married*!"

Her stepmother turned to her, her face set in stone. "He's getting a divorce and then we're going to get married."

"That's what they all say," she snapped. "Don't you watch daytime talk shows?"

"He's separated and has been for some time. He's been staying at the family's summer home here when he isn't in Washington." Karen looked down at the dishcloth in her hands. "We've been seeing each other for a while now." She looked up.

"Before he and his wife were supposedly separated." It wasn't a question.

"I'm not proud of it. It just happened."

Lorelei shook her head. *"It just happened?"*

"I love him and he loves me."

She bit her tongue, thinking how different this conversation would have been if she'd been the one having the affair. Her stepmother would be hitting the roof right now. Look how upset she'd supposedly gotten over James Colt being in the building next door to her stepdaughter. "You haven't said how you met him."

"Our paths crossed a few times while he was here building his summer home," she said. "We found we had a lot in common."

Lorelei wanted to ask what, but she wasn't ready to hear this. "You're serious." Of course her stepmother was. That glow she'd noticed. Karen was in *love*. That her stepmother would even consider an affair with a married man told her how head over heels she was with this man.

"With him possibly running for governor, the timing isn't good, but we're going to get married once the fallout from his divorce settles."

She couldn't bring herself to say that she wasn't holding her breath and neither should her stepmother. But she was so disappointed and angry right now that she couldn't deal with this. Karen had cautioned her about men since she was thirteen.

"Let me get the salad and we can go out on the deck and—"

"I'm sorry," she said. "I've lost my appetite." With that she turned and started for the door.

"Lorelei, wait."

She stopped at the door, closing her eyes as she heard her stepmother come up behind her. She thought of all the tantrums she'd thrown as a teen, all the arguments she and Karen had had over the years. They'd always made up and gotten through it.

"I'm sorry I've disappointed you."

"I am too, Karen." She started to open the door, felt her stepmother tentatively touch her back and flinched.

Her stepmother quickly removed her hand. "Disappointed in me or not you have to understand, I'm an adult. I get to make my own decisions, right or wrong." Her voice broke. "I'm still young. I've been lonely since your father died. Can't you try to be happy for me?"

Lorelei felt herself weaken, her love for her stepmother a constant in her life. Karen was right. She was still young and she'd been a widow for years now. Of course she was lonely; of course she wanted a man in her life.

"I'm trying," she said and turned to face her. "Tell me you aren't involved in what happened to the Sherman boy. Swear it on my life."

Her stepmother looked shocked. "Why would you ask—"

"Because I know you. For you to get so upset over James's questions about the case that you'd run to your lover and be seen, you must have something else to hide. Tell me the truth."

Her stepmother took a step back. "So, it was James who saw us and ran right to you to tell you. I should have known."

"He didn't run right to me. I cornered him, demanding to know why he would question you. But you still haven't answered my question," Lorelei said, that knot in her chest tightening. "Swear. On my life."

"Don't be ridiculous," Karen snapped and took another step back. "I would never swear to anything on your life. You're upset and don't know what you're saying. You should go before either of us says something we'll regret."

Lorelei felt tears burn her eyes. "You already have." With that, she opened the door and left.

CHAPTER TEN

AFTER LEAVING THE sandwich shop, James had felt at loose ends. He drove out to his family's ranch. *Ranch* was a loosely used term since no one had raised much of anything on the land. It was close to a hundred acres covered with pines. Some of it was mountainous while a strip of it bordered the river.

He and his brothers had talked about selling some of it off since they didn't use it, but Willie, their eldest brother, talked them out of it.

"Land doesn't have to do anything and someday you're going to be glad that it's there and that it's ours," Willie had said.

The remains of the double-wide trailer had been removed leaving a scorched area of ground where it had been. But James could see where grass was already starting to grow. It wouldn't be long before nature healed the spot.

James stood looking at the rolling hillsides, towering pines and granite bluffs. He was glad Willie had talked them out of selling even a portion of it. This land was all that brought them back here. It was the one constant in their lives. The one tangible in their otherwise nomadic lives.

That and the office building. He thought about Lori

wanting to buy it. He still thought of the place as Del's and felt himself balk at the idea of ever giving it up.

Back at the office, he found several notes tacked to his back door. Word had gotten out that he was in business. One was from an insurance company offering him surveillance work if he was interested. The other was from someone who wanted her boyfriend followed. He laughed, delighted that he had several new PI jobs if he wanted them.

But first he had to finish what he'd started. He drove out to Edgar Appleton's house some miles from town. Edgar owned a heavy equipment construction company. He and his crew had been working near where Billy Sherman's body had been found. One of his employees, Lyle Harris, had been operating a front loader that morning. He was about to dump a load of dirt into the ditch when a neighbor woman spotted the body and screamed—stopping him.

Edgar lived on a twenty-acre tract. His house sat off to one side, his equipment taking up the rest of the property. Several vehicles were parked in front of the house when James climbed the steps to knock. He could hear loud voices inside and knocked again.

A hush came from inside the house a moment before the door opened. Edgar filled the doorway. He was a big man with a wild head of brown hair that stuck up every which way. He was wearing a sweatshirt with his business logo on it and a pair of canvas pants. It appeared he'd just gotten home from work.

"If this is a bad time…"

"James Colt," Edgar said in a loud boisterous voice. "Bad time? It's always a bad time at this house. Come in!" He stepped aside. "Irene, put another plate on the table."

She yelled something back that he didn't catch just a moment before she appeared behind her husband wiping her hands on her apron. "You'd think I'm only here to cook and clean for this man." She smiled, her whole face lighting up. "Get on in here. I have a beef roast and vegetables coming out of the oven. I hope your table manners are better than Ed's. I could use some stimulating conversation for once." Her laugh filled the large room as she headed back to the kitchen.

"The meanest woman who ever lived," Edgar said so she could hear it. Her response was swift, followed by the banging of pots and pans. "I don't know what I would do without her."

"That's for sure!" she called from the kitchen.

"I can't stay for dinner. I probably should have called first," James said.

"Sorry, but you have no choice now," Edgar said as he looped an arm around his shoulders and dragged him in. "She'll swear I ran you off and I'll have to hear about it the rest of the night."

He had to admit, Irene's dinner smelled wonderful. He heard his stomach growl. So did Edgar. The man laughed heartily as he swept him into the dining room off the kitchen.

"I didn't come for dinner, but it sure smells good," he told Irene as she brought out a pan of homemade rolls. "Let me help you with that." He grabbed the hot pads on the counter and helped her get the huge pot out of the oven. It was enough food to feed an army, he saw. "Are there other people coming?" he asked as she directed him to a trivet at the head of the large dining room table.

"At this house, you never know," Irene said. "I like to be prepared. As it is, Ed didn't bring home half the crew tonight so I'm glad you showed up."

"Me too," Ed said as he sat down at the head of the table and began to slice up the roast. Irene swatted him with the dishtowel she took from her shoulder before she sat to his right and motioned James into the chair across from her.

"James, I want to hear it all," she said smiling as she reached for his plate and Edgar began to load it up with thick slices of the beef. "You know what I'm talking about," she said, seeing his confusion. "Is it true? You've taken over your father's private investigative business? We'll get to Melody and what happened to your trailer later."

"Sorry, I should have warned you," Edgar said with a laugh. "The woman is relentless." As he said it, he reached over and squeezed her arm.

For the rest of the meal, they all talked and laughed. James couldn't recall a time he'd enjoyed more. Seeing how these two genuinely cared about each other was heartwarming and Irene's dinner was amazing.

"I know you didn't come by for dinner," Edgar said when they'd finished and Irene got up to clear the table. James started to rise to help her but she waved him back down.

He explained that he was looking into his father's last case, the hit-and-run that killed Billy Sherman.

"We were working in that subdivision. You know Lyle, my front-end loader operator, was working that morning," Edgar said. "He was getting ready to fill in that ditch we'd dug when a neighbor lady came over with some turnovers she'd made for the crew. She saw

Billy lying there and started screaming." He shook his head. "It wrecked us all." Irene came from the kitchen to place her hand on the big man's shoulder for a few moments before taking the rest of the dirty plates into the kitchen.

"That was a new neighborhood nine years ago, new pavement," James said. "Did you see skid marks, any indication that whoever hit him had tried to stop?"

Edgar wagged his big head. "The sheriff, that was Otis back then, said the driver must have thought he hit a deer and that was why he didn't stop. Plus it was raining hard that night. I reckon the car was going so fast when it hit the boy—he was pretty scrawny for his age—that the driver hadn't known what was hit."

"But the driver had to have known it wasn't a deer, even if he didn't stop," James said. "There would have been some damage to the car, a dent or a broken headlight." Edgar nodded. "I would think the car would have had to have been repaired."

"You're assuming the driver was local, but even if that was the case, he wouldn't have had it repaired in town."

James thought of the next name on his list that his father hadn't gotten to: Gus Hughes of Hughes Body Shop in town. But Edgar was right. If it had been a local, then the driver would have gotten the car repaired out of town.

Irene came in and changed the subject as she served coffee and raspberry pie with a scoop of ice cream.

"I can't tell you how much I've enjoyed this meal," James told her before Edgar walked him to the door.

"I hope you find out who killed that boy," the big man said, patting him on the shoulder. "It's time he was put to rest."

LORELEI WOKE FEELING exhausted after a night of tossing and turning. She kept thinking about her stepmother and going from angry to sad to worried and regretful for the things she'd said. Her stepmother couldn't know anything about Billy Sherman's death. So why hadn't she sworn that? Why had she gotten even more upset and basically thrown Lorelei out of her house?

After a shower, she dressed for work. Owning her own business meant she went to work whether she felt like it or not. She had a couple of women she hired during the busiest seasons to help out, but she'd never considered turning the place over to one of them before this morning.

She reeled her thoughts back. What had she been doing nine years ago when Billy Sherman died? Working in a friend's sandwich shop in Billings, learning the business. Before that she'd had numerous jobs using her college business degree, but hadn't found anything that called to her. She'd always known that she wanted the independence of having her own business.

And what had her stepmother been doing nine years ago? Karen had her exercise studio and had been teaching a lot, as far as Lorelei could remember.

Frowning now, she tried to remember if it had been her stepmother who'd told her about Billy Sherman's hit-and-run or if she'd heard it on the news. Didn't she remember a phone conversation about it? Her stepmother being understandably upset since it had happened not that far from her house in that new adjoining subdivision.

Lorelei felt sick to her stomach and more scared than she'd ever been. She had to know the truth. But if she couldn't get her stepmother to tell her…

It was still early. She called her friend Anita and asked her if she wanted to fill in today, apologizing for the short notice. Anita jumped at the opportunity, saying she had nothing planned and could use the money.

"I had already made a list of the specials," Lorelei told her. "Everything you need is in the cooler. You just have to get the bread going right away. I'll be in to help as soon as I can."

Anita said she was already on her way out the door headed for the shop, making Lorelei smile. Her business would be fine. Grabbing her purse, she headed for her car.

WITH THE RISING SUN, James had awakened knowing he was going to have to talk to former sheriff Otis Osterman at some point. He had too many questions about how the sheriff had handled the investigation. According to his father's notes, Otis had refused to give him any information. James suspected it was one reason his father had taken a case that had still been active.

Del hadn't gotten along with the former sheriff and James had a history with Otis due to his wayward youth. So, he wasn't expecting the conversation was going to go well.

After getting ready for his day, he decided he would talk to Gus Hughes first, then swing by Otis's place out by the river. His father had already talked to Gus, but James thought it wouldn't hurt to talk to him again.

However, when he went downstairs to where his pickup was parked out back of the office building, he found Lorelei Wilkins leaning against his truck waiting for him.

He braced himself as he tried to read her mood. "Mornin'," he said, stopping a few safe feet from her.

She looked as if she didn't want to be there any more than he did. For a moment, he thought she would simply storm off without a word. "I want to hire you."

Of all the things that he'd thought might happen, this wasn't one of them. "I beg your pardon?"

"You heard me," she snapped, lifting her chin defiantly. "What do you charge?"

Good question. He had no idea. Legally, he wasn't a private investigator yet. The application and money had been sent in. He was waiting for his license. "If we're going to talk money, we should at least go somewhere besides an alley. Have you had breakfast?"

"I couldn't eat a thing right now."

"Could you watch me eat? Because I'm starved!" He gave her a sheepish grin. Even after that meal he'd had last night, he was hungry. He figured she might relax more in a public place. She also might not go off on him in a local cafe filled with people they both probably knew.

Because, he suspected before this was over, she would want to tell him what she thought of him.

Lorelei admitted this was a mistake as she watched James put away a plate of hotcakes.

"You sure you don't want a bite?" he asked between a forkful.

"I'm sure." The smell of bacon and pancakes had made her stomach growl, reminding her that she hadn't eaten dinner last night. But she still couldn't swallow a bite right now, she told herself. She just wanted to get this over with.

"So, are you going to do it or not?" she demanded.

He finished the hotcakes, put down his fork and pushed the plate aside. She watched him wipe his mouth and hands on his napkin before he said, "What exactly is it you want me to do?"

"I just told you," she said between gritted teeth. Leaning forward and dropping her voice even though there wasn't anyone sitting near them in the cafe, she said, "Find out the truth about my…" She mouthed, "Stepmother."

He seemed to give that some thought for a moment before he said, "Wouldn't the simplest, fastest approach be for you to ask her yourself?"

"I already tried that," she said and sighed.

"And she denied any knowledge?"

She looked away under the intenseness of those blue eyes of his. "Not exactly. She asked me to leave her house."

"Come on," James said, tossing money on the table before rising. "Let's go."

It wasn't until they were in his pickup that he said, "What is it you think I can do that you can't?"

"I thought you had some…talent for this."

"Like what? Throw my magic lariat around her so she tells the truth? Or use my brawn to beat the truth out of her?"

She mugged a face at him. "Of course not. I thought maybe you could break into her house and look for evidence."

Now they were finally getting somewhere, James thought. He disregarded the illegal breaking and entering part and asked, "What kind of evidence?"

She swallowed before she said, "A diary maybe. She used to keep one. Or…maybe a bill from like, say a… body shop for car repairs."

"What would make you think I'd find something like that even if nine years hadn't passed?"

"Because," she snapped, clearly losing patience with him. "If she was the one who hit Billy, then she would have had to have her car repaired, right? Has this thought really not crossed your mind?"

"My father already talked to Gus Hughes at his body shop."

She waved a hand through the air in obvious frustration. "Are you just pretending to be this dense? She wouldn't have taken it to the local body shop. She's smarter than that. She would have taken it out of town. It's not like she could keep it hidden in her garage for long."

"But she also couldn't simply drive it out of town either without someone noticing," he said.

"Maybe she did it at night."

He shook his head. "Still too risky. And how does she explain no car for as long as it was in the body shop?"

"It was summer. She always rides her bike to work in the summer. There must be some way she could get the car out of town to a body shop and get it brought back without anyone being the wiser."

"I have a couple of thoughts on the matter. In fact, I'm talking to someone on my list today about just that. I've already made inquiries of a half dozen body shops within a hundred-mile radius."

She sat back, looking surprised. "So, you *have* thought about all of this?" He didn't answer, simply looked at her. She let out a breath and seemed to relax a little. "You still haven't told me what you charge."

"Let's see what I turn up first, okay?"

Lorelei nodded and looked uncomfortable. "I'm starved. Would you mind stopping at a drive-thru on the way back to your office?"

He chuckled and started the engine. Out of the corner of his eye he watched her. She was scared, and maybe with good reason, that her stepmother was somehow involved.

He'd wanted to solve this case for his father. Also to prove something to himself. But right now he wanted to find evidence to clear Karen Wilkins more than anything else because of her stepdaughter. He wanted to put that beautiful smile back on Lori's face, even as he feared he was about to do just the opposite.

CHAPTER ELEVEN

AFTER JAMES DROPPED Lori off at her shop, telling her he'd think about what she'd asked him to do, he drove out to the river. It was one of those clear blue Montana summer days so he decided to quit putting it off and talk to former sheriff Otis Osterman. He'd save Gus Hughes for later, when he'd be glad to see a friendly face.

He put his window down and let the warm air rush in as he drove. He could smell the pines and the river and sweet scent of new grass. It reminded him of the days he and his brothers used to skip school in the spring and go fishing down by the river. One of his favorite memories was lying in the cool grass, listening to the murmur of the river while he watched clouds drift through the great expanse of sky overhead. His brothers always caught enough fish for dinner that he could just daydream.

The former sheriff lived alone in a cabin at the edge of the water. Otis's wife had died of cancer a year before he retired. He'd sold their place in town and moved out here into this two-room log cabin. His pickup was parked in the drive as James knocked. He knocked louder, and getting no response walked around to the back where he found the man sitting on his deck overlooking the river.

"Hello!" he called as he approached the stairs to the

deck. He didn't see a gun handy, but that didn't mean that there wasn't one.

Otis jumped, his boots coming down loudly on the deck flooring.

"Didn't mean to startle you," James said as he climbed the steps and pulled up a wooden stool to sit on since there was only one chair and Otis was in it.

"Too early for company," the former sheriff growled, clearly either not happy to be startled so early—or equally unhappy to see a member of the Colt family anytime of the day.

"I'm not company," he said. "I'm here to ask you about Billy Sherman's hit-and-run."

Otis gave him a withering glare. "Why would I tell you anything?" As if his brother Carl hadn't already told him.

"My father was working the case when he died. I've decided to finish it for him."

"Is that right? You know anything about investigating?"

"I worked with Del from the time I was little. I might have picked up a few things."

Otis shook his head. "You always were an arrogant little bastard."

"That aside, I'm sure you must have had a suspect or two that you questioned."

"Would have come out to your place and talked to you and your brothers but you felons were all too far away at some rodeo or other to have done it."

"Technically, none of us are felons," James said. "What about damage to the vehicle that hit him? You must have tried to find it."

"Of course we tried. Look, we did our best with what

we had to work with. Your father thought he could do better. But he didn't find the person, did he?"

"He died before he could."

"To keep his record intact."

James shook his head. He'd known this would be ugly. "My father didn't kill himself."

"You really think his pickup stalled on the tracks with a train coming and he didn't have time to get out and run?" Otis shook his head. "Unless there was some reason he couldn't get out." He mimed lifting an invisible bottle to his lips.

Bristling, James warned himself to keep the temperature down. If things got out of control, Otis would have his brother lock him up behind bars before he could snap his fingers. "Del did have a shot of blackberry brandy on occasion, but according to the coroner's report, he wasn't drunk."

"But he could have been trying to get drunk after the argument he had with a mystery woman earlier that day in town," Otis said. "At least, that's the story I heard. The two were really going at it, your father clearly furious with her."

James pushed off the stool to loom over the man. "If anyone started that lie, it was you to discredit my father. The only reason he would have taken an open case like Billy Sherman's was if he thought you and your brother were covering something up. If he hadn't died, what are the chances that he would have exposed the corruption in your department?"

"I'd be careful making wild accusations," Otis warned.

"Why?" He leaned closer, seeing that he'd hit a nerve. "It's never stopped you."

Otis held up his hands. "You've got your grandfather Colt's temper, son. It could get you into a whole pack of trouble."

James breathed hard for a moment before he took a step back. That was one of the problems of living in small-town Montana. Everyone didn't just know your business, they knew your whole damned family history.

"I'm going to find out the truth about Billy Sherman's death. And while I'm at it, I'm going to look into my father's death as well. You make me wonder if they aren't connected—just not in the way you want me to believe."

"You're wasting your time barking up that particular tree, but it's not like you have anything pressing to do, is it? You should be looking for the mystery woman."

James smiled. Otis's forehead was covered with a sheen of sweat and his face was flushed. "You would love to send me on a wild goose chase. Are you that worried that I might uncover the truth about how you and your brother handled the Sherman case? You're wondering if I'm as smart as my father. I'm not. But maybe I'll get lucky."

"Get off my property before I have you arrested for trespassing."

"I'm leaving. But if I'm right, I'll be back, only next time it will be with the real law—not your baby brother."

LORELEI COULDN'T BELIEVE what she'd done. Now that she was away from James, she regretted hiring him and planned to fire him as soon as she saw him. The man didn't even have a private investigator's license. What had she been thinking? He was worse than an amateur. He thought he was more trained at this than he was because he'd run a few errands and done some filing for his father.

It had been a spur-of-the-moment stupid decision and not like her at all. She usually thought things through. She blamed James for coming back and turning her life and her upside down.

Worse, as the day stretched on, she'd also had no luck reaching her stepmother. By almost closing time, she'd already sent Anita home and was prepping for the next day, angry with herself. Not even rock and roll music blasting in her kitchen could improve her mood.

She felt so ineffectual. Had she really suggested to James that he break into her stepmother's house and search for incriminating evidence against her? She groaned at the thought that he might have already done it.

If she really believed he would find such evidence, then why didn't she simply look herself? She had an extra key to the house and she knew when her stepmother should be at the studio.

But she also knew the answer. She was afraid she *would* find something damning and do what? Destroy it?

The front doorbell jangled. She looked up to see the very pregnant Melody Simpson waddle in. "Hey," the young woman called. "Am I too late to get a sandwich?"

She hurriedly turned down the music as she realized she'd forgotten to lock the front door. This was exactly the kind of behavior that was so unlike her.

"Not if you want it to go," Lorelei said, even though she was technically closed.

"Sure." Melody waddled up and studied the board.

"White bread, American cheese, mustard and no lettuce."

Lorelei nodded. "Twelve inch?" A nod. "Anything to drink? I have canned soda to go."

The young woman shook her head and stepped to the closest table to sit down. "My feet are killing me."

Not knowing how to answer that, Lorelei hurried in the back to make her a cheese sandwich. It felt strange seeing James's pregnant former girlfriend. Not that they had dated long before he'd left town. Still...

"I heard about you and Jimmy D," Melody called back into the kitchen.

"Pardon?"

"Breakfast at the cafe this morning early, whispering with your heads together. The two of you were the talk of the town before noon."

Lorelei gasped as she realized the rumors that would be circulating. She groaned inwardly. Because it had been so early, people might think that she and James had spent the night together!

That thought rattled her more than she wanted to admit. She could just imagine Gladys's Beauty Emporium all atwitter. The place was rumor mill central. She started to tell Melody that it wasn't what it looked like, but the explanation of her early morning meeting with James was worse.

"I just wanted you to know that I'm not jealous," Melody added.

That stopped Lorelei for a moment. Melody wasn't jealous? Why would she be jealous? She finished wrapping up the sandwich, bagged it and went back out front to find the woman had kicked off her shoes and was rubbing her stocking-covered feet.

She put the bag on the counter along with the bill. After a minute, Melody worked her shoes back on and limped over to her. As she dug a wad of crumpled bills from her jacket pocket, Lorelei said, "Why would you be jealous? I heard you were marrying Tyler Grange and having…" Her gaze went to Melody's very distinct baby bump. "His baby."

Melody continued to smooth out singles on the countertop, her head bent over them with undue attention.

Lorelei felt a start. *It was Tyler's baby, right?* "Have your plans changed?" she asked, finding herself counting the months by the size of Melody's belly. What if it was James's? And why did that make her heart plummet?

"Naw, my plans haven't changed. Tyler's going to marry me," Melody finally said as she finished. Lorelei realized Melody had been counting the bills. She took the fistful of ones. "It's just that I really cared about James. I want him to be happy. I guess if you can make him happy…" She sounded doubtful about that.

"Sorry, but it isn't like that between me and James."

Melody picked up the sack with her sandwich inside. "If you say so. Just don't hurt him. He's real vulnerable right now." With that, she turned and left.

Lorelei followed her to the door and locked it behind her. James vulnerable? That was a laugh. But as she headed back to finish up in the kitchen, she wondered why Melody would even think that.

Shaking her head, she tried to clear James Colt out of it. She hadn't seen him since this morning. She'd checked a few times to see if his pickup was parked out back. It hadn't been. She could have tried calling him—if she'd had his cell phone number.

She told herself she'd fire him when she saw him. She just hoped he hadn't done anything on her behalf and, at the same time wishing he had, but only if he hadn't found anything incriminating.

"SOUNDS LIKE YOU had quite the day," Ryan said when James stopped by the hardware store. "I can't believe that you threatened Otis. Wish I'd seen that."

They were in the back office, Ryan's boots up on the desk as he sipped a can of beer from the six-pack James had brought. After his visit with Otis, James had driven around trying to calm down. He'd stopped at a convenience store, picked up the beer and headed for Ryan.

The two of them had roomed and rodeoed together in college. Ryan always knew he would come back and run his father's hardware store. James hadn't given a thought to what he would do after he quit rodeo.

"You'd better watch your back," Ryan was saying. "Otis hates you and his brother is even less fond of you."

"I'm not afraid of that old fart or his little brother." He took a drink of his beer. "I'd love to nail Otis's hide to the side of his cabin."

"I wouldn't even jaywalk if I were you until you leave town again. You know how tight he is with his younger brother. What all did Otis say that has you so worked up?" his friend asked.

James chewed at his cheek for a moment. "He insinuated Del killed himself possibly over a broken heart because of a mystery woman or because he couldn't solve the Billy Sherman case or because he was a drunk and couldn't get out of his pickup before the train hit him."

Ryan raised a brow. "What woman?"

"According to Otis, my father was seen arguing with

a mystery woman earlier in the day before he was killed. Apparently not someone from around here since Otis didn't have a name."

"Seriously?"

"He was more than serious. He suggested I should find that woman. It was obvious that he's worried what I might find digging around in the Sherman case—and my father's death. I'm just wondering why he's so worried."

His friend took a long drink and was silent for a few minutes. "I've always wondered about your old man's accident."

"Me too. What was Del doing out on that railroad track in that part of the county at that time of the night? There are no warning arms that come down at that site. But the lights would have been flashing…" He shook his head. "I've always thought it was suspicious but even more so since I found out that Del told someone that he was close to solving Billy Sherman's case."

Ryan let out a low whistle. "Now you're a private investigator almost, investigate."

He smiled. "Just that simple?"

"Why not? Sounds like it's something you've thought about. Why not set your mind at ease one way or another?"

"Just between you and me? This is a lot harder than I thought. But you're right. I've already got half the town upset with me. Why not the other half?" He looked at his phone and, seeing the time, groaned. "I'd planned on stopping by Gus Hughes's garage. If I'm right, someone had to pay to get their car fixed out of town nine years ago."

"You're thinking it might have been Terry," his

friend said. Terry Durham worked for Gus. "Now that you mention it, Terry bought that half acre outside of town a little over nine years ago and put a camper on it. Could be a coincidence. Not sure how much he would charge to cover up a hit-and-run murder vehicle. But since he's usually broke…"

James drained his beer, arced the can for a clean shot at the trash in the corner and rose to leave. "Thanks. I think I'll stop by his place and have a little talk with him."

"Thanks for the beer. Best take these with you." Ryan held up the other four cans still attached to the plastic collars.

James shook his head. "I figure you'll need them if the rumors are true. Are you really dating the notorious Shawna Collins?"

Ryan swore as he hurled his empty beer can at him.

James ducked, laughing. "And you're warning *me* to be careful." He stepped out in the hall before his friend found something more dangerous to throw at him.

Although Del Colt had talked to Terry Durham according to his list—and checked him off—James wanted to ask him where the money had come for his land and trailer.

Terry lived outside of town on a half-acre lot with a trailer on it. James pulled into the woods, his headlights catching the shine of a bumper. In the large yard light, he recognized Terry's easily recognizable car and parked behind it. The souped-up coupe had been stripped down to a primer coat for as long as James could remember seeing it around town.

Getting out of the pickup, he started toward the camper. But stopped at the sight of something parked deep in the pines. A lowboy trailer. The kind a person could haul a car on.

The lowboy trailer was exactly what he wanted to talk to the man about and he felt a jolt of excitement. Maybe he could solve this.

Whoever had hit Billy Sherman would have had some damage to their vehicle or at the very least would have wanted to get the car out of town and detailed to make sure there was no evidence on it. One way to get the car out of town was on the lowboy. Terry Durham always seemed to need money. Add to that his proven disregard for the law and the huge chip on his shoulder, and you had someone who would look the other way—if the price were right.

Moving toward the camper again, he saw that there appeared to be one small light behind the blinds at the back. He knocked on the door. No answer. No movement inside. Was it possible Terry had come home and left with someone else?

James was debating coming back early tomorrow when he started past Terry's car and caught a scent he recognized though the open driver's side window.

He stopped cold, his guts tightening inside him as he glanced over inside the car.

Terry was slumped down in his seat behind the wheel, his eyes open, his insides leaking out between his fingers.

CHAPTER TWELVE

IT WAS DAYLIGHT by the time James had told the sheriff his story a dozen times before losing his temper. "I've told you repeatedly, I went out there to talk to Terry about a car he might have been paid to haul to another town."

"Whose car?" Sheriff Carl Osterman asked again.

James sighed. "Billy Sherman's killer whose name I don't know yet."

"You're back in town for a few days and now we have a murder. As I recall, you and Terry never got along. I recall a fistfight my brother had to break up out at the Broken Spur a couple years ago."

"That was between Terry and my brother Davey. I had nothing against Terry and I certainly had no reason to kill him. So, either believe me or arrest me because I'm going home!"

When the sheriff didn't move, James pushed out of the chair he'd been sitting in for hours and headed for the door.

"Don't leave town!" Carl called after him.

He held his tongue as he strode out of the sheriff's department to take his first breath of fresh air. It was morning, the sun already cresting the mountains. He felt exhausted and still sick over what he'd seen earlier.

After he'd called 911 and the sheriff had arrived, he'd

been ordered to wait in the back of Carl's patrol SUV while an ambulance was called along with crime techs. Eventually Terry Durham's body had been extricated from the car and hauled off in a body bag.

Even now, it took him a moment to get his legs under him. The last time he'd seen anything like that had been when a bull rider had been gored. He still felt sick to his stomach as he made his way to his pickup. He tried not to think about it. He'd wanted to ask Terry if someone paid him to take their damaged car out of town on that lowboy trailer of his nine years ago.

He'd been hoping the answer wasn't going to be Karen Wilkins. Terry wouldn't have done it for just anyone—unless the price was right.

Now he was dead. James feared it was because of the questions he'd been asking about Billy Sherman's death.

As he pulled up behind the office building, he saw that Lorelei's SUV was already parked behind her shop. He got out and was almost to his door, when she rushed out.

"I need to talk to you," she said. She smelled like yeast, her apron dusted with flour. There was a dusting of flour on her nose. He couldn't imagine her looking more beautiful.

But right now, he just needed some rest. He held up his hands. "Whatever it is, can we please discuss it later." He opened his back door and started to step in when she grabbed his arm.

"Are you sick or drunk?" she demanded.

He turned to look at her. She sounded like the sheriff because he'd had beer on his breath earlier. "I'm not drunk, all right? Lorelei, it's just not a good time. Whatever it is, I'm sure it can wait until I get some sleep."

"Rough night?" she mocked.

"You could say that."

Her gaze suddenly widened. "Oh, no. You found something. You went to my stepmother's and—"

He sighed, realizing why she'd been waiting for him to return. "I didn't go to your stepmother's." She'd hear about this soon anyway. "I went out to Terry Durham's and found him...murdered. I've been at the cop shop ever since."

She let go of his arm. "I'm sorry."

He nodded. "Now I just need a shot of brandy and a little sleep. I've spent hours answering the sheriff's questions. I can't take any more right now." She nodded and stepped back. "Later. I promise. We'll talk then." He stepped through his door, letting it slam behind him as he slowly mounted the stairs.

It wasn't until he reached the office door that he saw the note nailed to it.

Tearing it off, he glanced at the scrawled writing.

Get out of town while you still can.

Inside the office, he unlocked his father's bottom drawer and pulled out the .45 he would be carrying from now on.

LORELEI STARTED AT the sound of her phone ringing. She pulled a tray of bread from the oven and dug her cell out of her apron pocket. "Hello?"

"I hope I didn't wake you." It was her stepmother.

"No. I'm at work. I've been here for hours."

"You must be expecting a big day." Her stepmother sounded almost cheerful.

Right, a big day, she thought remembering her

encounter with James not long after sunrise. If that was any indication of how this day was going to go...

"I saw that you called yesterday," her stepmother said when Lorelei hadn't commented. "Sweetheart, I'm sorry about the way we left things. I had to get away for a while." With her lover? Lorelei didn't want to know. "I think we should get together this evening and talk. I'll make dinner. I thought you could come over after work." Her stepmother sounded tentative. "Please, Lorelei. You're my daughter. I love you."

She felt herself weaken. "Fine. But I need you to be honest with me."

"I am being honest with you. I don't know why seeing James upset me, but it had nothing to with Billy Sherman." A lie, she thought. "I was just worried that you were getting involved with him." Another lie? "He's all wrong for you." Yet another lie?

Lorelei closed her eyes to the sudden tears. "I'll see you this evening." She disconnected, hating this. They used to be so close. She feared everything had changed. Her stepmother had hidden a married lover. But that might not be the worst of it.

As she went back to work, she remembered what James had told her. Terry Durham had been murdered. She couldn't remember the last murder in Lonesome— then with a start, realized it would have been Billy Sherman's hit-and-run. James said he'd found Terry's body. He'd been so upset. Because he felt he might have caused it by asking questions around town from his father's list of people like her stepmother?

She felt a chill even in the warm kitchen. What if the two murders were connected? Hadn't she heard something about Terry getting beaten up after he tried to cheat during a poker game in Billings? But what if Terry was murdered because he worked at the local body shop and knew who killed Billy Sherman?

The thought shook her to her core. What if Billy Sherman's killer had felt forced to kill again? At the sound of a trash can lid banging in the alley, she quickly moved to the back door to look out in time to see James.

When she'd seen him coming in disheveled and exhausted she'd jumped to the conclusion that he'd been out on the town with a woman. It was reasonable given his reputation, but still she felt bad about how quickly she'd judged him. She'd been so ready to add this onto her list of reasons she couldn't trust the man. With a curse, she realized he'd probably thought she'd been jealous.

"Did you get some sleep?" she asked from the doorway.

"Some. Sorry I was short with you earlier."

She shook her head as if it had been nothing. As he joined her, she caught the scent of soap and noticed that his hair was still wet from his shower. He smelled good, something she wished she hadn't noticed. His wet dark hair was black as a raven's wing in the sunlight. It curled at the nape of his neck, inviting her fingers to bury themselves in it, something else she wished she hadn't noticed.

"You wanted to talk to me?"

"You look like you could use a cup of coffee," she said, stalling. "I have a pot on. Interested?"

He hesitated but only a moment. "Sure." He followed her into the kitchen at the back and leaned against the counter, watching her. She could feel the intensity of his gaze on her. She felt all thumbs.

Fire him. Just do it. Like ripping off a Band-Aid. Thank him and then that will be it. You can pretend that you were never so serious as to do something so stupid as hire him to investigate your own stepmother in the first place.

When she turned, he was grinning at her in that lazy way he had, amusement glinting in the vast blue of his gaze. His long legs were stretched out practically to the center of the kitchen as he nonchalantly leaned against her counter. "You want me to help you?"

She thought he meant the coffee and started to say that she had it covered.

"You aren't going to hurt my feelings," he said. "I figured you've changed your mind about hiring me. I don't blame you. Sometimes it's better not to know. And when it's your own stepmother—"

She bristled. "I didn't say I don't want to know if she's involved."

One dark eyebrow arched up. "So, what is it you're having such a hard time saying to me?" he asked as he pushed off the counter and reached her in two long-legged strides.

Lorelei swallowed the lump that had risen in her throat. The scent of soap and maleness seemed to overpower even the aroma of the coffee. Suddenly the kitchen felt too small and cramped. Too intimate.

She stepped around him to the cupboard where she kept the large mugs, opened the door and took down two. Her hands were shaking. "I didn't say I was going to fire you."

"No?" He was right behind her. She could practically feel his warm breath on the back of her neck.

She quickly moved past him with the mugs and went over by the coffee pot.

She heard him chuckle behind her.

"Do I make you nervous?" he asked as she filled both mugs shakily. When she turned around, he was back on the other side of the kitchen, leaning against the counter again, grinning. "I do make you nervous." He laughed. "What is it you're afraid I'm going to do? Or are you afraid I'm *not* going do it?"

"Sometimes you just talk gibberish," she snapped.

His grin broadened. "I want to know when you're going to do what I'm paying you to do."

"Paying me?"

She stepped toward him, shoved one mug full of coffee at him and waited impatiently for him to take it. She wished she'd never suggested coffee. The less time she spent around this impossible man the better. Right now, she wanted him out of her kitchen.

Seeing that he had no intention of going anywhere, she said, "We can talk in the dining room." With that she turned and exited the kitchen, her head up, chin out and her heart pounding. She told herself with every step that she hated this arrogant man. Why hadn't she fired him?

She slipped into a chair, cupping the mug in her hands, her attention on the steam rising from the hot coffee.

He slid into a chair opposite her and turned serious. "Let's face it, Lori. You don't want to know about your stepmother. So let's just forget it and—"

She reached into her pocket, pulled out the key and slapped it down on the Formica table. "That opens the back door to her house."

He stared at the key for a moment before he raised his gaze to her again. "You don't have to do this." She merely stared back, challenging him at the same time she feared she would change her mind. "Fine." He picked up the key and put it in his jeans pocket. Then he took a sip of his coffee.

"What does Terry Durham have to do with Billy's hit-and-run?" she asked.

He looked up in surprise. "I didn't say—"

"You didn't have to." She had a bad feeling that Terry's death had nothing to do with a poker game gone wrong.

"He works at the body shop. As you pointed out yourself, the vehicle that hit Billy would have some damage to it. How would you get it fixed without anyone being the wiser? Get it out of town quickly. Terry had a car-hauling trailer and now he's dead. Add to that, after the hit-and-run, Terry bought a piece of property and a small camper." James shrugged. "It's all conjecture at this point, but it stacks up. I start asking questions and now he's dead."

"What is it you'll look for at my stepmother's?"

"The person who owned the damaged car might have left a trail. Either a receipt from the body shop that fixed it. Or a lump sum withdrawal from a bank account to pay Terry off. But that's if they kept a record from nine years ago."

Her heart pounded. "Give me the key back."

He hesitated only a moment before he dug it out of his jeans and handed it over. "So, I'm fired."

Lorelei shook her head as she pocketed the key again. "No, I'm going with you." He started to put up an argument, but she cut him off. "It will be faster if I go. I know where she keeps her receipts, and her bank account records. Karen keeps everything. Come on," she said, pushing away her unfinished coffee. "She'll be at her studio now."

"You sure about this?" he asked.

"Not at all, but I can't do this alone and I have to know."

He met her gaze. "If what we find incriminates her, I won't cover it up even to protect you."

"You come with integrity?"

"It costs extra," he said to lighten the mood for a moment. "But seriously, if you want to change your mind, now's the time, Lori."

She didn't correct him. In fact, she was getting to where she liked her nickname, especially on his lips. "I'm serious too." She knew she couldn't live with the suspicion. "I have to know the truth before tonight. I'm having dinner at her house."

"Great," he said under his breath as he downed his coffee and rose from the table as she called a friend to come watch the shop.

CHAPTER THIRTEEN

JAMES PARKED IN the alley behind the house after circling the block. Karen Wilkins's car wasn't in the drive. Nor had there been any lights on in the house. He could feel Lorelei's anxiety.

He was about to suggest she stay in his pickup, when she opened her door and climbed out. Her expression was resigned. He could tell that she was doing this come hell or high water. She looked back at him, narrowing her eyes and he was smart enough not to argue.

Lori produced the key as they walked through the backyard. The sky overhead was robin egg blue and cloudless, the air already warming with the summer sun. A meadowlark sang a short refrain before they reached the back door.

He watched her take a breath as she unlocked the back door and they stepped in. "Does she keep an office here?"

With a nod, Lori led the way. The office was a spare bedroom with multipurpose use. There was a sewing machine and table and containers of fabric on one side. A bed in the middle and a small desk with a standing file cabinet next to it.

James headed for the filing cabinet only to find it locked. He looked at Lori who still hadn't spoken. He suspected she was having all kinds of misgivings about this but was too stubborn to stop it.

She opened the desk drawer and dug around for a few moments before she picked up a tiny wooden box that had been carved out of teak.

"My father gave her this." She opened the lid and with trembling fingers removed a tiny key and handed it to him.

He unlocked the top drawer and thumbed through the folders. Then he tried the second drawer. Karen's bank was still sending back the canceled checks nine years ago. He dug deeper and found small check boxes all labeled. She was certainly organized. He looked for personal checks from nine years ago, found the box, handed it to Lori. She sat down at the desk and began to go through them.

"You're looking for a check to Terry Durham or a towing company after Billy Sherman's hit-and-run so after April 10th," James said. "Also, a check to a body shop in another town." She nodded and set to work.

He found Karen's monthly account statement in the third drawer and quickly began to sort through them looking for a large withdrawal after April 10 from nine years ago. He'd just found what he was looking for when he heard a car door slam.

They both froze. "I thought you said she was working," he whispered.

"She was supposed to be. Maybe it isn't her."

James heard a key in the front door lock. "It's her." He grabbed the months he needed of the checking account documents and carefully closed the file drawer. He saw Lorelei pocket a handful of checks and slip the box into the top drawer as he motioned toward the closet.

He opened the door as quietly as possible. It sounded as if Karen had gone to one of the bedrooms on the other side of the house. The closet was full of fabric and craft supplies. There was just enough room for the two of them if they squished together. He eased the closet door closed as the sound of footfalls headed in their direction.

A moment later Karen came into the room. He heard her stop as if she'd forgotten what she'd come in for. Or as if she sensed something amiss? He tried to remember if they had left anything out that could give them away. He didn't think so. But if she opened the desk drawer she would see the check box. As neat and organized as she was, she would know.

He held his breath. He could feel Lori, her body spooned into his, doing the same. Her hair smelled like a spring rain. He could feel the heat of her, the hard and soft places fitting into some of his. He tried to think about baseball.

With relief, he heard Karen leave the room. The front door slammed and he finally let out the breath he'd been holding. A few moments later, a car engine started up. James waited until the sound died away before he carefully opened the closet door.

Lori stepped out, straightening her clothing, looking flushed.

"Sorry about that," he said, his voice sounding hoarse. She pretended she didn't know what he was talking about, which was fine with him. "Let's finish and get out of here."

He went through the bank statements and then Karen's retirement papers. That's when he found it. A large withdrawal of ten thousand dollars.

"Lori?" He realized that she hadn't moved for a moment. She was staring down at a canceled check in her hand. All the color had drained from her face. "What is it?" Without a word, she handed him the check.

The check had been made out to the bank for ten thousand dollars. He flipped it over and saw that the money had been deposited into Lori's account. "I don't understand."

"Nine years ago I looked into getting a loan to open a sandwich shop," she said, her voice breaking. "The bank turned me down. My stepmother had offered to cosign on the loan but I didn't want her risking it if I failed. I had no experience."

"And then you did get the loan," he said.

She nodded. "The president of the bank called, said he noticed I had applied for the loan and that he knew me and was willing to take a chance on me. He lied. It was all my stepmother."

She looked as if she might burst into tears at any moment as she put the check back in the box and opened the file cabinet to put the box away. He watched her relock the file cabinet and put the key back where she'd found it and close the desk drawer.

"I can imagine what you're feeling right now," he finally said.

"Can you?" She turned to face him. "I didn't trust my stepmother. I hired you and then I sneaked in here with you looking for dirt on her. Did we find anything? No. Instead, I find out that she took money out of her retirement to help me open my sandwich shop, the woman I've been at odds with for days because of you."

He didn't feel that was fair, but was smart enough not to say so. "I'm sorry. But we didn't find anything." Instead, he'd found a large withdrawal from a retirement plan but not to cover a crime. "No checks to Terry Durham or a body shop." He held up his hands. "So good news."

She merely glared at him before she pushed past him and headed out the back door. He double-checked the room to make sure they hadn't left anything behind and followed. By the time he reached the pickup, she was nowhere to be seen.

He climbed behind the wheel and waited for a few minutes, but realized his first thought was probably the right one. She'd rather walk back than ride with him. He started the engine and drove out of the alley.

Another great day as a private investigator, he thought with disgust.

CORA SWORE SHE had a sixth sense these days. She'd been in the living room knitting while she watched her favorite television drama when she had an odd feeling. Putting aside her knitting and pausing her show, she went into the kitchen and picked up her binoculars.

These special night vision binoculars had paid for themselves the first night she got them. It truly was amazing what a person could see especially since she lived on a rise over the river.

First she scanned the river road. Only one car parked out there tonight and she recognized it. The same couple that often parked out there on a weekday night. She thought for a moment, wondering if there was any way she could benefit from this knowledge and deciding not, scanned farther downriver.

Tonight not even a bunch of teenagers were drunk around a beer keg. Slow night, she thought, wondering why she'd thought something was going on.

Out of habit, she turned the binoculars on the Colt place. At first she didn't see anything since she wasn't really expecting to—until she saw a pickup coming through the woods on the Colt property with no headlights on. Had she heard the driver pull in? Or did she really have a sixth sense for this sort of thing?

She wondered as she watched the pickup stop on the spot where the burned-out trailer had once stood. James Colt? She waited for the driver to exit the rig. Western hat and a definite swagger, she thought, but she couldn't see the face because he kept his head down.

Following him with the binoculars, she watched as he went around to the back of his pickup and took out a box. It must have been heavy because he seemed to strain under the weight. To her surprise, he carried the box over to where the debris from the burned-out double-wide had been. He hesitated, then put down the box before going back to the pickup. He returned with a small shovel.

She watched, transfixed as he began to dig a hole into which he dumped whatever was in the box. Then he shoveled the blackened earth over the hole.

Shoving back his hat to wipe a forearm across his brow, Cora got her first good look at his face. She felt a start as she recognized him.

Her hand began to sweat because suddenly she was holding the binoculars so tightly, her heart racing in her chest. She watched former sheriff Otis Osterman carry his shovel and the empty box back to the pickup. A moment later he drove off.

LORELEI FELT ASHAMED and guilty and not just because of her stepmother. She'd blamed James for all this when she'd been the one who'd hired him. How could she possibly think her stepmother was involved in Billy Sherman's death? Worse, that her stepmother would try to cover it up? She hated too that she'd felt a wave of relief when they hadn't found anything incriminating. Had she been that worried that they would? She was a horrible stepdaughter. She promised herself that she would make it up to Karen.

The walk back to the shop helped. Fortunately, the moment she entered her kitchen, she had work to do. Anita had a lot done, but there was still more bread to be made before she opened at 11:00 a.m. She thanked Anita, paid her and sent her on home, needing work more today than ever.

When she'd come in the back way, she'd been thankful that James's pickup wasn't anywhere around. She recalled the two of them in the closet, her body pressed into his, and felt her face flush hot as she remembered his obvious…desire. Fortunately, he hadn't been able to feel her reaction to it. At least she hoped not.

"Lorelei?"

She spun around in surprise to see Karen standing in the kitchen doorway. She really needed to start locking the back door.

"Are you all right? You're flushed," her stepmother said as she quickly stepped to her, putting a hand on Lorelei's forehead.

"I'm baking bread and it's hot in here."

Her stepmother looked skeptical but let it go. "I hope you don't mind me stopping by."

She wiped her hands on her apron. "I'm glad you did."

"I know you're busy but I didn't want to do this over the phone. I'm afraid I have to cancel our plans for dinner tonight. I'm sorry. Something's come up."

Lorelei raised a brow, sick to the pit of her stomach at how quickly her suspicions had come racing back. "I hope it's nothing bad."

"No." Her stepmother looked away. "Just a prior engagement I completely forgot about." Lorelei nodded. "So, we'll reschedule in a few days." Karen let out a nervous laugh. "You and I are so busy."

"Aren't we though," she said, hoping the remark didn't come out as sarcastic as it felt. Her stepmother wasn't acting like herself. It wasn't Lorelei's imagination. She wanted to throw her arms around her and hug her although she couldn't thank her for the personal loan without telling her that she'd gone through her checks.

But at the same time, she wanted to demand her stepmother tell her the truth about what was going on. No matter what, she couldn't keep lying to herself. Something was definitely going on with her stepmother besides the affair.

"I'll call you." Her stepmother headed out of the kitchen.

"Mom!" Lorelei's voice broke. "Be careful."

Karen looked surprised for a moment. "You too, dear."

JAMES FELT AS if he'd been spinning his wheels. He knew no more about Billy Sherman's death than he had when he started this. Now he'd alienated someone he had been growing quite fond of since his return to town.

As he was passing a house in the older section of town, he recognized the senior gentleman working in his yard. James pulled up in front of the neat two-story

Craftsman with its wide white front porch. Getting out, he walked toward the man.

Dr. Milton Stanley looked up, a pair of hedge clippers in his hands. His thick white eyebrows raised slightly under small dark eyes. "You're a Colt."

He nodded. "James."

"You look like your father."

"My father's why I stopped when I saw you. Could we talk for a minute? I don't want to keep you from your work."

"I was ready for a break anyway." Milton laid down his clippers, took off his gardening gloves and motioned toward the house. "Take a seat on the porch. I'll get us something to drink."

James followed the man as far as the porch and waited. He could hear the doctor inside the house. Opening and closing the refrigerator. The clink of glass against glass. The sound of ice cubes rattling.

A few minutes later, the screen door swung open with a creak and Milton reappeared. He handed James a tall glass of iced lemonade and motioned to two of the white-painted wooden rockers. Each had a bright-colored cushion. James could imagine the doctor and his wife sitting out here often—before her death.

They sat. James sipped his lemonade, complimented it and asked, "You were coroner when my father was killed. I need to know if you ran tests to see if he was impaired."

The doctor drained half of his lemonade before setting down the glass on one of the coasters on the small round end table between them. James watched him wipe his damp hands on his khaki pants.

Milton frowned. "Why are you asking this?"

"Because of the case he was working on at the time of his death. It was ruled an accident by the sheriff, but I've since learned some things that make me think he might have been murdered."

"Murdered?"

"I'm not sure how, but I've only been working my father's old case a few days and already someone I wanted to talk to has been killed," James said. "I've always questioned my father's death but never more so than now. I've learned that he was close to solving Billy Sherman's hit-and-run."

The doctor frowned. "There was no alcohol or drugs in your father's system at the time of his death."

James blinked, swamped with a wave of relief. "None?"

"None."

The relief though only lasted a moment. "Then how did it happen?" Why didn't he get out of the pickup before the train hit him? Surely, he saw the flashing lights. Did he think he could beat the train? That wasn't like his father. Del was deliberate. He didn't take chances.

Milton shook his head. "Any number of things could have led to it. He might have had something on his mind and didn't notice the flashing lights. The train hit him on the driver's side. He might not have had time to get out. The pickup engine could have stalled. He could have panicked. You can't see that train because of the curve until it's almost on top of you. Your father's accident wasn't the first one at that spot. The railroad really needs to put in crossing arms." He picked up his lemonade and drained the rest of it.

James drank his and placed the empty glass on a coaster on the table. He could tell the doctor was anxious to get back to his gardening. "Thank you for your help."

"I'm not sure I was much help," Milton said and followed him as far as the yard. The doctor picked up his clippers and went back to work.

CORA STEWED. HER FAVORITE television drama couldn't even take her mind off what she'd seen. She tried to work it out in her mind. That was the problem. She wasn't even sure what she'd seen—just that Otis Osterman hadn't wanted to be caught doing whatever it was. Of that she was sure.

Putting her knitting aside again, she picked up her cell phone and muted the television. She let the number ring until she got voice mail. Then she called back. It took four times, one right after the other, before the former sheriff finally picked up.

"What the hell do you want, Cora?" he demanded.

"I bought myself one of those video recorders."

"What?"

"I was trying to learn how to use it and I accidentally videoed the darnedest thing. *You.* You're right there on my video."

"What. Are. You. Talking. About?"

"I couldn't figure out why you would be on the Colt property, let alone why you would dump a box of something into the ashes where the Colt's burned-out trailer had been, let alone why you would then cover it up with that little shovel you keep in your pickup."

She listened to him breathing hard and knew that she'd struck pay dirt. "I'm thinking James Colt would be interested in seeing my little video. Heck, I suspect he'd pay good money given how he feels about you.

Trespassing and so much more. So how much do you think my video is worth? Maybe I should just take it to the FBI."

Otis swore and Cora smiled. She could tell by the low growl on the other end of the line that she had him. She didn't care what he'd planted on Colt property. It was no skin off her nose. But she could certainly use a little supplemental income.

"You addled old woman. I don't know what you think you saw—"

"That's why I'm having this young person I met put the video up on the internet. Technology is really something these days. I bet someone has a theory about what you were doing, don't you? Even your brother the sheriff won't be able to sweep this under the rug—not after I make sure everyone knows the man in the video is a former sheriff. That should make it go viral, whatever that is. My new young friend assures me it's good though."

"Maybe I should come out to your place and we should discuss this," Otis said through what sounded like clenched teeth.

"I wouldn't suggest that. I get jumpy at night and you know I keep my shotgun handy. I'd feel terrible if I shot you."

"What do you want?" he demanded angrily.

"Five thousand dollars."

Otis let out a string of curses. "I don't have that kind of money."

"Well, not *on* you. You'll have to go to the bank and when you do, you tell them you borrowed money from me and want to pay it back. Just have them put it into my account. It's a small town. They'll do it. As soon as

ر

I get confirmation, I'll drop the video by your cabin. Maybe you'll have something cold for us to drink."

He growled again. "How do I know you won't make copies and demand more money?"

"Shame on you, Otis. They do say crooks are often the most suspicious people. I wouldn't have a clue how to make a copy."

"I want the camera too."

"Well, now that's just rude. I'm still learning how to use it. But I'll bring it when I bring the video. We can discuss it. With that night vision thing, the camera won't be cheap. Tomorrow then. Have the bank call me. Look forward to seeing you, Otis." She laughed. "In person. I've already seen enough of you in the movies." She laughed harder and disconnected.

Then she went to check her shotgun to make sure it was loaded, putting extra shells in her pocket, before she locked and bolted all the doors.

CHAPTER FOURTEEN

WHEN JAMES RETURNED to the office, he saw that it appeared someone was waiting for him. A bike leaned against his building in the alley with a young boy of about sixteen sitting on a milk crate next to it.

As he got out of his truck, the boy rose looking nervous. "Can I help you?" James asked.

"Are you the PI?"

He smiled. "I guess I am."

"I need to talk to you." He looked around to make sure there wasn't anyone else around. "It's about Billy."

In that instant, he realized who this boy must be. "Todd?" The boy nodded. "Does your mom know you're here?" The boy shook his head. "I'm not really supposed to talk to you without a parent present." Then again, he wasn't a licensed PI yet, was he?

"But I'll tell you what," he said quickly seeing the boy's disappointment. The kid had been waiting patiently. He couldn't turn him away especially when Todd might have valuable information. He glanced at the time. "What if we have another adult present who can advise you?"

Todd looked worried. "Who?"

"Hungry?" He asked the boy, remembering himself at that age. His father used to ask if he had a hollow wooden leg. Where else was all that food going?

Todd nodded but then hesitated. "What about my bike?"

"It's safe there." James pushed open the back door into the sandwich shop. Once that smell of fresh bread hit the kid there was no more hesitation.

LORELEI SAW JAMES first and started to tell him he was the last person she wanted to see—when she spotted the boy with him. Her gaze went from the boy to James in question.

"This is Todd. He's hungry." James turned to the kid. "What kind of sandwich would you like?"

"I suppose you don't have a hot dog?" the boy asked her sheepishly.

"Let me see what I can do. Would you like some lemonade with that?" The boy nodded and actually smiled. Her gaze rose to James.

He shook his head since he didn't have a clue what was going on. "We'll just have a seat. We're hoping you can join us. Todd wants to have a talk with us."

"With *us*?"

"You're going to be the adult in the group," James said.

She smirked. "I always am."

He smiled. "I knew I'd picked the right woman for the job. Mind if I go ahead and lock the front door while we talk so we aren't interrupted?" He didn't wait but went to the door and put up the closed sign and locked the door.

She did mind, even though it was past closing time. What was this man getting her into? She made Todd a mild sausage sandwich with a side of ketchup and mustard and poured three lemonades before bringing them out on a tray to the table. She put Todd's in front of him.

"So, what's this about?" she asked as she slid into the booth next to the boy. Todd had already bitten into his sandwich. He gave her a thumbs-up as he chewed.

"Todd was waiting for me behind my office. He wanted to talk to the PI." She raised a brow. "I explained to him that we probably shouldn't talk without an adult present. It's kind of a gray area."

Lorelei shook her head. "I'm not sure I want to be part of this."

"I have to tell him about Billy," Todd said, putting down his half-eaten sandwich. He took a drink of lemonade. "I know what my mom told you when you came over to see her. She forgot that I did have Billy's other walkie-talkie headset that night and that after that, she threw it away."

"You and Billy talked on the two-way radios the night he died?"

Todd nodded, looking solemn.

"About what time was that?" James asked.

"He woke me up. The electricity had gone off but I looked at my Spiderman watch. It was almost ten thirty. I told him not to do it."

James shot her a look before shifting his gaze back to the boy. "Do what?"

"He said he had to go out. That he'd seen someone walk by his house in the rain and that he needed to follow whoever it was."

"His mom told me that Billy didn't like storms," James said. "Why would he go out and follow someone?"

He picked up his sandwich, took a large bite and

chewed for a moment before swallowing. "Billy and I had this game we played. We pretended we were spies. We used to pick someone to follow. It was fun. They usually heard us behind them and chased us off. But sometimes we could follow them a really long way before they did."

"Who was he following that night?" James asked.

Todd shook his head. "He said he had to see what they were doing before he chickened out. I told him not to. He said the person was headed down the street in my direction and that I should watch for him and come out. I watched from the window, but I never saw him and then I fell asleep. I just figured he chickened out, like he said. Or his mom made him go to bed and quit using the walkie-talkies."

"How did you pick the people you followed?" James asked.

The boy shrugged. "Sometimes we would just see someone who looked dangerous."

"Dangerous?" Lorelei repeated.

"Sometimes we just wondered where they were going, so we followed them."

"So, Billy just saw someone out the window and decided to go out into the storm to follow them?" she asked, unable to hide her incredulity.

"I guess. It might have been someone he'd been following before that."

"Was it a man or a woman?" Lorelei asked.

"Billy said, 'I just saw someone outside my window. I have to follow and find out what they're doing.' He sounded…scared." The boy looked down at his almost empty plate. "When I heard you asking my mom about

Billy, I knew I had to tell you." He bit into what was left of his sandwich and went to work on it.

"Does your mom know about the call from Billy?"

The boy shook his head adamantly. "Billy and I took a blood oath not to ever tell our parents about our spy operations. But I think she was worried that I told Billy to go out that night and that everyone would blame me. I didn't. I swear. I tried to stop him." Todd's eyes shone with tears. Lorelei watched him swallow before he said, "I think he would have wanted me to tell you."

"Thank you, Todd. I'm glad you did," James said.

Lorelei touched the boy's shoulder. "You did the right thing."

He nodded, swallowed a few times and ate the last bite of his sandwich.

She looked across the table at James. He held her gaze until she felt a shudder at what they'd just heard and had to look away.

CHAPTER FIFTEEN

"ARE YOU OKAY?" James asked Lori after Todd left. He'd helped her clear the table, then followed her back into the kitchen.

"Fine," she said, her back to him.

"I forgot about your dinner with your stepmother tonight. I'm sorry. I hope I'm not making you late."

She turned in his direction, avoiding eye contact. "She cancelled. Something came up." He said nothing. Finally, she looked at him. "She's scaring me."

He nodded. "But maybe it has nothing to do with Billy Sherman. At least now we know why Billy went out that night. We just don't know who he was following or why." He sighed. "I'm sorry. I feel like I never should have started this." She didn't exactly disagree with her silence.

"Hey," he said. "How do you feel about a big juicy rib eye out at the steak house? I'm buying."

She smiled and he could tell that she was about to decline when his cell rang. He held up a finger, drew out his phone and, seeing who was calling, said, "I need to take this. Hello?"

"Mr. Colt?"

He smiled to himself. No one called him Mr. Colt. "Yes?"

"My name is Connie Sue Matthews. I heard you have

taken over your father's private investigations firm and that you've been asking questions about Billy Sherman's death."

"That's right."

"You probably know I was the one who found the body that morning. Could I stop by your office? I know it's after hours, but it's the only time I'm free this week. I might have some information for you." She lowered her voice. "I don't want to get into it on the phone."

He shot a look at Lori. He'd been looking forward to that steak but had really been looking forward to dinner with her. He hesitated only a moment, hoping Lori would understand. If this woman had any information for him... "You know where my office is?"

"Yes, I can be there in a few minutes."

"Use the back entrance. I'll see you then." He disconnected and looked across the room at Lori. Only moments before he was mentally kicking himself for digging into his father's unsolved case and here he was cancelling his dinner plans because of it. What was wrong with him? "I'm afraid I'm going to have to postpone that dinner invitation."

"Bad news?" she asked, looking genuinely concerned.

"No, maybe just the opposite." He could only hope.

CORA SAT IN the house, the shotgun lying across her lap. All the lights were out and there was no sound except when the refrigerator turned on in the kitchen occasionally. She'd always been a patient woman. She'd put up with her no-account husband for almost fifty years. She could sit here all night if she had to.

But she knew she wouldn't have to. She knew Otis

Osterman. He was a hothead without a lot upstairs. He'd stop by tonight and she would be waiting.

The fool would be mad, filled with indignation that she'd called him out. He wouldn't be thinking clearly. She reminded herself to make sure he died in the house after he broke in. She didn't want any trouble with the law—especially Otis's baby brother, Carl. But an old woman like herself had every right to defend her life—and her property.

Otis should have taken her deal. He'd regret it. If he lived that long.

And to think back in grade school she'd had a crush on him. He'd been cute back then, blond with freckles and two missing front teeth. She shook her head at the memory. That was before high school when she found out firsthand about his mean streak. But she'd taken care of it—just as she'd taken care of everything else all these years. If he came around tonight, this time he would leave with more than a scar to remember her by. Or not leave alive at all.

CONNIE MATTHEWS WAS a small immaculate-looking woman in her late fifties. She was clearly nervous as she stepped into his office. He'd had just enough time to pick up the room and close the door to the bedroom before she'd arrived.

She sat on the edge of one of the leather club chairs, her purse gripped in her lap as he sat behind his father's desk. Idly he wondered how long it would take for him to think of this office as his own.

"You said you might have information on Billy Sherman's death?"

Connie looked even more uncomfortable. "Those

boys, Billy and that Crane boy. I found them hiding in my bushes one day. They were always sneaking around, getting into trouble, stomping down my poor flowers. One day I caught them going through my garbage! Can you imagine? Billy said they were looking for clues. *Clues.* Clues to what, I'd demanded. And the Crane boy said, 'We know what you've been doing.' Then they laughed and ran off."

It sounded like typical boy stuff to James. He hated to think of some of the shenanigans he and his brothers had pulled. "Did you tell my father about this when he interviewed you?" James knew it wasn't in his father's notes.

She shook her head. "It seemed silly at the time because that young boy had lost his life. But what was he doing out in that storm in the middle of the night in his pajamas?"

"Since your house is the closest to where he was found, did you notice anyone outside that night? Hear anything?" He already knew the answer. *That* was in his father's notes. But Todd said that his friend was following someone.

"No, but I went to bed early. I don't like storms. I took some sleeping pills and didn't wake up until the next morning. By then the storm was over."

"What about your husband?"

"What about him?" Connie asked frowning.

"I wondered if he might have mentioned seeing anyone, hearing anything."

She shook her head. "George went to bed when I did so I'm sure he would have mentioned it, if he had seen someone or heard anything, don't you think? That's a busy road. Gotten even busier with all the houses that have come up. The mayor lives in the new section and I suppose you know that Senator Bayard lives just down the road from our place." She seemed to puff up a little.

That road was an old one used by a lot of residents who lived out that way. The subdivision had grown in the past nine years.

"Was there something more?" he asked. On the phone she'd sounded as if she might have new information. That didn't seem to be the case and yet she was still sitting across from him, still looking nervous and anxious. He waited, something he'd seen his father do during an interview.

"I hate to even bring this up, but I feel I was remiss by not doing it nine years ago," Connie finally said. "I think someone abducted that boy from his bed. Because what boy in his right mind would go out in a storm like that?" she demanded, clearly warming to the subject. "And I know who did it. It was the father." At his confused look, she said, "The *boy's* father, that ne'r-do-well, Sean Sherman. Weren't he and his wife arguing over the boy in the divorce? I think Sean snatched him out of his bed that night. That's why the mother didn't hear anything. The boy would have gone willingly with his own father otherwise he would have raised a ruckus, don't you think?"

"That is one theory. I wonder though how Billy ended up getting run over just blocks from his house?"

"Maybe the boy changed his mind, decided he didn't want to go with him and jumped out of the car. It would be just like his drugged-up father to run over the boy and then panic and take off."

James pretended to take notes, which seemed to

please the woman. "I'll look into that," he told her, and she rose to leave, looking relieved.

"I wasn't sure if I should say anything or not," Connie said. "But you haven't been around much so you don't know a lot about this town and the people who live in it. I thought you should know." She let out a breath, nodded and headed for the door where she stopped to look back at him. "I'd be careful if I were you though. If Sean Sherman killed that boy, he thinks he's gotten away with it for nine years." She nodded again as if that said it all, but seemed compelled to add, "I hired Sean one time to do some landscaping. He made a mess of it. When I refused to pay him…" She shuddered. "The man has a terrible temper. He's dangerous."

"Thank you, Mrs. Matthews."

"I believe in doing my civic duty," she said primly and left.

CORA HEARD THE sound of shattering glass in the basement of her small house and smiled. Otis was just too predictable. What was he thinking he was going to do anyway? Kill her? The thought made her laugh. He was a nasty little bugger, but she couldn't see him committing murder. No, he'd come out here to scare her.

She shifted the shotgun in her lap and waited. Her chair was in a corner where she would see him when he came upstairs. She could hear him moving around down there. After tonight, Otis was going to replace that window he'd broken and anything else she wanted done around here.

Over the years, she'd collected a few people who were indebted to her after she'd caught them in some nefarious act. Some paid her monthly, others paid in favors. She didn't like to think of it as blackmail. She preferred to call it penitence for misdeeds done. She never asked for more than a person could afford.

But she didn't like Otis. She would make him pay dearly—if she didn't shoot him on sight.

Her cell phone rang, startling her. She glanced at the time. Almost one in the morning. The phone rang again—and she realized no sound was now coming from the basement.

"Hello?" she whispered into the phone, planning to give whoever was calling a piece of her mind for interrupting her at this hour.

"I got your money," Otis said. "I'll put it in your account tomorrow. Why are you whispering?" He chuckled. "Oh, I hope I didn't wake you up."

She could hear what sounded like bar noise in the background. "Where are you?" she demanded.

"At Harry's as if that is any of your damned business," he snapped and disconnected.

She stared at the phone for a moment. Then she heard again a sound coming from the basement. Her blood ran cold. If Otis wasn't down there, then who was? Cora felt fear coil around her as she heard a sound she recognized.

A moment later, she smelled the smoke.

CHAPTER SIXTEEN

JAMES WAS AWAKENED some time in the night by the sound of sirens. Sheriff's department patrol SUVs and several fire trucks sped down Main Street and kept going until the sirens died away. He'd rolled over and gone back to sleep until his cell phone rang just after 7:00 a.m.

"Did you hear about the fire?" his friend Ryan asked. "That old busybody crossed the wrong person this time. Cora says someone set her house on fire, but I heard the sheriff's trying to pin it on her. Arson."

"You've heard all this already this morning?"

"The men's coffee clutch down at the cafe. You should join us. It's a lot of the old gang along with some of the old men in town. Pretty interesting stuff most mornings."

James shook his head and told himself he wouldn't be staying in town that long. His leg was better, and his ribs didn't hurt with every breath. It was progress. "Thanks for the invite," he said. "I'll keep it in mind."

"How is the investigation going?"

He was saved from answering as he got another call. "Sorry, I'm getting another call. Talk to you later?" He didn't wait for an answer as he accepted the call. At first all he heard was coughing, an awful hack that he didn't recognize. "Hello?" he repeated.

"I want to hire you." The words came out strained between coughs. "Someone tried to burn me alive in my own house last night."

"Cora?" The last time she'd said more than a few words to him, she'd been chasing him and his brothers away from her apple trees with a shotgun.

In between coughs, she said, "You're a private detective, aren't you?"

"Isn't the sheriff investigating?" he asked, sitting up to rub a hand over his face. It was too early in the morning for this.

"Carl? That old reprobate!" He waited through a coughing fit. "He thinks I set the fire, that's how good an investigator he is. I put myself in the hospital and burned down my own house? Idiot." More coughing. "You owe me, James Colt, for all the times you and your brothers trespassed in my yard and stole my apples."

He wanted to point out that she'd had more apples than she could ever use and let them waste every year. But they *were* her apples.

"The least you can do is prove that I didn't start the fire. Otherwise, the sheriff is talking putting me behind bars."

"I'll look into it," he said, all the time mentally kicking himself.

"Good. Don't overcharge me."

James disconnected. He lay down again, but he knew there was no chance he could get back to sleep. After Connie Matthews had left last night, he'd hoped Lori was still around. She wasn't so he'd gone out and gotten himself some fast food and then driven to Billy Sherman's neighborhood.

From there, he'd walked toward the spot where the

boy had died. He'd tried to imagine doing the same thing in a violent thunderstorm at the age of seven. Whoever Billy had seen couldn't have been some random person like anyone he and Todd normally followed. The boy must have recognized the person. But then why hadn't he mentioned a name to Todd? Or maybe there was something about the person that had lured him out into the storm. James couldn't imagine what it could have been.

An image from a movie during his own childhood popped into his head of a clown holding a string with a bright-colored balloon floating overhead. It had given him nightmares for weeks. A kid afraid of the dark and storms wouldn't go after a clown—especially one with a balloon.

LORELEI HAD DRIVEN past her stepmother's house last night only to see all the lights were out and her car wasn't in the garage. She'd been tempted to drive out to the senator's house to see if she was there. Earlier this evening on the news she'd heard that the senator and his wife were officially divorcing.

"They reported that they've been separated for some time now and believe it is best if they end the marriage," the newscaster had said. *"Senator Bayard said the divorce is amicable and that he wishes only the best for Mary."*

It had sounded as if Mary was the one who'd wanted the separation and divorce. Maybe she had. Maybe Lorelei had been too hard on her stepmother.

The news had ended with a mention of Bayard being called back to Washington on some subcommittee work he was doing. She wondered how true that was. Maybe

Fred and her stepmother had flown off somewhere together to celebrate the divorce.

What bothered Lorelei was that her stepmother felt
the need to lie to her. Or at the very least not to be honest with her. Like providing the loan for the sandwich
shop. Like falling in love without telling her. While
Lorelei didn't approve of her stepmother's affair, she
wanted her to be happy. She hated the strain in their relationship and promised herself that she would do what
she could to fix it when she saw Karen again.

After a restless night, she'd gotten up and gone to
work as usual. As she pulled in behind the shop to park,
James was standing by the back door of his office grinning.

"My license came today. It's official—I'm a private
investigator."

"Congratulations. You'll have to frame it and put it
up on your wall."

"I know it seems silly being excited about it, but I
am. It makes me feel legit. I also have a new client."
She raised a brow. "I'll tell you all about it over dinner.
I thought we'd go out and celebrate. I owe you a steak."
She started to argue, but he stopped her with a warm
hand on her bare arm. "Please? You wouldn't make me
celebrate alone, would you?"

She knew he could make a call to any number of
women who would jump at a steak dinner date with
him. When she'd awakened this morning, she'd promised herself that she would see her stepmother tonight—
if her stepmother was in town.

James waved the license in the air and grinned.
"How can a Montana girl like you say no to a slab of
grain-fed beef grilled over a hot fire?"

Lorelei laughed in spite of her sometime resolve to keep James Colt at arm's length. "Fine. What time?"

JAMES COULDN'T HELP smiling as he drove out to Cora's. Lori had agreed to have dinner with him. He hadn't been this excited about a date in… Heck, he wasn't sure he ever had been. That should have worried him, he realized.

Cora's house had sat on a hill. Smoke was still rising up through the pine trees and into the blue summer sky as he pulled in.

After parking, he got out of his truck and walked over to the firefighters still putting out the last of the embers. One of the fears of living in the pine trees was always fire. But the firefighters had been able to contain the blaze from spreading into the pines. The small old house though seemed to be a total loss.

"I'm looking for the arson investigator," James said and was pointed to a man wearing a mask and gloves and a Montana State University Bobcats baseball cap digging around in the ashes.

"I'm Private Detective James Colt," he said introducing himself.

The man gave him a glance and continued digging. "Colt? That your property next door?"

"Yep."

"A lot of recent fires out here." He rose to his feet and extended a gloved hand before drawing it back to wipe soot onto his pants. "Sorry about that. Gil Sanders."

James couldn't help his surprise. "Gilbert Sanders?" he asked, remembering seeing the name on his father's list. But why would his father be interested in talking to an arson investigator as part of Billy Sherman's hit-and-run?

"Have we met before?" Gil asked, studying him. "You look familiar."

"My father, PI Del Colt, might have contacted you about another investigation."

The man frowned. "Sorry. Can you be more specific?"

"He was investigating the hit-and-run death of a local boy about nine years ago."

Gil shook his head. "You're sure it was me he spoke with?"

"Maybe not." Now that James thought about it, there hadn't been any notes from the interview in his father's file. "I'm here about another matter. Cora Brooks called me this morning. Anything new on the fire?"

"It was definitely arson. The blaze was started in the basement. The accelerant was gasoline. It burned hot and fast. She was lucky to get out alive."

James nodded. "The sheriff seemed to think Cora started the fire herself."

The investigator shook his head. "I've already reviewed the statements from the first responders. The property owner was in a robe and slippers carrying a shotgun and a pair of binoculars. That's all she apparently managed to save. She couldn't have outrun that fire if she started it. Not in those slippers. I'm told she is in her right mind."

"Sharp and lethal as a new filet knife."

Gil chuckled. "She told first responders that she'd heard someone breaking into her basement. That's why she had her shotgun. Not sure why the binoculars were so important to her, but I don't see any way a woman her age could have started the fire in the basement and hightailed it upstairs to an outside deck. Not with as much gas as was used downstairs. I'm not even sure she can lift the size gas can that was found."

Cora was apparently in the clear. "Thank you. If I figure out why I saw your name in my father's case file…"

"Just give me a call. But unless it pertains to a fire, I can't imagine why he had wanted to talk to me."

James shook the man's hand and nodded at Gil's cap. "Go Bobcats," he said and headed back to his pickup. Too bad all his PI cases weren't this easy, he thought. He headed for the hospital to give Cora the good news. This one was on him, no charge. He knew she'd like the sound of that.

OTIS STUMBLED TO his cabin door hungover, half-asleep and ticked off. Whoever was pounding on his door was going to regret it.

"What the hell did you do?" his brother Carl demanded, pushing past him and into the cabin. The sheriff turned to look at him and swore. "On second thought, I don't want to know."

"If this is about that fire out at Cora's—"

"What else? I saw you yesterday. You were going on about the woman and last night her house burns down." Carl raised a hand. "There's an arson investigator out there. I told him that I think Cora did it for the insurance money, but he sure as the devil isn't going to take my word for it."

"I didn't do it." Otis stepped past him to open the refrigerator. He needed the hair of the dog that bit him last night. Pulling out a can of beer he popped the top, took a long drink and looked at his brother.

"How deep are you in all this?" Carl demanded.

"I did something stupid."

His brother groaned. "I wouldn't be here if I didn't suspect that was the case."

"I took something out to the Colt place. I was going to make an anonymous call and let you find it. I know you'd like to get that arrogant little turd behind bars as much as I would."

The sheriff swore. "Tell me it isn't anything explosive. You get anyone killed—"

"No, just some illegal stuff. Doesn't matter now. I'll get it hauled away. It was stupid. Then Cora saw me, said she made a video of me dumping it…" He hung his head again.

"Otis, swear to me you didn't burn down Cora's house."

The former sheriff looked up, his expression one of disbelief and hurt. "I was at the bar. You can check. I was there until closing. Even better about the time it was catching fire, I called Cora from the bar. See I have an alibi so I'm gold."

His brother swore.

"What's wrong? There will be a record of the call— just before I heard the sirens. So it couldn't have been me."

Carl told himself that his brother had been at the bar to establish that alibi, which meant Otis had hired someone to set fire to the place. He wished he didn't know his brother so well. "If it wasn't you, any idea who might have wanted Cora dead?"

Otis chuckled. "Anyone who's ever crossed her path."

"Let's just hope Gil Sanders doesn't find any evidence out there that would make him think you had anything to do with this."

CORA TOOK THE news as would be expected. She nodded, told James he'd better not send her a bill and ordered him out of her room.

A near-death experience didn't change everyone apparently, he thought as he left chuckling.

He was still wondering if the Gilbert Sanders on his father's list was the arson investigator and if so what Del thought the man could offer on the hit-and-run case.

Meanwhile, he tracked down Sean Sherman. His call went straight to voice mail. He left a message asking Sean to call him and hung up. Sherman lived in a town not far from Lonesome. If he had to, James would drive over and pay the man a visit.

With that done, he considered his father's list again. Connie Matthews had said something in her original interview with his father that kept bothering him. Lyle Harris had been operating the front-end loader the morning Connie had seen the body and stopped him from covering it up.

James knew it was a long shot. His father had already talked to the man and there wasn't anything in his notes that sent up a red flag. But he was running out of people to interview and getting worried that he'd missed something important.

At forty-five, Lyle Harris had quit his job with the local contractor after a work comp accident that had put him in a wheelchair. As James pulled up out front of his place deep in the woods, he noticed the ramp from the house through the carport to the garage. He recalled

Ryan telling him that he'd donated the lumber and the men Lyle·used to work with had donated their time to make the house more wheelchair accessible.

After parking, he got out and walked toward the house, changing directions as he heard the whine of an electric saw coming from the garage.

"Lyle!" he called. "Lyle, it's James Colt!" The sound of the saw stopped abruptly. He heard what sounded like a cry of pain and quickly stepped through the door into the large garage.

The first thing he saw was the wheelchair lying on its side. Past it, he caught movement as someone ran out the back door and into the pines. He charged into the garage thinking it had been Lyle who'd run out.

But he hadn't gone far when he saw that Lyle had left a bloody trail on the concrete floor where he'd crawled away from the wheelchair, away from the electric saw lying on the floor next to it, the blade dripping blood.

"What the hell?" he said, rushing to the man on the floor. He was already digging out his phone to call 911.

"No, don't. Please. Don't call. I'm okay," Lyle cried as he pressed a rag against the wound that had torn through his jeans to the flesh of his lower leg. "It's not fatal."

James stared at the man, then slowly disconnected before the 911 operator answered. "I just saw someone running out of here. What's going on?"

Lyle shook his head. "Could you get my chair?"

He walked over, picked it up and rolled the wheelchair over to the man, holding it steady as Lyle lifted himself into it.

"It looks worse than it is," Lyle said as he rolled over

to a low workbench. He grabbed a first aid kit. "But thanks for showing up when you did."

"That blade could have taken off your leg," James said.

"Naw, it wouldn't have gone that far."

Lyle winced as he poured rubbing alcohol on the wound then began to bandage it with shaking fingers. From what James could tell, the man was right. The wound wasn't deep. "You want help with that?"

"No. I'm fine," he said, turning his back to him.

"You're in trouble." Lyle said nothing. "And whatever it is, it's serious." James took a guess on how many times he'd seen Lyle's rig parked in front of the casino since he'd been back in town. "Gambling?"

Lyle finished and spun the wheelchair around to face him. "I appreciate you stopping by when you did. Now what can I do for you?"

He sighed. His father used to say that you couldn't help people who didn't want to be helped. He knew that to be true. He chewed at his cheek for a moment, thinking. "Were you gambling nine years ago when Billy Sherman died?"

The question took the man by surprise.

James saw the answer in Lyle's face and swore. "Connie Matthews said that if she hadn't seen Billy Sherman's body lying in that ditch when she did, you would have dumped dirt on him with your front-end loader and he would never have been found. She also told my father that she'd been surprised that you were already working that morning since you usually didn't start that early. In fact, she'd been afraid you were going to get fired since she'd heard Edgar Appleton, your boss, warning you before that day about coming to work late so often. She thought that's why you were there so early that morning and that still half-asleep, you didn't see the boy and would have buried him in that ditch. You would have known that the concrete had been ordered for the driveway. It was going to be delivered that day. Had you covered Billy's body with dirt, it would have never been found."

Lyle stared him down for a full minute. "Like I said, thanks for stopping by."

"I don't believe you ran that boy down, but I do wonder if you weren't hired to get rid of his body. Maybe hired is the wrong word. Coerced into making Billy Sherman disappear?"

"You can see your way out," Lyle said, wheeling around and heading toward his house.

CHAPTER SEVENTEEN

LORELEI COULDN'T BELIEVE that she'd agreed to have dinner with James. He'd caught her at a weak moment. The small table at the back of the steak house was dimly lit. A single candle flickered from a ceramic cowboy boot at the center. The candlelight made his blue eyes sparkle more than usual and brought out the shine of his thick dark hair.

If she had been on a real date, it would have been romantic. But this was James. A woman would be a fool to take him seriously.

James lifted his wineglass in a toast, those blue eyes taking her captive. "Thank you for indulging me tonight."

"My pleasure," she said automatically and realized she meant it as she lifted her own wineglass and tapped it gently against his. She couldn't remember the last dinner date she'd been on with a man. She took a sip of the wine. It was really good. "I'm surprised you know your wines."

He grinned. "You're impressed, aren't you?" He shook his head. "I called earlier and talked to the sommelier. I didn't want to look like a dumb cowboy."

"You could never be a dumb cowboy," she said, feeling the alcohol loosen her tongue. She'd have to be careful tonight. The candlelight, the soft music, the wine,

the company, it made her want to let her hair down—
so to speak. She'd pulled her hair up as per usual, but
in a softer twist. She'd worn a favorite dress that she'd
been told looked good on her and she'd spritzed on a
little perfume behind each ear.

She felt James's intent gaze on her a moment before
he said, "You look beautiful." His tone sent a tremor
through her that jump-started her heart.

Lorelei sipped her wine, fighting for a control she
didn't feel. "Thank you. I could say the same about
you." He'd worn all black from his button-up shirt to
his jeans to his new boots. The outfit accented his long
muscular legs and cupped a behind that could have sold
a million pairs of jeans. The black Western shirt was
opened just enough to expose the warm glow of his
throat and make her yearn to see more.

There'd been a time when she'd dreamed of being
with James Colt. When she'd fantasized what it would
be like if he ever asked her out. But he never had. Until
now. She had to remind herself that this wasn't a real
date and yet it certainly felt real the way he was looking at her.

She was surprised to see that she'd finished her wine.
James started to refill her glass—and not for the first
time. She shook her head. Given the trail her thoughts
had taken, the last thing she needed was more wine.

James suddenly got to his feet and reached for her
hand. "Dance with me."

She took his hand before the words registered.
Dance? She glanced at the intimate dance floor as he
drew her to her feet. No one was dancing. But he was
already leading her to it. He turned her to the middle
of the dance floor and pulled her directly into his arms.

He drew her close and she let him. She pressed her cheek against his shoulder knowing she couldn't blame the wine. Their bodies moved in time to the music as if they were one of those older couples who'd danced together for decades.

Lorelei drew back a little to look into his eyes and wanted to pinch herself. Not even in her fantasies had she dreamed of James Colt holding her in his arms and looking at her like this. She'd been only a girl and, like her Barbie dolls, she'd long ago stored all that away. And yet here they were.

She pressed her cheek against his warm shoulder again, closed her eyes and let herself enjoy this moment. Because that's all it was. A moment. Just like in the closet with him. The memory made her smile. He'd actually been embarrassed by his reaction to her.

The song ended. There was that awkward moment when they stood looking into each other's eyes. She was certain that he wanted to kiss her, but the waiter came by with their salads. The moment gone.

Her heart was still triple-timing as James walked her back to the table, holding her hand, squeezing it before letting it go.

"You dance well," she said.

He grinned. "My brother Willie taught me."

She laughed and felt herself relax a little. He had been about to kiss her, hadn't he? Another awkward moment before they dug into their salads, both seemingly lost in their private thoughts.

By the time their meals came they were talking like friends who owned businesses next door to each other. They'd both grown up in Lonesome so it made it easy to talk about the past and stay away from the future. That

moment on the dance floor had passed as if it had never
happened. She suspected they both were glad of that.
Otherwise, it could have made being business neighbors awkward. Neither of them wanted that.

ASKING LORI TO dance had been a mistake. Not that
James hadn't enjoyed having her in his arms. He'd loved
the sweet scent of her, nuzzling his way into her hair to
get at its source behind her ears. She'd smelled heavenly. She'd felt heavenly.

He'd lost himself in the feel of her, wishing the song
would never end. It was as if they'd called a truce,
shared no uncomfortable past, had only this amazing
few minutes moving together as one, in perfect sync.

And then the song ended and he'd looked at her and
all he'd wanted to do was kiss her. She'd parted those
lips as if expecting the kiss. He'd seen something in her
eyes, a fire burning like the one burning inside him.
And then the waiter had been forced to go around them
to put their salads on their table and he was reminded
of all the reasons he shouldn't get involved with this
woman. He wasn't staying. Getting the PI license was a
hoot, but he was a rodeo cowboy. If he solved this case,
then it would make all of this worthwhile. But once he
was healed, he would be leaving again. Long-distance
relationships didn't work. Just ask Melody.

But all that aside, he'd mentally kicked himself for
not kissing her when he had the chance. Maybe he'd
known deep inside that once he kissed her there was
no going back with this one. Lori wasn't like anyone
he'd dated—if you could even call it dating. The others
had known what they were getting into and had ridden
in eyes wide open.

Lori was different. She expected more. Would want more from him. More than he had to give at this point in his life. One of these days he'd think about settling down, but he hoped those days were still a long way off.

Even as he thought it, he couldn't help looking over at Lori as he walked her to her door later that night. He felt the pull of something stronger than the road, maybe even stronger than the rodeo, stronger than even his resolve.

"Thank you for a lovely evening and congratulations again," she said as she pulled out her keys and turned to unlock her door.

He didn't feel like himself as he touched her arm and gently turned her back toward him. "Lori." It didn't feel like his arms that drew her to him. Or his lips that dropped hungrily to her mouth. Or his fingers that released her hair and let it fall in waves of chestnut down her slim back.

Her perfume filled his senses as her arms looped around his neck and he pushed his body into hers until the only way they could have been closer was naked in the throws of passionate lovemaking.

The kiss and that thought sent a bolt of desire rocketing through him. He had never wanted a woman like he did this one. He felt humbled with desire. He wanted to be a better man. He wanted to be her man. He wanted her. For keeps.

He felt her palms on his chest, felt her gentle push as she drew her mouth from his and leaned back to look into his eyes. He saw naked desire as well as the battle going on there. She was as scared as he was.

She shook her head slowly. Regretfully? And pulled free of his arms. He watched her straighten, brushing her long hair back as she lifted the keys in her hand and turned toward the door again.

He let her fumble with the key to the lock for a moment before he took the keys from her and opened her door. Then desire still raging through him, he handed her the keys and took a step back. He feared that if he took her in his arms again there really would be no turning back. He looked at her and knew he couldn't do it. He wouldn't let himself hurt this woman.

"Thanks again for tonight," he said, his voice rough with emotion. "I'll see you tomorrow." He turned and hurried down the steps to his pickup. He hadn't noticed the car that had gone by. Hadn't heard it. Only the taillights turning in the distance made him even aware that anyone had driven past. Nor did he give it more than a distracted notice as he climbed behind the wheel and, thinking of Lori, allowed himself to glance back at the house.

She was no longer standing there, thank goodness. The door was closed and a light glowed deep in the house. He sat for a moment, still shaken before he started the engine and headed toward home, knowing he wouldn't be able to sleep a wink.

But to his surprise, he fell asleep the moment his head hit the pillow only to be assaulted by dreams that wove themselves together in a jumbled pattern that felt too real and too frightening. In the dream, he'd known that it wasn't just him who was in danger. Lori was there and he was having trouble getting to her when the little blond-haired girl appeared on her horse. She was laughing and smiling as she cantered toward him. "Watch this, Daddy!"

He half woke in a sweat. The nightmare clung to

him, holding him under even as he tried to surface. He was in uncharted waters on a leaky boat and it was impossible to swim with the concrete blocks that were tied to his ankles.

CHAPTER EIGHTEEN

LORELEI WOKE AND panicked for a moment, thinking she was late for work. She hadn't gotten to sleep until very late last night. It had taken her a while to process everything. James had kissed her. He'd called her Lori in a way that made her heart race. No one had ever given her a nickname. She hadn't been that kind of girl. Until James.

And that was the problem. He'd upset her orderly world. He'd made her burn inside with a need she knew only he could fulfill. He'd made her want to throw caution to the wind.

And then he'd been a perfect gentleman, unlocking her front door, handing her the keys and leaving.

She'd been shocked. But mostly...disappointed. She hadn't planned to invite him in. But he hadn't even tried. A man with his reputation? Surely, he had to know the power he had over women. He would know she was vulnerable after a kiss like that. So why hadn't he asked to spend the night?

Lorelei knew it was ridiculous that she was angry with him for not hitting on her. Everything the man seemed to do made her angry with him, even when he was well-behaved. Maybe it wasn't him. Maybe it was her who was the problem. Maybe he didn't find her attractive.

Those thoughts had her tossing and turning and losing sleep because of him. That too annoyed her with him.

She told herself that her life had been just fine before he'd showed up next door. Her stepmother was right. Having James Colt living next to her shop was a bad idea. The man was too…distracting.

As daylight crept into the room, she lay in bed staring up at the ceiling reliving the kiss, reliving the way he'd cupped the back of her neck, the way he'd buried his face in her hair, the way he said Lori.

"Oh, for crying out loud!" she snapped and swung her legs over the side of the bed. She was acting like a teenager.

The thought actually made her smile. She'd been so driven from middle school on that all she'd thought about was excelling in her school work so she could get into a good college. Then at college she'd worked hard to get top grades so she could get a good job. She hadn't let herself be a teenager and do what a lot of other teenagers did—like James Colt.

She'd missed so much. No wonder she'd never felt like this, she realized. Until now. Now she wanted it all. And she wanted it with James.

He had wanted her, hadn't he? That kiss… She'd seen the desire in his blue eyes. So why had he just walked away last night?

Because for the first time maybe in his entire life he was being sensible, something she'd been her whole life? Oh, that was so like him, she thought angrily as she stepped into the shower. *Now* he decided to be responsible.

JAMES THREW HIMSELF into work the next morning. His thoughts and emotions had been all over the place from the moment he'd opened his eyes. The cold shower he'd taken hadn't helped so he'd left the office early to avoid seeing Lori.

He knew it was cowardice, but after that kiss last night he didn't trust himself around her. That had been a first for him. Normally after a kiss like that, he would only avoid a woman if he didn't want to see her again. But Lori wasn't just some woman and that was the problem.

Because it was Montana, the drive to the next town gave him plenty of time to think—more than an hour and a half. In this part of the state, the towns were few and far between.

Alice Sherman's ex worked as a maintenance man at the local hospital. As it turned out, today was Sean's day off. A helpful employee told him that the man lived only a block away in a large apartment house.

James walked, needing to clear his head. On the drive over, he'd had plenty of time to think. Too much. He'd finally turned on a country station on the radio. Not that even music could get his mind off Lori Wilkins.

He went from wishing he hadn't come back to town to being grateful that he had because of her. He went from wishing he could get right back on the rodeo circuit to being too involved in not just this case to want to leave now. He knew the best thing he could do was give Lori a wide berth, but at the same time, he couldn't wait to see her again.

Now as he shoved open the front door of the large apartment house, he tried to focus on work. According to the mailboxes by the door, Sherman was in 322.

He turned toward the large old elevator and decided to take the stairs.

The man who answered the door at 322 was tall and slim and nice-looking. He was nothing like James had been expecting. Nor was the man's apartment. It was neat and clean, much like the man himself. "May I help you?"

"I'm James Colt. I'm a private investigator in Lonesome."

"Did Alice hire you?"

"No. I believe my father, Del Colt, was hired by you to look into the death of your son. As you know, he died before he finished the case. I've taken it over. I'd like to ask you a few questions."

Sean Sherman seemed to be making up his mind. After a moment, he stepped back. "Come on in. I'm not sure how I can help," he said after they were seated in the living room. "Alice and I were separated at the time and in the middle of a divorce. I was fighting for joint custody, but I would imagine she already told you that." She hadn't, but James had read as much in his father's notes.

"Were you in Lonesome that night?"

The man hesitated a little too long so James was surprised when he finally answered. "Yes." That definitely wasn't what Sean had told Del.

"You were?"

Sean sighed before he said, "I lied to your father about that. I had my reasons at the time."

"Then why tell me the truth now?"

"Because if it will help you find out who killed my son, then nothing else matters."

"But that wasn't the case nine years ago?" James asked.

"Other people were involved. It was a very traumatic time in my life. The divorce, arguing over Billy. I don't know if Alice told you this or not." He met James's gaze and held it. "I was having an affair. Alice found out and our marriage was over. The affair was a mistake, one I will always regret. I didn't want all of that made public and having it thrown in Alice's face. We'd lost our son. We were both devastated. The rest of it wasn't important."

"I understand drugs were involved?"

"I'll be honest with you. I couldn't take the pain of what I'd done, blamed myself for not being in the house with my family that night and I turned to drugs. It's taken me a long time to climb back out of that. Being honest is part of my recovery."

"If you were in Lonesome that night, but not at your house, where were you?" James asked.

Sean looked away for a moment before he said, "I was at Karen Wilkins's house."

He couldn't help his surprise. "She was the woman you were having the affair with?"

The man nodded. "I was in the middle of breaking it off with her."

"Were you there all night?" James asked.

"I think so. Things got very emotional. Karen left. She ran out into the storm. I started to go after her but turned back."

"She left on foot?"

He nodded. "But not long after that I heard her take her car and leave."

"What time was that?"

"I think it was about ten."

"You didn't go after her in your car?" Sean shook his head. "When did she come back?"

"I don't know exactly. I got into her booze, got disgustingly drunk and passed out; and when I woke up, she was standing over me distraught, screaming, crying and telling me to get out. It was daylight by then. I left and the only time I went back to Lonesome was for my son's funeral. I tried to mend things with Alice but…" He shook his head. "That's it."

James thought about it for a moment. "When you woke to find Karen home again what kind of shape was she in? I know she was upset. There was a thunderstorm that night. Was she still wet from being out in it?"

The man frowned. "No. Her clothes must have dried because they weren't wet. Stranger was the fact that she'd fixed her hair. She had to have been home for a while, I guess." He shook his head. "You can tell how out of it I was."

"She was wearing the same clothing though?"

"She was. She had to have been home for a while before she woke me up. I could tell that she'd had a shower." He shrugged. "I liked the smell of her shower gel."

James shook his head. If he knew anything about women who felt scorned, it was that they didn't calmly come home shower, fix their hair, put on the same clothing and then decide to wake you up to throw you out. So where had Karen been that she'd spent the night, taken a shower and gotten her clothes dried? He supposed it was possible that she'd gone to her exercise studio. They probably had showers there. Karen could even have a washer and dryer down there for all he knew. Still, it seemed odd.

"Did you hear any more from her?" he asked.

Sean shook his head. "That night pretty well ended everything in Lonesome for me."

"She's never tried to contact you?"

"Never. Nor did I ever contact her. It was over almost before it started. We both regretted it. I'm sure I could have handled it better than I did."

James thanked the man and showed himself out. He couldn't help being surprised about Karen. But at least now he knew why she was on his father's list. She'd been upset and out driving that night in the storm. Had she done something? Had she seen something?

He felt a start. But how had Del found out about her possible involvement in Billy's death? Sean hadn't told him and Karen certainly hadn't shared the information when James had tried to question her.

Had someone seen her that night?

LORELEI DID WHAT she always did on Sunday morning. She went to church; only today she was asked to help with the toddlers in child care during the service and jumped at it. She loved the job, especially toddler age. They were so much fun as they raced around, laughing and screaming and keeping her on her toes. Seriously, she later thought. What had she been thinking volunteering for this since she had thirteen toddlers between her and another volunteer? It was wonderful madness.

For several hours she forgot about everything, especially James.

Then it ended, parents picked up their children and she was facing what she did at home each Sunday after

church: cleaning house. Today, the place got an extra
good scrubbing even though it didn't need it. Her house
was small—just the way she liked it since she spent so
little time there.

She'd just finished when her doorbell rang. Her first
thought was that it was probably her stepmother. They
often did something together on a Sunday every month
or so. But when she opened the door, it was James standing there. She blinked in surprise and then horror as she
realized what she was wearing. Leggings and an over-
sized sweatshirt that hung off one shoulder. Her hair
was pulled up in a high ponytail. She never wore much
makeup, but now she wore none. And she smelled like
cleaning solution.

"We need to talk," he said without preamble as he
stepped in, seemingly not even noticing her appearance.

"Iced tea or beer?" she asked as she followed him
into the kitchen.

"Beer." He looked around. "Nice house."

"Thanks." She took two beers from the refrigerator
and handed him one as she led the way into the small
living room and curled up on one end of the couch. He
took the chair next to it, looking uncomfortable.

"If this is about last night—"

"No," he said too quickly. "I mean." He met her gaze.
"No. It's about your stepmother." Lorelei groaned in-
wardly and thought, *Now what?* "I drove over to Big
Timber and talked to Sean Sherman this morning."

She frowned. "Billy's dad?"

He nodded. "He told me something. Are you aware
that your stepmother was seeing him nine years ago?"

James could have told her almost anything about her
stepmother and she wouldn't have batted an eye. Karen

had proven to her how little she knew about the woman who'd raised her.

"What do you mean 'seeing' him?" When James merely looked at her, she let out a cry and shot to her feet. "If you're trying to tell me that my stepmother is a serial philanderer with married men…"

"It might be worse than that," he said. "Sean told me he broke up with her that night. Upset, Karen left the house in the storm, at first on foot, but later came back for her car."

Lorelei had moved to the fireplace but now put her free hand over her mouth, her eyes filling with tears as her heart dropped like a stone, bottoming out.

"We don't know that she was the one who hit Billy—" he choked out. "But she went somewhere. When she returned to her house, she'd either gone straight to the shower, fixed her hair and dried her clothing and put on the same outfit before confronting Sean who'd passed out after being into her booze, or…"

She rolled her eyes. "Or what?"

"She'd been somewhere and showered and fixed her hair before returning to the house to make it look as if she'd been home longer than she had."

Lorelei removed her hand from her mouth and took a drink of her beer without tasting it. She thought she might throw up. "All you have is Sean's word for this, right?" she asked, already looking, hoping, for a way that none of this could be true.

"He's on the wagon, in a program that requires him to be honest, he said, which is why he was willing to talk now. I called Alice on my way back. It's true."

"What am I supposed to say?" she asked, her voice breaking.

"I'm worried about your stepmother. Do you have any idea where she is?" She shook her head. "I've been trying to reach her. From what I can tell she hasn't been home. Neither has the senator."

"Maybe they ran away together to celebrate his divorce," she said. "She thinks he's going to marry her."

"I hope she is with him. I would hate to think that she's alone. It might be my fault that she's left town. I need her side of the story."

Lorelei couldn't believe this and yet she could. It explained why her stepmother had gotten so upset that James was digging into the old hit-and-run case. Because she had a whole lot to hide. But Lorelei couldn't let herself think that her stepmother had killed that boy. She wouldn't.

"I'm sorry to be the one to tell you," he said, sounding as miserable as he looked. "I wish…" He shook his head. He didn't need to say it. She had her wishes too.

She put down her half-full beer. "I'll let you know when I hear from her."

James finished his beer, set the empty bottle on the small table by the chair and rose. He had taken off his Stetson when he'd come in. It now dangled in his fingers by the brim. She couldn't help but think about those fingers on her face, in her hair, last night as he'd kissed her. He'd been so gentle, his caress soft, his callused fingertips sending shivers through her.

He took a step toward her. She couldn't move, couldn't breathe, couldn't think. She felt her eyes widen as he leaned toward her and brushed his lips over hers. "About last night," he said, his voice low. "It was the best date I've ever had." He drew back, his gaze locking with hers before he turned and left.

CHAPTER NINETEEN

JAMES FELT AS if he'd been kicked in the gut by a bronc. But he'd come this far. He couldn't stop now. He had to finish his father's case. That meant finding Billy Sherman's killer—no matter where the path led him.

When his phone rang, he hoped it would be Lorelei. If not her, then her stepmother. But it was Lyle Harris.

"I've been thinking. I want to talk," Lyle said. "Can you come here?"

"I'm on my way." He turned and went back the way he'd come, turning and going east on a dirt road until he came to the small homemade sign that marked the way into Harris's place hidden in the pines.

James tried not to be anxious, but he'd known that there was more to Lyle's story. He'd just never thought he was going to hear it. Because Lyle was afraid of the person who'd hired him to cover up the body? Or out of loyalty to that person? Either way, James thought, he needed a break in this case. And this just might be it.

He parked, got out and checked the garage shop first before going up to the side door of the house. At his knock, Lyle called, "Come in."

Shoving open the door, he stepped first into a mud room, then a hallway with a lot of doors. "Lyle?" No answer. He felt his skin prickle as he realized belatedly that he might be walking into a trap. The garage had been large, easy to see if someone had been hiding to jump him.

You're getting awfully paranoid.

"In the kitchen," came Lyle's voice.

He headed slowly down the hall, pushing aside half-open doors on his way. True to his word, Lyle was in the kitchen, which had been remodeled to accommodate a man in a wheelchair.

"I was just making chili," Lyle said, his back to him. "My stepmother said no one eats chili in the summer." He turned then to look at James. "I do." Wheeling back to the pot on the stove, he stirred, turned down the heat, and putting down the spoon spun around. He looked nervous, which made James nervous too. "I called you at a weak moment. I'd just talked to my mom on the phone."

"Does that mean that you've changed your mind about telling me the truth?" James said, hoping that's all there was to this.

"Look, I know you're going to keep digging. I've heard around town. A lot of people are getting upset."

"They shouldn't be unless they have something to hide."

Lyle laughed. "Hey, in case you haven't noticed, Lonesome is a small town. It's tight, man. I don't think you realize the position you're in. This is dangerous because you've stirred things up after nine long years when everyone thought it was over."

"Why would they think that? Billy Sherman's killer was never found. Why would people not want the boy's killer to be found?"

"I'm going to level with you," Lyle said. "I think you're an okay dude. Well-meaning enough but treading where you shouldn't be treading unless you have a death wish. So, you're right. I *was* told to cover up the body in the ditch before anyone saw it—especially the neighbors' kids. But I was told it was a coyote."

"A coyote?"

"I saw the blood on the road where it had been hit that morning when I came to work. I had no reason to think otherwise. It was god-awful early in the morning. I was half asleep, half loaded too. I climbed up on my front loader—"

"You didn't go look at the coyote?"

"Why would I? I just loaded up the bucket and was about to dump it when that woman came out and started screaming. That's the truth."

James realized that he believed him. "There's just one thing you left out. Who told you it was a coyote?"

Lyle looked down at his feet for a long moment. "You see all these ramps out here? You see this kitchen? You think the state picked up the bill?" He shook his head. "My friends and the people I worked with did all this."

James felt an icy chill begin to work its way up his spine. "You ever think that the person who told you to bury the…coyote…was lying to you?"

Lyle met his gaze with an angry one. "No, I did not. Because I admire the hell out of the man who told me to do it. It's the kind of thing he would think to do if he saw a dead coyote in the road in a nice neighborhood where he thought it might upset the kids. You think he would have done that if it had been a little boy lying in that road?"

"I don't know. I guess it depends on who we're talking about." He watched Lyle's temper rise and fall before the man turned back to his chili. James thought he knew where this was headed. He didn't want it to be the man and his wife that he'd had dinner with a few nights ago. He didn't want to believe it and yet he knew that Lyle couldn't be talking about anyone else.

"Edgar told you about the coyote, didn't he? He's the one who told you to come in early and cover it up. You didn't question it because you'd been coming in late and he'd been threatening to fire you. And like you said, you would do anything he asked you—even before your accident."

"It *was* a coyote," Lyle said as if trying to convince himself. "You say otherwise and you're going to destroy a good man. You don't want to do that in this town unless you're planning to leave and never come back. It might already be too late anyway."

James left the man to his chili, hearing the warning, knowing well enough how small towns worked. He suspected his father had made an enemy while working the case and it had gotten him killed.

He felt sick at the thought of Edgar Appleton being involved. He was thinking of the dinner that night, the love he saw between husband and wife, as he climbed into his pickup and started the engine. He didn't want to believe it. Worse, he didn't want to confront the man. Edgar and Irene were good people. But his father always said that even good people made bad decisions and ended up doing bad things sometimes.

Still… He'd turned around and driven through the dense pines toward the main road when he heard it. A rustling sound followed by the distinct rattle. His blood froze as his gaze shot to the passenger side floorboards of his pickup.

He hadn't noticed the paper sack when he'd gotten

in. His mind had been on what Lyle had told him. Now though, it drew his attention like a laser as the head of the rattlesnake slithered out, its body coiling, the head rising as the rattles reached a deafening sound.

James slammed on the brakes, throwing the pickup into Park as he flung open the door and bailed out. Even as he did he felt the snake strike his lower calf, sinking its fangs into the top of his cowboy boot.

CHAPTER TWENTY

As EDGAR APPLETON opened the door, James grabbed his hand and dropped eleven rattles into his palm. He saw the man's startled expression. "What the—"

"Someone put a rattlesnake in my pickup," James said and reached down to draw up his jeans pant leg to show where the snake had almost bitten through the top of his boot before he'd dragged it out and killed it, cutting off the rattles. "Want to guess why?"

The older man frowned. "If you're suggesting—"

"I was at Lyle Harris's house when the snake was put in my pickup. Nine years ago, you told Lyle Harris to bury the body."

Edgar blinked. "You should come in. Irene is out working in the garden. I can see that we need to talk." He turned and walked into the dining room.

Through the window, James could see Irene bent over weeding in the huge garden. He turned to Edgar, wishing this hadn't brought him to this house of all places. He waited, sick at heart.

The older man sighed and dropped into a chair, motioning for James to take one as well. But he was too anxious to sit. He stood near the window and kept waiting.

"Irene and I had been to a movie and stopped for milkshakes at the In-N-Out. We were headed back. It was pouring rain. Irene was driving. There was a car pulled off to the side of the road. Irene went around it and hadn't gone far when she hit something. She stopped, terrified of what she might have run over. We'd both been distracted by the car beside the road. Because of the storm, I had wanted to stop and see if the person needed help, but Irene was anxious to get home. She was worried that she'd left the oven on." He rubbed a hand over his face.

"You didn't check to see what she'd hit?"

"Of course I did," Edgar snapped. "I got out and ran back through the rain. I knew it hadn't been a person. It had been too small." He looked up at James, holding his gaze with a steady one of his own. "It was a coyote. I shoved it off the road. On the way home, I got to thinking about all those kids in that neighborhood seeing it on their way to school. Coyotes remind me of the dogs I've had over my life. So I called Lyle and told him to come in early and make sure it was buried before anyone got up."

"How did the coyote turn into a little boy's broken body?"

"I don't know." He lowered his voice, looked toward the garden. Irene still had her back to them. "I'm telling you the truth."

James didn't know what to believe. "What time was this?"

"A little after ten, I think."

"Did you see anyone else out that night? Did you see Billy?"

"No one other than the car pulled off the road."

"You didn't notice who was in the car or the make or model?"

"It was an SUV, like half the town drives. On top of that the night was pitch-black and with it raining hard… It was tough enough to see anything that night." Edgar swore. "Don't look at me like that. I can tell the difference between a coyote and a kid." His voice broke. "When I heard the news about Billy Sherman…" He looked out the window to the garden. "Irene was beside herself. My wife didn't even believe me. She really thought that I would cover up that child's death to protect her."

"I think you would too," James said. "But if you had, I think it would have eaten you up inside after all these years. I also don't think Irene would have let you."

The older man nodded, smiling sadly. "You're right about that. I'd hoped your father would find out who did it." He met James's gaze. "Find out who killed that boy. Do it for all our sakes."

He saw Irene headed back in. "About the snake—"

"I'll talk to my guys, if that helps, but Lyle has some of his own friends who I have no control over."

"Thanks. Give Irene my regards," he said and left.

LORELEI HAD ALREADY made up her mind that if she didn't hear from her stepmother today she was going to track her down. The day seemed to drag even though she was busy most of it. She was still reeling from what she'd learned from James about Karen and Sean Sherman. How could you think you knew someone so well, only to realize it was a lie?

All day long she'd thought James might stop in for a sandwich. He didn't. She wondered if he was avoiding her. Or just busy with his case. He'd already dug up so much about her stepmother, she feared it would get worse. So maybe not seeing him was good news.

That evening as she locked up, she noted that James's pickup wasn't parked out back. She felt a strange tremor of worry that something might have happened to him. Since he started asking questions about Billy Sherman's death, at least one person had been murdered.

She was almost to her stepmother's house when she saw her pull in. The garage door went up and her stepmother's car disappeared inside. Lorelei pulled in as the garage door closed. She didn't know what she was going to say now that she was here. Accuse Karen of yet another affair? Or of murder and covering it up?

Maybe all her stepmother had been hiding was her relationship with Billy Sherman's father and the divorce that followed. But was there more? Lorelei feared there was.

She climbed out of her SUV and walked to the front door. She didn't have to knock. The door opened and her stepmother was standing there with such a resigned look on her face that Lorelei wanted to cry.

Without a word, Karen stepped back to let her in. She followed her into the kitchen where her stepmother opened the refrigerator and pulled out a bottle of wine. Opening it, she poured herself a glass and, without asking, poured another. She set Lorelei's in front of her at the breakfast bar, then walked into the living room to sit down.

For a moment, Lorelei stared at the wine. Then impulsively, she picked it up and downed it before turning her phone to Record and walking into the living room. Even as she did it, she felt as if she was about to betray the woman who'd been her mother. But if Karen had killed that boy…

"I'm at a loss as to what to say to you," Lorelei said as she watched her stepmother sip her wine.

"And yet here you are." There was defiance in her words, in her look.

"You had an affair with Sean Sherman. You destroyed his marriage. Did you also kill his son?" She'd thought her words would get a quick and violent reaction.

Instead, her stepmother took another sip of her wine and set the glass down on the end table next to her before she spoke. "I hate small towns. I told your father that when we moved here. It's like living in a fishbowl." She met Lorelei's gaze. "You were the best part of that marriage. I'd always wanted a child and couldn't have one of my own. I felt like you were my flesh and blood daughter, but I wasn't happy. I loved your father, but he definitely wasn't the love of my life. He couldn't… satisfy me."

"Could anyone?" She regretted the retort at once, sighed and sat down as a long silence fell between them.

"When Fred and I get married, I'm going to put this house up for sale," Karen said, looking around. "I'll sell the studio as well since we're going to get an apartment in Washington. We'll come here in the summer so it's not like I'm leaving forever, and you can always come visit us in Washington if you want to."

"What about Billy Sherman? You were upset and out driving that night."

Karen got a faraway look in her eye for a moment. "I loved Sean and he loved me. But he was determined to go back to his wife even knowing it would have never worked." She made eye contact again. "Remember when I told you that some women always go for the bad boys?" She chuckled. "That was me. And maybe you since I've seen the look in your eye whenever James Colt's name is mentioned."

"I'm nothing like you," Lorelei said, shaking her head.

Her stepmother chuckled again. "Sean had a wild side."

"What about Fred? Does he have a wild side?"

Karen looked away.

"It's all going to come out," Lorelei said. "Everything. James isn't going to quit, and neither am I."

Her stepmother looked at her again and she saw resignation in Karen's eyes. She felt her heart drop as her stepmother said, "That was one of the worst nights of my life."

When Lorelei spoke, it came out in a whisper. "What did you do?"

Karen took another drink of her wine. "I drove around. I was upset. I wasn't thinking clearly. I was crying and it was raining. I couldn't see anything so I pulled over beside the road. I knew I shouldn't be driving in the condition I was in and yet I couldn't stay in the house with Sean, knowing he was leaving me. My chance of happiness had been snatched away and right or wrong, I blamed Alice."

Lorelei lifted a brow. "After you stole her husband, you blamed her because her husband was going back to her?"

"You can't steal anyone's husband," she snapped with obvious disgust. "That's just what wives say so they don't have to take responsibility for their husbands being unhappy with them."

"I'm sorry, but that sounds like an excuse for what you did," Lorelei said and then quickly waved it away. "I don't care. Are we finally getting to what you did that night?"

"I was sitting in my car crying when this car went by. I heard this *thump-thump* and the brake lights came on and a man jumped out and ran back through the rain. The driver had run over something. I could see a small form lying in the road. The man kicked it off to the edge of the ditch with his boot, ran back and jumped into the car and they drove away."

Lorelei's heart had lodged in her throat. "You saw who killed Billy Sherman?"

"It wasn't Billy. I got out and went over to see. At first I thought it was a dog, then I realized it was a coyote. It was a young one. I picked the poor thing up. It was dead. I don't know where I planned to take it. As I said, I wasn't in my right mind. It doesn't make any sense now, but right then I felt this connection to that dead animal. I started walking down the road holding this dead animal in my arms and crying. I didn't know where I was going or what I was going to do with it."

Lorelei saw the pain in her mother's face, then the anger.

"I decided to leave it on Alice's front doorstep. She was killing me. I wanted her to suffer."

"As if she wasn't suffering enough?"

Karen looked away. "If you'd ever been in love—"

She thought of James and how he'd turned her life upside down. "So you left this dead coyote on her doorstep?"

"That was what I'd planned to do. But as I started by the house I saw her. She was out on her porch having a cigarette. She stubbed it out and went inside, slamming the door. I realized how small and cruel and juvenile my plan was so I turned around and headed back. I can't tell you how badly I felt about all of it, the affair, the people I'd hurt, but most of all the pain in my heart. I wanted so desperately to be loved like I felt I deserved." She glanced at Lorelei. "No offense to your father. He did the best he could, but he—"

"Back to Billy," she said, cutting her off.

Karen nodded. "I hadn't gone very far when I realized there was someone behind me. I turned and..." She swallowed, tears filling her eyes. "It was Billy. He'd been following me."

CHAPTER TWENTY-ONE

JAMES WAS HEADED back into town from the Appleton house when he got the call from Lori. He heard it at once in her voice. "What's wrong?"

"I need to see you." The quaver in her voice sent his pulse rocketing.

"Are you all right?" She had him scared.

"Just meet me at your office, okay?" Her voice broke. "It's important."

"I'm headed there right now," he said and sped up. "Just be careful." But she'd already disconnected.

As he pulled into the alley behind their buildings, she climbed out of her SUV and started toward him. The look on her face made him rush to her and pull her into his arms. She leaned into him for a moment, resting her head on his shoulder, before she pulled back.

He saw the plea in her eyes. Whatever was wrong, she needed to get it out. "Let's go upstairs," he said as he opened the door. He felt a draft, accompanied by a bad feeling. Slowly he began to climb upward, hesitating just before the top to peer down the hallway. Empty. But he could see the door to his office standing open.

Moving closer, he could see that the wood was chewed from where the lock had been jimmied. He wanted to send Lori back to her car. Or into her shop, but he also didn't want to let her out of his sight.

"Stay behind me," he whispered as he pulled his weapon. A cone of light from inside the office shone golden on the hallway floor. He watched it as they moved quietly toward it. But no shadow appeared in the light. No sound of movement came from within the office.

At the door, he motioned Lorelei back for a moment before he burst into the office, his weapon raised and ready to fire. He saw no one and quickly checked the bedroom and bath. Empty.

Turning, he saw Lori framed in the ransacked office doorway. "Who do you think did this?"

"Someone worried about what I've discovered in the case," he said without hesitation as he holstered his gun and, ushering her in, locked the office door and bolted it. Turning to her, he said, "Tell me what's happened. I can see how upset you are."

She reached into her pocket and pulled out her phone. A moment later, he heard Karen Wilkins's voice—and her stepdaughter's.

WHEN THE RECORDING ENDED, Lorelei turned off her phone. At some point, she'd taken the chair James had offered her along with the paper cup of blackberry brandy.

"So, when Billy came face-to-face with your stepmother he screamed and ran into the storm. She didn't go after him. She didn't see him again."

She nodded. "You heard her. She swears it's true. She took the dead coyote into the trees and then she walked back to her car and drove home."

"Billy was killed in the same block from where your stepmother said she'd pulled off the road. I have a witness who saw her car there. Unfortunately, there were no video cameras in that area because of the empty lots and construction going on at the time. The witness killed the coyote just after ten that night. I need to know what time she saw Billy. And what time it was when she returned to her car and where she went after that. She didn't go home until daylight. Sean was at her house waiting for her. He said that she'd fixed her hair and wasn't wet from the storm. So where had she been?"

Lorelei shook her head, drained her blackberry brandy and rose. "I need to go home and try to get some rest. I have to work early tomorrow."

"I'm sorry you got dragged into this," James said as he got to his feet as well. "You look exhausted."

"I am. I knew she was hiding something." She met his gaze. "I honestly don't know what to believe. I thought she and my father had a good marriage. I was wrong about that. I was wrong about so many things. I thought I knew her. Now... I'm not even sure she's telling me the truth. What will you do now?"

"I'll talk to her. I'll tell her what you told me. I won't tell her about the recording. If I can establish a time sequence..."

"You think she did it, don't you?"

"I think she might have blotted it out of her memory. As she said, she wasn't in her right mind. Picking up a dead young coyote and carrying it down the street to play a mean joke? Clearly she wasn't herself."

"But upset enough to run over a little boy on her way home and not remember?" Lorelei shook her head. "We've already established that she's dishonest about at least her love life. We both know there is a part of her story that she's leaving out."

He stepped to her and took her shoulders in his big

hands. His touch felt warm and comforting. She wanted to curl up in his arms. "I'm going to find out who killed Billy. Please, I need you to be careful. Someone doesn't want me to know the truth. I doubt they found what they were looking for in my office. I'm afraid of how far they might go to cover up their crime. I don't want you involved."

She smiled sadly. "Too late for that."

"But promise me you won't do any more investigating on your own."

She was too tired and drained and discouraged to argue.

"I'll see you tomorrow?" he said, meeting her gaze.

She nodded numbly and he let her go but insisted on walking her down to her car. He'd wanted to follow her home, except she wasn't having it. It was flattering that James cared, but she wasn't some helpless woman who relied on a man. She wasn't her stepmother. Lorelei wanted a man in her life, but she didn't need one.

"I'm fine," she assured him. "I'm more worried about you."

"Indulge me. Please. Call me when you get home, so I know you made it okay. Promise me?"

JAMES DIDN'T CARE what Lori said. He was going to follow her home to make sure she was safe. He felt as if he'd dragged her into this. Just being associated with him could be bad enough. Add in her stepmother...

As she drove away, he reached for his keys and swore. He'd left them upstairs in his shock at finding his office broken into and ransacked, not to mention the information Lori had gotten on her stepmother.

He turned and rushed upstairs in time to hear his

phone ringing. The phone and his keys were on his desk. He scooped up the phone, thinking it might be Lori. It was Gilbert Sanders, the arsonist investigator. He glanced at the time and had a feeling the man wouldn't be calling now unless it was important.

He picked up the call on his way out the door.

"I was thinking about what you said about your father wanting to talk to me about a hit-and-run case he was working on," Gilbert said after a few pleasantries were exchanged. "I couldn't imagine why he'd want to talk to me about anything but a fire. But then I remembered. I *did* talk to him. He told me he was working on a case about a young boy who'd been killed, right?"

"Right. Billy Sherman."

"But that wasn't why your father called me. He wanted to know about a house fire. One fatality. The wife."

James frowned. "Whose fire?"

"His own. Del Colt wanted to know about the fire that killed his wife."

"I don't understand," James said as he reached his pickup and stopped. "My mother died of cancer."

"It was his first wife."

James couldn't speak for a moment. "His *first* wife."

"I'm sorry, you didn't know that your father had been married before?"

"No. What did you tell him about the fire?"

"Just that it had been ruled an accident, a faulty lamp cord. But I wasn't the one who handled that investigation. It was my uncle, the man I was named for, Gilbert T. Sanders, who did the investigation. Your father asked me to look into it for him. Something must have come up in his investigation of the hit-and-run that made him believe the fire that killed his first wife had been arson and was somehow connected to his case."

This made no sense. "Did you look into the fire?" James asked as he climbed into his pickup. Lori would probably be home by now and probably trying to call him.

"I did. I think your father might have been right."

"Wait, right about what?"

"The fire that killed his first wife," Gilbert said. "My uncle suspected it was arson, but there were extenuating circumstances. An eyewitness swore he saw the lamp ignite the living room."

"Who was the eyewitness?"

"Sheriff Otis Osterman. He was the first person on the scene. But I saw in my uncle's notes on the case that there was a string of small fires that summer around Lonesome. There was a suspect at the time."

James felt all the air rush from his lungs as Gilbert said, "Freddie Bayard, now Senator Fred Bayard. Freddie had apparently been a firebug since he was little. But there was no proof and his father, also a senator, made Freddie untouchable. The boy was sent away to a private school where his father promised he would get him the help he needed. In the report, there was also mention of Del and Fred being at odds, some rivalry that went back years."

"How is that possible?" James asked. "I didn't think Fred moved here until about ten years ago."

"His grandparents lived here and he stayed with them more than he stayed with his parents. His father was in DC a lot of the time and he and his mother weren't close. I'm not sure how any of this will help with your investigation."

"Me either, but thank you for letting me know." James pulled in front of Lori's house. No lights on. No Lori. She hadn't come straight home or she would be here by now. Fred Bayard was involved with Karen Wilkins and Lori was involved because of it.

He felt a tremor of fear. Why hadn't Lori gone straight home like she'd planned? Had her stepmother called? Had something happened?

He started to call Lori's cell when he knew where she'd gone. Making a sharp U-turn in the middle of the street, he headed toward her stepmother's house.

As he drove, he couldn't get what Gilbert Sanders had told him out of his mind. He called his brother Davey only to get voice mail. He tried his brother Tommy. Same thing. He was about to give up when he realized the brother he needed to ask was his eldest brother, Willie.

"What's up?"

"Did you know Dad was married before?" he demanded.

Willie hesitated before saying, "Who told you that?"

"You just did! And you never said anything?" James couldn't believe this.

"Why would I? It had nothing to do with our family," Willie said. "Also, it was too painful for Dad. I wanted to protect him. They were married less than a month when she was killed. Luckily, he met our mom."

"Protect him from what?" James demanded.

"Heartbreak. He blamed himself for her death. Like us, he was on the rodeo circuit all the time. He'd left her alone in a house that had bad wiring. He didn't need to be reminded of the past. That's why I didn't tell you or the others."

"How did you find out?" he asked as he pulled up in front of Lorelei's stepmother's house.

"Otis Osterman told me. He was the cop who investigated the fire. He threw the fact that Dad left his wife in a house with faulty wiring in my face the first time he hauled me in on some trumped-up charge. I told him that if he ever said anything like that to me or my family again, I'd kill him. Apparently, he believed me."

"I'm getting another call," James said, hoping it would be Lori. "We'll talk about this soon." He disconnected from Willie and said, "Lori?"

Silence. He realized that the other call had gone to voice mail. He listened, still hoping it had been Lori. It was one of the out-of-town body shops he'd called inquiring about a vehicle being brought in from Lonesome nine years ago after Billy Sherman's death. He didn't bother to listen to the message. Right now he only cared about Lori. He couldn't shake a bad feeling that she was in trouble.

LORELEI HAD GRUDGINGLY promised to go straight home and call James when she arrived. Her intentions had been good when she'd left him. Until her stepmother called crying and hysterical.

"What's wrong?" Karen didn't answer, just kept crying. "Mom."

Calling her mom seemed to do the trick. "We broke up."

It took Lorelei a minute to realize that she must be talking about the senator.

"Why?"

More awful sobbing, before her stepmother said, "It was all based on a lie. How could I have ever trusted that he was really in love with me? Or that he wasn't just marrying me so I couldn't testify against him?"

At those words, Lorelei felt shaken to her soul. Marry her so she couldn't testify against him? "What are you talking about?"

"That night on the road. Billy." She was sobbing again. "I left out that part. When I was walking back to my car, Fred picked me up. On the way to my car..." More sobbing. "He ran over something in the road. It didn't seem like it was anything. I told him about the coyote... He didn't stop to check but he did look back in his side mirror. I saw his expression. I knew it wasn't a coyote."

Lorelei felt her blood run cold. Her stepmother was sobbing.

"I was so upset and freezing and there didn't seem to be any damage to his vehicle."

"He took you to his house," Lorelei said, seeing now how it had happened with her mother and the senator.

"He was so kind, so caring. I wanted to believe in him." More uncontrollable bawling.

She didn't need her stepmother to tell her what had happened after that night. Fred had been afraid that Karen could come forward with what she knew. He must have seen how much she'd needed a man in her life. He became that man to protect himself. Until Karen finally admitted the truth—and not just about the night Billy Sherman had died.

Lorelei had known women her own age who went from one man to the next, desperate to have someone in their lives. She'd felt sorry for them. She felt sorry for her stepmother. Karen would have been flattered at the senator's attention. She'd been lonely, had needed a man so desperately, that she would rather live a lie than admit the truth about her relationship with Fred Bayard.

Until now.

"You told him what you told me," Lorelei said.

"I knew you were right," her stepmother wailed. "James was going to find out. Fred became so angry. It's over." She began to cry harder.

Why hadn't she noticed how unhappy Karen had been? Why hadn't she known what her stepmother had been going through? Because Karen had seemed happy. And because Lorelei had been busy living her own life, seeing what she wanted to see.

"Mom, I'm almost to your house." But she didn't think Karen heard her. "Mom?" She kept hearing her stepmother's words. *I knew it wasn't a coyote.*

She could hardly make out her stepmother's next words, "Someone's at the back door. It can't be Fred. He's promised to go to the sheriff…" Then Karen's voice changed, and Lorelei knew her stepmother was no longer talking to her. "What are you doing here? I thought—"

Lorelei heard what sounded like the phone being knocked out of Karen's hand. It made a whishing sound as it skittered across the hardwood floor.

She couldn't make out the words, but it sounded like Karen and a man arguing. Then to Lorelei's horror, she heard her stepmother scream followed by a painful cry an instant before she heard the sound of what could be a body hitting the floor.

"Mom?" she cried into the phone. Silence. Then footfalls. The line went dead.

Her hands were shaking so hard on the wheel that she had to grip it tightly. She was calling 911 as her stepmother's house came into view and she saw the smoke.

CHAPTER TWENTY-TWO

THE SMOKE SEEMED to be coming from the back of the house. The man had come in the back door. Lorelei knew who the man was, knew what he'd done and why. But as she made a quick turn and swung down the alley, she was surprised to see him jump into his large dark-colored SUV. She sped toward him as he ducked behind the wheel and took off in a hail of gravel. But not before she'd seen his license plate number. The senator had vanity plates.

She hit her brakes behind the house and bailed out of her vehicle. She could see smoke rolling out of the open back door. She was running toward the house when James came running around the side of the house toward her.

"My stepmother's inside," she screamed over the crackle of the blaze. "The senator was here. I heard him attack her, then set the house on fire." She could see flames rising at the kitchen windows.

"Stay here," James ordered as he pulled off his jean jacket, and putting it over his head ran into the open back door and into the smoke and flames.

Lorelei stood there, feeling helpless. She could hear sirens growing closer. The fire trucks would be here soon. But soon enough? She wanted to race into the house through the smoke and flames and find James, find Karen. She felt her panic building. James was here because of her. He couldn't die because of her.

She began to cry tears of relief as she saw him come out of the smoke carrying Karen. She ran to him as the first of the fire trucks pulled up out front along with an ambulance and the sheriff.

"She's unconscious," James said, coughing. "But since she was on the floor, I don't think she breathed in much smoke."

Lorelei wiped at her tears as she ran to keep up with him as he carried Karen toward the waiting ambulance. James had risked his life to save her stepmother. She loved this man. The thought whizzed through her mind as they reached the sidewalk and were immediately surrounded by frantic activity as James handed over Karen and the EMTs went to work on her.

"Want to tell me what's going on here?" the sheriff asked as he sauntered up to Lorelei.

"My stepmother was attacked and left in a burning house to die," she snapped. "That's what happened. I saw the man who assaulted her and started the fire. I was on the phone with her when he attacked her. I was only a block away so I saw him running away as I drove up. I took down his license number. But I also saw his face. It was Senator Fred Bayard."

Carl started to argue that she had to be mistaken. "Fred is a godsend to this community. Without him and the donations he'd made—"

Karen, now conscious, pulled off her oxygen mask. She narrowed her gaze on the sheriff, stopping the EMTs from loading her gurney into the back of the ambulance.

"Senator Fred Bayard tried to kill me and then he set

my house on fire," her stepmother said through coughing fits. "He also killed Billy Sherman. I know because I was in the car with him. He didn't stop to see what he'd run over. He just kept going. He would have killed me too."

The EMTs got the oxygen back on Karen as she gasped for breath.

"If you don't arrest the senator," Lorelei said, turning to the sheriff, "I will call the FBI and tell them that you refused to pick up the man who assaulted my stepmother, started the fire and left her to die. I don't think you want them looking into the other things you and your brother have done over the years to cover up crimes in Lonesome."

The EMTs loaded Karen into the ambulance. "I have to get to the hospital," she said and pushed past the sheriff.

"I'll take you," James said, suddenly at her side. He put his arm around her as they hurried to his pickup. She leaned into him, for once happy to have someone to lean on.

As she climbed in and he slid behind the wheel, she told him what her stepmother had told her on the phone before she'd heard Karen being attacked.

"When I drove up, I saw him running from the back of the house," she said. "He tried to kill my stepmother to cover up his crime." She fought tears, fearing that Fred would get away with it. The sheriff certainly didn't have the guts to arrest him.

Sheriff Carl Osterman swore as he watched the ambulance leave, siren blaring and lights flashing. James Colt and Lorelei Wilkins took off behind it. When had those two become so tight, he wondered. He'd thought Lorelei had more sense. Shaking his head, he watched the firefighters trying to put out the blaze and then sighing, climbed into his patrol SUV and headed out to the senator's place.

He knew how this was going to go down so he was in no hurry. It would come down to the senator's word against the woman he'd just broken up with and Lorelei, a younger woman protecting her stepmother. Not the best witnesses especially if all this had been caused by a domestic disagreement between the senator and Karen Wilkins. He certainly didn't want to take the word of a hysterical woman.

As he pulled up in the yard in front of the large summer house, he slowly got out. He wasn't surprised when Fred came out carrying a small suitcase and walked toward his helipad next to the house in a clearing in the pines.

Carl followed him. "If you have a minute, Fred?"

"Sheriff, good to see you. Actually, I don't. Something's come up. My chopper should be here any minute. I need to get to the airport. Government business."

The senator smelled as if he'd taken a quick shower, so quick that there was still that faint hint of smoke on him. "We have a problem," Carl said.

Fred smiled. "I'm sure it's nothing that you can't handle, Sheriff. It's one of the reasons I backed your campaign. Please don't tell me I supported the wrong man."

He could hear the sound of the helicopter in the distance. "You did back the right man," Carl said, bristling. "But money can only buy so much. This time I'm going to have to take you in for questioning, Fred. Lorelei Wilkins saw you leaving her stepmother's house. You stepped over a line. What you did can't be undone."

The senator shook his head. "I was at her house. I'm not sure what happened after I left, but I had just broken up with her stepmother. Karen was overwrought, threatening to kill herself. Of course Lorelei is going to blame me if the woman did something…stupid."

"It's more serious than that, I'm afraid, Fred. Karen regained consciousness. She says you assaulted her and set her house on fire. Lorelei was on a phone call with her stepmother and heard it all. Karen also says that you killed Billy Sherman—that she was in the car that night and will testify in court that you didn't even stop."

"She's lying. I told you. I broke it off. She'd say anything to get back at me." The helicopter came into view.

Carl pulled out his handcuffs. A part of him had known that this day was coming and had been for years. Fred had gotten away with numerous crimes over the years since he was a boy. Back then he'd been a juvenile, his father a respected senator, his grandparents churchgoing people. But now that the man's house of cards had started to tumble, the sheriff suspected a lot more was about to come out.

Worse, Carl knew that he and Otis would be caught in the dirt once it started flying. He laid his hand on his weapon and slowly unsnapped the holster. Fred saw the movement, his eyes widening. The senator had to know that there was an easy way out of this for Carl, for his brother. If Fred were dead there would never be a trial, a lot of old cases wouldn't come to light.

"I hope you'll come peacefully, senator," Carl said. "But either way, you're going to have to come down to the station for questioning." He met the man's gaze and held it for a long moment.

Fred swore. "All the things I've done for your two-bit town." He angrily pulled out his phone and called his attorney.

"I'll tell the helicopter pilot that you won't be going anywhere for a while," Carl said, then turned back to the senator. "By the way, I heard from Gilbert Sanders, the state arson investigator, earlier today. He told me that he's reopening the Del Colt fire case. He thinks he has some new evidence." He watched Fred's spray-on-tanned face pale. "He was especially interested in talking to you."

"The statute of limitations on arson is five years."

"I guess you forgot. Del's first wife died in that fire. There is no statute of limitations on murder."

CHAPTER TWENTY-THREE

LORELEI FOUND HER stepmother to be in good spirits when she stopped by the hospital the next morning. Karen had a concussion from the blow the senator had dealt her and a mild cough from the smoke, but she was going to be fine.

"The prosecutor said he didn't think I would be arrested for withholding evidence," Karen said. "I'm just glad to be alive. But I can't stay in Lonesome. I should have left a long time ago."

She took her stepmother's hand. "You stayed because of me."

Karen smiled. "You always did give me the benefit of the doubt. I will miss you, but you need to get on with your life. You need not worry about me anymore."

She wasn't sure about that. "You put up the money for my shop from your retirement account."

"It was the right thing to do. I inherited the house and your father's money. It's what your father would have wanted me to do."

"I'm sorry things didn't work out for you," Lorelei said.

"I chose the wrong men for the wrong reasons." She shook her head. "I've learned my lesson. Don't look at me like that. Even old dogs can learn new tricks."

Lorelei laughed. "You're still young. There's some-one out there for you."

"I hope so." She took a ragged breath. "What's going on with you and James Colt?"

She shrugged. "We had a moment, but now he's done what he set out to do. Solve his father's case. I'm sure he'll be going back on the rodeo circuit."

"I'm sorry."

"I'm sure it's for the best," Lorelei said. "I heard you're getting out of here today."

"I'm thinking of going to Chicago. I'll be back for the trial, if Fred's case goes to trial. But first I have to tie up some loose ends with the insurance company and the house. I've had an offer for the exercise studio and I've decided to take it. I'm looking forward to a fresh start in the big city."

She squeezed her stepmother's hand. "Please keep in touch."

"You know I will. You're my daughter." They hugged and Lorelei left before she cried. She would miss Karen. Her stepmother had been the last link she had with her father and the last reminder of her childhood. With Karen gone, she had no family left here.

The thought made her sad as she drove to her shop. Anita had volunteered to come in and work, which Lorelei had happily accepted. Given everything that had happened, she needed a little time off. Karen thought she was like her because of James Colt. Was he her bad boy? He had played that part in high school and for some time after, but she no longer thought of him that way. He was her hero. But he was also a rodeo cowboy at heart. The circuit would be calling him now.

As she got out of her SUV, James drove up. Just seeing him made her heart soar. Yesterday evening he'd gone to the hospital with her, but she'd sent him home after the doctors checked him over. He had smoke inhalation and she could tell he needed rest. He'd called to make sure she and Karen were both all right late last night. She hadn't had a chance to talk to him since.

He got out of his pickup and sauntered toward her. Had she really not noticed how good-looking he was that first day when she'd seen him again after all the years? She could laugh about it now. She'd thought his hair was too long, that he dressed like a saddle tramp, that he was too arrogant for a man who obviously lacked ambition. So why did he seem perfect now? He hadn't changed, but the way she saw him definitely had, she realized. She'd gotten to know the man inside him and fallen in love with him.

The thought struck her at heart level like a blow. She'd had the thought yesterday after he'd gone into a house on fire to save her stepmother. This time the thought carried no raw emotion. It just happened to be the truth.

And now he would be leaving Lonesome, leaving her.

"I'm starved," he said, grinning as he joined her.

"You're always starved," she said with a laugh.

He put his arm around her as they headed into the back of her sandwich shop. He did it casually and yet it sent a jolt through her. "What's the special today?"

"Pulled pork. Your favorite."

He looked over at her and smiled. "You know me so well. Anita must be working. Thank goodness since I don't want you going anywhere near my sandwich."

She thought of that day when she'd added hot sauce

and sliced jalapeños to his sandwich—and he'd eaten every bite of it. "I'm still sorry about that."

"Sure you are," he said with a laugh as he headed for his usual table. "Have an early lunch with me?"

Lorelei nodded, fighting tears. She didn't want to think about the days he would no longer stop by. When his pickup wouldn't be parked in the alley next door. When she wouldn't see him. "Let me place our orders. I'll be right back. Iced tea or lemonade?"

"Both." He looked so happy. He'd solved his father's last case. Why wouldn't he be happy? But she feared it was more about going back on the rodeo circuit.

JAMES TOOK HIS usual seat at the booth and looked out on the town. Funny how his attitude toward Lonesome had changed. It had been nothing more than a stopover on his way somewhere else for so many years. He realized that he hadn't appreciated it.

Now he felt more a part of the place. It was a good feeling, one he would miss if…when he went back on the rodeo circuit. He'd done what he'd set out to do. Solve his father's last case. Still, it felt unfinished. There was the question of his father's death. He thought the truth about it still might come out—if as he suspected Otis had something to do with Del Colt's death.

The senator's arrest had a domino effect. The feds had stepped in and taken over the case. Gilbert Sanders turned over new evidence to the prosecutor regarding the Del Colt case along with other fires that were quickly attributed to Fred. He was being held without bail.

A small-time criminal Otis Osterman had arrested back when he was sheriff was picked up and charged for drug possession. He copped a plea, giving up Otis as the one who'd hired him to burn down Cora Brooks's house. The prosecution, closely watched by the feds, began looking into how other investigations had been handled by both Carl Osterman and his brother Otis. Under pressure, Carl had resigned, and the reign of the Osterman's was over. More of their misdeeds would be coming out, James knew.

He dragged himself out of his thoughts as Lori appeared with a tray full of food and drinks. "I'm sorry. I could have helped you with that."

She gave him a dismissive look. "I do this for a living. I can handle it."

He watched her slide into the chair across from him and take everything off the tray. He'd never imagined he would have these kinds of feelings for Lorelei Wilkins and yet he did. Once, it had been flirting. Now... Now it was so much more. She had a pull on him stronger than gravity.

"What will happen now with the case?" she asked after they'd tucked into their sandwiches in companionable silence.

"Probably the most Fred will go down for will be assault, arson and manslaughter even if the prosecution can prove he set the fire that killed my father's first wife. He might get some time in prison, but probably not much. But his career is over. He'll be a felon. He won't even be allowed to vote, own a gun or hold office in most states and there are countries that won't allow him in."

She put down her sandwich. "It's not enough. What about Billy?"

James shook his head. "I doubt a jury will convict

him on that because of lack of evidence. Karen says he ran over something. All Fred has to do is lie and say he didn't. It's her word against his. There apparently wasn't any damage to his large SUV."

"He's in a position where he can lie and there will be people who will believe him over my stepmother."

James couldn't argue that. "Taking away his career and ruining his reputation will hurt the most. He'll lie, say he was railroaded by a scorned woman. That he was innocent of all of it. But he ran from your stepmother's house after assaulting her and setting her house on fire. Add to that the other fires... His reputation is toast."

He watched her pick at her sandwich as if she'd lost her appetite. "Do you think he would have married Karen?"

She shook her head. "I think she realized there was no happy ending with the lie between them. She would have always questioned his love for her."

James reached across the table to cover her hand with his own. "People disappoint us but ultimately we're all human. That's what my dad used to say. We do what we have to do to survive. For some, that's lying, cheating, stealing and even killing. For others it's small lies and secrets. My dad was good at uncovering them and finding a little justice or at least peace for those in pain. I understand now why he loved doing this."

"So you're hooked on the PI business?" She'd said it jokingly, but he knew at the heart of her question what she was asking. This year's rodeo season was in full swing. He was healed. There was nothing to keep him from getting back to his life. He'd accomplished what he'd set out to do. Solve his father's last case—with Lori's help. If he didn't go soon...

Lori. He looked into her face, saw her compassion, her spirit, her desire that mirrored his own. How could he leave her for months to go back on the rodeo circuit? But then how could he not? He wasn't getting any younger. He didn't have that much time left in the saddle and there were a lot of broncos he'd yet to ride.

LORELEI STOOD IN the kitchen of her shop after James left. He'd said there were some things he had to take care of and that he would see her later. She and her friend Anita were prepping for the next day and getting ready for the lunch crowd. It was Saturday and a beautiful summer day. There would be a lot of picnickers coming for her special weekend basket.

"I keep thinking about everything that happened," she said, voicing her doubts out loud. "It doesn't feel over."

"I'm sure it's going to take a while to process everything." She and Anita had been good friends in high school. While Lorelei had gone to college, Anita had married her childhood sweetheart, had babies and settled in Lonesome. Lorelei looked up to her since Anita had definitely had more life experience because of it.

"I keep thinking about something Karen said. She heard a car go by moving fast when she was in the trees getting rid of the coyote. She hid, so she didn't see the car or the driver. She said that's when she realized that she couldn't do what she'd been doing anymore. That she needed to find a man who appreciated her and wanted to marry her and that things were really over between her and Sean."

Anita stopped to plant one hand on her hip. "Where are you going with this?"

"I'm not sure. Right after that, she stepped back on the highway in the pouring rain and was picked up by the senator," Lorelei said. "Of course, Karen thought it was fate."

"Until the senator hit Billy."

"That's just it. Karen said he ran over *something* in the road. Not that he *hit* something."

"I'm not sure I see the difference."

"That car that sped by too fast while Karen was hiding in the trees, what if that's the driver who actually hit and killed Billy Sherman?"

"But you don't know who it was."

"No. Minutes later the senator would pick up Karen and run over something in the road and not bother to stop." She grimaced. "He must have seen the boy lying on the road in his rearview mirror."

"Well, you know what kind of man he is already," Anita said.

"But what if Billy was already dead? What if the senator panicked, thinking he had killed the boy and believing Karen would know he'd done it? When he looked back in his side mirror, he would have seen the boy's clothing. From that moment on, he had to keep my stepmother from ever telling so he seduced her that night."

Anita shuddered. "And when he realized he could no longer trust her, he tried to kill her and burn down her house."

"Maybe that's what he planned all along. I really doubt he would have married her and yet he couldn't break up with her for fear of what she might do. He must have felt trapped. How ironic would it be if he was innocent?"

"Innocent is not a word I would use with him, but I

see what you mean," Anita agreed. "But how can you prove that Billy was already dead, hit by the car before the senator's vehicle drove over the remains?"

"I have no idea," Lorelei said. "But I'm going by Alice Sherman's today. My stepmother was going to stop by her house, but I talked her out of it. Karen wanted to send her a card to tell her how sorry she was about everything. She's now decided that to change she needs to apologize to those she hurt."

"Not a bad idea."

"No, but I think Karen showing up there might not be a great idea. So I said I'd drop off the card she wrote instead. I wanted to see if Alice might remember a car flying past that night. My stepmother said Alice had been outside smoking a cigarette when she'd seen her but had gone back inside. I would imagine she'd been at the window making sure Karen kept going past."

Anita looked skeptical. "Are you sure she'll want to talk to you? I mean, you are Karen's daughter. But what's the worst that can happen? She'll throw you out."

"That's a pleasant thought," she said as she tossed her apron in the bin and headed for her SUV parked outside. But she had to try.

She noticed that James's pickup was still parked in the alley. She considered sharing her theory with him but decided otherwise. There was a good chance that the senator had been the one to hit Billy in that big SUV of his with the huge metal guard on the front. Questioning Alice Sherman probably wouldn't go anywhere anyway.

On top of that, she could see a shadow moving around in the upstairs apartment. Was James packing? Would he tell her goodbye?

JAMES HAD LOOKED around the office, his gaze lighting on his private investigator's license. He'd taken Lori's advice. He'd framed it and put it on the wall next to his father's. It had felt presumptuous. But he liked the look of it there.

He knew he should start packing. He needed to pick up his horse and trailer. He turned and saw the Colt Investigations sign in the front second-story window. He should take that down. He'd already had several calls from people wanting to hire him as the news had swept through Lonesome.

The crazy part was that he would never have solved it without Lori's help. He still didn't know what he was doing. He was playacting at being a PI. But it had given him some experience. Maybe with more…

The worst part was that something was still nagging at him about the case. He told himself that the FBI would get to the bottom of any questions he might have. Everything was in good hands.

He turned to look at his framed PI license hanging on the wall over the desk next to his father's again. He felt torn about leaving. When he thought about Lori he wasn't sure he could leave. But would he regret it later if he didn't go at least one more year on the circuit? It would probably be his last.

His cell phone rang. "Congrats," Willie said. "You're all over the news. Dad would be proud."

"Thanks."

"I suppose I know what you're doing. Packing. Did I hear you might catch up to us in Texas?"

"Thinking about it."

"What? You aren't already packed? What's going on?" James knew he had to make a decision. He still didn't know how or why his father had died that night on the railroad tracks. He feared that he never would.

He'd been offered more cases since the senator's arrest. Maybe he could make a living at this PI thing. He and Lori had found Billy Sherman's killer. They'd made a good team.

"I'm packing," he told his brother. "I'll let you know, but probably Texas." He disconnected. But something was still nagging him. About the case? About leaving?

He stepped over to the desk and sat down. Earlier, he'd filed the case away. Now he pulled it out. There were his own notes in with his father's. Would his father be proud?

What was bothering him? He flipped through the file, stopping on the coroner's report. He'd read it over when he'd first started the case. Billy's injuries had been consistent with being hit by a vehicle. Numerous bones had been broken but it was a massive head injury that was listed as cause of death.

Numerous bones had been broken, he read again and looked through the list. Billy's right arm had been shattered and was believed to have been run over by the vehicle's tire after initial impact.

He picked up his phone and called Dr. Milton Stanley. He figured the man would be out working in his yard and was surprised when he picked up. "This is a bit unusual, but I was looking at the coroner's report on Billy Sherman. I need to know if this is consistent with a small boy of seven being struck by a large vehicle."

"It would depend on the size of the car. If it was a large SUV or pickup or a small car, the injuries would be different. The state medical examiner did this autopsy. Send me the report and I'd be happy to give you my opinion."

James glanced around the office and spotted his father's old fax machine. "I can fax it to you. I don't have a copy machine."

The doctor laughed. "How about a computer? No? If you're going to stay in business, son, you need to get into at least the twentieth century. Just take a photo of it with your phone and send it to me."

He'd just hung up, wondering what it was he was looking for when his cell phone rang. When he saw it was one of the out-of-town body shops he'd called, he remembered that one of them had called him back but he'd never listened to the message or returned the call. He'd forgotten about it with everything else that had been going on.

"You still looking for a vehicle that might have been involved in a hit-and-run?" a man asked.

He wasn't and yet he heard himself say, "What do you have?"

"I saw the message you left about looking for a damaged vehicle after April 10th nine years ago. I killed the message before my boss saw it," the man said. "Otherwise, no one would be calling you right now."

Did the man want money? Was that what this was about? "So why are you calling me?"

"After that date you mentioned, we had a car come in. It was late at night on a lowboy trailer. My boss had it dumped off. He pushed it into one of the bays. He didn't know I was still in the garage. I was curious so after he left I took a look at it. It wasn't the first car that rolled in that was…questionable. This one bothered me because there was blood on it and…hair."

Even as James told himself that this wasn't Billy's hit-and-run, he felt his heart plummet. This vehicle had been involved in a hit-and-run somewhere. Unless this guy was just leading him on. "Why didn't you report it?"

"My boss was an ass but I needed the job. My old lady was pregnant."

"You don't work there anymore?" He waited for the man to ask for money.

"I won't after this. I was suspicious so I bagged the hair and a scrap of clothing that was stuck in the bumper. Now I find out that the clothing matched the description of what that boy was wearing. I also took a piece of clean cloth and I wiped up some of the blood and put it into the bag for insurance. Look, I could get in trouble for this in so many ways. But now I've got a kid and when I heard about the trial of that senator for running over that boy… I want to see him hang."

So did James. "The FBI is going to want that bag with the evidence in it and your statement. Will you do it?"

Silence, then finally, "What the hell. My old lady says it's bad karma if I don't. It's been bothering me for the past nine years."

"They'll also want the make and model of the car."

"No problem. I even took down the license plate number." He rattled it off and James wrote it down. He was frowning down at what he'd written, when the man said, "It was a mid-sized sedan. I took a photo. Hold on, I'll send it to you."

A few moments later, the photo appeared on James's phone. By then he knew deep down what he'd been fearing. The car wasn't Senator Fred Bayard's large black SUV. The license plate number had been wrong as well.

Heart in his throat, he stared at the car in the photo and remembered where he'd seen it. Parked in front of Alice Sherman's house.

CHAPTER TWENTY-FOUR

LORELEI WAS ABOUT to give up. After ringing the door-bell several times and finally knocking at Alice Sherman's door, she still hadn't been able to raise anyone. She'd seen the car in the garage so she suspected the woman was home. There had been a news van parked outside when Lorelei had driven up, but it left after she hadn't gotten an answer at the door.

She was about to leave the card from her stepmother when the door opened a crack.

"What do you want?" Alice wore a bathrobe and slippers. Her hair looked as if it hadn't been washed in days. The woman stared at her, clearly not having a clue who she was.

"Mrs. Sherman, I'm—"

"It's not 'Mrs.' You're a local. I've seen you before. You one of those reporters?"

"No," she quickly assured her before the woman could close the door. "I'm Lorelei Wilkins. I own the sandwich shop in town. I just stopped by to—"

"Wilkins?" She grabbed hold of the door as if she needed it for support. "You're related to Karen?"

"She's my stepmother. She's in the hospital—"

"Like I care." Tears welled in Alice's eyes. "I hate her. I hope she dies."

"I'm sorry." Lorelei was still holding the card in her hand.

"What's that?"

"It's a note from my…from Karen."

Alice's eyes widened. "She sent you with a card for me? How thoughtful after what she did to my life," she said, her voice filled with rancor. Suddenly the woman opened the door wider. "You should come in."

That had been her hope originally, using the card as an excuse. But now she wasn't so sure. "I don't want to disturb you—"

"Too late for that. Come in."

Lorelei hesitated for a moment before stepping in. As she did, Alice Sherman snatched the card from her hand.

"Sit." She tore into the envelope. "Did she tell you what she did to me?" Alice didn't wait for an answer. "She destroyed my life and now everyone is going to know and she and her boyfriend are going to pay. It's just too bad my ex-husband isn't going to prison too."

"The senator's not her boyfriend anymore," Lorelei said as Alice motioned her into a chair. This was clearly not the best time to be asking questions about Billy's death, she thought. But then again she couldn't imagine a time that would be. The senator's arrest and Karen's part in it had obviously opened the old wounds— wounds Lorelei suspected hadn't ever started to heal.

"But he *was* her boyfriend," Alice said, showing that she had been listening. "Karen lied to protect him and herself after they killed my boy."

Lorelei took a seat. She watched her read the card not once, but twice before she ripped it up and threw it into the fireplace.

Alice reached into a container on the hearth, drew out a match, struck it and tossed it into the shredded paper. Flames licked through the card in a matter of seconds before dying out.

"What did you really come over here for?" Alice asked, turning to face her. "It wasn't to bring me a card from your mother."

She didn't correct her. She thought of Karen as her mother. "You're right. I had wanted to ask you about the night Billy died."

Alice looked surprised. "Why? The cops have Billy's killers."

"I was hoping you could help me with something. Karen was in the pines not too far from here when she heard a car go racing past."

The woman's eyes narrowed. "The senator."

Lorelei shook her head. "He didn't drive by until minutes later when Karen was walking back up the road toward her car. I was wondering if you saw the vehicle go by? If you might have recognized it."

"I had other things on my mind besides looking out the window."

She couldn't help her surprise or hide it. Alice was looking at her expectantly, waiting as if almost daring Lorelei to call her a liar. "It's just that you saw my stepmother."

"I don't know what you're talking about." Alice rubbed the back of her neck as she turned to look at the ashes in the fireplace, her back to Lorelei.

"My mother had been headed for your house but when she saw you and when you saw her, she changed her mind."

Alice picked up the poker and began jabbing at the charred remains of the card lying in the bottom of the fireplace. "I just told you I didn't look out the window."

Lorelei felt a chill move slowly up her spine. One of them was lying and this time, she believed it wasn't Karen. A thought struck her as she watched the woman's agitation increasing with each jab of the poker. "She said you quickly disappeared from the window. Not long after that, she heard the car go racing by." The chill moved through her, sending a wave of goose bumps over her flesh.

In that instant, she knew. Worse, Alice knew that she'd put it together. Lorelei shot to her feet, but not quickly enough. Alice spun around, the poker in her hand, getting between Lorelei and the door.

Brandishing the poker, the woman began to make a wailing sound. Lorelei took a step back and then another as she shoved her hand into her pocket for her phone and looked for a way out.

The wailing stopped as abruptly as it had started. Alice got a distant look in her eyes that was more frightening than the wailing. "I saw her out there through the rain. She'd taken my husband, destroyed my family. I knew Sean had broken it off with her. I knew that was why she was out there in the rain. I hated her. I just wanted her dead. Then I saw her turn and head back up the road toward her house."

Lorelei felt her phone in her pocket, but she didn't dare draw it out as Alice advanced on her, brandishing the poker.

"I went into the garage and got into my car. I opened the garage door, hoping it wouldn't wake Billy. I planned to be gone for only a few minutes. I knew exactly what I had to do. She'd asked for it and now she was going to get what she had coming to her."

Lorelei bumped into the kitchen table. She glanced

toward the back door, but knew she'd never reach it in time. Alice stopped a few feet away. Her eyes looked glazed over as if lost in the past, but Lorelei didn't dare move as she took in her surroundings—looking for something she could use for a weapon.

When Alice spoke, her voice had taken on a sleep-walking kind of sound effect. "It was raining so hard, the night was so dark. I saw the figure running down the road. I hit the gas going faster and faster. The rain was coming down so hard, the wipers were beating franti-cally and…" Alice stopped talking, her eyes wide with horror. She began to cry. "I didn't know. How could I know? It was so dark, the rain… I didn't know." The poker wavered in her hands. "What was he doing out there in the storm? I thought he was in bed. I thought…" She looked at Lorelei, her gaze focusing and then hard-ening as her survival instincts took over. "I thought I killed Karen. She took my husband and then my son.

"And now I'm going to take her daughter."

Lorelei's cell began to ring, startling them both.

JAMES TRIED LORELEI'S cell on his way over to Alice's. At lunch, he remembered their discussion. Something had been nagging at Lori too, he realized. The same thing that had been bothering him.

Karen had said that the senator ran over something. Not hit something. That had been the clue the whole time. When the call to Lori went to voice mail, he called Karen. She said she'd just gotten home from the hospital after being released.

"Have you see Lorelei?" he asked, trying not to sound as worried as he was.

"She was going over to Alice Sherman's house. I had a card I wanted her to deliver."

James swore. "Call 911 and tell them to get over there. I'm on my way. Lorelei could be in trouble."

He sped toward Alice Sherman's house. He remembered Karen saying that she'd heard a car go racing past while she was in the pines getting rid of the coyote. That was after seeing Alice—and after Alice saw her walking down the road in the rainstorm. He desperately wanted to be wrong.

Just the thought of what Alice might have done, what she'd been living with… If he was right, she'd killed her own son and then covered it up. What would she do if forced to face what she'd done? That was what terrified him. If Lorelei asked too many questions…

He was almost to Alice's house. He could see Lori's car parked in the driveway. He just prayed he was wrong, but all his instincts told him that she was in trouble. He just prayed he could reach her in time.

CHAPTER TWENTY-FIVE

ALICE RAN AT HER, swinging the poker, aiming for her head. Lorelei had only a second to react. She grabbed the back of the wooden chair next to her at the table and heaved it at the woman. The chair legs struck the poker, knocking it out of Alice's hands and forcing her back. The poker clattered to the kitchen floor and then skittered toward the refrigerator away from both of them.

Shoving the fallen chair aside, Alice came at her like something feral. "You and your boyfriend just couldn't leave it alone. Billy is buried. Why can't you let him rest in peace?"

"Alice, you don't want to do this," Lorelei cried as she managed to get on the other side of the kitchen table. "It was an accident. You didn't know it was Billy."

But the woman was shaking her head as she suddenly veered to the right. She thought Alice was going for the poker on the floor in front of the refrigerator deeper in the kitchen. She decided to make a run for it. She had just come around the end of the table and was headed for the living room and the front door beyond it at a run when she heard the gunshot. Sheetrock dust and particles fell over her, startling her as much as the loud report of the gun.

"Take another step and the next bullet will be for you," Alice cried.

Lorelei turned slowly to look back. The woman held the gun in both hands, her stance a warning that she was no novice at this.

"We're going to go for a ride," Alice said and motioned with the gun toward the door to the garage.

Lorelei had seen enough movies and read enough thrillers to know that you never wanted to be taken to a second location. That was where someone would eventually stumble over your shallow grave. Or their dog would dig up your remains. It was how you made the headlines.

But she also thought that as desperate as Alice appeared, maybe she should take her chances. From the look in the woman's eyes, she would shoot her here and now—just as she'd warned. Maybe during the drive Lorelei might see an opportunity to get the upper hand.

Out in the garage, Alice ordered her behind the wheel. As she climbed in, Alice got in the other side and ordered, "Start the car. I will shoot you if you do anything but what I tell you."

The key was in the ignition. As Alice hit the garage door opener, Lorelei snapped on her seatbelt, started the car and drove out of the garage.

"Go left."

She turned onto the street, her brain whirling. So far Alice hadn't buckled up. Lorelei was debating what to do when she saw James's pickup racing up the other side of the street. She swerved in front of him hoping to get his attention.

"What do you think you're doing?" Alice demanded, shoving the gun into her face as they sped past James. Had he seen her? Had he seen Alice and the gun pointed at her head?

"You called him!" Alice screamed. "I told you not to do anything stupid, but you did." She had turned in the seat and was looking back.

In her rearview mirror, Lorelei saw James make a U-turn and come after them. He had seen her, but Lorelei realized it had been a mistake to draw his attention. James couldn't save her. Alice would kill her before that.

Worse, Alice had put down her window and was now shooting at James. In the rearview mirror, she saw the pickup's windshield shatter.

Lorelei swerved back and forth as she tried to keep the woman from getting a clean shot at James. He'd knocked out the rest of the windshield and was still coming up fast behind them. She swerved again and Alice banged her head on the window frame.

"You silly fool," the woman screeched, turning the gun on her. "I told you. Didn't I tell you? You've left me no choice."

Lorelei hit the gas again. She knew she had to act fast. Alice was too close to the edge. It would be just like her to pull the trigger and then turn the gun on herself. She slammed her foot down hard on the gas. The car jumped forward, the speed climbing quickly.

"What are you doing?" Alice cried. They were on the straightaway almost to the spot where Billy had died.

Alice was screaming as if she'd realized where they were. "No! No!" She took aim and Lorelei knew what she had to do.

Keeping the gas pedal to the floor, she suddenly swerved to the right. The car bounced down into the shallow ditch. Alice, still not belted in, was slammed

against the door, throwing her off balance in the seat
as she tried to aim the gun at her.

But Lorelei didn't let up on the gas as she pointed
the vehicle toward the stand of pines in the empty lot
across from where Billy died.

"I should have killed you at the house!" Alice
screamed as she took aim at Lorelei's head.

The car bucking and bouncing across the field, she
let go of the steering wheel with one hand to try to grab
for the gun. The shot was deafening, but nothing like
the sound when the car hit the trees.

JAMES COULDN'T BELIEVE what he was seeing. He'd never
felt more helpless as he watched Alice's car leave the
road. It roared down into the ditch then headed for
the pines. He hit his brakes, barely getting his pickup
stopped before the car crashed into the pines.

He leaped out and ran toward the wrecked car. Steam
rose from the engine. He could see that the front end
of the car was badly damaged—mostly on the passenger side. Lori had been behind the wheel. As he raced
to that side, Connie Matthews came out of her house.

"Call 911. Hurry!" he yelled at her as he reached the
driver's side door and saw that the window had been
shot out. He felt his heart drop. Had Alice shot her? Is
that why the car had left the road, why it had crashed
into the pines?

Inside he could see Lori. Her airbag had gone off
and was now deflated over the steering wheel with Lori
draped over it. There was blood dripping onto the deflated airbag.

He noticed it all in a split second as he tried unsuc-
cessfully to open her door. Past her, he could see Alice.

She'd gone through the windshield and now lay partly sprawled across the hood. She hadn't been wearing her seatbelt. Nor had her airbag activated.

James could hear sirens headed their way. He put all his weight into opening the door, surprised when he looked down and noticed his own blood. He'd taken a bullet in his arm but hadn't even realized it.

The door groaned and finally gave. In an instant he was at Lori's side. He felt for a pulse, terrified he wouldn't find one. There it was. Strong, just like her. He felt tears burn his eyes as relief rushed over him.

"Lori?" he said as he knelt beside the car. "It's going to be all right, baby. It's all going to be all right now. You're a fighter. Don't leave me. Please, don't leave me."

Soon he heard the EMTs coming, telling him to step aside. He rose and moved away, running a hand over his face as he watched them go to work. One of the EMTs noticed he was bleeding and pulled him aside.

More sirens and more rigs pulled up. Workers rushed past with a gurney for Lori. He turned away as he saw them checking Alice. It had been clear right away that she was gone.

He didn't remember going back to his pickup and following the ambulance to the hospital. Just as he didn't remember calling his brothers. Just as he didn't remember the doctors taking care of his gunshot wound or giving his statement to a law enforcement officer. All he'd thought about was Lori.

Hours later, he was walking the floor in the waiting room, when Willie arrived, followed soon after by Davey and Tommy. The surgeon had come in shortly after that to tell him that Lori had survived and was in stable condition.

"You should go on home and get some rest," the doctor told him. "You won't be able to see her until later today anyway."

He hadn't wanted to leave, but his brothers had taken him under their capable wings. When he'd awakened hours later in his bed, he'd gotten up to find them sitting in their dad's office. His arm ached. He'd looked down at the bandage, the horror of what had happened coming back to him.

"I just called the hospital," Willie said as James walked into the room. "I talked to a nurse I know. Lorelei's good. If she keeps improving as she has, you can see her later today."

James's knees felt weak with relief as he dropped into his father's office chair his brother Tommy had vacated for him.

"Now tell us what the hell has been going on here," Willie said. "Tommy went out to get us something to eat and came back with newspapers. You're a famous detective?"

"Not quite or Lori wouldn't be in the hospital right now," he said.

"Lori, is it?" Willie asked, grinning. "We saved you something to eat and made coffee. You fixed up the place pretty nice. But I think you'd better tell us what's been going on."

When he finished telling them between bites of breakfast washed down by coffee and a pain pill, his brothers were staring at him.

"You're good at this?" Davey said and laughed.

"Not quite," he said. "I almost got myself and Lori killed."

"You solved the case," Willie said.

James shook his head. "I almost got Lori killed."

"It's pretty clear to me what's going on here," Davey said. "James is in love."

His three brothers looked at him as if waiting for him to deny it. But he couldn't. It was true. He loved Lori. He repeated it out loud. "I love Lori."

His brothers all laughed, stealing glances at each other as if they couldn't believe it. James was the last one they'd have expected to get serious about anyone.

"Wait, what are you saying? You're giving up rodeo?" Tommy said.

LORI OPENED HER eyes and blinked. She thought she was seeing double. No, not double, quadruple. Four men dressed in Western attire standing at the end of her bed. All tall, dark and handsome as sin. One in particular caught her eye. She smiled at James and closed her eyes again.

When she woke up again, James was sitting by her bed. "I dreamed that there were four of you," she said, her hoarse voice sounding strange to her. "Four handsome cowboys."

He rose quickly to take her hand. "My brothers."

"I haven't seen them in years. They're…gorgeous."

James grinned down at her. "You're still drugged up, aren't you."

She nodded, smiling. "I can't feel anything but this one spot on my head." She reached up to touch her bandage. "Alice shot me."

"Fortunately, the bullet only creased your scalp, but it did give you a concussion and bled a lot. The doctors had to stitch you back up, but you're going to be fine." He squeezed her hand. "You scared the hell out of me, Lori. I thought for sure…" She saw him swallow. "I wish you would have told me you were going to see Alice."

"You were busy packing."

It was true. He'd planned to leave. He'd put the case behind him even though something had been nagging at him. "You hadn't been gone long when I got a call from one of the auto body shops that had fixed her damaged car after the hit-and-run. When I saw the photo of the car…"

"The senator didn't kill Billy," she said.

"No, he did apparently run over part of his body though and he didn't stop. Not to mention what he did to your mother. So he's still toast."

She nodded and felt her eyelids grow heavy. "I thought you might have already left."

He shook his head. "I'm not going anywhere. You rest. I'll be here."

Lorelei closed her eyes, hoping the next time she woke he wouldn't be gone and that this would have been nothing more than a sweet dream.

WILLIE COLT STOOD in the small second-floor office about to propose a toast. James had dug out a new bottle of blackberry brandy and paper cups.

"To my brother James," Willie said. "The first of the brothers to take his last ride."

There was laughter followed by rude remarks, but as James looked around the room at his brothers he'd never been happier. It had been so long since they'd all gotten together. "I've missed you guys." He still couldn't believe that they'd dropped everything and come running when he'd needed them.

The four of them had always been close, but definitely lived their own lives. They'd see each other at a rodeo here and there, but often went months without talking to each other. But when the chips were down, they always came through. They would squabble among themselves as boys, but if anyone else got involved, they stood together.

"You're really doing this?" Davey said, throwing an arm around his brother. "You're going to marry this woman?"

James nodded, grinning. "I really am. Well, I'm going to ask her to marry me. She hasn't said yes yet. I thought I should wait until she's not doped up on the drugs they're giving her for the pain."

He'd been to the hospital every day. Lori was getting better. She was strong, just as he knew. She had bounced back fast and would be released from the hospital today.

"When are you going to ask her?" Davey wanted to know.

"I'm not sure. Soon, but I want to do it right, you know." He looked over at Tommy who'd wandered behind their father's desk and was now inspecting both James's and their father's private investigator licenses.

"You'll miss the rodeo," Davey predicted.

He couldn't deny it. "Not as much as I would miss Lori. I don't expect you to understand. I wouldn't have understood myself—until I fell in love."

Davey laughed. "I've been in love. It comes and goes. Mostly goes."

"I'm talking about a different kind of love other than buckle bunnies on the circuit," he said. "I can't even explain it. But you'll know it when it happens to you."

"So you're sticking with this PI gig?" Willie asked. "It sounds even more dangerous than bronc riding."

James chuckled. "Sometimes it definitely is. But I like it. I see why Dad liked it. Lori has her sandwich shop. Not sure what we'll do when we have kids."

"Wait a minute. *Kids?*" Davey said before the others could speak.

"She's not pregnant."

Willie chuckled. "You haven't even…"

"Nope. We literally haven't gotten that far." He grinned. "But I know she'll want kids. I'm just hoping she'll want to start trying right after the wedding."

Willie was shaking his head. "Boy, when you fall, you fall hard. You sure about this?"

"I've never been more sure of anything," he said. He couldn't describe what it had felt like when he'd leaped out of his pickup and run toward Alice Sherman's car. The driver's side window had been blown out. There was blood everywhere. His knees had threatened to buckle under him when he'd realized that Lori had been shot.

"I'm thinking about building out on the ranch," he said. "There's plenty of room for all of us. As long as there are no objections." There were none. He knew that right now his brothers couldn't see themselves settling down. Eventually they would and the land would be there for them all.

"You going to keep the name, Colt Investigations?" Tommy asked. It was the first time he'd spoken since they'd come back from the hospital.

James studied him. "I guess, why?"

"Any chance you might want a partner?" his brother asked. Everyone turned to look at Tommy.

"Are you serious?" Davey sounded the most surprised. "You just turned thirty. You have a lot of rodeo ahead of you."

Tommy shook his head. "I've been thinking about quitting for some time now. I guess I was waiting for someone to go first." He smiled at James.

"You have even less experience at being a private investigator than James," Willie pointed out. "No offense."

"It can't be that hard," Davey joked. "If James can do it."

"Right, nothing to it. James and Lorelei both almost got killed," Willie said, sounding genuinely worried.

But Tommy didn't seem to be listening. "Look at this office. I could start by getting it up to speed technologically." He continued, clearly warming to the subject. "We could invest in computers, an office landline, equipment and even filing cabinets."

James realized that his brother was serious. "You've given this some thought."

Tommy nodded. "I didn't work with Dad as much as you did, but I could learn on the job while I helped do whatever you needed done. Didn't you say a lot of the jobs you've been offered were small things like Dad used to do, finding lost pets, tracking cheating husbands and wives, filming people with work comp injuries Jet Skiing, that sort of thing. What do you say?"

"I actually think he's serious," Davey said with a shake of his head.

Willie had been watching them. "It sounds like a pretty good deal. We all know we can't rodeo forever."

"I say great," James said, surprised and yet delighted.

He stepped to his brother and started to shake his hand, but instead pulled him into a bear hug. "Let's do this."

Willie was smiling broadly. "You could change the name to Colt Brothers Investigations."

"I like that," James said and looked to his brother. Tommy smiled and nodded. He looked at Willie and Davey. "That way if the two of you ever—" Before he could get the words out, Davey stopped him.

"Not happening," Davey said. "I have big plans. None of them include getting myself shot at unless it's by an irate boyfriend as I'm going out a bedroom window."

They all laughed. Willie had been quiet. As James looked at him, his older brother winked at him. "Let's just see how it goes, but I know one thing. Dad would have loved this," he said, his voice breaking. He lifted his paper cup. "To Dad." They all drank and James refilled their cups.

"There is one more thing," James said. "One of the investigations I'll be working on involves Dad. I don't think his death was an accident." As he looked around the room at each of his brothers he saw that they'd all had their suspicions. "Maybe we can find out the truth."

"I'll drink to that," Davey said, and the rest raised their paper cups.

CHAPTER TWENTY-SIX

LORI LOOKED FORWARD to James's visits each day at the hospital. And each day she'd waited for him to tell her he was leaving. She knew she was keeping him in town and hated that he felt he had to stay because of her.

I'm fine, she'd told him yesterday when he'd come by. *I know you're anxious to get back on the rodeo circuit. Please don't stay on my account.*

I'm not going anywhere, he'd said. *I just spoke to the doctor. Told me that you're going to be released tomorrow. Which is good because I have a surprise for you.*

A surprise?

Yes, a surprise and no I'm not giving you any clues.

She'd been allowed to dress but had to wait for a wheelchair to take her down. She'd begun to worry that James wouldn't show up. Maybe that was the surprise, she'd been thinking when he walked in. She felt a wave of relief wash over her and felt herself smiling at just the sight of him.

He grinned. "Ready to blow this place?"

She nodded, a lump in her throat. He'd stayed for her. He had a surprise for her. She tried not to, but her heart filled like a helium balloon even as she warned herself that this was temporary. James never stayed anywhere long, and he'd been here way past time. Those boots of his would be itching to make tracks.

He wheeled her down to his pickup and helped her into the passenger seat. "I want to show you something," he said as he started the engine. "You feel okay, comfortable, need anything?"

She laughed. "I'm fine," she said as she buckled up her seat belt and settled in, wondering where he was taking her. "Still no clue as to this surprise of yours?"

James shook his head, still grinning. The radio was on to a Western station. Lorelei felt herself relax. She breathed in the warm summer air coming in through the open window. She was alive. Suddenly the world seemed bigger and brighter, more beautiful than she remembered—even the small town of Lonesome.

When she voiced her euphoric feeling out loud, James laughed and reached over to take her hand.

He gave it a squeeze, his gaze softening. "It sure seems brighter to me too, being here with you."

Lorelei felt her heart fill even more and float up. She felt giddy and as hard as she tried to contain her excitement, she couldn't as he headed out of town. She glanced over at him, again wondering where he was taking her.

He turned off onto a dirt road back into the pines and kept driving until the road ended on the side of a mountain overlooking the river. He stopped, cut the engine and turned toward her.

She wasn't sure what surprised her more, that he'd brought her here or that he seemed nervous.

"Do you like it?" he asked, his voice tight with emotion. She must have looked perplexed because he quickly added, "The view. I'm thinking about building a house on this spot. What do you think?"

She looked out at the amazing view. "It's beautiful."

He was thinking about building a house here? This was the surprise? "How long have you been thinking about building here?"

"For a while now," he said. "Do you feel up to getting out? There is a spot close by I wanted to show you."

JAMES HAD NEVER been so nervous in his entire life. He'd climbed on the back of rank horses without breaking a sweat. He'd even ridden a few bulls he shouldn't have in his younger days. He'd been stomped and almost gored and still, he'd never hesitated to get back on.

But right now, as they walked through the wildflowers and tall summer grass toward his favorite spot, he felt as if he couldn't breathe.

He couldn't help being nervous. He'd planned out his life and Lori's and he wasn't even sure she wanted to marry him. They'd been through a lot in a short time. They'd gotten close. But they'd had only one date. One kiss.

It had been one humdinger of a kiss though, he thought with a grin.

As he walked, he reached into his pocket and felt the small velvet box. The engagement ring was an emerald, Lori's birthstone. The moment he'd seen it, he'd known it was perfect for her. He just hoped she liked it.

He took his hand out of his pocket, leaving the ring in its box. He had to do this right, he thought as he glanced over at her. Her bandages had been removed all except for one. The headaches were only occasional and minor. The doctor had said that she was good to go.

"This isn't too much for you, is it?" James asked, his voice sounding tight.

Lori laughed. "I'm fine, James. Are you sure you're all right though?"

His laugh sounded even more nervous than he felt. He was glad when they reached the outcropping of rock. "This is my favorite spot."

"I can see why," she said, smiling up at him. "It's beautiful."

He reached down and picked a couple of wildflowers, held them in his fingers for a moment before he offered them to her. As she took them, he watched her expression soften. Her brown eyes seemed to turn golden in the summer sun. She was so beautiful that she took his breath away.

"Lori." He swallowed.

"James?" she asked, suspicion and concern in her voice.

"I'm in love with you." He spit out the words so quickly that he had to repeat them. "I'm madly in love with you." He waited for her reaction.

LORELEI COULDN'T HELP being shocked. He was looking at her as if he couldn't believe she really hadn't seen this coming.

"I brought you here because this is where I want to build our house. I know this is fast," he added quickly.

"And maybe out of the blue," she said, unable not to smile. "We've never even been on a real date."

"You didn't think dinner at the steak house was a real date? How about when we danced?"

She nodded and felt her cheeks warm. "That did feel like a date."

He grinned as if not as nervous as he'd been before. "How about when we kissed?"

She nodded as she felt color rising to her cheeks.

He cocked his head as he looked at her. "We packed a lot into a few weeks time, you and me. We solved a mystery together and almost got killed."

Chuckling, she said, "I suppose you could say we got to know each other."

His grin broadened. "I remember being in the closet with you."

She flushed and had to look away. "If that's your idea of courtship—"

"My idea of courtship is to spend every day loving you for the rest of my life."

"James, I know you feel responsible for what happened to the two of us and that's why you're saying this. But what about the rodeo?" she asked.

"I'm not asking you out of guilt, although I do feel responsible. I jumped into my father's case not realizing how many lives I was risking—especially yours. But over this time, you've changed me."

She couldn't help her skeptical look.

He laughed. "Changed me for the better. You've made me see what it is I want out of life. I want to be with you. When I almost lost you—"

"You didn't lose me. Once you realize that I'm fine, you can go back to the rodeo—"

"I'm not leaving. I figured I had maybe another year or two max. It was time, Lori. I love rodeoing, but I love you more."

Lorelei watched him drop to one knee. Reaching into his pocket, he came out with a small velvet box. "James?" She felt goose bumps ripple across her skin.

"Lorelei Wilkins? Will you marry me and make me

the proudest man in the county?" he asked, his voice breaking.

"James."

"I want to go on dates with you, dance, kiss and make love. But I want to do it right. I want to do all of it with my wife. Say yes. You know you love me."

She laughed. "I do love you, Jimmy D."

He opened the small velvet box. "I saw this ring and it reminded me of you. One of a kind."

"My birthstone," she said. "Oh, James, it's beautiful." She met his gaze as tears filled her eyes. "Yes. Yes, I want to do all those things with you. As your wife."

He slipped the ring on her finger and rose to take her in his arms. The kiss held the promise of many days living on this mountainside overlooking the river. She could hear the laughter of their children, smell the sweet scents of more summers to come and feel James's arms around her always, sheltering her, loving her.

CHAPTER TWENTY-SEVEN

LORELEI WANTED TO pinch herself as she stared into the
full-length mirror at the woman standing there.

"You look beautiful," her stepmother said as she
came up beside her. They smiled at each other in the
mirror. "Such a beautiful bride."

"I'm doing the right thing," she said. "Aren't I? I
know it's sudden. James and I hardly know each other."

"Hush," Karen said as she turned to her. "I've never
seen anyone more in love than the two of you. You
know James. And he knows you. I could see this coming for years. He was always trying to get your attention back in high school. You used to blush at just the
sight of him."

"I still do," Lorelei confessed with a laugh. "It's the
way he looks at me."

Her stepmother laughed. "I've seen it. It's the way
every woman wants to be looked at. The way every
woman wants to feel. You're very lucky."

"He makes me happy."

"I can see that." Karen looked at the time. "Ready?"

Lorelei took one last look at the woman in the mirror.
She was glowing, radiating happiness and excitement.
Life with James would never be dull. Anita had offered
to buy the sandwich shop. At first Lorelei had been surprised that her friend would think she wanted to sell it.

I just assumed you'd be working with James in the PI business until the babies start coming, Anita had said with a wink.

She'd laughed at the thought, but only for a moment. *James mentioned the same thing. He says he can't do it without me.*

When she'd mentioned selling the sandwich shop to James, he'd been excited to hear that she was going to do it. *We'll change the name of the business to Colt Investigations.*

No, Lorelei had said. *I think it should be Colt Brothers Investigations. I won't be working there. I'll be too busy. We have a wedding to plan, a house to build and decorate to get ready for the babies we're going to make.*

I do like the sound of that last part, he'd said with a laugh. *Let's get on that right after the wedding.* And he'd kissed her.

"Shall we do this?" her stepmother asked, bringing Lorelei out of her reverie.

Lorelei nodded. She couldn't wait.

The church was full to overflowing. Her three bridesmaids were ready. So were the three Colt brothers, but all she saw was James standing at the end of the aisle, waiting for her. The look in his eyes sent heat rocketing through her. Last night he'd told her about this vision he'd had of a little girl of about two on a horse.

I know she's ours, he'd said. *Our little girl.*

She'd had the same dream. *I've seen her. She has your blue eyes.*

Lorelei took a step toward James and their future. She wanted to run to him, to throw her arms around him, to tell him again and again how much she loved him, how much she wanted him.

But instead, she took another slow step and then another. There was no reason to run. They had the rest of their lives together.

* * * * *

COLD CASE KIDNAPPING

Nicole Helm

For the reluctant heroes.

CHAPTER ONE

GRANT HUDSON HAD been well versed in fear since the age of sixteen when his parents vanished—seemingly into thin air, never to be seen or heard from again. So, as an adult, he'd made fear and uncertainty his life. First, in the military with the Marines and now as a cold case investigator with his siblings.

Privately investigating cold cases didn't involve the same kind of danger he'd seen in Middle Eastern deserts, but the uncertainty, the puzzles and never knowing which step to take was just as much a part of his current life as it had been in the Marines.

And if he focused on seemingly unsolvable cases all day, he didn't have time to think about the nightmares that plagued him.

"Your ten o'clock appointment is here."

Grant looked up from his coffee. His sister was dressed for ranch work but held a file folder that likely had all the information about his new case.

Hudson Sibling Solutions, HSS, was a family affair. The brainchild of his oldest brother, Jack, and a well-oiled machine in which all six Hudson siblings played a part, just as they all played a part in running the Hudson Ranch that had been in their family for five generations.

They had solved more cases than they hadn't, and Grant considered that a great success. Usually the answers weren't happy endings, but in some strange way, it helped ease the unknowns in their own parents' case.

Grant glanced at the clock as he finished off his coffee. "It's only nine forty-five."

"She's prompt," Mary agreed, handing him the file. "She's in the living room whenever you're ready."

But "whenever you're ready" wasn't part and parcel with what HSS offered.

They didn't make people wait. They didn't shunt people off to small offices and cramped spaces. Usually people trying to get answers on a cold case had spent enough time in police stations, detective offices and all manner of uncomfortable rooms answering the same questions over and over again.

The Hudsons knew that better than anyone—particularly Jack, who'd been the last person to see their parents alive and had been the only legal adult in the family at the time of their disappearance. Jack had been adamant when they began the family investigation business that they offer a different experience for those left behind.

So they met their clients in the homey living room of the Hudson ranch house. They didn't make people wait if they could help it. They treated their clients like guests... The kind of hospitality their mother would have been proud of.

Grant had made himself familiar with today's case prior to this morning, but he skimmed the file Mary had handed off. A missing person, not out of the ordinary for Hudson Sibling Solutions. Dahlia Easton had reported her sister, Rose, missing about thirteen months ago, after her sister had disappeared on a trip to Texas.

Dahlia Easton herself was a librarian from Minnesota. Dahlia was convinced she'd found evidence that placed Rose near Sunrise, Wyoming—which had led her to the HSS.

Ms. Easton hadn't divulged that evidence yet, instead insisting on an in-person meeting to do such. It was Grant's turn to take the lead, so he walked through the hallway that still housed all the framed art his mother had hung once upon a time—various Wyoming landscapes—to the living room.

A redhead sat on the couch, head down and focused on the phone she held. Her long hair curtained her face, and she didn't look up as Grant entered.

He stepped farther into the room and cleared this throat. "Ms. Easton."

The woman looked up from her phone and blinked at him. She didn't move. She sat there as he held out his hand waiting for her to shake it or greet him in some way.

It was a strange thing to see a pretty woman seated on the couch he'd once crowded onto with all his siblings to watch Disney movies. Stranger still to feel the gut kick of attraction.

It made him incredibly uncomfortable when he rarely allowed himself discomfort. He should be thrilled his body could still react to a pretty woman in a perfectly normal way, but he found nothing but a vague sense of unease filling him as she sat there, eyes wide, studying him.

Her hair was a dark red, her eyes a deep tranquil blue on a heart-shaped face that might have been more arresting if she didn't have dark circles under her eyes and her clothes didn't seem to hang off a too-skinny frame. Like many of the clients who came to HSS for help, she wore the physical toll of what she'd been through in obvious ways…enough for even a stranger to notice.

He set those impressions and his own discomfort aside and smiled welcomingly. "Ms. Easton, I'm Grant Hudson. I'll be taking the lead on your case on behalf of HSS. While all six of us work in different facets of investigation, I'll be your point person." He finally dropped his hand since she clearly wasn't going to shake it. "May I?" he said pointing to the armchair situated across from the couch. His father had fallen asleep in that very chair every single movie night.

"You look like a cowboy," she said, her voice sounding raspy from overuse or lack of sleep, presumably.

The corner of his mouth quirked up, a lick of amusement working through him. He supposed a cowboy was quite a sight for someone from Minnesota. "Well, I suppose in a way I am."

"Right. Wyoming. Of course." She shook her head. "I'm sorry. I'm out of sorts."

"No apologies necessary." He settled himself on the chair. She didn't look so much out of sorts as she did exhausted. He set the file down on the coffee table in between them.

"I have all the information Mary collected from you."

"Mary's the woman I talked to on the phone and emailed. I thought she'd…"

"Mary handles the administrative side of things, but I'll be taking the lead on actually investigating. I can get Mary to sit in if you'd feel more comfortable with a woman present?"

"No, it isn't that. I just…" She shook her head. "This is fine."

Grant nodded, then decided what this woman needed

was to get some sleep and a good meal in her. "Have you had breakfast?"

"Um." Her eyebrows drew together. "I don't understand what you're..."

"I'd like you to recount everything you know, so we might be here a while. Just making sure you're up for it."

"Oh, I'm not much for breakfast."

He'd figured as much. He pulled his phone out of his pocket and sent a quick text to Mary. He wouldn't push the subject, but he wasn't about to let Dahlia keel over either. He slid the phone back in his pocket.

"I've got your file here. All about your sister's trip to Texas. The credit card reports, cell phone records. Everything you gave us. But you said you had reason to believe she ended up here in Wyoming."

"Yes," Dahlia agreed, putting her own phone into a bag that sat next to her. "Everything the police uncovered happened in Texas," Dahlia said. "But she just... disappeared into thin air, as far as anyone can tell me, but obviously that isn't true. People can't just disappear."

But they did. All the time. There were a lot of ways to make sure a person was never found. More than even Grant could probably fathom, and he could fathom a lot. Which was why he focused on one individual case at a time. "So, there's no evidence she ever left Texas?"

"She took one of those DNA tests, and it matched her with some people in Texas," Dahlia said earnestly, avoiding the direct question. "She was supposed to go to Texas and meet them. She never made it to the people—at least the police there didn't think so. When all the clues dried up, I decided to look at Rose's research. The genealogy stuff that prompted her to take the DNA test. I researched everything she had, and it led me to a secret offshoot of the Texas family that wound up in Truth, Wyoming."

Grant tried not to frown. Because, no, there wasn't proof Rose Easton had left Texas, and also because no one in Sunrise particularly cared to think about Truth, Wyoming. "Ah" was all he said.

"It's a cult."

"It was a cult," Grant replied. "The Feds wiped them out before I was born." Still, people tried to stir up all the Order of Truth nonsense every few years. But there was no evidence that the cult had done anything but die out after the federal raid in 1978.

"Doesn't everything gone come around back again?" Dahlia asked, nervous energy pumping off her. "And if this line of our family was involved then, doesn't it mean they could be involved now?"

Grant studied the woman. She looked tired and brittle. It didn't diminish her beauty, just gave it a fragile hue. Fragile didn't cut it in these types of situations, but here she was. Still standing. Still searching.

She was resting all her hopes on the wrong thing if she was looking into the Order of Truth, but she believed it. She was clearly holding on to this tiny thread for dear life. So Grant smiled kindly. "Let's see your evidence."

HE DIDN'T BELIEVE HER. No different than any of the police officers and detectives back home or in Texas. Once Dahlia uttered the word *cult*—especially one that had been famously wiped out—people stopped listening.

Grant Hudson was no different, except he was placating her by asking for her evidence. Dahlia didn't know if that was more insulting than waving her off or not. Honestly, she was too tired to figure out how she felt about much of anything.

She'd driven almost eighteen hours from Minneapolis to Sunrise in two days and had barely slept last night in the nice little cabin she'd rented. She was too anxious and tangled up about this strange connection. Too amped at the thought of *hope* after so long.

"I think you probably have all the evidence you care about," Dahlia said, trying to keep her tone even. "I know investigators are obsessed with facts, but facts haven't helped me. Sometimes you have to tie some ideas together to find the facts."

Grant studied her. It had been a silly thing to say, that he looked like a cowboy, but it was simply true. It wasn't just the drawl, it was something about the way he walked. There were the cowboy boots of course, and the Western decor all around them, but something in the square jaw or slightly crooked nose made her think of the Wild West. The way he hadn't fully smiled, but his mouth had *curved* in a slow move that had left her scrambling for words.

"We are investigators, and we do have to work in the truth," Grant said, still using that kind veneer to his words, though Dahlia sensed an irritation simmering below them. "But I think you'll find we're not like the police departments you've dealt with. I'll admit, I think the cult is the wrong tree to bark up, but if you give me reason to change my mind, I'll bark away."

The tall slender woman who'd let her in the house entered the room pushing a cart. She wore adorable cowboy boots with colorful flowers on them and Dahlia had no doubt when she spoke, it would be tinged with that same smooth Western drawl Grant had.

It was easy to see the two were related even if Grant was tall and broad and...*built*.

There was something in the eyes, in the way they moved. Dahlia didn't have the words for it, just that they functioned like a unit. One that had been in each other's pockets their whole lives.

People had never been able to tell that about her and Rose, aside from being named for flowers. It took getting to know them, together, to see the way they had learned how to deal with each other and their parents. The rhythm of being a sibling.

Dahlia had been turned into an only child now, and she didn't know how to function in that space. Not with her parents, who had given up on Rose when the police had. Not with her friends, all of whom were more Rose's friends than hers and who wanted to be involved in a tragedy and their grief more than they wanted answers.

Only Dahlia couldn't let it go. Couldn't hold on to her old life in this new world where her sister didn't exist.

Not dead. Not gone. She didn't *exist*.

"I told you I'm not a breakfast eater," Dahlia said sharply and unkindly. She might have felt bad about that, felt her grandmother's disapproval from half a country away, but she was tired of caring what everyone else felt.

Grant apparently felt unbothered by her snap. "So consider it lunch." He looked at his sister. "Thanks, Mary."

She nodded, smiled at Dahlia, then left. Grant immediately took a plate and began to arrange things on it.

Dahlia figured he'd shove it at her, and she had all sorts of reasons to tell him to shove it down his own throat.

Instead, he set it next to the file folder. Picking a grape and popping it into his own mouth before pouring himself some coffee.

Dahlia knew she'd lost too much weight. She understood she didn't sleep well enough, and her health was suffering because of it. She'd seen a therapist to help her come to terms with Rose's disappearance.

But no amount of self-awareness or therapy could stop her from this driving need to find the truth.

She didn't know if Rose was still alive. She was prepared—or tried to prepare herself—for the ugly truths that could be awaiting her. Namely, that Rose was dead and had been all this time. Her sweet, vibrant sister. Murdered and discarded.

It wasn't just possible, it was likely, and yet Dahlia had to know. She couldn't rest, not really, until she had the truth.

And if you never find it?

She simply didn't know. So she'd keep going until something changed.

Grant continued to eat as he flipped through papers that were presumably the reports and information she'd emailed to Mary.

Dahlia wasn't hungry, but she hadn't been for probably the entire past year. Still, food was fuel, and this food was free. She could hardly sidestep that when her entire life savings was being poured into hiring Hudson Sibling Solutions and staying in Wyoming until the mystery was solved.

She finally forced herself to pick a few pieces of fruit and a hard-boiled egg and put them on a plate. She'd been guzzling coffee for days, so she went for the bottle of water instead.

"Tell me why you decided to come all the way out here." He said it silky smooth, and whether it was the drawl or his demeanor, he made it sound like a gentle request.

She knew it was an order though. And she knew he'd ignore it like everyone else had. It was too big of a leap to take, and yet...

"Rose found out our great-grandfather was married before he married our great-grandmother. And he had a son from this first marriage. A man named Eugene Green."

Grant's expression didn't move, but something in the air around them did. Likely because he knew Eugene Green to be the founder of the Order of Truth.

"That's not exactly a close relation, is it? Something like a half great-great-uncle. If that."

"If that," Dahlia agreed. Her stomach turned, but still she forced herself to eat a grape. Drink some of the water. "But it was in Rose's notes."

Grant flipped through the papers again. "What notes?"

Dahlia moved for her bag and pulled out the thick binder she'd been carting around. "After the police decided it was a cold case, they returned her computer to me. I printed off everything she'd collected about our family history. *That's* what took her to Texas. She had a binder just like this. With more originals, but she scanned and labeled everything. So I recreated it. The Wyoming branch and Texas branch of the family are one and the same. It connects."

Grant eyed the binder. "Ms. Easton..."

"I know. You don't believe me. No one does. That's okay." She hadn't come all this way just for someone to believe her. "And you can hardly look through it all. But there is this." She pulled out the piece of paper she'd been keeping in the front pocket of the binder. "The picture on the top is from security footage of the gas station in Texas where Rose was last spotted. That's Rose," she said pointing to her sister. "No one can identify the man with her, but he looks an awfully lot like the picture on the bottom. A picture of Eugene Green from my sister's notes."

Grant didn't even flick a glance at the picture. "Eugene Green is dead."

"Yes, but not everyone who might look like him is."

Grant seemed to consider this, but then people—law enforcements, investigators, even friends—always did. At first. "Can I keep this?"

Dahlia nodded. She had digital copies of everything. She wasn't taking any chances. If HSS took all her information and lost it, discarded it or ignored it, she'd always have her own copies to keep her going.

"Did you have anything else that might tie Rose to Truth or Wyoming?" Grant asked.

No, she hadn't come here thinking HSS would believe her, but she'd…hoped. She couldn't seem to stop herself from hoping. "No, not exactly."

"Can I ask why you couldn't have told us this over the phone?"

Dahlia looked at the picture. Every police officer she'd talked to about it told her she was grasping at straws. That the Order of Truth was gone, and all the Greens had long since left the Truth area. That the man in the picture wasn't *with* Rose. He was just getting gas at the pump next to her.

"I'm not sure I could explain it in a way that would make any sense to you, but I needed to come here."

Grant nodded. "Well, I'll look into this. Is there anything else?"

Dahlia shoved her binder, sans security picture, back in her bag and then stood. He was dismissing her now that he understood her evidence was circumstantial—according to the police.

She was disappointed. She could admit that to herself. She'd expected or hoped for a miracle. Even as she'd told herself they wouldn't care any more than anyone else had, there'd been a seed of hope this family solving cold cases might believe her.

She should end this. The Hudsons weren't going to do any more than the police had, and she was going to run out of money eventually. "If you don't have anything new in a week, I suppose that will be that."

His eyebrows rose as he stood. "A week isn't much time to solve a cold case."

"I don't need it solved. I just need some forward movement to prove I'm paying for something tangible. If you can prove to me the Order of Truth has nothing to do with this—irrefutably—that'll be enough."

He seemed to consider this, then gave her a nod. "You're staying at the Meadowlark Cabin?" Grant asked as he motioned her to follow him.

Dahlia nodded as she retraced her footsteps through the big stone-floored foyer to the large front door with its stained glass sidelights. Mountains and stars.

"How long are you planning on staying?"

Dahlia looked away from the glass mountains to Grant's austere face. "As long as it takes."

Again, his expression didn't quite move, but she got the distinct feeling he didn't approve. Still, he said nothing, just opened the front door.

"I'll be in touch," he said.

She forced herself to smile and shake his outstretched hand.

Just because he'd be in touch didn't mean she was going to go hole herself in her room at her rented cabin in Sunrise. No.

She planned on doing some investigating of her own. She'd come here hoping the Hudsons could help, sure, but she'd known what she really needed to do.

Help herself.

CHAPTER TWO

"DID YOU KNOW about this?"

Mary looked down from where she was situated on her horse. She adjusted the reins in her hands and then studied the paper Grant held. Mary frowned. "Is that Eugene Green?"

"Your new client seems to think he's involved."

Her frown deepened. "Did you mention that he died like fifty years ago?"

"I did. I also mentioned the Feds wiped out the Order of Truth in the seventies. You're supposed to do a better job of weeding out the pointless cases."

Mary's frown turned into a blank look she'd perfected. People who didn't know her might consider it a nonreaction, but Grant was her brother. He knew better. And he knew he'd pay for it later. But his irritation with cult nonsense overrode self-preservation at the moment.

"Did she seem *pointless* to you?" Mary asked, her voice calm if icy.

"Not until she pulled out this picture."

"So she's misdirected. Following the wrong lead. People do that kind of thing. Even us." Mary's horse puffed out a breath, energy pumping off the large animal. It was ready for a run, for some work.

But Mary kept the horse still, waiting for Grant to respond in some way.

There were a million dead ends when it came to investigating cold cases. A lot of retracing steps and looking at the same evidence over and over again, trying to find a different angle or shed a new light. And, yes, sometimes an investigator went down the wrong path. More than once.

Even him.

Still, Grant wanted nothing to do with Truth. He'd never found the cult stories interesting the way some people did. Maybe it was the family connection, even if it didn't connect to him. Because like Dahlia and Rose Easton, he had broken branches of a family tree too.

Grant had always felt in line with his mother's track of thinking on the matter. Best not to dwell on it. Best to leave it alone.

Besides, the ghost town of Truth had never done anything except give him a bad feeling—one he now recognized as the same bad feeling he'd gotten in the Marines before something had gone FUBAR.

But their client thought Truth had something to do with her case, and unless Grant's people skills were rusty, he was willing to bet Dahlia Easton wouldn't let that angle go without some proof. So, he had to prove to her she was on the wrong path, and then maybe he could help her find the right one.

"I'm taking one of the dogs," Grant muttered.

"Better clear it with Cash," Mary replied, and she didn't smile exactly, but Grant could read the smug satisfaction all the same. "And make sure to use the business credit card for gas."

Grant rolled his eyes. "I'm not Palmer."

"You're all men, and men are constantly forgetting important details. At least the men I know."

Before he could respond to that, Mary urged her horse forward, and it more than willingly obliged, leaving Grant standing in a cloud of dust.

Grant considered the horse stables. He could take one over. Cash's dog barn was on the other side of the property, as was the cabin where he lived with his eleven-year-old. Izzy would be at school, which meant Cash would likely be training his dogs. Cash trained all sorts of dogs, search and rescue, detection, even some service dogs.

But if Grant took a horse over, he'd have to come back and deal with the aftercare. He wanted this trip done with ASAP. So he got his truck and drove the dusty path from the main part of the ranch to Cash's little corner of it.

It was a sunny fall day, warm enough, but the air would go cold the minute the sun started dipping toward the horizon. The sky was a dark blue, and the land of the Hudson Ranch stretched out around him in rolling hills and long plains that led to those timeless craggy mountains in the distance. No matter what he'd seen out there in the world, Sunrise and this ranch had always been home to the most beautiful sky in the whole world.

He'd always known he'd come back here. The military had been a side trip. To get out of Jack's hair. Assuage some of the restlessness inside of him. See the world. Fight for his country. *Do* something outside of Sunrise and everyone who knew him and defined him by his tragedy.

But he'd always known when that side trip was over, he'd be back here. Working the same land his great-great-great-grandfather had.

Grant came to a stop next to the dog barn, a squat red

building where Cash housed all his dogs. Cash himself stood outside in front of a line of dogs. If he'd been in the mood for it, Grant might have found some amusement in how much the sight reminded him of soldiers standing at attention awaiting their orders.

Grant parked and got out, then walked toward his brother as Cash made a hand signal. The dogs all sat in unison. Another hand movement, they all laid down.

Only once Cash was satisfied every dog had its stomach on the ground did he turn to Grant. "What's up?"

"I need a dog for a job. Few hours tops. Nothing special. More company than anything." Grant had no desire to head out to that eerie place alone.

Cash nodded, studied his pack. "Willie." He gave a sharp whistle, and a brown-and-white shepherd got up and trotted over to them. "Don't feed him scraps."

"You're always telling me that."

"Yeah, and you're always ignoring me."

Grant chuckled. True enough. He planned to continue to do so. Who could resist those soulful canine eyes just begging for a treat?

Cash made some more of his hand gestures and different sounding whistles, and Willie bounded up into Grant's truck.

"This about the Easton missing person case?" Cash asked, closing the truck door behind the dog.

"Yeah. How'd you know that? I thought you were keeping your nose out of cases."

"I try, but between Anna and Palmer's big mouths I end up knowing far more than I want to." Cash glanced back at the house. Though Grant knew Izzy was at school, he also knew that's who his brother was thinking about.

Cash would have taken a more active role in cases if he wasn't worried about his daughter's safety or his own as a single father. Which was why, even though he tried to keep his nose out of things, he'd inevitably ask…

"So, what was the Wyoming connection?"

"Tenuous at best," Grant replied. He didn't want to get into it, but no doubt Cash would hear about it one way or another. The only way to prove it didn't bother him was to be the one to tell him. "She thinks it connects to Truth."

It was Cash's turn to chuckle. "Isn't it funny how the one of us the most afraid of Truth got picked for lead investigator on a case that connects to it?"

"The case doesn't connect to Truth. The Easton woman just thinks it does. I'm headed there to prove to her she's wrong." He knew he should leave it at that, but Cash always knew how to needle him into giving up more information than he cared to. "I'm hardly afraid."

"Fifteen-year-old Grant sure was."

"Yeah, well unless you and Palmer have concocted yet another plan to attempt to scare the—"

"Oh, it wasn't an attempt. We scared the living daylights out of you."

Grant rolled his eyes. "I went to war, Cash. I'm not afraid of Truth, Wyoming. Or you and Palmer for that matter," Grant muttered, adjusting his cowboy hat on his head. He got into his truck, ignoring his brother's mocking laughter.

Truth be told—a fact he'd never admit to his brothers—he'd rather be back in the Marines than spend the next few days in Truth, but he'd learned a long time ago, a man didn't always get what he'd rather.

TRUTH, WYOMING, was a ghost town. Dahlia wasn't surprised. Everything she'd read about it told her that after the federal raid had ended in three dead FBI agents, ten dead cult members and the rest of the adults jailed for life, no one had wanted anything to do with the town except the occasional tourist to gawk at the scene of tragedy.

But no one stayed. No one built inappropriate tourist attractions. It had been the site of something gruesome that no one understood. A fascination, surely, but not one to spend more than a few hours in.

So, no, Dahlia wasn't surprised the buildings were empty or that here on the rock cropping she'd climbed to look down at the town, the land stretched out, gray and brown and deserted and what she figured most would find unappealing.

What did surprise her was the way the ethereal beauty of the area struck her someplace deep inside. It was nothing like home. No green, no sparkling lakes, no fall colors. The land stretched out in all directions, the same grayish color, routinely interrupted by strange rock formations—some skinny and jagged reaching for the sky. Some big fat columns of earth. But it didn't feel like some alien planet. It felt alive and vibrant.

It felt…*right*. As if she belonged down there, walking the length of the abandoned street. She didn't understand the feeling at all. It made her want to cry. Inexplicably.

You're just exhausted, she told herself as she climbed back down the rock. What had she expected to find here? Signs of her sister? Or any civilization? She was exhausted and it was affecting her decision making.

But she walked down what had once been Main

Street, and she knew she should feel out of place. Creeped out, maybe, but there was only a thrumming curiosity that had her poking her head into doors. She didn't know what she was looking for or what she was hoping to prove. She was just following instinct...or her gut...or something.

The same something that had pushed her to leave her life behind and come here to begin with. Everything had frozen in place once Rose had disappeared. Dahlia didn't know how to unfreeze it without figuring out... something. *Something.*

She walked into a building that had clearly once been a restaurant of some kind. A few tables were still scattered around the main room, a counter ran along the far wall, with an empty display case that looked like it might have once been filled with baked goods.

Dust and grime stuck to every surface. No one had been here lately. That was clear. Even if they had, why would they leave evidence of it? And what would she do if she found it?

She should have gone back to her rental cabin and slept. This was a waste of time. She should be searching the Green family and their connection to hers, not some Wyoming ghost town.

Maybe her parents were right. She couldn't think straight. She should commit herself until she could again. But Dahlia knew she hadn't had any sort of mental break. Maybe she had let emotions affect her decision-making, but she...

She had to see this through. The right way though. Taking care of herself had to start being a priority.

She stepped out of the abandoned building and then stopped abruptly. A shudder moved through her. That odd peace she didn't understand evaporated. Replaced by the feeling of being watched.

She swallowed at the bubble of fear. Her eyes darted from side to side as she stood rooted to the spot. She didn't see anything out of the ordinary. She held her breath and listened, trying to discern something beyond the gentle rustle of the wind.

A faint high-pitched sound cut the silence, then was hushed by a quiet command. Dahlia told herself to move, but fear kept her frozen in the doorway. *Run! Hide! Scream!*

She did none of those things. She couldn't. Apparently in a flight-or-fight response situation, Dahlia went with neither.

A soft yip—like from a dog—echoed through the air, and then a large brown-and-white dog appeared around a corner. Relief coursed through her. She nearly sagged against the doorway behind her. Just a dog. Just a—

"Willie. Sit."

It was a man's voice. Sharp and commanding. And the dog immediately plopped its butt on the dusty ground a few yards away. She didn't see the man, but something about actually hearing a voice, or maybe the dog itself, prompted Dahlia into action. She scurried back into the building, crouching behind the wall so that no one could see her from outside.

She pressed her back against the wall. She tried to hold her breath but realized belatedly that wouldn't be sustainable.

How would she know when the man was gone? Would the dog sniff her out? Why was she acting like she needed to hide when she had just as much right to be here as anyone else? As far as she could tell, the land was public property and...

She heard the dog, the faint panting noises, the padding of paws closer and closer and closer until...

"Closing your eyes doesn't stop the bad guy from coming, Ms. Easton."

Dahlia blinked her eyes open and looked up at the tall shadow of a man who stood in the doorway. She hadn't realized she'd screwed her eyes shut in some childish instinct.

Embarrassment washed over her more than fear when she recognized the man.

She frowned at Grant Hudson's disapproving face. "What are you doing here?"

"Shouldn't that be my line?"

She hadn't expected...this. At all. He'd been so dismissive. "You're investigating."

"I said I would."

"I didn't think you'd actually look into Truth."

"You said you needed proof it didn't connect." He held out a hand, and it took Dahlia quite a few ticking seconds to realize he was offering to help her to her feet. She found she didn't want to slide her hand in his but couldn't say why. So she went against instinct and took it.

Firm and callused, he grasped her hand and leveraged her to her feet. The minute she was upright and steady, he immediately let her hand go. He strode back out to the street without another word.

Dahlia didn't know what else to do but follow, like the dog.

"Is this proof enough?" he asked, waving to the empty town around them.

Dahlia followed the path of his hand with her gaze. Even knowing she hadn't been watched but instead was running into the investigator she hired, something had changed. She didn't feel that sense of belonging anymore. Only foreboding.

"Proof that she isn't in Truth right this moment. But that's about it."

Grant sighed. "Ms. Easton, you should understand—"

"I know. I'm very well aware she could be dead." People didn't seem to understand that hope didn't mean she was ignoring the very real possibility her sister had been murdered. That thought plagued her, haunted her, just as much as that tiny sliver of hope that Rose was alive somewhere did. That's why she needed the truth.

The dog made another whining noise. Grant looked down at the animal with a faint line of confusion on his brow. "Go," he offered.

The dog took off down the empty street, and Grant followed him, so Dahlia followed Grant. The dog led them down an alley between two buildings that had been enveloped by some kind of winding vine. It was a narrow alley, and even with the bright sunshine overhead the area was shadowed and dark. Dahlia shivered at the cooler temperature here, looking over her shoulder as goose bumps popped up along her arms.

When she looked forward again, Grant had stopped and was frowning in the same direction she'd been looking. But he shook his head and pressed forward through the alley.

Once on the other side, Dahlia was surprised and confused to find a kind of walled courtyard. Thick, tall stone walls were built along the perimeter—the alley apparently the only way in or out. There was no roof, only the bright blue sky, and there was nothing of note in the courtyard. Just a square of dusty ground and a few patches of grass or brush.

But the dog continued yapping, and as Grant strode over to the corner where it stood, Dahlia's unease intensified. She moved slowly toward where Grant was crouched. He was staring at a small piece of something on the ground.

"What is it?"

"Casing," he replied somewhat absently.

"What does that mean?"

"Someone shot a gun here. And not that long ago." Grant studied the small object, frowning. "Could have been someone target-shooting. It could be a lot of things." He stood, but there was something…off. He held himself differently now. The frown on his face was more serious.

"So, why do you look so…perplexed?"

He looked up, studying their surroundings with a cold detachment that made her aware she was alone with a virtual stranger in a very isolated landscape. Stuck in this little courtyard, as no doubt Grant could block off the one exit before she could make it out.

When his eyes met hers, they were dark and not at all comforting. "Let's get you back to town."

CHAPTER THREE

SOMETHING WASN'T RIGHT. Grant didn't believe it had anything to do with Truth. But it definitely had something to do with the woman driving in front of him.

Grant glanced in his rearview mirror. He'd half expected someone to follow them out of Truth. Half expected *something* to happen, though he couldn't have said what.

He wished he'd had time to investigate, but instinct told him to get Dahlia out of there, and he was still enough of a soldier to follow his instincts.

She hadn't argued. Oh, she'd looked at him a bit like he might be the Devil sent to take her to hell, but she'd done as he said. Walked back to her car, gotten in, then waited for him to bring his truck around so he could follow her back to Sunrise.

He glanced at the rearview again. He couldn't shake the feeling someone had been watching them. He hadn't seen any evidence of that. It was just a feeling.

But added to the lone shell casing, they needed to do a full-blown search of Truth. Much as he was loath to admit it.

It could be unrelated. People went to Truth sometimes. High school kids went out on a dare. Yahoos driven by stories on the internet went out to do whatever rituals they thought might make something happen. That casing could mean anything.

But there'd been a mark on the wall—mostly scrubbed off—that made Grant suspicious *something* was going on in Truth even if it had nothing to do with the missing Easton sister. *Or* the cult.

But he had to get Dahlia tucked away before he could deal with that. She pulled her car off the highway. Surprisingly not a rental, but a compact sedan registered to Dahlia Easton of Minneapolis, Minnesota.

He'd called Zadie, an old family friend now with the sheriff's department, to get him that information. Taking her own car rather than flying or even renting for a few weeks spoke of something longer than a brief trip to check things out.

But Dahlia herself wasn't the case. The missing sister was. And now, for Grant, the case included figuring out what was going on in Truth.

It was a short drive off the highway to the cabin Dahlia was renting. Just inside Sunrise's borders, it was secluded—a pretty little cabin in a pretty little spot.

But she'd do better somewhere with a little bit more foot traffic. Grant didn't believe anywhere was don't-lock-your-doors safe, but Sunrise was about as close as a person could get. She should be closer to people who would, if nothing else, notice if something fishy went on. Then the gossip chain would let the Hudsons know before anything bad happened.

Dahlia got out of her car, and she gripped her bag so hard her knuckles were white. She stayed close to her car as Grant got out of his truck. "You didn't have to follow me here."

She wasn't comfortable with him, and he understood.

He wished he could give her more space, but something was off. The safety of a client came before their comfort.

Still, Grant whistled for Willie to get out of the car. She seemed to relax a little bit around the dog.

"I'm just going to have a look around," he said, trying to sound casual as Willie ambled over to sit next to her.

She looked at the dog. Then him. "Look around what?"

"The cabin."

She shook her head. "Why on earth would you do that?"

"Ms. Easton, did you get the sense you were all alone when you were in Truth?"

"Yes. Yes, it was peaceful actually. Until you came along." She lifted her chin. She might be exhausted, maybe even a little fragile, but she had some fighting spirit in there.

"And what happened when I came along?"

She shook her head. "I don't know. I guess I just… felt your presence or whatever. Not in a woo-woo way. I heard the dog. I…" She trailed off, frowning, but she didn't continue.

He didn't know who might be following her. Who might be hanging around Truth. But he knew there was something off, and he had to wonder if it was something she'd brought with her from Minnesota.

"Would anyone have followed you here? To Sunrise?"

"From Minnesota?"

"Maybe you hired a private investigator? Or there's a

family member worried about you? Anyone who might not have wanted you to come here alone."

She blinked, shaking her head. But he knew that was a knee-jerk response. She really needed to consider the possibilities. Maybe she would after he was gone. "I'm just going to do a quick perimeter check. You stay put."

"I—"

He didn't give her a chance to argue. He strode off, the stay-put order being not just for her but Willie as well.

He didn't expect to find anything. Once he got Dahlia situated, he'd head back to Truth, maybe with Palmer and Anna, and go over the things he'd seen, but he had to make sure all was good here first.

He walked around the side of the cabin. The backyard was a small patch of green. Trees created a kind of frame, and Ursula—the lady who kept the cabin—had colorful blooms in pots all over the back porch.

He studied the windows. There were blinds on them, but they weren't drawn. Right now it was too sunny to get a good look inside, but at night with the lights on, anyone would be able to see what Dahlia was doing.

Grant studied the small backyard, walked the perimeter of it and almost passed the small indentation in the scrubby grass. But then there was another one, where grass met a dusty patch of dirt. And then another—this one, clearly a footprint. Too big to be Dahlia's, or Ursula's for that matter.

Lawn care? Ursula's son? Grant studied each footprint, following its progress toward the house, crossing every potential culprit off the list. Ursula's son lived in Houston and hadn't visited since Christmas. God knew she told everyone who listened that little complaint. Ursula didn't hire out lawn services. She believed in handling things at her rental properties herself.

Grant came to a stop at the cabin. The footprints led right up to the structure on the side. There was a window right in front of him, and if he shaded his eyes to look inside, he could tell it was a bedroom.

Dahlia's bedroom.

Dread curled in his gut. Much like back in Truth, it could be a lot of things. Some Peeping Tom, a burglar, either potentially unrelated to Dahlia.

But they were problems, related or not.

Unfortunately, Grant was struggling to believe all this didn't connect. The timing was too suspect. Everything too…centered around her.

He finished his perimeter check, debating whether to tell Dahlia about the prints. Maybe he could just convince her to go home. Not mention…anything.

A frustrating line of thought. It wasn't his job to protect her feelings or assuage her fears. It was his job to get answers.

He made it back around to the front. She sat on the porch stair scratching Willie behind his ears. She looked up at Grant as he approached, her enjoyment of the dog going cold as their eyes met.

She stood.

Grant thought there was probably a gentle way to put it, but he didn't have it in him to find out. Not when her hair glittered in the sun, and those blue eyes looked at him with such distrust, made worse by the dark circles under her eyes.

"There are footprints leading up to that back window that looks into your bedroom."

"Footprints," she echoed.

"Not yours."

Her eyebrows furrowed, and she looked back at the cabin, then the world around them. "It could be the... the owner. The cleaning service. It could be..."

Grant wished he could agree, but he knew everyone who would have been walking around the cabin, and none of them had a size twelve military-style boot.

"Dahlia, I think you might be in danger."

GRANT'S WORDS DIDN'T make sense. Not when applied to her. So Dahlia laughed. It seemed the only possible reaction. "I'm not in any danger."

"Someone is watching you. If you don't think it could be someone looking out for you, it's someone who wants something else from you."

"I wasn't being followed. No one followed me."

"You're certain?"

But of course she wasn't. Not when he'd introduced the possibility she was in danger. Something had happened to Rose. Didn't that mean something could happen to her? All because Rose had started digging into the past. And then Dahlia had in order to find Rose. "How can I be certain of anything?"

Something on his face...softened. She certainly wouldn't call his expression kind or his demeanor gentle, but her words seemed to affect him. Some way.

"I don't think it's safe for you to stay here until we figure this out."

Dahlia looked behind her at the pretty little cabin. *Someone is watching you.* "Where would I go?" she said, though she hadn't precisely meant to say it out loud—certainly not as a question geared toward him.

"Why don't you grab your things and come to the ranch for a bit? We'll figure everything out."

"But…you're strangers."

He nodded. "Ones you hired to find your sister."

"Yes, to solve a cold case. Not to…protect me or whatever this is."

Any hint of that earlier softness hardened again. "Ms. Easton—"

"Oh, don't drawl 'Ms. Easton' at me. My name is Dahlia. I don't understand why you think I'm in danger. I don't understand—" she flung her arms up in the air "—any of this."

"Neither do I. That's why I think it'd be smart if you came to the ranch so we can go over your case piece by piece. Determine if there's a real threat."

"What's the other option?"

"Coincidence."

Dahlia huffed out a breath. "None of this feels like a coincidence."

"No, it doesn't. I believe that's my point. Still, we can't be sure until we investigate. Now, if you'd rather stay here—alone, unprotected and isolated—it's a free country. If you'd like to use the full services of HSS, you can pack up your things and follow me back to the ranch."

"I don't care for ultimatums."

"I don't care for interfering clients, but here we are."

When she glared at him, he winced a little. She wasn't sure why. Surely, he was being honest. He didn't seem like the kind of man who felt bad about a little honesty.

But he let out a sigh. "I apologize. You're free to do as you wish, Ms. Easton—*Dahlia*. I'm inviting you to the Hudson Ranch while we analyze the potential threat to you, but if you don't feel comfortable, you certainly can make your own decisions."

His businesslike voice meant to appease her was far worse than him calling her an interfering client.

"You could also go home. Trust us to—"

"No." Going home wasn't an option. Not until she had answers.

"Somehow I figured," he muttered, clearly disapproving of that response. "So? Stay or go?"

She needed more time to think. She needed sleep. She needed…help. That was why she'd come here. That was why she was planning on spending every last cent on finding Rose. Grant had been dismissive of her belief there was a cult connection, but he'd gone to Truth. Right away. He'd investigated.

It was more than anyone else had done.

"I just…" She shook her head and swallowed the words back down. Grant wasn't her friend or her confidant. He was her employee. A partner at best. He didn't need to hear about the emotional circles her brain was running in. "It shouldn't take me too long to pack."

He nodded firmly. "Good. I'll wait in the truck."

She nodded, grateful he wasn't trying to enter the cabin. He'd give her space, if not the opportunity to really figure this out.

She stepped inside the cabin. She hadn't had time to appreciate or enjoy it. Now it was tainted by the knowledge someone had been… In Grant's theory, someone had been watching her through her bedroom window.

She stepped into said bedroom and looked at the big window that overlooked the backyard. Pretty. Peaceful.

And someone had allegedly been standing right there. Watching her.

And she'd been clueless. She shuddered against the bolt of fear and unease, then turned to grab her things.

"I can't believe I'm doing this," she muttered to herself. It was insanity. A scam. Maybe she was about to meet her end just as Rose had. Because she was pretty sure on the Hudson Ranch she *could* just disappear. Still, she shoved the few belongings she'd taken out back into her suitcase.

Maybe she *should* go home. Maybe—

Grant was there—suddenly, silently. Like he could simply will himself to appear in her doorway without making any noise.

"Stay here. Lock the door. And whatever you do, don't open it up for anyone." Before she could say anything, he was gone, practically like he'd vanished. But not before she'd watched a gun appear in his hand like magic.

She stood there, suitcase in hand, and then the dog from before padded into the room. He plopped himself right in front of her like he was some kind of guard dog.

It was now clear in a way it hadn't been this whole time.

Dahlia had no idea what she'd gotten herself into.

CHAPTER FOUR

GRANT MOVED BACK OUTSIDE, hand on his weapon as he scanned the world around the little cabin.

Someone was out there. Not just *had* been out there, but was there right now. Watching. Maybe waiting.

He wasn't about to leave—with or without Dahlia— knowing someone might follow. Maybe Dahlia wasn't in immediate danger, because someone had been watching her for some time and nothing had happened, but there were no good reasons for being watched.

Grant took a second to look back at the cabin, grateful Dahlia hadn't followed and Willie had obeyed the order to stay put. Then Grant moved forward. He'd had that watched feeling when he'd been waiting in the truck, but that wouldn't have been enough for him to act.

Sometimes a soldier didn't fully leave behind that watched feeling. But he'd seen the flash of something in his rearview mirror. Just at the curve of the road. He wasn't going to go straight for it though. He was more tactical than that.

He didn't follow the length of the road, he moved through the yard, using the truck as a kind of cover, hoping to move around enough to get a different angle at the road and see beyond the curve without who or whatever he'd seen knowing.

He held his gun and moved silently and quickly, eyes trained on where he'd first seen the flash of something. As he moved up the slight rise of land at the edge of the yard, he saw it again.

A figure darting too quickly out of sight to tell much about. It could have been a man or a woman. No sense of coloring. Just a shadow—human—then gone.

Grant ran after it, determined to get some clue as to who was watching his client. He pushed away thoughts of strange twists of fate bringing him a case that connected to Truth and all he struggled to forget. He let the mechanics of the all-out run block all those thoughts. There was only one target: whoever was watching them.

But the figure had too much of a head start, and as he came to the curve of the road, he knew going any farther would leave Dahlia alone and too far out of his reach to help if someone else was involved or the runner doubled back.

Grant came to a stop, scanning the landscape. He scowled, and after one last look around and another minute to return his breathing to normal, he turned and walked back to the cabin. He kept his instincts honed to the world around him, but he knew in his gut whoever had been there was long gone.

It ate him up that he couldn't follow, but he'd need to get Ms. Easton somewhere safe first.

There was more to this whole thing than that woman had let on. Well, he'd give her the benefit of the doubt. Maybe she didn't know what she'd gotten herself into. Sometimes that happened, especially with cold cases that weren't quite as cold as people thought.

It did not ease his frustration any. He returned to the cabin, tested the door. She'd followed his instructions and locked it. At least she could follow directions sometimes.

He knocked and waited for her to answer. When she pulled the door open, Willie was still right next to her.

Grant crouched and gave the dog a scratch behind the ears. "Good dog," he murmured, then stood and studied Ms. Easton.

She was looking a little rough around the edges. He had enough sisters to know not to say that out loud. "I saw someone, probably whoever's been watching you, but unfortunately they were too far away to pursue safely. I think it's all the more reason for you to come stay at the ranch."

"Why would someone be watching me?"

He'd also worked with enough clients to know not to give them—particularly the nervous ones—all the possibilities. "Hard to say. We'll figure it out. Let's head on back to the ranch. Why don't I drive you?"

"I have a car." She gestured helplessly at it.

"I know. Let's just leave it here for the time being. A little misdirection."

"Misdirection," she echoed.

She was in some kind of shock maybe. He moved around her and grabbed the suitcase she'd had clutched in her hands when he'd first come in. "Come on," he said, gesturing her forward and then striding through the front door as if he had no doubt she'd follow.

But he did actually have a few doubts. He made it to the truck before he allowed himself to look over his shoulder. She was following, Willie at her side, but clearly not convinced this was the best course of action.

He got in the driver's seat and texted his sisters to get a room ready and be around so they could help Dahlia feel more comfortable about her stay. When she finally got into the passenger seat, Willie jumping over her lap and then scrambling into the back, Grant weighed his words.

"We're going to let the police and Ursula know that someone was poking around the cabin, watching through the windows. And everyone at Hudson Ranch will be on the lookout for anyone following you. We'll get to the bottom of it in no time."

Grant started the truck and pushed it into Drive.

"This sounds like a lot more than investigating a cold case."

"Cold cases sometimes warm up, Ms. Easton." While he wanted to write it off as some kind of Peeping Tom, the facts just didn't add up. "And when they do, we protect whoever is in the cross fire."

IT WAS PROBABLY supposed to be comforting, but Dahlia couldn't relax sitting in the passenger seat of Grant's truck. He kept those dark eyes trained on the road and his mouth in a firm, tense line.

Dahlia glanced behind her at the dog, who sat in the backseat panting happily.

If this was the *cross fire*, as Grant had so helpfully put it, she supposed it wasn't all bad. And she supposed if the cold case was warm, that meant—had to mean—they were on to something with Truth.

He retraced the route she'd taken this morning. From her cabin to the sprawling Wyoming ranch. She hadn't known real people lived like this. The Hudsons had to be loaded. She didn't know anything about ranching, but the sheer size of their operation had to cost a bundle. And while she knew she was paying for the Hudsons' services, she didn't think even that would fund all this. Even if they had a hundred cold cases they were solving for a fee.

Grant pulled the truck to a stop in front of the house.

"What about talking to the police?" she asked. Something about the house was so…inviting. Comforting. She had a hard time trusting it.

"Yeah, we'll take care of all of that at dinner." Grant got out of the truck, the dog bounding after him. Dahlia had no choice but to follow.

Grant was carrying her suitcase toward the house, and the dog ran off into the fields barking happily, and Dahlia could only scurry after Grant's long-legged strides.

"At dinner?"

"My oldest brother. He's Sunrise's sheriff. We'll tell him all about it at dinner. Just a forewarning though, whatever my brothers say about me and Truth, it isn't true."

She just stared at him. *Me and Truth.* Like he had some kind of deep dark secret about the place she was *sure* connected to her sister's disappearance.

He laughed, and that was something of a surprise in and of itself. Thus far, he'd been stern or overly polite. Not *amused.*

"I'm sorry," he said, and seemed genuinely apologetic. "Not in some scary I-was-in-a-cult way. Truth's been a ghost town since we were born. I think you can imagine what teenage boys do in ghost towns, but if you can't, they spend a lot of time trying to scare the tar out of each other."

"Oh."

He opened the front door and gestured her in. She

hesitated, because surely everything she was doing was silly. She could hear her father's voice in her head: *Everything too good to be true usually is.*

But Grant was inside with her things. He handed the suitcase off to Mary, who was apparently waiting for their arrival.

"I know the Meadowlark Cabin is so cute and a great place to relax," she said, reaching forward and taking Dahlia's arm. "But we've got a nice room for you, a private bathroom, and you'll be safe and sound until everyone can get to the bottom of everything."

And then Dahlia was being firmly maneuvered deeper into the gorgeous house. She glanced back at Grant, who was standing there still looking like that stern cowboy.

But he'd investigated. He'd warned her about someone watching her. And he'd laughed when telling her about teenage shenanigans.

Mary led her up a staircase. "This is sort of the guest wing," she explained. "So, you'll have privacy for the most part in this hallway, and there's an en suite bath in your room."

Before Dahlia could protest once again, Mary kept right on. "I know it likely feels strange to come stay at a stranger's house. But I just want you to know this isn't out of the ordinary for us. We've put up clients before. Sometimes it's easier to accomplish things if people are on the premises."

But this wasn't about accomplishing things. It was, allegedly, about keeping her safe.

Mary opened a door and gestured Dahlia inside. The room was spacious and beautiful. The walls a buttery yellow with floral prints. There were lace curtains over the big windows. The bed had that Western quality of somehow looking both feminine and inviting and big and sturdy.

"If there's anything I can do to put you at ease, if you want to have someone join you—your parents, a friend? There's no extra charge for that. There's a lock on the door, a phone in the room. Bathroom is through there with any toiletry you might need, but if not, ask. Think of it as a bed-and-breakfast."

"I'm not paying you for a bed-and-breakfast."

Mary smiled kindly. "You're paying us for a service. This is part of the service if it needs to be. Unpack. Relax. I'll come get you for dinner."

There was nothing to say. Mary was already gone, leaving Dahlia alone in this...truly perfect room.

She stepped to the window and pulled the lace curtain back, looking out over the ranch. Everything about it was beautiful. The grassland, the mountains in the distance, the buildings and fences that dotted the landscape looking both old and impeccable at the same time.

Rose would love it because it was generations and roots and legacy. She would be throwing herself into these people, what they knew and how they all connected.

But Dahlia wasn't her sister. She couldn't get past how wrong this all felt. No matter how genuine Mary seemed or how capable Grant *was*. She didn't belong in their home.

Someone *had* been watching her though, she couldn't deny that or be okay with it. She'd felt it at times and brushed it off. It irritated her that Grant didn't believe the connections she'd found, even as she understood why he'd be skeptical, but he *had* protected her and listened to her even when he didn't believe her.

She supposed there was something noble in what the Hudsons were doing, trying to solve cold cases. She'd picked them for not just their proximity to Truth but because the story on their website had been about their own parents' cold case.

Dahlia wanted to believe they cared because of that connection even if her own cynicism held her back sometimes, but this seemed too good to be true.

And her father had always warned her about that.

She sighed and stepped away from the window. She didn't unpack. She just…sat down on the bed and tried to get a handle on her roiling emotions.

The next thing she knew, someone was knocking at the door. She'd fallen asleep, clearly, though she didn't remember lying down. Drowsily, she got back up and realized outside the sun was starting to set.

Mary was at the door with that kind smile on her face. "Hungry?" she asked.

Dahlia didn't have a chance to respond before Mary was leading her out of the room, back down the stairs, through the living room she'd initially met Grant in and then to a whole new wing of the house.

She heard voices—raucous but pleasant—before she entered the room. Mary led her into the spacious dining room dominated by a long table and *lots* of people. The chairs at the table were nearly all full. Grant and three carbon copies of him, a woman who was currently arguing loudly with one of them and then a girl not more than ten or eleven who was feeding scraps to the three dogs patiently waiting under the table.

The table itself had a huge family-style meal, bowls

and platters overflowing with food. It looked like Christmas or some big family celebration, but Dahlia could tell by the way they acted, it was just the norm for them.

Mary gave her arm a little tug and then gestured her to a seat. "Dahlia, this is everyone," she said, as the voices around the table quieted. "We've got the brothers Jack, Cash, Palmer, and you know Grant. My sister Anna. Cash's daughter Izzy. Don't bother trying to remember all the dogs' names. Half of them look alike, and they're all running around constantly. Now, you sit right here and help yourself."

Dahlia was already overwhelmed, and she wasn't sure she'd caught any of those names. None of this felt... right. She cleared her throat and did not sit down. "I do appreciate this. I really do. But I shouldn't be interrupting your family dinner. I'm not paying for room and board. I'm—"

"We charge for work. That's honest," Jack said, with a firm nod. "We don't charge for hospitality—not when we've got plenty to spare. Now, sit and eat up. You need it."

Dahlia didn't know how to argue with that, particularly coming from a stony-faced man who looked even more like a cowboy out of an old Western than Grant did, complete with shiny star badge pinned to his shirt.

Dahlia slowly sank into the seat. Grant himself put a heaping pile of mashed potatoes on her plate before passing them along to Mary next to her.

He gave her a reassuring nod. "I'd advise you listen. No one argues with Jack's hard head and wins."

So Dahlia did just that.

CHAPTER FIVE

GRANT HADN'T SLEPT WELL. He'd gone over Dahlia Easton's case again and again, adding his own experiences, and felt no closer to a lead than he had when the Peeping Tom, or whoever was watching her, got away.

He wanted to prove that Eugene Green and Truth had nothing to do with her sister's disappearance, but no matter how little he *thought* they connected, he hadn't found a way to prove they didn't.

And that bothered him.

Still, he was up at dawn with his brothers to handle the necessary ranch chores. Some things they hired out, but the brothers always met in the mornings to handle a few jobs like all the Hudsons had since they'd arrived in Sunrise over a hundred years ago.

He met them at the stables, same as every morning since they'd been kids. But only Palmer and Cash were there.

"Where's Jack?"

"Went in early," Palmer said, pulling his hat lower on his head against the rising sun. He looked like he'd been out late last night, probably drinking, but Grant said nothing about that, as he was already in a terrible mood.

"Said he was going to take pictures of those footprints and write up a report. Have one of his deputies check around, see if anyone's seen anything suspicious," Cash added.

"That's good." Grant envied him. It was an actionable step to take. Take a report. Collect evidence. *Do* something instead of read the same reports over and over again.

"She's a looker," Palmer offered.

Grant could have pretended he didn't know who his brother was talking about, but he didn't see the point. "She's a client," Grant replied irritably. And sure, pretty as a spring day. But she was barking up all kinds of wrong trees.

Case in point: Eugene Green. "Cash, you looked at the file?"

Cash nodded in assent as they all got up on the horses. They didn't have to talk about what they were doing today. Jack kept a strict calendar and schedule, and he always made sure everyone knew what their role for the day was.

"What do you make of this attempt at a Eugene Green connection?"

"Well." Cash took his time responding as their horses walked side by side through the cool, pretty morning. "The security picture she's got is grainy at best, but you can't discount some similarities to Eugene Green."

"The guy was a lunatic. He could have had kids all over the country," Palmer added.

"Ones that wouldn't necessarily know a thing about him," Cash pointed out.

"It could also be a coincidence," Grant said. "Reaching."

"Could," Cash replied, and once again let silence settle over them. Because Cash was never in a hurry. He took his time to draw any conclusions. "But it's not the only connection to Eugene Green. The missing sister was all up in these DNA tests and whatever."

"Can't those things be wrong?" Palmer asked.

"Anything can be wrong. But it could just as easily be right." Cash looked over at Grant and shrugged. "I know you want to. I get why. But we can't discount the facts."

"I'll take over this one if you want." Palmer flashed a grin. "I'd take Red *very* seriously."

Grant didn't know why that comment set his teeth on edge. His brother was forever saying things like that and making his way through the female population of Sunrise and just about every surrounding area. And somehow, he hadn't ticked off the wrong woman yet.

"Take her over to Mrs. Riley this morning. She'd know all about the Green family tree and all that. More than any DNA ancestry site or just about anyone else. I know you don't *want* it to connect to Truth, but we all know how cold cases like this go. Any little connection can lead you to a bigger one."

It was a solid idea and an honest lecture. Grant didn't care for either from his little brother. "Maybe *you* should take over the case?"

Cash looked wistful for a fraction of a second before he was shaking his head and nudging his horse in the other direction. "Gotta get Izzy off to school. Then I'll be working with the dogs. Call if you need anything."

"Dumb thing to say," Palmer muttered once Cash was out of earshot.

"Well, he should take some cases. He can't *never* leave the ranch just because he's got a daughter."

"His choice," Palmer replied.

Because when push came to shove, the two younger brothers tended to stick together. And Grant didn't have Jack here to be on *his* side, though no doubt Jack would be.

So Grant worked with Palmer in mostly silence until breakfast time, then broke off and headed back to the house. Cash's suggestion was a good one. He'd take Dahlia over to the library today and maybe stop by the sheriff's department and check on things.

It wasn't going to connect to Eugene Green. It probably wasn't going to connect to anything. But for all of Dahlia Easton's more…fragile tendencies, she was determined to see this through. Stubborn, no doubt.

So, if nothing else, he had to *disprove* a theory that was going to lead her on a wild-goose chase. And maybe Cash was right and they could find some bigger more plausible thread to tug.

He couldn't help but think of the way she'd clearly been so lost and overwhelmed at dinner last night. He couldn't blame her—the Hudson clan could be overwhelming even when you were one of them—but he knew in part it was hard for her, because they were a family, and she was missing a piece of hers.

But so were they. And had been since their parents had gone missing all those years ago. He should have said something about it, should have made the connection to her so she might have felt some…sliver of comfort.

But he'd just filled up her plate and watched to make sure she ate and then let Mary handle things from there.

He was the investigator, and his job was to find answers. Even knowing there might never be any answers to give.

He got to the stables and took care of his horse before walking back to the house. He saw a figure sitting on the side porch and realized that flash of red meant it wasn't his family or a ranch hand but the woman in question.

He walked toward her, though there was an odd, errant bolt of a thought that told him he should turn around. Go anywhere but forward. But that made absolutely no sense, so he walked forward. To the porch, to Dahlia.

She sat on the little rocking chair his grandmother had liked to do her knitting on in the summer. In the here and now, Dahlia had a mug of coffee cupped between her hands. Her red hair whipped around in the breeze, and she watched him approach with careful eyes.

She looked exactly right there, like she'd been born to sit on his porch and wait for him to arrive. Which was the strangest damn thought he'd ever had, perhaps, in his entire life and left him completely mute.

She didn't say anything either. For a lot longer than made sense. Eventually she broke the silence.

"I expected a *howdy* maybe."

His mouth quirked. "Fresh out." His voice sounded gruffer than it should have, so he cleared his throat. "The library in town has all sorts of things on Truth, as does the genealogy society, which has an office in the library. Why don't we eat breakfast and head over? We'll stop by the sheriff's department, see if they've found anything about the guy watching you."

She didn't say anything to that, just kept watching him with those careful eyes. Wary.

He didn't have any right to be frustrated, but it bothered him all the same. For reasons he couldn't begin to sort out. "It must be hard to trust perfect strangers, even if you are paying them. Doesn't hurt my feelings. But I do know things would be easier if you'd give us a chance."

"I'm here, aren't I?"

"You are. And just about always looking for the rattlesnake to strike." He could understand it and still be frustrated by it. Apparently that was going to be his predominant feeling around Dahlia.

But the breeze teased the red waves of her hair, and her blue eyes held his in an eerie silence that settled over him like a touch.

Okay, maybe not the *predominant feeling.*

Then she blinked and gave a little nod. "You're not the enemy is what you're getting at, and treating you like one probably doesn't move the needle any closer to finding answers."

"That's a good way of putting it."

"I've been looking for help for a year. Someone, anyone to take me or Rose seriously. Even my parents don't."

He thought she might break at the mention of her parents. She looked on the cusp of tears and Grant wanted to back away from *that*. She straightened her shoulders though. Blinked back the tears.

"I've been fighting *everyone* for answers. Even the people who've helped… It only lasts for so long. At a certain point, you can only depend on yourself."

He hadn't expected her words to cut him off at the knees, but they did. Because he knew that feeling. Was so well acquainted with it, it had helped build HSS—the fact that, eventually, he and his siblings hadn't had anyone else to lean on. They'd learned that when faced with something difficult, they could only trust themselves.

But he had his siblings. He had family and roots, and Dahlia Easton didn't seem to have much of anything.

"At a certain point, I hope you feel like you can depend on us, but even if you never feel that way, we'll see this through. That's a promise."

She looked down at her coffee. He wasn't sure it was disagreement or just feeling overwhelmed, but she didn't lift her gaze again when she spoke. "When do we go to this library?"

DAHLIA HADN'T WANTED to eat breakfast. She'd slept better last night than she had since she'd left Minnesota, but her stomach still roiled and made it hard to feel like eating—even if last night's dinner had been delicious.

Still, much like last night, somehow Grant maneuvered her into eating a small plate of eggs and toast. And, though she didn't plan on admitting out loud to anyone, it did make her feel sturdier. More like she was capable of surviving this strange new world she found herself in.

Maybe—she could admit in the privacy of her own head—she hadn't been taking care of herself very well. Maybe she needed to if she was going to actually get to the bottom of Rose's disappearance.

Then she'd had to go out with Grant and climb into his big intimidating truck, this time without her dog friend as company. She did have Rose's binder replicas though, and she clutched them too hard as Grant drove them into town.

"Do you think your library will have something my sister didn't?"

"It's possible. Not everything's on the internet, especially when it comes to a small town like Sunrise, and it seems as though Rose didn't make a connection to Wyoming until she got to Texas, right?"

"As far as I know."

"So, she didn't make it here. Which means there might be records or clues into the family connection that might lead us to an answer."

He didn't believe it was Truth or Eugene Green. She kept telling herself it didn't matter. People believing her hadn't mattered this whole time, so why should it start now?

But she found herself wanting to explain to him until he agreed with her. Luckily, she'd learned when to keep her mouth shut, even when she didn't want to. Maybe her parents had taught her something worthwhile after all.

He didn't try to fill the silence as he drove—off the sprawling Hudson Ranch and toward the town of Sunrise.

It was beautiful. The whole area—ranch or driving or even the cute little western town. Dahlia had always planned on visiting the West at some point. Make it out to Yellowstone or even Colorado, but school and then work had taken up most of her time, and when she finally went on vacations, it was always with Rose, who preferred cities or old museums on the East Coast.

But there was something so open and vast about Wyoming. Sunrise was just a postage stamp of a town that clustered around the main thoroughfare. And in the distance, craggy peaks that felt intimidating or awe-inspiring depending on the moment.

Grant pulled his truck into a parking spot in front of

a squat stone building that didn't look like much, except old. But as they got up and walked to the door, Dahlia noted the little details that made it special. Impressive little cornices shaped like books. Tiny books carved into the wood frame around the door. She followed Grant inside. Small, definitely, but…warm. Inviting. So much more so than the new, more industrial-like building her library was housed in back home.

The woman behind the desk looked up, then straightened a little as if she recognized Grant. When she flashed him a smile, Dahlia was *sure* she recognized him.

"Hi there, Freya," he offered somewhat absently, like he didn't notice the woman brighten the minute she laid eyes on him.

"Morning, Grant." Her eyes flicked to Dahlia, and the smile dimmed a little. But she held firm. "Here for work?"

Grant nodded, then gestured at Dahlia. "This is Ms. Easton."

"Hi," Freya offered, and though she was definitely speculating about some things based on the way she gave Dahlia a once-over, Dahlia didn't feel any animosity. Exactly.

"Is Mrs. Riley in?"

"Just like always," Freya said, trying to share a conspiratorial eye roll with Grant, but Dahlia watched him miss it, as he was already looking deeper into the library, presumably for Mrs. Riley.

"Thanks," he said, not giving poor Freya a second look. Dahlia moved to follow Grant, but something about Freya's crestfallen expression made her stop.

"I love what you've done with this place. It's so inviting. I'm a librarian in Minnesota, and everything is so...bureaucratic. I can't make any choices about decor without like three people writing off on it."

"Oh well. Probably a little bigger than this, huh?" Freya sounded wistful again.

"But not nearly as special."

The corner of Freya's mouth tugged up, and she looked around as if seeing the library with new eyes. "Thanks. It really is cozy, isn't it?"

"I love it." She smiled and then followed Grant, who was waiting by a door with a somewhat impatient frown on his face.

Once she approached, he knocked on the door.

Dahlia felt like she should probably keep her mouth shut, but Grant seemed totally ignorant. "She likes you."

He frowned at her, then over at Freya. "She dated my brother."

Well, that did change things, Dahlia supposed. She glanced back at Freya. "Well, regardless of what she *did*, she's currently very into *you*."

Grant grunted and said nothing more as the door opened to an older woman. She looked at Grant, then Dahlia.

"Your turn, huh?" the woman said to Grant.

He nodded. "Mrs. Riley, this is Dahlia Easton. Ms. Easton, this is Mrs. Riley. She runs the historical society, the genealogical society and knows just about everything about the history of Sunrise."

Mrs. Riley eyed Dahlia with some suspicion. Dahlia wondered if this was the small-town distrust of outsiders she'd read about but never experienced.

"Come on in then." She waved them into the cramped room. Shelves lined two walls filled with labeled binders and boxes. She had a little table in the middle of the room—also filled with stacks of folders, books and binders. Then the two chairs in the room were filled with stacks as well.

"So, what are you wanting to know?"

"I'd like to ask for your discretion before we show you anything," Grant said.

Mrs. Riley grinned, a flash of a woman with *some* sense of humor. "You can ask."

Grant sighed but didn't argue with her. "Ms. Easton's sister was tracing her family tree when she disappeared over a year ago. Ms. Easton found some…loose connections to Sunrise and—"

"Not to Sunrise," Dahlia interrupted. "To Truth. To the Greens."

Grant closed his eyes as if in pain. Mrs. Riley's bland expression went into a furious scowl, but Dahlia paid no heed. She took her binder, opened it to the page that had led her here and handed it to Mrs. Riley.

The woman looked at the page, then back at Dahlia, eyes narrowed as she pointed to the section on the Greens. "How'd you find out about this?"

"Wait. *You* know about this Texas connection?" Grant asked Mrs. Riley.

"Of course I do," the woman replied with a sniff. "I made sure I knew every last inch of that family so they could never hurt mine again." Then her gaze turned to Dahlia, and it was *cold*. "Guess you're one of them."

"It's a loose connection at best," Dahlia replied, but that didn't win her any favors.

"*Loose* wouldn't matter to the Greens." Mrs. Riley tapped her bright pink fingernails on the book. "The cult was big into blood ties and rituals. He'd have known his tree backward and forward. He'd have known about *you*. Which is why I asked, how'd you know about this?"

"I didn't. My sister did research and took a DNA test." *And disappeared.*

"Eugene Green is dead, Mrs. Riley. We all know that," Grant said, as if he said it firmly enough, this woman would simply have to accept it.

Mrs. Riley huffed. "Maybe. Maybe not. There're rumors, and some of them connect to Texas."

Grant muttered something that sounded like "God save me from conspiracy theories," but Mrs. Riley didn't seem to catch it.

She turned away from the binder Dahlia held out. "I don't need any Greens hanging around *my* office."

"You're not—" But Grant didn't finish the sentence. Mrs. Riley folded her arms across her chest and just glared.

It wasn't exactly a dead end, Dahlia assured herself as she followed Grant out of the small office. If Mrs. Riley knew about conspiracy theories that connected to an alive Eugene Green in Texas, there was a chance someone else in town knew about it.

She waved at Freya as they passed, and Grant gave the woman an absent nod at best before they stepped back into the pretty fall morning.

"I'm sorry about that. I did *not* see that coming, but I should have."

"It's not a big deal."

"It is to me. It isn't right to hold people accountable for some random offshoot of a family you didn't even know about." He sounded strangely vehement. Like he'd…maybe dealt with similar before.

"It isn't right my sister is gone," Dahlia said gently. "The world doesn't work on what's right."

He grunted, clearly not loving that answer. What must it be like to be a man who went through life thinking he could make everything right simply through sheer force of will?

"The sheriff's department is just down the street. How about a walk?"

Dahlia thought he made the suggestion for himself. He was a contained man, but frustrated energy pumped off him. So she agreed and fell into step beside him as they walked down the sidewalk.

She still clutched the binder to her chest. She looked down at it, then at the frustrated man next to her.

"It isn't about me. Mrs. Riley being upset. It's about her…life. I don't know what the Greens did to her, I don't need to know in order to understand."

"That's very generous of you," Grant replied. He looked down at her, and something in his expression softened. "You want it to be a lead, but they're just stories. And Mrs. Riley is going to tell *everyone*, so it's going to be all stories and conspiracy theories. I think there's one about aliens? It's going to get ridiculous, and I just want you to understand these aren't leads. If there was any truth to all the stories that fly around about Truth and the Greens, the authorities would have found that out a long time ago. It's not hope. Trust me, I have been there, and all it does is prolong the pain."

She wanted to bristle, but she heard a world of experience in his words. He had been there, she knew, because they had the story of their parents' disappearance on their website. They promised dedication and hard work because they knew what not having answers felt like.

Still felt like.

"How does it not eat you alive?" she asked, her voice a mere whisper. She knew she shouldn't ask. It wasn't polite, and what's more, she was almost certain she'd hate the answer.

"It's always eating you alive," Grant replied softly. "You just have to do other things while it does."

Which was *dire* and not at all hopeful. "Forever?"

"If it's forever." He glanced at her. All dark-eyed intensity. But also…a pain under it all. She supposed it drove him—all of them. She'd only been missing her sister a year. They'd been missing their parents for over a decade.

"So, you still have hope for your parents?" she asked, *had* to. Because it seemed hope was the source of the pain, but Dahlia knew it was also the source of everything that kept *her* going. Did that die at some point? Would she be left with…nothing?

"I wish I didn't," he said, looking away, jaw clenched. Unknown years of pain in every syllable of those words.

"That's not a no."

He stopped in front of a door and hesitated, which didn't seem to fit the man at all. But in the end, he didn't respond to her. He gestured at the door that read *Sunrise Sheriff's Department*.

"Come on. Let's go talk to my brother."

CHAPTER SIX

JACK HAD FOUND the footprints at the rental cabin, and he had a deputy working on questioning anyone who might have been around the Meadowlark Cabin while Dahlia had been there. There were no clear answers on who might be watching her. Unfortunately, it wasn't looking good they'd find any, unless they caught the watcher in the act in the future.

Grant didn't like it. The idea she might be in danger and the idea the woman who was stirring up Truth talk would be under his roof for the foreseeable future.

But she'd answered Jack's questions carefully and concisely. She'd asked a few of her own about what she should be doing to keep herself safe.

She seemed to be in better shape than she had yesterday, and he didn't know why that gave him some odd sense of satisfaction. Like he'd had anything to do with it, even if he *had* all but tricked her into eating breakfast this morning.

After Jack was satisfied, Grant drove Dahlia back to the ranch in silence. He'd give her credit, she didn't seem to mind the silence. It settled over them easily enough. He supposed they were both lost in their own thoughts, worries. Hopes.

He scowled at the road in front of him. He didn't

allow himself to think much on *hope*. He focused on reality. Facts. Probability.

In all *likelihood*, his parents were long dead. If they weren't, it still wasn't a *good* story. But no matter how his brain told him those things, over and over again since he'd been a teenager, his heart still wanted a different outcome.

Which was damn foolish.

He pulled the truck in front of the house. He wasn't sure what to do with Dahlia. Usually when he investigated a case, the person looking for answers wasn't his responsibility to cart around.

Maybe he'd dump her on Mary while he tried to figure out what the next step would be to get ahead of all the Truth gossip.

When Dahlia got out of the car, Grant heard the yip of a dog. Willie came racing around the corner and zoomed straight for Dahlia. Jumping and yapping happily as if they were long-lost loves.

Dahlia knelt and accepted the dog's excited kisses while she rubbed him down. "There's my hero."

Something uncomfortable and unacceptable tangled low in his gut as she smiled at the dog. For a second, her worries had lifted, and he wished with an intensity the situation didn't warrant he could give her that kind of happiness long term.

But some cold cases were never solved, as he well knew.

That's not a no.

He *knew* his parents were dead. Knew it.

Palmer appeared on the porch. "Good. You're home. I've got something to show you." He glanced at Dahlia. "You and Willie can come too, Ms. Easton."

Her smile faded as she stood. "I suppose that means it's about me."

Palmer shrugged apologetically, then waved them to follow. Not through the house but around it, back where Willie had run from. Grant walked toward the fence that wrapped around the front and back yards— more for decoration and land demarcation rather than keeping the animals in one place or the usual functional ranch fences.

As they walked, Willie kept right next to Dahlia. She seemed to relax around the dog, so Grant made a mental note to see if Cash would let Willie stick around the main house until they figured out if Dahlia was safe.

"Are you the brother the librarian dated?" Dahlia asked as they walked.

Palmer looked back at Grant with raised eyebrows. "Freya? Yeah, we went out a few times a few years ago."

Dahlia frowned at him, as if she objected to his term *date* when explained in that way. But she didn't know Palmer. A few dates *was* about as close to a relationship as he ever got.

"So, it was nothing serious for Grant to worry about," Dahlia continued.

"Grant?" Palmer laughed. "She's always had a thing for Grant. Long before she went out with me, but he doesn't date local women." Palmer grinned at him over Dahlia's head. "Or much at all. Everyone knows that. Including Freya."

"I'm glad we can discuss everyone's private life so openly, but I'd prefer to focus on the case." Grant didn't shove his hands into his pockets like he wanted or hunch his shoulders. He remained passive. Blank.

Palmer jerked a thumb in Grant's direction but leaned

down to stage-whisper conspiratorially to Dahlia. "All work, no play, this one."

Grant didn't like the serious bolt of anger and frustration that shot through him when Palmer was just being Palmer. Trying to get a rise out of him. It wasn't anything Grant hadn't heard before.

Dahlia smiled a little at Palmer's quip, but she didn't quite jump in as Palmer likely hoped or Grant expected.

"I suppose it's important work," she said instead.

Palmer rolled his eyes but stopped at the fence line around the front yard. "Found some footprints. Not any of ours and shouldn't be a ranch hand's." He glanced at Dahlia and tried to smile reassuringly. "Doesn't mean they're not, of course."

Grant wanted to swear, but he held it in. All the tension that had gone out of her shoulders at Willie's arrival was back.

"I don't really understand this," she said, looking at the clear set of footprints in the mud.

"Did you call Jack?" Grant asked.

Palmer nodded. "Took some pictures and sent them over. Deputies are all tied up, but they'll be by eventually. Haven't told Cash yet. He's going to flip."

"Why?" Dahlia asked, directing the question at him rather than Palmer.

"Cash...worries," Grant said, trying for diplomacy. "Izzy likes to wander."

"The daughter," Dahlia said, chewing on her bottom lip. "Should I not stay here? I don't want to bring trouble to your door. That isn't—"

"We can handle it," Grant assured her. "You've got the sheriff living on the premises, along with trained investigative professionals. We have a great security system, which Palmer can assure you is some of the best."

"I make sure of it. Plus, this guy here is a war hero."

Dahlia's eyes widened as she turned to him again. "War hero?"

Grant tried not to react to the term. He hated it. He hadn't done anything special—except survive when a lot of men hadn't. "I was a Marine. Doesn't make me a war hero."

"That's not what the paper said when he came home."

"Can we focus on the task at hand?" Grant said, failing at keeping the snap out of his tone. "Dahlia, I'd like you to go inside. I'm going to look around and see what else I can find."

She frowned at that, then looked down at Willie sitting next to her. "I'd like to look too. I feel like…" She struggled over whatever she wanted her next words to be. "I just want to know what I should keep an eye out for. Does that make sense?"

Grant exchanged a look with Palmer. He didn't really want Dahlia tagging along, but it was hard to refuse someone who wanted to learn in order to protect themselves.

"I'll go break the news to Cash before he hears it through the grapevine. Text if you find anything else. Jack will call Mary when they've got a deputy on the way, but it won't hurt to have it checked out before they get there."

"All right. Tell Cash we're keeping Willie with us for the time being."

"Will do." With that, Palmer left, and Grant had to decide how best to handle a woman and a dog when he'd much prefer to search alone.

"Grant, I really don't understand why someone would be watching me."

"Neither do I, which is why we're going to get to the bottom of it. We're going to see how far we can follow these footprints." He looked the way the footprints were pointing. There was no clear glimpse *into* the house from here, but that didn't mean they hadn't searched for other places. "Now, make sure you follow me. We don't want a bunch of extra prints. We want the police to know exactly what they're looking at."

Dahlia nodded solemnly. "What about Willie?"

"Willie knows how to follow orders."

"Oh."

Grant studied the footprints, then hopped the fence a good few feet away so he wouldn't disturb them. Willie wriggled under the bottom rung, but Dahlia stood there looking unsure.

She was dressed in jeans and tennis shoes and a winter coat, and the fence was low and easy to climb over, so he wasn't sure what held her back. "Do you need help?"

"No." But she looked so unsure as she awkwardly maneuvered over the fence. Grant took a step toward her as if to steady her. But she got on the other side without tripping or toppling over.

She offered him a rueful smile. "I'm not very athletic." She steadied herself on the fence instead of his outstretched hand. "I can follow directions though."

He thought about yesterday when she'd gone off to Truth by herself. He supposed he hadn't directed her *not* to, but it didn't exactly speak to compliance.

Still, he gestured her forward, because she definitely deserved to know what to be on the lookout for when she was the target.

DAHLIA FOLLOWED GRANT, though her tennis shoes weren't holding up very well against the mud they tramped through. But it was a fairly good landscape to see footprints in.

Or so said Grant. He pointed to little marks, indentations and holes and actual outlines she could see. There were paw prints and other signs of animal activity. He explained each of them to her patiently and as if it were important information to know.

She supposed for him it was. So she listened and filed away what she could. But she'd never been an outdoorsy person. She preferred books and being able to control the temperature of the room she was in.

They walked and walked, and every once in a while, Grant would stop, crouch, study another print. When they were human, or he thought they were, he pulled out his phone and took a picture.

Willie followed along, right beside her, never darting off, though sometimes he would stop, sniff and let out a faint *woof.*

Dahlia had always wanted a dog, but her father and Rose had been allergic, and then when she'd finally moved out at Rose's insistence, her apartment hadn't allowed pets. She should think about getting one in the future, but she couldn't seem to see a future anymore.

There was just finding Rose or finding out what had happened to her. Everything else was…not important.

So she walked with Grant. In silence. Dahlia didn't usually mind that, but the conversation with Palmer had given little glimpses into Grant the man. Which she supposed was none of her business, but she was staying under their roof for the time being. They were helping her.

Why not know more?

"So, Jack is law enforcement, Cash handles the dogs, and Palmer is the security. Mary does all the administrative work, but what do you and your other sister specialize in?"

"Anna is a private investigator. She likes the flexibility of going off and working for herself when she needs to."

He did not answer in regard to himself. When she slid in a little mud, he immediately reached out and grabbed her arm, helping her stay upright. Once she was, he immediately dropped it and kept on walking.

"And you?" she pressed. It wasn't usual for her to press, but something about this man's tight-lipped nature made her want to.

He shrugged, knelt and studied another print. "I fill in where needed."

"Jack of all trades?"

"Guess so. They all started this when I was still deployed, and they weren't sure when I'd be coming home. This is animal," he said, standing again and then moving forward.

There was something about the way he said *deployed*, devoid of just enough emotion to make her curious. He didn't sound bitter or resentful, but there was a tenseness to him when he or Palmer spoke of his military career.

She thought military made perfect sense. He was so…large. So self-possessed. It wasn't hard at all to imagine him in military camo holding one of those big intimidating weapons. If that was what Marines did. She didn't know.

But Palmer had called him a war hero.

"Where were you dep—"

"Look, it's not interesting. The military is the military. I didn't do anything special. I'm not a hero. I joined the Marines at eighteen. I did my time, went on a few deployments, did as I was told, watched out for my brothers and when my final time was up, I came home. Beginning and end of story."

Dahlia didn't argue with him, though she inexplicably wanted to. She couldn't imagine being any kind of soldier, away from home, in this weird system of guns and violence and war. So it *was* kind of interesting... intriguing. Courageous.

But she could also imagine why he might not want to talk about it. So she bit her tongue and kept following Grant, Willie happily trotting beside her.

The next time Grant crouched at a print, even Dahlia could see it was a footprint. They were more toward the back of the house now. If she put her feet where the prints were, she'd be looking at the back window.

She studied the house, trying not to let the fear take over like it had yesterday. But that was the window to the room she was staying in. Not that whoever stood here would be able to see in, but after yesterday, everything about this felt ominous and terrible.

"Both of these full prints are very similar to the one outside the cabin yesterday," Grant said, taking pictures from different angles. "Which leads me to believe it's the same person."

Dahlia nodded. Same person. Someone was...stalking her, basically. And as she wasn't interesting and hadn't made any enemies in her life, there seemed to be only one logical conclusion.

"If someone..." She struggled with the next word,

emotionally and being able to say it past all that emotion. "If someone murdered Rose, they wouldn't want people poking around her disappearance, would they?"

She thought she might surprise him with the question, but he only looked grim. Like it had already crossed his mind. Like he already believed it.

A shudder of worry went through her. Her parents had warned her she was getting in over her head. Were they right?

"It's only one theory," Grant said gently, but she knew just by the fact he was *being* gentle, it was the most logical one.

"Even if it's true, even if she's dead, I can't give up. I have to find out what happened."

"Even if it puts you in danger?"

Dahlia looked from the footprint to the mountains in the distance. Such a pretty place, and someone out there was watching her. But they hadn't done anything to hurt her.

The *yet* seemed to hang in the air around her.

"I can't live with myself if I go back home. If I put it all away. I just can't." She met Grant's direct brown gaze. Maybe he didn't understand or couldn't, but maybe she didn't need anyone to understand except herself. "I'd rather risk something than try to live under the weight of not doing anything."

For a moment they stood there staring at each other in a grave silence. Then, finally, he nodded. "Let's go inside and update Jack and talk to Palmer about increasing some security measures."

CHAPTER SEVEN

GRANT MADE SURE Dahlia got back to her room, Willie in tow, then had his usual afternoon meeting with his siblings.

They discussed increased security, which wasn't the first time. Cold cases were often just that, cold, and came with no immediate danger, but they'd found themselves in a few questionable situations before, which had led Mary to develop a coding system, just like security threat levels.

Today, they moved the ranch's security level from green to yellow.

Of course, this meant that Cash was missing from the HSS meeting, as he likely wouldn't let Izzy out of their remote cabin for the foreseeable future. Mary and Anna thought it was a travesty, but Grant figured none of the rest of them were parents, so they didn't really get a say in how Cash decided to keep his child safe.

"It has to be an out-of-towner," Jack said, clearly frustrated neither he nor his deputies had come up with any leads yet. "Maybe someone followed her."

Grant had gone through the same reasonings. Tried to convince himself this had nothing to do with Sunrise or, worse, Truth.

But there was absolutely no evidence to the contrary.

"Someone had been at Truth. Before she got here.

That shell casing I found wasn't old, but it wasn't brand new."

"Kids," Jack scoffed.

"I want to believe that too."

"Look, if *Grant* is willing to consider the possibility of Truth being involved, I'd say that's some damning evidence right there," Anna put in.

"I'm not saying Truth is actually involved." Though Grant realized with every passing step in this investigation, he had a harder time dismissing it out of hand. "I'm saying someone has been hanging out in Truth lately. I'm saying Dahlia's being followed only after making the connection to her family history and Truth."

Grant looked at his older brother, whose expression gave nothing away.

Jack had taken care of them since the moment their parents had disappeared. He'd kept the ranch going, made sure they did their homework and were fed and became responsible adults. Even though Grant had been sixteen himself, in a lot of ways, Jack had stepped into the role of father despite the small two-year age difference between them.

Grant had done everything he could to earn Jack's approval, and it was hard now not to wither under his older brother's stare. But these were facts.

"My deputies will keep asking questions," Jack said. "If she feels comfortable, I think it's best if she stays here until we get to the bottom of it."

"I agree," Grant said with a nod. "I think she will too, depending on how long it takes. But she's pretty determined to get to the bottom of what happened to her sister, even if it's bad news."

For a moment they were all silent because they knew

that even when you were determined, even when you never gave up, sometimes answers never materialized.

"I could post a deputy out here tonight. Be on the lookout for someone."

"If Palmer and Anna are good with it, I think we should just take turns in house. We'll have a better sense of who should be coming and going anyway."

"It's a big ranch."

"It is. But we all know nothing is getting by Cash as long as Izzy is there. We've got the cameras at the entry points. We stay up and watch them, maybe we can catch this guy."

"He's not setting the cameras off with movement," Palmer said. "I can change from motion-induced to twenty-four seven surveillance, but we'll have to up the security budget for the month."

"All in favor?" Jack asked, because he ran the business like a democracy even when he'd rather be dictator.

But wouldn't they all?

Everyone raised their hands, and Mary noted down the agreement so she could handle the funds. They tackled some other admin details, but Dahlia was their sole client right now, and with an active threat against her, it was hard to think about much else.

They ended the meeting and parted ways to go handle their individual jobs or chores. Grant *wanted* to throw himself into ranch work, but instead he settled in the big armchair in the office and went through Dahlia's binder all over again.

Eugene Green. Grant didn't for a second believe conspiracy theories. The man was dead, and the picture Dahlia had that *resembled* Eugene Green was grainy and fuzzy at best.

But she didn't think it *was* Eugene Green. She had said it could be someone that *looked* like him.

Grant flipped to the family tree again. Dahlia's family was an offshoot of what appeared to be a very normal branch that hadn't ever settled in Wyoming but had gone down to Texas. Before Dahlia had been born, her father had gone to college in the Midwest and married a native Minnesotan, which is how she and her sister had ended up there.

He looked at the picture again. The woman identified as Rose Easton was just as grainy as the man, and the picture was black and white. There was a resemblance, he supposed, somewhere around the mouth and nose, between the woman and Dahlia. The resemblance between this man and Eugene Green as a young man easier to see.

But nothing about it was concrete, and Grant preferred to deal in concretes.

How was he going to find one?

He had to put it aside for dinner. One of the strictest family rules was everyone made it to dinner unless they had a *really* good excuse. Dahlia was already there when he entered the dining room. She still looked uncomfortable, but Willie was curled up behind her chair, and she was listening to Anna talk animatedly at her.

He took the seat next to her, and she offered a small smile as Anna continued to chatter and Mary brought out the food. It was the same kind of dinner as last night, except Cash, Izzy and a lot of the other dogs were missing. Dahlia was still quiet, but who could blame her with Anna and Palmer dominating the conversation like they usually did.

When they were done with dinner, he felt like he

should say something to her about the fact that following the Eugene Green theory might lead them in the opposite direction, about the plans to keep her safe, so she could sleep tonight.

But in the end, she seemed content to talk to Mary and pet Willie, so Grant escaped the dining room with Palmer and went to their little security center—a small room on the first floor that had once been a porch before the house had been added on to in the fifties. It housed any of Palmer's security equipment, the guns they kept registered in their name locked in their respective safes and a computer.

Palmer booted it up. "I've changed all the cameras to run twenty-four seven like we discussed. It'll record everything, and I've armed the system on the house, but if we're worried the peeper might turn dangerous, we should keep physical watch."

Grant nodded in agreement. "Until we figure it out. Mary's always around, and I'll stick close to Dahlia."

"Yeah, I just bet you will."

Grant didn't rise to the bait. It wasn't worth it. "If her sister was murdered, this could be more dangerous than we originally thought."

"Always that possibility in a cold case. We're ready for it. I'll take the first shift," Palmer said. "Anna's second. You're the early bird, so you get third."

"All right. But come get me if anything is funny."

"Feeling territorial?"

Grant sighed. "How long are you going to try to get a rise out of me using that tactic?"

"Long as I think it might be true. I mean, she was interested in Freya's interest in you."

"I'm pretty sure that was to clear the way with Freya like some sort of ill-fated matchmaker."

"Nothing wrong with Freya."

"Nothing wrong with minding your own business either."

"Go get some shut-eye, bud."

Grant knew it was in his best interest to do just that. If Palmer took a four-hour shift, then Anna took a four, it would put him waking up at 4:00 a.m. Not much earlier than he usually got up, but he'd do better tomorrow if he got a good night's sleep and didn't stay up looking over every detail of the case he already knew by heart.

So, though he *wanted* to, he left his materials where they were in Mary's office, went to his room, got ready for bed and turned off every facet of his mind that wanted to think about Dahlia Easton and her case.

A trick he'd learned in the military that served him well. Still, sometime later, he awoke with a start, the taste of sand and blood in his mouth. An old dream he hadn't had in a long while making his heart pound like he'd just run a marathon. He sat up in bed in the pitch-black and focused on getting his breathing back to even.

It was a mix of things—no one terrible memory from his service. A blend of them. A firefight here, a sniper there, sometimes his Marine brothers, sometimes his family members.

And this time a certain redhead who he certainly didn't want in his dreams, let alone as pale and bloody and very clearly dead as she had been.

It was hard—harder than it should have been—to get his breath back, so he slapped on his bedside light and did what he'd had to do almost every night when he'd first come home.

Focus on the little watermark on the ceiling. Count. Disassociate. Until his heart beat the way it should. Until his lungs moved easily—inhale, exhale—no hitch, no gulping for breath.

Just home and the reality that his days of war were behind him. He glanced at his clock: 3:15 a.m. Well, there was no point going back to bed for forty-five minutes when it'd likely take him that long to fall asleep after the nightmare.

So he got up, got dressed and went to find Anna in the security room. She was in the rolling chair, feet propped up on the table. She sipped a Coke while she watched the screens and clearly had earbuds in, so she didn't hear his approach.

Still, when he tapped on her shoulder, she didn't jump or startle at all. She just looked up at him, then swiveled around to face him as she pulled one of the buds out of her ear.

She frowned at him. "You're early—and looking a little ghostly," Anna said, studying him with way too perceptive hazel eyes. She looked almost exactly like their mother and acted *nothing* like her. She was the baby of the family, so Grant couldn't say how purposeful that was. She'd only been eight when Mom and Dad had disappeared, and sometimes Grant wondered how much of either of them she fully remembered.

"I'm fine," Grant muttered. He'd gotten a handle on the physical effects of the dream, but the emotional ones lingered.

"Haven't looked that way since—"

"I said I'm *fine*." He looked at the monitors Anna had been studying. "Nothing, huh?"

She paused as if deciding whether or not to argue,

then swiveled back to look at the screens. "Not a thing. If he knows we're looking…"

"I think he'd have to be local to know we're looking."

"You were the one who told Jack he *could* be local. Besides, *he* could also be a *she*. You don't know."

Grant resisted rolling his eyes at his sister. Sure, it was possible, but it was a big boot print to be looking for a woman. He almost pointed that out, but something… moved. Grant's eyes narrowed. "Did you see that?"

"A shadow," Anna confirmed, leaning forward.

"That's way too close to where I saw a footprint this afternoon. The one that looked into Dahlia's room." He didn't like it, so he was already reaching for his gun.

"You can't go out there alone."

"Can. Will. Wake up Palmer. And get Dahlia out of that room."

"Don't you think—"

It would take too long. It would all take too long. "Get her out of that room," he repeated, then ran for the back door.

CHAPTER EIGHT

DAHLIA WAS ROUSED from sleep by a pounding on her door and the sound of a dog whining. Once she finally woke up enough to understand the noise—and how it couldn't mean anything good—she threw back the covers and rushed to the door.

She wasn't sure why she expected it to be Grant or why something in her chest sank when it was Anna instead.

"Hey, sorry to wake you," Anna said, reaching down to pet Willie. She was calm and even smiled, so maybe this wasn't…terrible.

"I… It's fine. What time is it?" But Anna had taken her arm and was pulling her forward and out of the room, Willie padding after them. Which didn't seem good at all when it was still dark everywhere.

"We might have caught our friend, but if he knows you're in this room, we just want to go above and beyond careful and get you into an interior room. If you're the target."

Target?

Why was she a target for anything?

But she knew there was only one answer to that, and it meant Rose was dead. So she pushed the thought away. Had to.

Anna pulled her down the hall, and Dahlia felt like

she had no choice but to go. It was only when she was halfway down the corridor that she realized she was in her pajamas. Shorts and a baggy tee, fine enough, but not wearing a *bra* underneath. The floors were cold on her bare feet, and everything made her shiver.

Anna, on the other hand, was dressed like it was the middle of the day. Jeans, sweater, cowboy boots.

"Um." Dahlia hugged herself as the chill sank deeper.

Anna looked back. "Oh man, you're cold. I'll get you a sweatshirt or something. Let's just get you into our wing first."

Our wing?

It was a big house. Sprawling, really, and maybe like the wings had been added on over the years as the family expanded.

They crossed through the living room, where a big window overlooked the front yard. It was still only dark out there, but Dahlia saw the flash of red and blue lights.

"The police are here."

"Yeah. Hopefully they're arresting the jerk." Anna looked back at her and then offered another smile. "Don't worry. It's all probably harmless. We're just being super cautious with the active part of this case."

Active? As though Rose missing *wasn't* active. Which made Dahlia's stomach twist into more knots.

They went through the dining room and then up a new set of stairs and down another hallway. Mary stepped out of a door in this hallway, also dressed as if it were the middle of the day, though her outfit was a little bit more *business* than Anna's ranch wear. Slacks, a button-down shirt and a cardigan.

Dahlia felt more and more out of place.

"Oh, I'm sure you're freezing," Mary said immediately. "I'll grab you a robe."

"She needs socks too," Anna piped in before pulling Dahlia into yet another room. This one was small and shaped oddly, all weird angles and stained glass windows. The furniture was old, definitely antique, and Anna nudged her to sit down in one of the fuzzy chairs. Willie flopped down right at her feet.

Mary quickly appeared and handed Dahlia a soft robe and big fuzzy socks. "You just put those on and warm up. The police have already arrived, so it won't be long before we know more."

It was then Dahlia noted the gun at Anna's hip. The way Mary had closed and locked the door. They could act calm and cheerful, but this was serious. And somehow Dahlia felt…at fault for it all. Surely they'd been living completely normal lives before she'd hired them.

"I'm sorry this is happening. I… If I'd known it would cause so much trouble…" She trailed off, because what would she have done? Certainly not stopped looking for Rose and answers.

"Ms. Easton—Dahlia, this is what we do," Mary said. "We have processes in place to deal with this kind of thing because it's always the risk you run when you take on a case—cold or otherwise. We're all well trained to deal with threats. So, please, don't feel responsible for actions that aren't your own."

"Yeah, this is a piece of cake," Anna added.

The room fell into silence, and Dahlia had to look at the sisters. There wasn't much resemblance. Anna was more on the fair side, everything about her dress and demeanor screamed *tomboy*. Mary had darker hair and eyes and seemed all around more…prim.

It reminded her of her own sister. They each took after a different parent in looks and definitely had different personalities. Rose was so outgoing, so ready to try new things and dive into new experiences.

It still didn't make sense to Dahlia that she was the one doing *all* this. Rose was the tenacious one. Dahlia swallowed at the lump in her throat and focused on the stained glass window of a mountain with a big star at the top.

She wasn't sure how much time passed, but she put on the robe, the socks and warmed up a little.

Eventually there was a tap at the door, and Mary unlocked and opened it. Dahlia could hear Grant's voice, though he hadn't stepped in the room far enough for her to see him.

"The police arrested the guy. Jack will question him. For now, everyone can probably go back to sleep. There is just one…slight oddity to the whole thing. He's a kid."

"A *kid*?" Anna repeated.

"If I had to guess? I'd say not a day over sixteen." He stepped farther into the room, and Dahlia leapt to her feet, heart slamming into her ribcage.

"You're bleeding."

"Oh." Grant lifted a hand to his mouth and pulled it back, examining the blood. "Was a little shocked to find a kid, so he got a lucky shot in." Then Grant shrugged like it was nothing.

And his sisters kept throwing out questions like it didn't matter.

"But he wasn't armed?" Anna asked.

"Had a gun on him, but he didn't pull it. Can't say I know what to think about the whole thing. The police will do some investigating, make sure his prints match the others, and he's the only one, but—"

"You're *bleeding*," Dahlia interrupted, because she was still standing here, heart beating too hard, staring at the smudge of blood at the corner of his mouth. Didn't anyone, least of all *him*, care?

All three sets of eyes looked at her with varying amounts of consideration.

Then Mary smiled kindly. "I'll get something to clean it up." She stepped out of the room, Anna at her heels.

"Yeah, I'll help you."

So, it was just her and Grant alone in this strange room. In this strange new version of her life.

"I've had a lot worse than a busted lip from some kid," he offered, as if *that* were some kind of comfort. "You really don't need to worry about it."

Dahlia turned away from him, because no matter what he said, she just hated the sight of blood. Hated knowing—no matter how Anna or Mary acted—that this was about her.

She stared hard at that mountain of stained glass.

"Dahlia," Grant said, and it wasn't the way he usually spoke. All stiff orders and frustration. There was a note of softness he only usually deployed at those family dinners. He was also closer than he had been. "I can't tell you not to be afraid, but I can assure you that HSS will do everything to get to the bottom of this while keeping you safe."

She swallowed. She felt like spun glass. Like every time she got her footing in this terrible situation, some earthquake came along. She didn't want to be weak. She didn't want to cry.

She just wanted to find her sister. She cleared her throat, calling on every last piece of strength within her. "It's very disorienting. I guess I just need to find my footing." *Again.*

"You're doing just fine." He gave her shoulder a little squeeze. Friendly. Reassuring. But when he released her, his hand moved down her shoulder blade. It was a casual move, just the way a hand would fall off a shoulder as someone pulled it away.

But it twisted through her like something else and made her breath hitch.

He cleared his throat and created distance between them—almost as if he felt it too.

Clearly she was delusional. Sleep deprived. "I'm very tired."

"I'm sure you are. We'll keep an eye on the security cameras until we know for sure this kid acted alone, but you're fine to go back to your room and sleep."

She nodded as Anna and Mary came back in with a little first aid kit, smiling over something they'd said to each other in the hallway.

"You want me to take you back to your room? All the hallways are confusing till you get used to it," Anna said.

"Sure. Thanks." Anna stepped back into the hall, and Dahlia followed, Willie always at her heels, but she found herself looking back at Grant, who was standing there letting Mary dab away the blood on his face.

He looked so...strong. Like some Western movie hero. A tiny bit beat up, but noble and true and right. *You're doing just fine.* It was the strangest thing. How easy it was to believe when *he* said it. Because he looked like he knew. Like all his convictions *had* to be right, or the world would crumble into dust.

But he didn't believe her about Truth or the Greens. Because he didn't want to, not because there wasn't evidence.

So he wasn't her friend. He wasn't her protector. He wasn't anything, except a man she paid to help.

But the way he'd touched her shoulder kept her awake for the rest of the night.

CHAPTER NINE

GRANT NEVER DID get much sleep after that. What he wanted to do was head down to the sheriff's department immediately, but Jack would want everything on the up and up, which meant no HSS interference until later.

It worried Grant that the perpetrator was a minor. That parents or the juvenile detention center—when they didn't have a local one of those—would complicate getting answers.

But he did his chores, ate his breakfast and waited for Dahlia to emerge from her room. Once she did, he'd take her down to the police station and figure out if there was anything to go on.

The phone in his pocket began to ring as he walked back to the house from his second round of morning chores. The caller ID showed the library's number, and Grant hoped it would be Mrs. Riley with some information or lead now that she'd realized her reaction to the Green connection had been overboard.

"Hudson," Grant answered.

"Hi, Grant. It's Freya."

Grant winced. Good Lord, this was not what he needed. "Hi, Freya."

"I thought I should call you. I know you were working with that redhead yesterday, and Mrs. Riley wasn't very helpful."

"No, she wasn't." Grant stepped into the house, stamping his boots on mats meant to pick up all the ranch mud.

"Well, she was complaining to Mr. Durst about it this morning. About the Greens. Mr. Durst obviously pointed out that they're all dead and so on. But…"

"But?"

"I shouldn't stick my nose in this, I know, but the redhead was really nice. And I wanted to help. And…"

"What is it Freya?"

"Mrs. Riley said something about how she's connected to the Greens? Dahlia, right?"

"Very loosely, it seems. A century ago or something. All that genealogy stuff. You know how that goes. Turns out everyone's related half the time."

"Well, yes, but Mrs. Riley was talking about how the redheaded Greens were always the bad ones. She seemed so…angry, and it was just kind of weird. Even Mr. Durst told her she was being ridiculous."

Redheaded Greens? Eugene Green had been bald and so had the man in that picture with Dahlia's sister. But there were other Greens. He didn't want to remember all the pictures of Truth in its heyday.

"Thanks, Freya. It's good to know that's what people are saying. Can you do me a favor?"

"Anything."

He winced at the fervor in her tone. "If the gossip mill starts winding up, will you do what you can to stop it? Or at least correct it. No one needs Mrs. Riley stirring people up into thinking this is some kind of direct connection to the Greens or Truth."

"Sure, Grant. I can do that."

"Thanks, I appreciate it."

"No problem. Anytime. Really."

"I'll see you around, Freya. Bye." He pressed End, feeling the way he always did. Uncomfortable, guilty. There was nothing wrong with Freya. She was a sweet woman. And, okay, he could admit he'd known she was going out with Palmer to see if *he'd* pay attention, but he just…wasn't interested.

He was complicated. And there was no point in throwing those complications out for everyone in town to know when they already talked about his family plenty.

Once his boots were clean, he left the mud room and went into the kitchen. Dahlia stood there alone, except for Willie at her feet, staring out the window over the sink. She held a mug of coffee but didn't seem to hear him enter.

The sunlight streamed in, making her red hair glow, like a flame. And then there were those blue eyes, lost and hurting, and he wanted to…

What the hell is wrong with you?

He should be thinking about Mrs. Riley assuming this was some kind of bad Green mark on her. The way Mrs. Riley spread gossip around town, everyone would believe it by the end of the day. Freya would try to turn the tide, but people loved a story.

He should know.

As if she finally sensed him there, she turned to look at him. She didn't register any surprise or discomfort at him just standing there *staring* at her.

"Do you know any more?" Dahlia asked without any kind of greeting.

"Not really. We can head down to the station whenever you want, confer with Jack."

She nodded. "I'd like to do that right away."

"Of course. But have you eaten anything?"

She looked down at the coffee, then made a face. "I really… I'm not a breakfast person. And it feels strange to…"

She trailed off as he began to open the pantry. He wasn't going to force a full meal on her, but he wasn't about to take her to the police station without something in her stomach. He found the variety pack of granola bars Anna loved so much and held out the box to her. "Pick one."

She hesitated.

He shook the box. "You feel better when you eat, don't you?"

She huffed out an irritated breath but then took one. "Happy?"

"I will be once you eat it."

This time she scrunched up her nose, but she opened the bar and took a bite. But she kept…staring at him.

It took him a few uncomfortable seconds to realize there was a *reason* her eyes kept drifting to his mouth. And they were none of the ones he'd been imagining.

It was because that's where he'd been bleeding last night. It wasn't even really swollen. There was just the little cut on his lip where the kid's elbow had knocked it into his tooth.

"I guess you're doing okay, then," she said after a few bites of granola bar.

"It was really nothing."

She nodded. "I just don't know how to make sense of it all. People don't get hit in my world. There aren't disappearances and stalkers and all this."

He didn't say the obvious. It *was* her world now, whether it made sense or not.

He also didn't say what he should tell her—that the town was going to look at her like the Devil now that Mrs. Riley undoubtedly shared a bunch of wrongheaded rumors. And unfortunately for Dahlia, her red hair wasn't any different than a big red A in this instance.

But maybe once they got to the bottom of whoever was watching her, she'd have enough answers to head back to Minnesota, and it wouldn't matter.

Why that thought settled so uncomfortably in his chest wasn't worth thinking about. "You want to grab anything before we head into town?"

She shook her head. "No, I'm ready."

DAHLIA FELT OKAY. More sturdy than not. She hadn't slept well, but whoever had been watching her had been caught, and it was both a relief and maybe a lead.

She desperately wanted a lead.

But when Grant pulled up in front of the sheriff's department, dread pooled in her stomach. Whoever had been watching her—a *teenager*—was in here.

"Jack will likely ask you a few questions. Hopefully he'll be able to give us some information to go on, but even if he doesn't, just the fact this guy is in custody is a new lead to follow."

Dahlia knew Grant was trying to assure her, so she attempted to smile and nod and feel reassured.

But she just kept thinking about how her sister was probably dead, and this *child,* essentially, might know something or be involved. There might be answers here, and for this entire year, the quest for them had driven her. Even knowing Rose might be—probably was—dead.

Faced with the possibility of confirmation…

"Dahlia," Grant said, with that rare gentleness that made her want to cry. "There's a reason my family specializes in cold cases. It's because they're unique. The way they drag out to the point where answers start to feel like as much of a curse as not knowing. We get it. So we can sit here as long as you need, or I can go in alone."

"It's just… I guess I never fully understood that an answer doesn't really change anything, does it?" She looked out the windshield, desperately trying to hold it all together. "If she's…gone, she's still gone. Whether I know or not."

Grant nodded along. "But you want to know. Or you would have given up a long time ago, Dahlia. A lot of people do."

She let out a shaky breath. He was right. Her parents had given up. Her and Rose's friends. Everyone had said *enough*, and she hadn't been able to. She sucked in a steadying breath. "Okay. I'm ready."

They both got out of the truck, and Grant met her at the front. He put his hand on her back and guided her inside. It was a friendly offer of support. Made all the more poignant by the fact everyone had…stopped offering that. Everyone wanted her to give up. Either be sad or get over it. Not stay mired in the what-ifs.

But Grant and his family understood. Dahlia hadn't realized how much she needed that. How much she missed feeling like someone…cared.

Of course, it was their job, and she was paying them, so it wasn't real care. But it still felt like a weight lifted.

He opened the door, and his hand stayed on her back as they entered. It was a small office, and the woman behind the desk looked up. She obviously knew Grant, but something odd flickered in her gaze when she took in Dahlia.

Still, she smiled and greeted Grant. "Your brother's back in the holding room."

Grant nodded and led Dahlia past the front desk. Jack was standing in a hallway and didn't greet them when he saw them, just nodded his head in a *follow me* gesture. So they did. Back to a little room with a big window. Jack pointed at the teenager inside, sitting next to a woman in a black suit.

"Do you know him?"

Dahlia swallowed and looked through the mirrored window. She studied the teen's face, desperate for any kind of recognition. And found none. "No."

Jack nodded as if that's what he'd expected. "Let's go into my office and have a chat."

He led them to the same small room she'd been in yesterday answering his questions. The same fat black cat slinked off the desk when Jack shooed it.

Jack Hudson did not seem like the type of man to care for a cat, but Dahlia hadn't asked questions then and didn't plan to now.

"Who is he?" she asked.

"His name is Kory Smithfield. Sixteen years old. A year and a half ago, he was reported missing by his parents in Austin, Texas."

Dahlia thought her knees might buckle, but she stiffened them and steadied herself by holding on to the back of a chair. She was afraid if she sat on it she'd never get back up. "Texas."

Jack nodded, his expression nothing but stoic. "We asked him some questions, talked to his parents. They can't come get him, and I didn't get the impression they were that interested in having him home at this point. We're going to have to send him to the juvenile center in Cody, at which point, finding answers is going to get complicated."

"Where's he been living since he went missing?" Grant asked.

"He wouldn't say. Pretended like he didn't run away, but it's clearly him. He also refused to admit he was following or watching Ms. Easton. Which is fine. We have proof. I'd like to bring Dahlia in to talk to him, but we'll need a lawyer present to make that aboveboard, and the parents weren't paying."

"So, what? It's a dead end?" Dahlia asked. Even though... Texas. If he was connected with Texas and had somehow wound up here in Wyoming...

He wasn't the man in the security footage with Rose, so maybe she was making too big of a leap to think it connected.

But it had to, didn't it?

"Not exactly." Jack paused, as if grappling with something significant. His cool gaze moved from Dahlia to his brother. "Grant, he has a tattoo."

She felt Grant stiffen next to her. Neither brother said anything, but their reaction made her think of her research, of all the things she'd read about the cult she was somehow connected to.

"He has an Order of Truth tattoo?" Dahlia demanded.

Grant scowled but said nothing. Jack didn't confirm, but *obviously* that's what it was.

"It connects. He *connects*. You can't deny it. You can't keep denying it. He was watching me. He has an Order of Truth *tattoo*. You have to let me talk to

him. You have to let me ask him some questions. You
have—"

"The only thing I *have* to do is follow the letter of
the law," Jack replied stiffly. "I let you go in there, and
the entire stalking case against you goes up in smoke."

"I don't care!"

"Dahlia."

She whirled on Grant. "I don't. I don't! He has something to do with my sister's disappearance. Maybe he
killed her, and I don't care if he's sixteen or sixty. I will
find out what happened to my sister. I *will*."

"Take a breath," he said gently.

But boy, that was the *wrong* thing to say. "Take a
breath? This is the first hint of a lead I've had, and
you're trying to stand in my way when I hired you all
to *help*." She was not going to cry. She wasn't.

Grant put his hand on her shoulder. It should have
infuriated her, but there was something about the heavy
weight of a big hand and the serious way he looked at
her. None of the dismissiveness she was used to from
men and law enforcement.

He didn't say anything to her though, instead he
moved that serious gaze to his brother. "We don't want
to impact any potential case, but surely there's *some*
way she can ask this kid a few questions. Or you could
on her behalf."

"I've asked him plenty. He's not talking."

"Jack."

Dahlia didn't think Jack would relent. He was like a
mountain. Absolutely no give. She expected that from
Grant as well, but whatever passed between the brothers—something Dahlia didn't see or understand—had
Jack blowing out a breath.

"I have to move him to a cell until we can transport him. Which means I'll have to walk him down the hallway. And there's no reason you couldn't…also be in the hallway."

What was she going to do with a hallway passing? She almost argued some more, but Grant looked back at her with a nod like *This is as good as it's going to get.*

Her mind scrambled for some idea as Jack moved back out of his office and to the holding room she'd looked into.

The teen still sat there looking calm. Maybe a little irritated, but not nervous. Not worried.

Dahlia couldn't imagine running away from home and then being picked up by the police and not being sad and scared.

"Stay here," Jack ordered. "Whatever you ask, whatever he says, it's completely inadmissible in a court of law. So just keep that in mind."

Grant's hand was on her back again, like he'd keep her there if necessary. Still, she didn't know what to say. What to ask. *Where is my sister? Why are you watching me?*

Jack went into the room, said something to the kid before he got to his feet. He was handcuffed, then Jack pulled him out of the room. Dahlia couldn't seem to find words, because the boy laughed and smiled like this was just a fun game.

"I didn't even know sheriffs were real. Sounds fake to me," the boy was saying. "Not good enough to be a real cop?"

Jack said nothing, but he met Dahlia's gaze over the teen's head. Which made the boy look over at her.

He looked at her, and while she saw nothing that

made her feel like she knew him, there was something
about the way he stared at her that made her feel…ex-
posed. Like he knew exactly who *she* was.

Then he smiled at her, and her blood ran completely
cold. She couldn't force *any* words out of her mouth.

He tried to lean forward, but Jack jerked him into
place. Still, Dahlia heard exactly what the boy whispered.

"You'll be with your sister soon."

CHAPTER TEN

GRANT DIDN'T THINK the move through. He simply reacted. He reached out, meaning to get a hand on the
kid, but Jack was faster, stepping between them. "He's
going to a cell," Jack said icily.

When that little bastard had *threatened* Dahlia. Grant
looked down at Dahlia. She'd gone white as a sheet,
and no wonder.

"Dahlia." But he didn't know what to say.

She raised her blue eyes to his, looking a bit like a
shell-shocked victim. "You heard him, right? You heard
what he said."

Grant nodded. He wanted to say something reas-
suring, but he came up empty. The kid had mentioned
Dahlia's sister without prompting. He had an Order of
Truth tattoo.

Damn it.

"What do we do if we can't ask him questions? How
do we get answers if Jack is all 'letter of the law' about
this?" Dahlia demanded. Some of her color was coming back, so that was good.

But they weren't going to get anywhere with Jack.
Not when he thought he had a good case against the kid.
Not when everything about this was going to stir up
everything...*everything*. "I have my ways. Come on."

He got her out of the station before Jack was finished

with the kid. Jack would no doubt want to lecture them on what they could and couldn't do.

Typically Jack's work as sheriff didn't interfere with the cases HSS worked because even amongst the suspicious missing persons, many of them committed suicide or died accidentally. The few murder cases they'd found and worked on had involved mostly dead people, so there was nothing active to put Jack in a complicated position with his job.

But this? Dahlia's sister's cold case disappearance now intersected with a current stalking case. That tied to the Order of Truth.

Damn. Damn. Damn.

This wasn't even about him being wrong. He could deal with that. What he couldn't—or didn't want to—deal with was the way this would, yet again, tear up his hometown. A town that had perhaps only in the past ten years started healing from what happened at Truth.

And it would bring up *everything* with his parents' disappearance once more. Grant didn't just dread it. He wasn't sure how he was going to *stand* it.

He unlocked his truck and waited for Dahlia to climb in. She was clutching her hands together, looking like she was about ready to jump out of her skin.

"We've got his name. Where he came from. The tattoo. It's a lot to go on," Grant offered, hoping to relax her some. He pulled out of the station parking lot with the thought of heading home. He and his siblings would all start researching Kory Smithfield ASAP.

And going down those old traumatic roads that led to the Order of Truth.

"What about that casing we found in Truth?" Dahlia asked.

"Jack's got that too, so he'll see if it matches the gun the kid had." But that was another thing that bothered Grant. When he'd wrestled that kid to the ground, the kid had tried to get away. But he hadn't tried to use his gun on Grant. He hadn't been a particularly adept fighter either. He hadn't wanted to be caught, but there'd been no thirst for violence in his reaction.

And yet, the smile he'd given Dahlia, the whispered words, they were *chilling*. As was the thought of that boy with that gun trailing around after Dahlia, watching her.

"The casing could tell us…something, right?"

He wouldn't say what he was thinking. Because unfortunately, without a body, even a murder weapon didn't mean much. But he tried to smile reassuringly at Dahlia. "It's definitely a lead of some kind."

"Wait. Stop," Dahlia said, reaching across and placing her hand on his over the steering wheel. She pointed at the library out his window as he slowed to a stop in the middle of Main Street. "I think we should go see Mrs. Riley. She said she made sure she knew all about the Greens. She might know if Eugene had sons, nephews, someone who looked like him. Maybe they aren't in Truth, but they're somewhere if that boy had a tattoo."

Grant hesitated. It was strange how much he wanted to protect her from the truth. Mostly he didn't mind being a little abrasively straightforward. But he supposed most of the people he dealt with were his siblings and ranch hands, so it suited the circumstances.

Dahlia was… Well, he didn't know how to explain it. She was soft, but she was strong. She was always on the verge of breaking apart but somehow always pulled it back together. And she was doing something he couldn't do anything but respect.

Finding answers for her family, no matter what it took.

So he didn't want to tell her Mrs. Riley wouldn't see her or answer her questions. That she'd likely already spread it around town that Dahlia was the next coming of cults and Greens and Truth nonsense. And the arrest of Kory Smithfield was only going to exacerbate the problem.

But apparently he didn't have to tell Dahlia any of that.

"I know she won't want to speak with me," Dahlia said earnestly, and her hand was still over his on the steering wheel. "But you could go talk to her. I could just…wait somewhere. Here in the truck or hang out in the library. I could go over to the general store if you think she'll see me and not talk. You go in and ask her questions, and I'll stay out of sight."

Grant wondered if even he could get through to Mrs. Riley since she knew Dahlia was his client, but he'd try. *After* he got her somewhere safe. "I'll take you back to the ranch and—"

"We don't have time for that."

They did have time—there was always time—but she had her first real lead in over a year. He understood why she wouldn't want to have patience now when, finally, it felt like something might move forward.

But she very clearly hadn't accepted the situation yet, or at least the implications as they connected to *her*. If she thought he was going to leave her alone for a second, she was *sorely* mistaken.

"Dahlia." He didn't want to be the one to put the thought in her head, though it was hard for him to understand how she hadn't arrived at the same conclusion yet. "What he said to you back there was a *threat*. Which means the possibility there is still someone out there who might want to cause you harm is high. You're not going to be out of my sight unless you're safe inside the ranch house until we know who else might be after you. And why."

IT WASN'T THAT Dahlia didn't understand what Grant was saying. Once he said it out loud, she went back over the whole experience and sort of…processed the situation. She'd been so focused on the sister part—the confirmation that boy knew something about Rose—she hadn't even fully grasped that her seeing Rose soon was… probably a death threat.

Rose was dead.

And she was sitting in some strange cowboy's truck in the middle of small-town Wyoming, thinking he could help her find answers.

Dahlia let out a slow breath and carefully sucked it in. She felt like she was on the verge of breaking into a million pieces, but she simply wouldn't let herself.

You're not going to be out of my sight unless you're safe inside the ranch house until we know who else might be after you. And why.

He wanted to help. He wanted, for whatever reason, to help keep her safe. He was worried. She knew it was business, not personal, but to be worried about her when it had nothing to do with her mental state felt…oddly like a huge weight had been lifted off her shoulders.

"But I agree with you," he continued when she didn't say anything. "Mrs. Riley might have more answers about the Greens still around and that might be a lead. I'm going to take you back to the ranch though."

Dahlia looked out of the passenger side window at the pretty little town and the sunny fall afternoon as

Grant began to drive again. She had hired the Hudsons to look into this. Investigate. Find the connections. And here Grant was doing just that, all the while protecting her from a potential threat.

Going back to the ranch was what she should do. She was hardly going to *ignore* a death threat, but going through her binders in that beautiful room just made her feel like screaming. Which was ridiculous, because aside from a scenery change, that was about what she'd been doing for the past year. And now there was a *lead*. She should want to pore over everything again.

She turned to Grant, studying his profile while he drove. He was no different than Jack. An immovable mountain made up of certainty and strength of purpose. She wished she could emulate it.

Or get through to it. "Grant…" But she didn't have any experience laying out her feelings for people. She hated to ask for anything, hated to be seen as a burden. She *liked* being self-sufficient. She didn't mind being the one everyone forgot about, because that meant no one was paying too close attention to her.

Because when they did, they tended to think her strange or, since Rose disappeared, unhinged.

Grant spared her a glance, then his gaze dropped to where she realized she still had her hand rested atop his on the steering wheel.

She pulled it back and dropped it in her lap like it wasn't her own appendage. There was just something… comforting about him. She didn't know why. He was abrupt sometimes. She knew he tried to be gentle, but he wasn't especially *good* at it, even if she did appreciate the attempt.

"I know it's hard to sit around and wait. Or worry,"

Grant said. Because for all his inability to be gentle, he *did* have understanding. True understanding. In a way no one else in her life seemed to. Which was a comfort, Dahlia supposed.

"It's all I've done for a year, and now there's *finally* this…piece. I don't know how to fit it in, but it's a piece. He said, 'your sister.' He *knows* about Rose. I can't go back to the ranch and sit in that room and stew just because…"

"Just because he *threatened* you? That's not a *just* because in my world, Dahlia. It's a big damn *because*."

Dahlia sighed and looked away out the window as the landscape passed. Mountains and fall colors. Such a pretty place, and her sister had likely been murdered. For some reason, that runaway teenager thought she would be next.

She thought about the cranky woman at the library who'd immediately taken against her. That woman had said… "Mrs. Riley told us they would know about me. That they knew their tree backward and forward, and a loose connection wouldn't matter, it was still a connection. But if Eugene Green has been dead fifty years, who was she talking about in the here and now when she said, 'they?'"

Grant frowned at the road ahead of them. He clearly didn't like the connection to Truth or the Greens, but he was no longer trying to talk her out of it. "Listen, Mrs. Riley is…difficult. Her father joined the cult when she was a teenager. Her mom left her dad because she saw it for what it was, but the dad took some of the kids in there with them, and then… Well, her brother was one of the people who helped bring in the Feds. He always told her their father had tried to escape, but once you're initiated into the Order, you can't leave. Not alive anyway."

Dahlia listened to that reasoning. It explained some of the woman's animosity, she supposed.

"They all died. Her father, her brothers—the ones who were involved, the ones who tried to bring it down. The remaining Rileys have always... Well, they're bitter. Understandably."

"But they're also *knowledgeable*, Grant."

His jaw tightened, but he didn't argue with her. "We just have to be careful about how we approach her. It's a lot of trauma. All this happened before I was born, but for my entire childhood, it was such a...sore subject for everyone. It affected the whole town, generations of families. All of whom lost people."

He didn't say it, but she heard it all the same. *Just like you.*

He sighed before he continued. "And the thing is, this kid and his tattoo... It doesn't just stir up old, bad memories for people here. It means someone out there is still..." He shook his head. "I can't believe I'm saying this, but it means everything we thought *ended* back in 1978 didn't actually end. And that's going to hurt a lot of people."

"They've already been hurt. And so has my sister. Just because time has passed doesn't mean the hurt isn't still there. Surely you of all people know that."

"People want it to be over," Grant said stiffly.

"But it's *not*."

He spared her a glance, and she thought he was going to argue with her further, but instead he reached across the space between them abruptly. He pushed her head down, enough so that she let out a little yelp of pain. "Stay down," he ordered.

A second before something exploded.

CHAPTER ELEVEN

GRANT KEPT ONE hand pushing Dahlia's head down away from the windows and one hand with a death grip on the steering wheel as the truck jerked beneath them.

Someone had shot out his tire. It was better than shooting Dahlia's *head*, but it still wasn't good.

He was halfway between town and the ranch, a stretch of highway that didn't see much traffic that wasn't a member of his family. Which meant this was very carefully planned and not good for either him or Dahlia.

He couldn't drive well on the flat tire, particularly in his best approximation of a crouch in the hopes that any other shots that went off didn't actually hit him or Dahlia. He had a gun, but it was locked in the glove compartment, and if he couldn't drive his way out of this, he supposed he'd have to shoot his way out.

Something uncomfortable and a lot like dread curled in his gut. He hadn't had much luck shooting since he'd come back from the Marines. The few times he'd sucked it up and forced himself to target practice, all his former accuracy and skill seemed to be completely and utterly gone.

So he'd stopped trying.

But now someone was shooting *at* him and Dahlia, and he was going to have to be able to do something about it. Whether his brain wanted to cooperate or not.

The truck was screeching metal now, tire rim against concrete at a bad angle that meant the whole thing could flip if he wasn't careful. Driving much longer like this was almost as dangerous as getting shot at.

So he slammed on the brakes, and Dahlia let out a little yelp as the seat belt kept her from slamming into the dash. He ripped the keys out of the ignition. "Keep your head down," he ordered, releasing her head and shoving the key into the hole on the glove compartment. He unlocked it, then scanned the world around them as he pulled his gun out.

He spotted the shooter in the rearview mirror—up on a ridge and working his way down it. But as far as Grant was concerned, that was the least of his problems. There were three other men moving out from various protected areas—moving to circle them.

He didn't have much time. And if there were any more men hiding, they were probably in for a world of hurt.

But he didn't let his mind go down that road. He could only deal with the threat in front of him. He turned to Dahlia. "You're going to stay in the truck. Call 911. I'm going to take care of it."

"Take care of what?" she demanded, though she was definitely shaken, crouching there low enough her head wasn't visible in any of the windows.

But it was then a few things dawned on him. One, the shooter on the ridge hadn't shot again, though he could have. Two, the three men who were currently moving to surround the truck didn't appear to have weapons— not visible or drawn anyway.

Which meant this wasn't simply an attempt to murder Dahlia, or anyone looking into Rose's disappearance.

It was something else.

"Just stay put," Grant said, and then he had to trust she would. He opened the door, keeping the shooter behind him in sight. He waited to see if the man would lift the gun and aim it at him, but he simply kept moving down the ridge and toward the road.

Grant turned his attention back to the much closer men. Even if they didn't have visible guns, he didn't like the idea of them surrounding the truck. Even if they didn't want to kill anyone, nothing they wanted could be *good*.

"I think you fellas have the wrong people," he called out to the man closest—the one coming for the front of the truck, while the other two spread out to the east and the west respectively. He eyed the open door's side view mirror and saw the other man still climbing down the rock he'd been perched atop.

None of the men responded to him. They just kept advancing. Grant adjusted the grip on his gun, trying to focus on the goal rather than the anxiety clutching at his chest. He had to keep Dahlia safe.

Had to.

"Come any closer, and I'm going to have to start shooting," Grant warned. He aimed at the man in front. "We've called the cops, so why don't you all turn around? Go back where you came from."

They seemed wholly unafraid, though they didn't keep moving forward. The man in front studied Grant. "Is it true? Do you have her?"

Grant squeezed his hand in an attempt to keep it from going numb like the rest of his body seemed to be doing. "Who?" Grant said, and the three men answered in succession.

"The true one."

"The answer."

"Our promised."

Grant had seen a lot of terrible things. He'd been scared and freaked out more times than he liked to count. But this was possibly one of the creepiest damn things he'd ever encountered.

"That's not going to work for me. I warned you about taking another step."

But the man in front took one. So Grant got off a shot—aiming for a few feet in front of the forward-moving man. The shot went shorter and way wider than he'd anticipated.

He cursed under his breath. *Not now. Now when it matters.*

The men did stop advancing. They didn't turn around and run away or anything, but they stopped taking steps.

"Give us the woman," the man he'd shot at said in an authoritative tone. "And you'll be rewarded."

But there was something…familiar about him. The voice or the way the man in front stood. Grant moved toward him, gun still held and pointed at him. But the man didn't move or even eye the gun warily. He stood, chin held high, eyes on the truck as if he were trying to catch a glimpse of Dahlia.

Not going to happen.

It was when Grant got close enough to see the man's ear that it finally dawned on him who it was. "Lyle?"

"Lyle's dead," the man said flatly. But it *was* Lyle Stuart. He'd been one of Jack's buddies in high school, but once Mom and Dad disappeared, Jack had cut ties because Lyle made trouble wherever he went. And Lyle was *always* recognizable because he was missing half his ear from a dog attack when he'd been a kid.

Lyle had left Sunrise years ago. Grant couldn't remember where he was supposed to have gone, but he did remember it was not long after Mom and Dad disappeared. Jack had said it was a good riddance type situation.

Now, all these years later, here Lyle was. Older, definitely having lived some hard years, but Lyle Stuart. Part of this damn cult that had somehow been revived.

And they wanted Dahlia.

"I've got some bad news for you, Lyle. Dead or alive, you're not getting her."

DAHLIA FOLLOWED INSTRUCTIONS for a while. She'd called 911, though it had been hard to give the dispatcher enough information. She didn't know enough about the area to give first responders an idea of where they were. The dispatcher kept asking her questions she didn't know the answers to.

"Jack Hudson will know where we are," she'd finally said. "The sheriff in Sunrise, Wyoming."

"Sunrise, Wyoming," the dispatcher repeated. "Stay on the line, miss."

Dahlia did, but she wasn't really paying attention to what the dispatcher said, because a loud *bang* exploded through the air. Dahlia dropped the phone and looked up over the dash, eyes frantically searching the area.

There was a man in front of the truck and two other men on either side of the truck. Grant was moving toward the man in front, but no one seemed hurt. Or scared. While her heart was racing and her palms were sweating.

Phone forgotten, everything forgotten except someone *shooting*, she watched as Grant stopped in front of the man who now stood in the middle of the road as if he were blocking the truck, when the truck was leaning at such an angle, she didn't have any reason to believe it *could* go.

It was almost like they were squared off. They were a good ten feet apart if not more, and they were talking, though she couldn't hear what they were saying. Grant had his gun pointed at the man, but the expressions on their faces weren't antagonistic, exactly.

More wary. Waiting. Considering.

She looked out the passenger window, then the opening left by Grant leaving the driver's side door open. The other two men were watching the exchange, though sometimes they would turn their gaze to the truck, and Dahlia would duck down—not sure why she felt like she didn't want them to even see her when they no doubt knew she was in the car.

She twisted in her seat, still crouched, and carefully poked her head up—inch by inch—until she could see out the back. A man stood there as well, gun pointed at Grant's back.

Dahlia did *not* like that.

But no one was immediately shooting. Still, she couldn't understand why Grant wasn't looking back, wasn't worried about the man with the gun. Surely he knew that man was there.

"Lord of Truth," the man in front of Grant yelled, raising his hands up to the sky. "Help us."

The two other men on either side of the truck began to do the same. They just kept shouting those words over and over, looking up at the sky like something might drop down and save them. Dahlia looked back at the man with the gun. He was moving again toward the truck. Toward her.

She knew this was about her just by the way the man looked at her through the back window of the truck. He was zeroed in on her, while the other men shouted about truth and help.

She wanted to cover her ears. It was only the voices of three men, but the repetitive words were so loud and alarming.

She heard the back door of the truck creak open, and she no longer saw the gunman in the windows. She looked wildly for Grant, but he was no longer standing off with the man in front, who was still chanting at the sky in time with the other men.

Maybe it was him. She looked back at the door, and a gun barrel appeared. "Get out of the truck," an unfamiliar voice said, though the face was hidden behind the door itself.

She didn't have anything to use as a weapon. Didn't know what to do except…refuse. "No," she replied as she looked around wildly. There had to be something she could use as defense, but as she looked to the right of her, she noticed one of the other men advancing toward the door.

It was locked, but that didn't make her feel safe, particularly since he was still yelling words about truth and help. She didn't *see* a gun, but that didn't mean he didn't have one.

Maybe this was what happened to Rose.

She looked back at the gun pointed at her. It was beyond surreal. Maybe it was not being able to see the man behind it, or how little experience she had with guns, but it was almost impossible to believe it could kill her.

But maybe it killed Rose. Could she convince this man to keep her alive and take her to wherever he'd taken Rose? Maybe she'd die, but maybe she'd know?

Before she could act on that irrational thought, the gun disappeared. She heard a distinctive male grunt and then a clattering sound. She scrambled over to the driver's side to see through the windows.

Grant was grappling with the gunman. He took an elbow to the stomach but barely even winced as he pivoted and jabbed his fist up, hitting the man squarely in the jaw. The man stumbled back and into the truck on a grunt. Meanwhile the shouts from the other men continued to echo outside.

She thought maybe she heard sirens beyond all that noise and prayed help was on the way, because she didn't have the slightest idea what to do.

The gun. Guns. The man had been holding a gun and so had Grant, but where were they now? She peeked her head out of the doorway and saw them both on the ground. One right by the gunman's boot and the other a few yards away, almost in the ditch next to the roadway.

She didn't know how to use a gun, but if she got them both, she could give them to Grant. And none of these screaming men could get them.

She slid out of the truck and onto shaking legs, but she focused on the guns. She crept toward the one by the ditch because she didn't want to get in the way of Grant's grappling. Grant landed another punch, but the man refused to go down.

Dahlia took another shaking step toward the gun. She could do this. She could help. But she heard movement next to her, and when she turned, one of the yelling men was too close. No longer yelling. Just staring at her and *smiling*.

She wanted to bolt. Just start running and screaming in the opposite direction, but she was only two steps maybe away from the gun. She took another step, but he reached out.

She jumped away, but he never stopped smiling or advancing. He didn't lunge. He didn't speak. Just kept moving for her, arms outstretched.

"Don't move another muscle."

Dahlia froze in time with the man, because it was Grant's voice, low and lethal. When she got it through her head he was talking to the man—not her—she looked over at him.

He had a gun—not the one she'd been going for but presumably the original gunman's, who was crawling on the ground, gasping for breath as blood leaked out of his mouth.

Sirens sounded, and two police cars appeared on the rise. The man next to her and the other shouting man ran. Back from wherever they'd come, still shouting about truth and gifts.

Dahlia took a few halting steps after them. They might know who killed Rose. They might have answers.

"Dahlia."

She looked at Grant and realized he, too, was bleeding. Like…badly. The entire bottom of his shirt was slowly becoming soaked with blood, and it was his *own*. It was then she saw in the hand that didn't hold a gun, he held a knife. Covered in blood.

Her stomach threatened to roil. "Grant," she said, not knowing what else to say. He'd been *stabbed*. She moved haltingly for him, but she had no idea how to fix a stab wound.

The police were coming. She could hear them shouting now as they approached, guns drawn. She looked around, but the man who'd been crawling was gone. *Gone.*

And Grant was bleeding and… She had to do something. Something. But Jack ran over.

"About damn time," Grant muttered.

"He's hurt. He's… He needs an ambulance," Dahlia babbled at Jack, whose face went from worried to a blank kind of coolness Dahlia couldn't believe. Grant was his *brother.*

He started talking into a com unit. Barking out orders as he put his hand on Grant's shoulder.

His face betrayed nothing, but there was a slight shake to his hand as he placed it there.

"The men. They…they tried to… You have to follow them."

Jack's gaze turned to hers. It cooled even more. "We'll handle it."

"I'm fine," Grant said, but he didn't sound himself, and he still hadn't moved. The gun was still pointed where the man had been. He still held the dripping knife. He still bled.

But another officer came running. He held a little white box Dahlia assumed was a first aid kit.

"Why don't you get out of the way," Jack said to her. "Take a seat in one of the cruisers. We'll have questions for you once we take care of Grant."

Dahlia wanted to argue. To *help.* But Jack moved in such a way that he blocked her view of Grant, and he spoke with the other officer in quiet tones she couldn't make out.

Dismissed. No, ordered away. Jack clearly blamed *her* for what had happened, and was he wrong? She'd cowered in that truck, and then even when she'd finally attempted to do something, Grant—bleeding—had been the one to stop the man from getting her.

She backed away from Jack. From Grant. She blinked a few times as she shakily moved for the cruisers still flashing lights though the sirens were off. The men who'd stopped Grant's truck, all gone.

Had any officers followed those men? Maybe she should just run after them. They wanted her. Why not go see why? Better than…this horrible feeling of uselessness and guilt.

But another person arrived, this time in a truck just like Grant's. Mary and Anna got out, and while Anna made a beeline for Jack and Grant, Mary came right for Dahlia.

"Are you okay?" She reached out and took Dahlia by the elbows so that she had to focus on Mary rather than Jack blocking her from Grant or the men who'd run off into the rocks and ridges.

"Grant…"

"They'll take him to the hospital, and I'll take you home. He's fine. Standing on his own two feet, right?" She slid her arm around Dahlia's waist and began leading Dahlia to the truck. Dahlia watched over her shoulder, but between Jack, Anna and the other deputy, she couldn't actually see Grant.

She turned her attention to where the men had gone. "The police…"

"They'll see if they can find who tried to hurt you

and get answers," Mary said, giving her a reassuring squeeze and delivering her to the passenger side of the truck.

"But they didn't try to hurt me," Dahlia said, turning to look at Mary. That man had been close, but even when he'd tried to take her arm, it hadn't been violent. He'd been *smiling*. Grant was the one they'd fought. The one they'd hurt.

Mary looked back at her for a long minute. "Dahlia, maybe they didn't physically hurt you, but that doesn't mean they didn't hurt you in other ways." She opened the passenger door. "Get in now. We'll sort it all out back at the ranch."

She didn't want to leave Grant. Or this place that felt like maybe it had answers to Rose's disappearance.

But Mary smiled and squeezed her elbows again. "Dahlia, we're going to help. But there's nothing more to be done in the middle of the road."

We're going to help. They hadn't given up. They'd found something, and Grant had protected her. This was more forward movement than she'd had the entire thirteen months Rose had been gone. She should be happy, excited that there were real leads to follow.

So why did she just want to cry. She swallowed at the lump in her throat. "Are you sure he's okay?" she asked on a whisper.

"If he wasn't, I'd be over there. Go on now. Get in the truck."

So Dahlia finally did.

CHAPTER TWELVE

"I'M FINE," GRANT SAID to his older brother. Perhaps for the three hundredth time. He didn't know why he was saying it. It wouldn't ever get through Jack's hard head. He glanced in the rearview mirror at his sister sitting in the back as the cruiser sped toward the hospital with lights and sirens going. He wouldn't get through her hard head either.

A very annoying Hudson trait.

"You were stabbed," Jack said through gritted teeth, every part of his body so tense Grant was pretty sure if he reached out and poked Jack, he'd shatter into a million pieces.

Tempting. But the throbbing pain in his stomach kept him from doing much moving. "Yeah, better than shot," he muttered. He adjusted in the chair, then hissed out a breath. It still pissed him off that guy had managed to stick him with that knife, but his focus *had* been on the gun and getting it away from being pointed at Dahlia. But this was a flesh wound at most.

"They wanted to kidnap her." Grant stared hard at the road that would lead them to the hospital. Where he'd get poked and prodded and stitched up and no doubt sent home in a few hours' time. He felt a little sick at the prospect of *hospitals*. But that was hardly the only thing bothering him. "They were chanting all this crazy stuff about *truth*. Lyle Stuart—and I *know* it was Lyle—said, and I quote, 'Lyle's dead.' This is real cult stuff. And they want Dahlia. They called her 'the answer.' 'The promised' or something. She's the target, and *she's* in danger."

"Yeah, and you're the one bleeding through your bandage."

Grant didn't even bother to look down at said bandage. Paying more attention to all the ways he hurt wasn't going to help. "Did you send any deputies after them?"

Jack flicked a glance at him, his hands flexing on the steering wheel. "I only had one to spare."

Grant stared open-mouthed at Jack for a good minute before speaking again. "Damn it all to hell, Jack. What were you thinking?"

"That I didn't want you or any of my deputies to die?"

"I'm not about to die from a flesh wound. And furthermore—"

"Furthermore, Deputy Brink tracked them for a bit. I've instructed her to put together a search party. They'll comb the area and get some leads. We're certainly not going to let any Order of Truth copycats wreak havoc on our town."

Grant would have preferred to have been part of that search party rather than on his way to any hospital, but at least Jack had sent a team.

Then his brother went and ruined that *at least*. "I think we should back off this."

Grant looked back at Anna, even though it hurt, because if he reacted to his brother's flat-out *absurdity*, it wouldn't be pretty. "Please tell me he's kidding."

Anna looked at Jack, then Grant, as if deciding which side to take. Because Anna was never scared of taking a side. Or making up her own. But she kept her gaze on Jack. "So, what you're suggesting is we back off. Let that woman get taken by some unhinged cult, or copy-cat cult, and probably be killed just like her sister?"

"That is *not* what I'm suggesting," Jack replied darkly. He pulled to a stop at the ER entrance and switched off his sirens and lights. "We'll discuss it later."

Grant wanted to argue, but he also wanted his infuriating stab wound stitched up so he could stop bleeding through bandages. He didn't want to end up worse for the wear because of how much blood he'd lost.

So he got out of the car before Anna could help him, which made Jack growl. Grant didn't feel the least bit chagrined. His brother was being an overbearing jerk.

Not unusual.

Anna came up behind him and linked arms with him. "He's just shaken because you're hurt. It feels like a failure, so he'll be grumpy, but you know as well as I do he's not going to let that poor woman dance in the wind. Besides, Chloe's the one he put in charge of the search team, and you know she'll be thorough."

Chloe Brink was a fine cop, but... "I should be out there."

Anna shook her head. "Like hell you should."

They walked into the hospital and talked to the ER attendant, and then after what felt like hours, Grant was through all the rigmarole of being admitted and waiting for someone to come stitch him up.

The entire time, he replayed the moments in his head. What he could have, or should have, done differently.

What all this meant for Dahlia. "They wanted her," he muttered to Anna.

She looked up from her phone. "Yeah, but they stabbed you."

"Which proves just how dangerous they are."

Anna shrugged.

The doctor came in and stitched him up, telling him how lucky he was and how he needed to take it easy and—*blah, blah, blah.* As if sensing an unresponsive patient, the doctor handed Anna the recovery instructions and the prescription for pain medication Grant had no plans on taking.

Then Anna started talking about horses with the doctor, the young man clearly flirting with her. She laid on the charm and flirted right back. Once the doctor *finally* left, saying they could too, Grant glared at his sister.

"Really? I've been *stabbed* and you're flirting with the doctor?"

"He was cute," Anna said with a grin.

They walked back out of the hospital. Everything in him kind of throbbed, but he'd rather feel the pain than be all zapped out on painkillers.

Been there, done that, no repeat performance, thanks.

Jack was in the parking lot pacing next to his cruiser, his phone to his ear.

"Uh-oh," Anna muttered. "Bad Jack vibes."

"Are there good Jack vibes?"

"Good point," she said with a laugh.

Jack ended his phone call as they approached. He studied Grant in silence for a few moments before he seemed satisfied Grant wasn't going to just keel over. "So?"

"Doctor says he'll be fine," Anna said because Grant knew Jack wouldn't believe *his* recounting of what the doctor said. "Needs to rest, but it didn't hit anything important."

Jack nodded. "That's good news. Unfortunately I have some of the bad kind."

"Of course you do," Anna said.

"The man who stabbed you? They caught up with him pretty easily…because he was dead."

"Dead?"

"Shot in the head."

Grant was…stunned. "I didn't…"

"No, but someone did. And left him there while they disappeared. Seemingly into thin air."

Grant had to bite his tongue to keep from telling his brother he should have handled things differently. It wasn't fair. Jack had more to worry about than getting to the bottom of this—the safety of his citizens and deputies chief among them.

But Grant should have gone after them himself, stab wound be damned.

"This situation is too dangerous," Jack said, relying heavily on the "I may be your brother, but I was also your father more or less" tone that Grant hated. *Hated.* It was that tone that had sent him to the Marines, at least partially. "We're turning it *all* over to law enforcement. The case. The woman. Beginning and end of story."

Grant didn't say anything to Jack, because it was pointless. Like talking to a brick wall or worse.

But like hell this was the end.

DAHLIA REALLY COULDN'T get over the kindness of Mary. Not only did the woman make her lunch and insist she eat, but she also seemed to understand what Dahlia needed even when Dahlia couldn't articulate it.

She didn't insist Dahlia rest. Instead she brightly suggested Dahlia help with some of Mary's administrative tasks. They were simple—filing mostly—but it helped ease some of that useless feeling and kept her mind engaged enough not to fall apart, but not so engaged she actually had to *think*.

When the phone rang, Dahlia jerked in surprise. She'd been reliving those moments on the road over and over again, trying to work out what she should have done differently as she'd filed the stack of papers Mary had given her.

Mary answered the phone, and Dahlia shamelessly listened in. At first Mary sounded businesslike, then relieved. "Okay. Yes. Yes." There was a flicker of something. Her cheerful demeanor slipping for just a moment. "All right. I'll tell her. Uh-huh. See you soon."

Mary smiled brightly as she hung up the phone and turned to Dahlia at the filing cabinet. "Grant's all stitched up and on his way home. Good to go. He'll be back in the saddle in no time."

But there was something else. Something bad. Dahlia sucked in a breath, bracing herself for… She didn't know what.

"Unfortunately, the deputies couldn't find the men who stopped you guys."

"Oh."

"At least right away." Mary reached out and put a gentle hand on her arm. "I'm sure they'll discover clues to help them search, and this is a concrete crime for them to investigate."

Still, Dahlia got the feeling there was more to it, and

Mary was purposefully keeping it from her. She wished she knew Mary better so she could demand whatever information. But at the end of the day, Mary wasn't her friend. She was just part of the organization Dahlia was paying to help find her sister.

And now things were…complicated. Because there was an *active* crime, and the police were involved, and she was somehow…a target in all this.

She wasn't going to ask what Mary was keeping to herself. It didn't feel right in the moment. But that didn't mean she couldn't start…being active. Making some of her own decisions.

Since Grant had found her poking around Truth, the Hudsons had taken over, and she'd let them. She couldn't let that continue. Not with Grant hurt. Not knowing she was some kind of bizarre cult target for whatever reason.

So, she focused on what she knew how to do. What she *could* do. "Mary, do you have anything about the Order of Truth? When I was doing my research, I focused on Eugene Green and his family more than the cult itself. Maybe I need to learn more about this cult."

Mary hesitated, which seemed a rare thing for the woman who was always very composed. "I'm not sure…"

"I can't just sit around. I…" She couldn't explain what she felt to Mary, or she'd end up crying. "I have to do something. And the only thing I'm any good at is research."

Mary nodded as if she understood not just what Dahlia was saying but, on a deeper level, what it meant. "Jack and Grant never wanted anything about the cult around. It was a leftover reaction from my parents. We weren't allowed to talk about it growing up or even joke about it. You see—" Mary waved it away "—it has always been a very sore subject in our house, and Jack and Grant were the oldest, so they took it to heart the most."

Dahlia understood there was more to that story but also that it was none of her business. "I guess I could just do some internet searching," Dahlia said, thinking aloud.

"Oh, don't do that. There's so much bad information. People love to sensationalize a cult. Just...stay here for a second."

Mary disappeared and Dahlia waited, then went ahead and finished filing. It gave her hands something to do. It gave her mind some sense of accomplishment.

When Mary returned, it was with a stack of books. "I'm not sure how Anna's going to feel about this, but I wanted to get them to you before Jack and Grant get back. Maybe it's part and parcel with being the youngest and how little she remembers of my parents, but Anna's always been obsessed with the cult business against the rest of our wishes. These are all hers. If she kept these, they have better information than you'll find on the internet. I promise."

She handed the books off, and Dahlia took them. The top title was *Order of Truth: Fact and Fiction*.

"Take them to your room. Keep them out of sight if you think Grant might be in there. I'll let Anna know you have them, and if she has an issue with that, we'll figure it out."

"Thank you," Dahlia said, even though what she really wanted to say was *Why would Grant be in my room?* "I think I'll go do some reading then. Can you..." She trailed off. She'd see Grant at dinner, and Mary had assured her he was fine multiple times, but still, she just...wanted to see for herself. But for some reason the comment about Grant and her room made this all feel...awkward. "If you ever need more help with things, it makes me feel useful."

Especially since, at most, she could afford maybe another week of their services and their generosity. She needed answers and she needed them quick. So she moved through the maze of a house to her room.

When she got there, she shut the door behind her and looked through the titles. When she'd been researching before coming to Sunrise, it had been all about Eugene Green and how he connected to her, to Texas, to Truth. So, she'd learned some things about the Order of Truth, but not really the inner workings, the beliefs and all that. It hadn't seemed pertinent. Because everything was about genealogy and blood connections.

But the men had been...chanting, reaching for the sky. It had to be some kind of...ritual? Or something related to the cult. She flipped through indexes, trying to determine what kind of information she wanted.

Not the raid or the murders. She wasn't ready to delve into all that. But what did the group believe? What was *their* truth?

Lord of Truth! Help us! They'd shouted.

So, who was this Lord? She found a chapter in one of the books titled "Lord of Truth" and began to read. It didn't seem to be based on any religion she was familiar with. It was a mix of things—nature and signs, but mostly the bottom line seemed to be Eugene Green himself.

He was the Lord of Truth. Only Eugene and his descendants knew the truth.

Dahlia felt a cold chill run through her at the word *descendants*. She wasn't a direct descendent of Eugene Green and neither was Rose, so it made no sense that these men wanted her.

But Mrs. Riley had said they would know their tree. They would know about her.

But maybe that was only part of it. Maybe it was *Rose* knowing about them.

A knock sounded at the door and Dahlia jumped a foot. She looked around a little wildly and realized she'd been reading for some time now. The light outside was dim instead of bright afternoon.

"Dahlia?"

It was Grant's voice. She wanted to throw open the door, see for herself he was all right. But Mary's warning about Grant not seeing the books had her grabbing them all and shoving them frantically under the bed. "Just a minute!"

It was ridiculous. Like she was a child sneaking Harry Potter again when her parents didn't approve. But she supposed as much as she wanted it to be different because she was an adult, it wasn't, because this was Grant and his family's house.

Not hers.

She tried to steady her uneven breathing and the odd nerves that moved through her. She wanted to *see* he was all right, and she didn't want to face what had happened.

But it was time she stopped being such a coward.

She opened the door and tried to manage her best approximation of a smile. He stood there looking just as he had this morning. Maybe he was a little pale, but he stood on his own two feet and didn't seem to hold himself any differently.

He was fine and whole.

"I just wanted to make sure you're all right," he said, his eyes warm and kind.

"Me? You're the one who was hurt." She wanted to reach out and touch him. Assure herself he was as real and sturdy as he seemed. But there was all this space between them, and it felt like some kind of wall.

"I'm sorry," he offered stiffly.

But she couldn't fathom what he was apologizing for. "For what?"

"They got away. Now Jack's got a crime to investigate, and he will—him and his department—do an excellent job."

"I wish I found that convincing."

He pulled a face. "I wish I could feel more convincing, but the truth is their hands are tied by the law in a way mine aren't. I won't be giving up on this, Dahlia. I want you to know that. I won't rest until we find who's after you. And I am not bound to the laws Jack is."

He said it so earnestly. Like it was a vow or a promise. Like her safety was important to him personally. Like he'd protect her.

"I'm not sure anyone has ever..." She trailed off, because it was a foolish thing to say, to feel. She was *paying* him, and she couldn't keep doing it for much longer. So she needed to figure out how to protect herself. "Grant, I need you to do something for me."

"What?"

"I need you to teach me to fight."

CHAPTER THIRTEEN

GRANT FOUND HIMSELF at a loss for words. She looked a little healthier than she had when she'd first come to them, but she was still on the frail side. She was a librarian and tended toward skittish. She'd told him herself she wasn't athletic. He just…couldn't picture her throwing a punch.

But anyone could learn—that or how to shoot a gun. Anna had always taken to shooting and fighting, but it had been Mary's natural inclination to avoid those things, and still she'd learned. Grant considered her marksmanship a personal triumph. He had taught her, after all.

Before you lost the ability.

"I can see what you're thinking," Dahlia said, sounding *almost* peeved. "And you aren't wrong. I'm weak. I don't know the first thing about protecting myself, except to walk with my keys between my fingers in a dark parking lot, but that's just it. I spent my whole life avoiding the dark parking lot. The sketchy situation. I can't avoid this. And I *hate* what happened today. Not just because you were hurt but because I just sat there and let it happen. I hate the fact I hid and didn't know what to do. I was *weak*."

"You went for the gun. You didn't hide. The fact that

you're here, still standing, after all you've been through, isn't weakness."

But she was having none of it. "I did hide for a while, and I only went to the gun to keep it from them. I don't know what to do with a gun. And if they're going to keep coming after me, I should know how to fight or shoot or something."

"I'm going to be here." He had to resist the urge to take her by the shoulders. To press all of his assurances into her like he could tattoo them on her. "We're all going to be here protecting you."

"Not forever," she replied, clearly troubled.

He didn't know why it bothered him that she was already thinking ahead to that. He didn't know why he wanted to...just protect her. When his sisters had been growing up, he'd been all about giving them the skills to protect themselves.

Nothing about his reaction to Dahlia ever made any sense. But she *was* speaking logically, even if something deep inside him rebelled at the thought. "We can do that. Teach you some self-defense."

She let out a breath as if she'd been afraid he'd refuse the request. "Thank you." Then she took a step forward, hesitated. But seemed to sort of gather herself, or her courage, and reach out. She put a hand on his arm and looked him right in the eye. "I'm so sorry you were hurt."

It was such a genuine flat-out apology—something that had not existed in his life as a Hudson or in his life as a Marine. He could only stare back at her. What did someone *say* to that? Who just came out and apologized with no equivocations or attempts to pick a fight?

She cleared her throat and let her hand drop, which

felt like a loss. For a moment it was like he was reconnected to some old pieces of himself he'd thought he'd lost.

Which was a particularly ridiculous thought. "I've survived worse."

Her eyebrows drew together, and he forgot that people who weren't military or his family didn't always have that same dark sense of humor or slightly warped way of looking at things.

"Were you hurt in the military?"

Grant shrugged. "Here and there. Nothing major. Never sent me home over it."

This did not assuage her concern or smooth out the furrow in her brow. "Is that why you don't like talking about it?"

There was something about her blue eyes, the way she looked at him that felt like looking *into* him. He'd swear she was hypnotizing him if he believed in such things.

"I survived my injuries. No, I don't see the need to recount them, but they don't weigh on me. They are what they are."

"Then what does weigh on you?"

If anyone else had asked that question, he would have tensed. He would have barked out a rebuff as a response or said nothing at all. *Anyone* else.

But it was Dahlia, and she was just…different. And open. She had no preconceived opinions about him. No opinions on his military experience or what he wore to the tenth grade homecoming. She apologized and stumbled in the mud and loved dogs. She had her own demons, and somehow…that made him want to share his own.

"I was lucky. Not everyone was. Not just…making it home in one piece but being able to bear the weight of what you see."

Her hand rubbed up and down his elbow for a second. Comfort, or an attempt at it. "I'm not sure I'm bearing the weight of anything very well lately," she said, her voice quiet. Sad.

He couldn't help himself. He lifted his own hand and rested it over hers on his elbow. He smoothed his thumb over the top of her hand. "Not all weights are meant to be borne easily. Certainly not loss and grief. Those are the weights you have to learn to carry in whatever ways you can. You've come this far, Dahlia. And I am intimately acquainted with the strength you need to push forward when everyone tells you to let it go. Jack and the family… We may not have gotten our answers, but we stuck it out a lot longer than anyone else. We exhausted every option. I'm proud of that, and it made the weight easier to carry eventually."

Her hand was small and warm, the skin soft where his thumb brushed. For a moment her eyes dropped to their joined hands, and he saw the little hitch in her breath and felt something he really wasn't allowed to feel when it came to a client.

Maybe it wasn't a Hudson rule, but it damn well should be.

She looked up then, pinning him with that blue gaze. "I know you said you're not a war hero, but why do people *think* you're one?"

It was enough of an uncomfortable and unwanted topic that he managed to pull his hand away instead of getting lost deeper in this moment that was feeling more and more dangerous.

"Why are we having this conversation?" he asked. "We'll be late for dinner."

"Right." She looked away and attempted to smile as her hand dropped off his arm, but it faltered. "Sorry. I'm not usually nosy."

"So, why are you now?"

"I...don't know."

"Can I be nosy for a second?"

She sucked in a breath and let it out like she was preparing herself. When she looked at him again, she had her pleasant but distant smile on. "Sure."

He shouldn't ask. He should keep his big mouth shut. It was one hundred percent none of his business. She was a client, and regardless of her answer, it changed nothing. And still the words came out anyway. "There's no one waiting for you back home?"

"Well, my parents, but they're not really waiting for me."

"That's...not what I meant."

Confusion lined her face, but then she seemed to clue in. If the blush creeping into her cheeks was anything to go by.

"Oh. No. There's...no one."

Grant should maybe laugh it off or say something about needing to know for safety reasons or something ridiculous. But he didn't. "Ready for dinner?" he asked instead.

And she nodded and followed him out of the room.

DAHLIA HAD GONE through dinner wondering if Grant had used some sort of...distraction tactic on her. Flirt with the mess of a woman wanting to learn to fight, and she'll forget all about it.

Or something.

But the next morning at breakfast, Anna and Palmer were waiting for her. "Grant said you wanted to learn some self-defense." So he'd listened. And done something about her request.

"Oh, well, yes." She tried not to look around the kitchen and into the big dining room and failed. "Is he around?"

"I sent him back to bed. He looked *terrible*." As if realizing this was the wrong thing to say to the woman who felt slightly responsible for his *stab* wound, Anna quickly continued on. "That was at like five this morning. He's refusing to take the pain meds, so he just didn't sleep well. I bet he'll be back down any minute for some breakfast. Everything else is just fine on the Grant front."

"That seems generous, Anna," Palmer said, clearly teasing as he earned himself a glare from his sister. Then a hard jab to the stomach that had Palmer doubling over a little.

"The element of surprise is your first lesson," Anna said, back to smiling. "That and eat a solid breakfast." They all turned as they heard a noise—Grant entering the kitchen.

Dahlia didn't think he looked terrible, but he hadn't shaved or combed his hair, so he did look a little dangerously disheveled. It made her stomach do little flips. She didn't even *know* this man, not really, and her silly immature reaction to him was really starting to be a problem.

"How's it going, champ?" Palmer greeted.

"Just fantastic," Grant grumbled. But he looked over

at Dahlia and managed a smile, if a little gruff around the edges. "Morning."

"Good morning," she replied. "I could make—"

"Mary already made you two plates," Anna interrupted, pulling the refrigerator door open. "She said you're both on the 'on the mend' diet. Lots of protein and liquids."

"I'm not injured," Dahlia protested.

"No, but you're *way* too skinny, and Mary loves to mother. She's on horse duty this morning, but she instructed me by threat of pain and suffering to warm up your meals and make sure you eat." Anna popped one plate into the microwave as she said this. "Go on into the dining room. I live to serve."

Palmer gave an exaggerated laugh. "That's a new one."

Still, Grant and Palmer moved into the dining room, so Dahlia felt like she had to as well. She took a seat in the chair that seemed to be *hers*, while Palmer and Grant spoke of some ranch thing and sipped their coffee.

Anna entered soon enough, carrying two plates she set in front of Dahlia and Grant. "Eat up or face the wrath of Mary, a surprisingly alarming force if provoked."

Dahlia tried to smile. Her appetite hadn't returned any on its own, but the food was always so delicious once she started, she'd manage to eat the whole meal. Maybe she was learning to feed her body even when it seemed to not want to be fed.

"We'll go over some basic protection moves and how to use a gun," Palmer said, as if this were a normal thing to discuss over breakfast. So casual. "Anna and I will show you the self-defense moves since Grant has to rest, but he'll teach you how to shoot."

"Maybe she'd do better with a female teacher," Grant offered, shifting in his chair, then wincing. Dahlia wished there was anything she could do to take the pain away.

"Or someone more on par with a beginner's skills," Palmer said, clearly teasing Anna.

But Anna didn't seem interested in rising to the bait. "Grant's the best shot, by far. And he's the most patient out of any of us, but Mary or I can do it if you want."

"Hey, I can be patient," Palmer replied.

"Yeah, getting out of bed maybe," Anna grumbled.

"I don't really..." Dahlia swallowed. She wanted their help so badly, had even asked Grant for it, but it seemed like too much. "I appreciate—"

"Dahlia," Grant interrupted. "You need to stop thinking you're some kind of burden to us."

She looked at him, arrested by how simply he cut to the heart of the matter when she wasn't sure she'd even realized that was the clearest verbalization of her thoughts.

"But..." She'd always felt...a bit like a burden to everyone. And she'd worked very hard to shrink herself down, shut herself out, so no one thought she took up too much space or asked for too much.

Rose's disappearance had been an odd turning point in her life, giving her a courage and determination she'd never had. So maybe it required a change in how she looked at the world around her.

Not a burden but a person who took an opportunity when it was offered.

"This whole thing is to help people," Anna said, gesturing around the house. "Because we've been there. So, no burdens."

"It has to be a business," Palmer continued. "Realistically. But that doesn't mean it isn't more than that too."

"There's a reason we keep a running ranch along with it," Grant added. "That's about money and legacy. This is about...us."

"Trust me, the three of us? We don't offer *anything* out of the goodness of our hearts," Anna said.

Dahlia found herself glancing at Grant. He didn't argue with Anna, but Dahlia felt like he should have. He'd been *stabbed* in an effort to keep her safe. *That* was goodness.

"Eat," Grant told her gently. And she didn't know what else to do but that.

CHAPTER FOURTEEN

THE DAYS PASSED with very little forward movement. They kept Dahlia on the ranch, watched over by someone or cameras or a dog at all times. In the mornings, Grant or one of his siblings worked on her with either self-defense or shooting.

Jack's sheriff's department found nothing. It frustrated Grant, but when he was being fair, he realized that whatever kind of copycat group this was had been avoiding detection for some time, so just because law enforcement *knew* of them didn't mean it would make them easy to find.

If the group had really found Rose Easton and murdered her, as seemed likely, they'd spent over a year keeping everything under wraps—from law enforcement, private investigators and Dahlia herself.

Much as he didn't *want* to, Grant knew he needed to go back to Truth and poke around. The police had done it multiple times, but Grant just got the feeling there was something more there. And if not...well, at least it felt like *doing* something.

Because teaching Dahlia how to shoot was slow torture in the "this woman is very off-limits to me right now" department. And the very uncomfortable realization that the man he'd been before he'd been deployed would not have cared and done something about it anyway.

He found her with Anna in the little gym they had in one of the outbuildings. They were both breathing a little heavily, likely having been at self-defense practice for a half hour or so.

He didn't dare show up sooner, because watching her learn to punch and block and break holds should *not* have affected him in any way, but it did.

"Dead Eye is here," Anna announced cheerfully when she caught sight of him. "Just in time. I've got a few calls to take." Anna walked over to him, lowered her voice as she passed. "I'm going to be scarce for a few days, FYI."

"Am I the only one you're telling?"

"You and Mary," she replied, then flashed him a grin. "Don't go telling big brother on me. I know a guy who knows a guy. Might be able to get me some info. Might not. I'll be back by the weekend."

He resisted the urge to lecture Anna on being careful. He couldn't say they were alike in many ways, but while Jack, Palmer *and* Cash all wanted to lock her up in a room and pretend like she was still a little girl, Grant understood the restlessness. The need to get out there and take some risks.

But he was still himself and a man and a big brother. "Be careful."

"I was born careful," she replied. Which was a flat-out lie, but there was no use in arguing the point with her. He let her go instead. Just like all his siblings had let him go once upon a time.

When she was gone, he turned to Dahlia. She was standing a little uncertainly on one of the mats. Her gaze was on the gun in his hand, but she raised her eyes and forced a smile.

"I really appreciate—" At his scowl, she waved him off, but she smiled, and this one was genuine, not forced. She had the sweetest smile, not saccharine or anything. Just sort of like they were rare and special when she doled one out.

"It's not a *thank you* this time. Promise," she said. She gave the gun another sideways glance. She'd learned the safety rules and shot it a few times, but she didn't care for the noise or impact.

Dahlia approached him, and he got the impression she was trying to choose the right words to say. She was always so careful with her words, and he had to wonder what had made her that way.

"I appreciate you teaching me how to use it." Then her shoulders drooped and she let out a really long sigh. "I just really hate it."

It was his turn to smile. "Yeah, I can tell."

She wrinkled her nose. "I know I'm a weakling."

"Hardly. Mary's not a fan either. She learned because it's a necessity out here, and it helped put Jack's mind at ease, but she's no fan. Cash won't touch guns around Izzy. They aren't toys. It's okay to be uneasy about them. Better than liking them *too* much."

She nodded. "I appreciate that. So, we could be done with this side of things since I could at least hold one and point it at somebody if I had to?" she asked hopefully.

"And we'll work really hard to make sure you don't have to," Grant said firmly. He'd make it his mission.

Her smile was back, though it wobbled a bit. "Um. The thing is. We've settled in. We've regrouped. I've got…very minimal self-defense skills, sure, but I have to *do* something. I'm running out of money, and before you tell me yet again the money doesn't matter, try to understand it matters to *me*."

He didn't *like* that it did, but he could understand it anyway. Pride and that need to feel like she had some control over her life. Still, he didn't need to dwell on the fact if she ran out of money, she'd leave.

"I was thinking about heading out to Truth this afternoon," he offered instead, though he hadn't really planned on telling her.

But he could admit, here in the privacy of his own mind, he wanted to spend time with her. Even if it was torture. It was the kind that reminded him not everything had broken irreparably in the Middle East.

"Jack won't approve, which means if you want to come, it'd just be us. And Willie. And we'll probably have to lie to my siblings. At least some of them. So you could tag along, as long as none of that bothers you."

She chewed on her bottom lip, and since he didn't want to look at *that* and let his mind wander, he looked at the curls around her temple that had fallen out of the hair tie she had most of her hair pulled back in.

"Well…" she began, not meeting his gaze "…speaking of lying."

Grant didn't need to feign surprise. "*You've* been lying?"

She looked up at him through her lashes. "It's not so much lying as omitting some facts you may not care for." She tried for a reassuring smile. "It's just, those chants really bothered me, and it pointed out a small hole in my research."

"What kind of hole?"

"I'd researched the Greens, how they connected to my family and what the cult *was*, sure, but not really the actual beliefs or rituals."

Grant usually had a good poker face, but nope, not when it came to the Order of Truth. "You've been researching the cult." It sat in his gut like a weight.

Dahlia looked pained. "Mary mentioned you wouldn't like that."

It frustrated him. That Dahlia looked guilty when she had every right to do whatever the hell she wanted. That his sister was going around discussing anything to do with the cult or his feelings on it with *anyone*. "Oh, Mary did, did she? And who else knows this is what you've been up to?"

"Well—" she blew out a breath "—I am sorry. Anna knows too, but that's it. We've kind of been discussing it, and I just—I *am* sorry. I know it bothers you, but I kept thinking that if maybe I understood…what they thought, what they did, it would give us some clue as to where they were or…" She reached out, just a light finger brush against the sleeve of his coat. "I *am* sorry."

"You don't owe me any apologies for doing what you think is best." Not that he could agree, even if she *was* right. His father had always warned him Truth was dangerous. Because it wasn't just about murderers and religious zealotry. It was about taking advantage of people desperate for something to believe in. Something to belong to.

He didn't think Dahlia was desperate, but she was alone. The few things she'd said about her family didn't paint a close picture. She was here in a place where she didn't really know anyone, trying to find her sister's *murderer*. It wasn't that he thought she was susceptible for falling for a cult. It was just all so dangerous and she had so very little support.

"I don't want you to be mad at me," she said when the silence between them stretched out.

"I'm not," he said, automatically. Being mad at her didn't have anything to do with what he was feeling. He hesitated to tell her the truth. "It's dangerous business. I know you don't need me to tell you that. It's just, I'm not even sure I can explain it. Truth has always been a shadow in this town, a boogeyman of sorts. I don't know anyone whose family wasn't affected, even if it was generations ago. My own parents included, and it was just...we were raised with the belief you don't go poking into Truth. It's an open wound." He sighed. "Anna, of course, loves poking at an open wound."

Her mouth curved very little, as if she agreed with his assessment of Anna, but she sobered quickly. "I don't want to poke at anything. I just want to find out what happened to my sister."

"I know. That's why even if I'm uncomfortable, I can't be angry with you."

"So, if you're all frowny and gruff, it's discomfort, not disapproval."

"Frowny and gruff? I think you've been spending too much time with my sisters."

She smiled a little, some of the gravity leaving her expression. He wished it would lighten any of the weight inside of him.

"It's a dangerous situation in a lot of ways. Particularly if we're wading into a murder investigation. Even if I understand, even if I even think it's a necessary step, poking into the Order of Truth is dangerous. And tricky. I worry about you."

Her eyes widened a little. "No one ever worries about me."

"Well, you can't say that, because I do."

She looked up at him, expression perfectly serious, but searching too. He didn't know what she was searching for. Didn't know if he wanted to give whatever it was if he could.

"Do you worry about everyone you help solve cold cases for?" she asked after a long pause, her voice quieter. More hushed.

He shook his head. "No." He could elaborate on that. Explain how his cases were rarely murders or dangerous, and never had to do with psychotic cults. But he didn't.

So they simply stood staring at each other. There was more he should say or a subject to change or something. His gaze certainly shouldn't drop to her mouth, and his body *definitely* shouldn't lean forward like she was some magnetic force he was pulled to.

But she didn't step back. She didn't break his gaze or do anything to *stop* him. He could have kissed her, easy enough. But the moment stretched too long, got too big in his head. And a loud, sharp bark interrupted any forward progress he'd thought of making.

Willie ran in, tail wagging, so it wasn't any kind of warning bark. Just an excited one. Grant looked at his watch. Had to, instead of risking a glance at her. Noon.

Grant cleared her throat. "That's the lunchtime signal."

"Right. Sure. So, lunch and then we'll go out to Truth…without telling anyone?"

Grant nodded. And felt, not at all for the first time, that he'd never get used to the man he'd become after leaving the military and returning home.

DAHLIA FOLLOWED GRANT INSIDE, and they ate lunch with Mary and Palmer. Then Grant encouraged her to grab a bag and any of her notes she thought might be helpful, and then they headed out to his truck to drive to Truth, Willie at her heels.

It was a strange and probably terrible thing that she was thinking more about the way Grant had looked at her in the gym than she was about her notes and what she might want to investigate once they got to Truth.

She should be thinking about Rose. About murder and danger and wondering why knowing Rose was dead didn't bring her any sense of closure.

But she thought about the way Grant's eyes had moved to her mouth. The way he'd seemed…closer. The way no matter how she told herself she was probably hallucinating, it had seemed like he'd at least *considered* kissing her.

She was a terrible person. At least, that's what she kept trying to convince herself. But somewhere on the quiet drive over to Truth, she had the realization the voice in her head arguing with the trajectory of her thoughts sounded an awful lot like her mother.

Grant had said he *worried* about her, which was hard to fathom when her whole life she'd been told no one really *had* to worry about her. She was a good girl, who followed the rules and would never dream of stepping out of line. So what was there to worry about?

Rose had been the wild one. *And look where that got her.*

Again, her mother's voice. Not her own. If she had a friend in the exact position she was, would she be telling her friend she was a terrible person for thinking about more than just her sister? Or would she remind that friend that tragedy or not, she was still alive.

And for the first time in a long time, the thought felt like an optimistic one.

It wasn't just Grant and the possibility that he might inexplicably be interested in her. It was his whole family. The way they treated her more like family than her own did.

He was *worried* about her safety. She wanted to play it off like…it was just his noble heart. All that military stuff and wanting to help and protect people.

But it felt different, Grant's worry, than anything the rest of his family did. Even if they were nice and compassionate, the way Grant looked at her *was* different.

And your sister is dead.

But you are alive.

She snuck a look at Grant. His gaze was on the road ahead, and he looked so serious. There was a way his siblings treated him, and the kind of indulgent look he gave them when they did, that made her think he hadn't always been quite so stoic. Like maybe the military had hardened him.

But he was hardly all tough outer exterior. There was a softness underneath it all. Or maybe that wasn't the right word. Something hidden.

Willie stuck his head between the front two seats, pushing his nose against her shoulder until she twisted around to give his ears a scratch. "I've always wanted a dog," she said absently.

"Why don't you get one?"

"Oh, both my father and Rose are—were allergic. Then when I was on my own, my apartment didn't allow pets."

He seemed to think that over. "I don't want to tell you what to do, but at some point you've got to realize you're the adult and get to make the choices in your life for you, not other people. And I only say that because it was a strange realization I had when I got out of the military."

"I don't think you can compare leaving home and going to *war*."

He shrugged. "Depends, I guess, on how much your childhood felt like a war zone. Metaphorically."

She wanted to keep arguing with him, but it was the word *metaphorically* that kept the words lodged in her throat. Metaphorically, it had been a bit like a war. Her parents forever throwing volleys at Rose, and Rose forever hurling them right back. And Dahlia somewhere in the middle just trying to hide.

Grant didn't say any more, but he pulled his truck off the highway and onto the country road that led to Truth. Dahlia watched the landscape, and even though she knew the men that had stopped them in the road, the men who'd killed Rose could be out there, she felt that same strange sense of peace as they came up on the ghost town.

She knew she was supposed to be appalled because of what had happened here, but… "It's such a pretty place."

He pulled the truck to a stop, and she could *feel* his disapproval, even if he didn't say it out loud.

"I know you can't look past what you know happened here, but there's something peaceful about it."

"You don't have to justify your feelings to me, Dahlia. You get to feel what you want. Kinda like you get to make the choices you want."

He started getting out of the truck, but she felt stuck for a moment. He didn't sound mad or dismissive, just like it was obvious. *You get to feel what you want.*

It was…revolutionary. Maybe because she'd led such a small life, but she was used to…defending herself at every turn. To always feeling like the odd man out who had to change what she thought or felt to suit everyone else. To stop all that metaphorical war.

He came around to her side of the truck and opened the door for her. But there was concern in his expression. "You okay?"

She swallowed. Sure, she was fine. Just having her whole worldview upended since the disappearance of her sister. "Yeah." She forced herself to get out of the truck, and Willie jumped out after her.

They stood there, shoulder to shoulder, surveying the abandoned town of Truth. Dahlia felt lost. For so long, the simple act of finding Rose had given her a goal. Something to fight for and toward.

She still wanted to find Rose's killer—she really did—but the confirmation she had to be dead was… disorienting.

And then Grant pointing out all these things she didn't *have* to do. All these old thought patterns and behaviors that didn't suit her.

Who *was* she?

Grant's hand covered hers, his fingers threading through hers. A gesture of support. He gave a little squeeze. Reassurance.

"Come on. Let's go poke around," he said.

Maybe she didn't know who she was anymore, or maybe she'd never known. Maybe she'd always been afraid. But she'd spent the last year doing the unthinkable, leading to this moment where she was holding hands with a handsome cowboy, determined to find answers.

So, she'd figure it out. She'd figure it *all* out.

CHAPTER FIFTEEN

GRANT DIDN'T KNOW what he was looking for, but that often happened with cold cases—even ones that got a little warm. You had to look and be open for anything.

Even holding hands with your off-limits client.

It was meant to be a comforting gesture, and he felt like it had worked. But it was…more to him. Like reaching out and forging a connection when he'd spent the last year at home struggling to make connections.

She had such strength in her, but she still seemed a little reluctant to use it. He was getting the impression it came from a childhood of shrinking herself into a mold that didn't fit, and he knew…

His parents had been wonderful, but losing them the way they had, had put him and all his siblings in a kind of box. A mold they were expected to fill, and it had chafed, so he'd gone off to war.

And lost who he was.

Not the time. At all. They were here to find clues, not make some kind of large-scale realizations about life.

But he didn't let her hand go. She seemed to need that connection to move forward, and he didn't mind it himself. It took his mind off the throbbing pain in his side where the damned stab wound never stopped reminding him he'd been hurt.

"Remember that place where we found the bullet thing?" Dahlia asked.

"The casing, yes."

"I was reading, and that was like a holy place where they did rituals and things. Maybe they still do. Maybe that's why a casing was there."

"Do their rituals involve guns? Because even last week on the highway, only one of them had a gun and was using it."

"No. That is something I noticed about a lot of the literature. They don't believe in modern weapons. Though there was a whole section on how Eugene Green stockpiled semiautomatic weapons in a bunker. So, I guess it's your typical 'do what I say, not what I do.'"

Grant nodded grimly, and they walked through the alley and into the enclosed area. It didn't surprise him they did rituals there. It had always given him the creeps, the way the stone seemed to block out everything except the sky. Making you a target.

He didn't particularly want to go back in there, but they *had* found the casing there. So someone had been around. Maybe they'd just been doing target practice, maybe it had been kids, but maybe…there were more clues to be found.

She hesitated at the opening to the enclosed courtyard, which made him feel good about his own pause.

"They chose this place and built these walls because they said it was sacred ground containing some stones that were found here."

Grant looked at the dirt beneath his feet. "They didn't leave the stones?"

"No, they made them a kind of traveling altar for the Truth Prophet. As much as they settled here, there's this sense they always knew they had to be…mobile? Or nomads? Kind of like they needed to cling to this idea of being persecuted."

"Truth Prophet. Who listens to that garbage?"

Dahlia moved forward, and their fingers slid apart. She dropped his hand. "Desperate people do desperate things."

He felt chastised, though he didn't know why. He'd probably seen a lot more people do a lot more desperate things than she ever had. But she moved forward into the walled courtyard. The afternoon sun was high above lighting up the odd shadowed circle of earth and her with it.

The sun gleamed on her red hair. She looked like some kind of goddess. Ancient and powerful. He couldn't paint, couldn't take a picture in focus to save his life, but he somehow wanted to memorialize that moment where she looked…otherworldly and somehow perfectly at home. Here.

Perfect.

She looked away from the walls to him, then frowned. "What is it?" she asked.

"You're beautiful."

She opened her mouth, then closed it, clearly flustered. Part of him thought he should apologize. It wasn't *appropriate.* But it was true, so he didn't know how to pull it back.

She swallowed, visibly, looking up at him with those big blue eyes. Willie wagging his tail between them, as if he were an eager onlooker.

"Well, um. Thanks," she finally said when he couldn't quite come up with the right collection of words.

Grant shrugged. "Just true," he managed. Then he

looked around the courtyard. "We found the shell casing right there," he said, pointing. "Was there anything about this place in particular in the books? Like it's special beyond sacred or…"

She shook her head. "Some things were specific, but they were more generic about where things happened. They never named Truth as their town or any of the waterways or mountains they considered sacred, just some of the things they did there. They didn't even specify this place, except that it was a stone circle and sacred because of what was found in the earth. Maybe there's another one somewhere too, but I figured since we knew this one existed, it was probably the one they were talking about."

Grant nodded along. He didn't understand adult people falling for this hocus pocus, sacred and prophets and what have you. Sure, a kid might be predisposed into whatever worship they were brought up in, but people choosing this… It made no sense to him.

Dahlia still stood in the center, squinting up at the sun now. "One thing the books all agreed on was the Truth Prophet is always a Green. They believe in blood and genetic ties. Sort of like the monarchy, but it's more about who's…powerful or connected to the truth, I guess."

He could see that she felt…bad about that. Like somehow she was connected to all this idiocy when she'd never stepped foot here before this month.

"You're not a Green."

She looked over at him. "No, but they want me for some reason." She seemed to grapple with telling him something. He found he didn't want to press. Whatever was on her mind, he wanted her to tell him of her own volition.

You have a real problem.

"They believe in sacrificing people. I think that's what they did here."

The word sacrifice gave him a cold chill, and he could tell it bothered her too. Though even without studying, he knew the Order of Truth believed in human sacrifice. It was part of why they'd been such a story. "None of their so-called sacrifices were done with a bullet."

"No, they weren't," Dahlia agreed. She moved around the courtyard, Willie at her heels. She looked so alone. Like the world was on her shoulders, and Grant knew what that felt like. It didn't matter if people wanted to help you when you felt like there was some wall between you and the people. A wall you didn't know how to tear down or cross or ask for help through.

So, he followed her path around the area, wishing every step didn't cause a spiking pain through his stomach. But it was better than being numb on painkillers. He kept following her path until he was behind her as she studied the ground where they'd found the mysterious casing.

"Dahlia, what's on your mind? Hopefully you know that even if I don't agree, you can tell me. It doesn't change anything." Because he sensed that reluctance in her, and he couldn't help but wonder if she'd been talking to Mary or Anna about it, she would have just said it.

He didn't want to be the reason she didn't speak her mind. Didn't make suggestions.

She turned to face him, chewing on her bottom lip.

She looked up at the sun again, then down at Willie. "Rose is blond," she said at length.

"Okay."

"The Greens who are the prophets? They always had red hair. It was a kind of...symbol."

He saw now what she was grappling with. It pained him that she could even think that connected her. "Dahlia, you're not a Green."

"Does it matter if I know I'm not if they think I am? I wasn't into it the way Rose was, but genes are science. It's DNA and chromosomes and... Does me having Green blood change who I am? No. But it makes me someone important to them."

It was why they wanted her. Why they'd been willing to hurt him but not her.

"Grant..." She looked up at him imploringly. Like she needed him to be on her side, and he had a very bad feeling he wouldn't want to be. "I think I need to let them take me."

DAHLIA KNEW HE wouldn't *agree* with the idea, but she hadn't expected him to laugh. She frowned at him as he laughed and laughed.

Then he seemed to get some dust in his nose and sneezed. He winced and kind of doubled over, clearly in pain from the whole thing.

And maybe it served him right for laughing, but she still felt bad. Especially when he let out a quiet string of curses, still bent over.

"Are you okay?" She reached out, hand on his shoulder, one on his jaw, needing to offer some comfort. Maybe it was his own fault for laughing, but she still felt at least partially responsible for his *stab* wound.

He straightened, tilted his head back and breathed deeply, but still winced because that likely hurt too.

"Guess I deserved that," he muttered. Then he reached up and patted her hand that was still on his jaw. But she didn't drop her hand, and then he just sort of left his there.

They stared at each other for the longest time, and she knew this was…secondary. Whatever they were starting to feel for one another didn't belong in a creepy cult, deserted ghost town on the search for her dead sister.

But it was something good in a sea of all that had been bad, and she wanted to cling to it like a life jacket. She could feel what she wanted. She could *do* what she wanted. She wasn't beholden to everyone else.

So when he took her hand off his jaw, she wanted to protest. Until he pulled it toward his mouth. He pressed his lips to her palm, holding her gaze the whole time. She would have said it was offhanded, but it *wasn't*. Because his mouth had touched her skin and that wasn't something friends just *did*. Certainly no friends she'd ever had.

He opened his mouth, and she braced herself for some apology or explanation. But instead of saying something that would make her feel foolish or angry, he closed his mouth.

Instead of excuses or walking away or letting Willie or anything distract him, like what had happened back in the gym, he leaned down and gently placed his mouth to hers.

And it was gentle, but it wasn't timid. It was careful, but he wasn't holding back. There was a sweetness to it and a heat. A deep longing sense of something inside of her clicking into place. Like this moment was exactly where she belonged.

When he eased away, it wasn't so much like an ending, but more like the natural ebb and flow of something. Come together, step apart. *Don't let go.*

And still she had no words, because that kiss was better than anything she'd ever read about. Any movie she'd sighed over. Maybe because it wasn't just fuzzy feelings of "wouldn't that be amazing?" Maybe it was just…reality was better than imagination.

With the right kind of man, anyway.

She looked up at him, not sure she understood the expression on his face. Maybe because it reflected so many things deep under the stoic mask she knew was more habit than who he was.

He was real and human and flawed, and so was she, and…she didn't know how this could happen in the middle of the worst year of her life. But that only seemed to make it more precious.

"Probably not the place for this." He didn't let her go, exactly. He smoothed his hand down her arm, then eased away, but not completely. Not like distance.

"Probably not."

He let out a long careful sigh. "I can't let you be taken, Dahlia. I get it. Why you'd think that'd be a solution. I'm not sure I wouldn't think the same thing in your position. But self-sacrifice isn't the answer here."

"Then what is?"

"I don't know. Sometimes it takes a while to find an answer. But I can't let anything happen to you. Professionally. Personally."

She felt a little flutter of panic because this was not expected. This was not what she'd come here for. Could a kiss change the course of her life? She very much wanted to see if it could. When she never, ever got what she wanted. Not really. "We don't even know each other," she said, her voice little more than a whisper.

"I wish I could agree with you. But you feel right, Dahlia."

It took her breath away. Probably because she knew he didn't say things he didn't mean. Because he wasn't prone to exaggeration or sparing feelings. If there was anything she was sure of when it came to Grant, it was that the truth was as sacred to him as this place had been to the cult that wanted her.

But if they took her, she could find answers. And if they didn't want her dead because of dumb things like bloodlines and red hair, didn't that mean she had some power in the situation?

He lifted her chin with his fingertips, forcing her to look him in the eye. "It isn't an option. I need you to promise me you understand that."

She decided to use his own words against him. "I wish I could agree with you and promise you that."

He frowned, but he didn't drop her chin. He didn't step away, and she realized she'd braced herself for him to do just that. And it wasn't fair. At every turn, Grant had not done what he wanted at the expense of what she wanted. He'd listened, considered, and even when he'd disagreed, it hadn't changed how he treated her, how he looked at her.

How he kissed her.

It was hard to know what to do with that when her agreement with everyone had always been the condition to their love.

"Okay," he said at last, his fingers still gently pressed

to her chin. But his eyes darted to the left, and everything about him tensed, though he stood completely still. When he moved, it was a blur and he moved her with him.

He had her pressed up against the wall, the stone cold against her back, him hard and warm against her front. It might be enjoyable if he wasn't looking at the top of the wall, if their bodies being pressed together was about that kiss earlier and not about him shielding her body with his.

"Grant."

"I heard something," he murmured. "We're definitely not alone. And this place is too open."

She realized he had his gun in one hand while another wrapped around her elbow like he was about to guide her somewhere.

"We'll move carefully out of here." He glanced at Willie, who was standing guard at the entrance. If he sensed anyone, he didn't show it, except in maybe the fact his tail wasn't wagging. But he didn't bark or growl.

"They want me, and not dead, maybe I should be the one protecting you," Dahlia said, worrying over his stab wound.

Grant's expression got even harder. "Just because they want you alive at first doesn't mean they always will. Keep that in mind before you go sacrificing yourself to your sister's memory."

It hurt, she supposed because it poked at a truth, and what she *had* been thinking. That she'd be safe even if it was scary. But maybe Rose had thought that too. Maybe a cult full of psychopaths and sociopaths only had so much use for a person, even if they were a red-headed descendent of a Green.

"I'll apologize for that later," he muttered irritably, taking her elbow. He moved her, always keeping his body sort of wrapped around hers, her back against the wall. Protecting her.

She knew he'd do it to anyone. It was who he was—a protector, a hero. But still, even though it wasn't personal to *her*, it was still something that made her heart stumble. That and even though he'd been harsh, which was just his natural way of things, he admitted the need to apologize.

They reached the opening of the courtyard, and Willie came to attention while Grant looked out, surveying the area presumably for people. "I don't see anyone, but someone is out there."

Dahlia remembered how she'd felt the last time she'd been here. In the end, she'd chalked up that feeling of being watched to the dog and Grant, but maybe there was more. Maybe someone was *always* here.

But they'd looked through the town and found no sign of people, and maybe she wouldn't know what signs to look for, but Grant would.

"Come on," he said, gently moving her out of the courtyard and into the alley, still blocking her as best he could.

They made it to the road when Willie let out a low growl, and Grant turned toward where the dog was focused, but Dahlia felt drawn to look to the right instead. Down the length of the abandoned street.

There was a figure in one of the broken windows. A shadow or…a person. She opened her mouth to tell Grant, but she caught the flash of something familiar. She stood stock still for longer than she could count.

Surely it was a dream. A hallucination. She'd finally had that psychotic break her parents were so worried about.

But the figure didn't vanish. It moved from the window to the empty doorway. The figure—the person—appeared as real as anything else. "Rose," she whispered.

Just as Grant whirled around and shot.

CHAPTER SIXTEEN

DAHLIA'S SCREAM ECHOED in Grant's ears even as he pushed her onto the ground. The man on the ridge disappeared, so Grant didn't think his shot had been in time. But he was ready for a return volley.

Dahlia struggled against him.

"Stay down. Someone could shoot back," he ordered.

"It's her," Dahlia said, still struggling.

Willie trembled next to her—not in fear, but because the dog was eager to track down the threat. But Grant could hardly leave Dahlia here without protection. So Willie had to stay.

Why did you bring her?

More screams echoed in his head, but he knew they weren't real. Or at least real in this moment. Old screams. Old smoke and explosions.

He really did not need this now.

"It's her. I saw her. Grant, I saw her," Dahlia kept saying. But he couldn't get his brain to click in. "Why'd you shoot at her?"

Lincoln is down. Get out of here, Hudson.

He squeezed his eyes shut against the old voices. He hadn't run. At least there was that. In the moment he could have saved himself, he hadn't. Unfortunately, his attempts to save his superior officer had been in vain.

"Grant?"

"Yeah," he said, or tried to say. It seemed to come out dry and dusty like the desert. But he opened his eyes. Focused on Dahlia. At some point, Dahlia had stopped struggling against his hold but shifted in it so she could look at him.

"What is it?" He could see the concern on her face and knew he had to put the past behind him. But it wrapped around him like a fist, a vision he couldn't shake.

"There was a man on the ridge over there," he said. Because he wasn't about to tell her what was going on in his mind, and he had to focus on the important facts for now. "He ran away, but he could circle around."

"What about Rose?"

He took a deep breath, using all those coping mechanisms the discharge therapist taught him. Breathe. Visualize. Ground himself. But it was hard when he also knew they were in danger. He couldn't compartmentalize the way he should with a gun in his hand, a current threat and old pain. "What about Rose?"

"I saw her. She was in that building." Dahlia pointed down the street.

Grant kept breathing carefully. He stared at the building, trying to ascertain if anything he saw was real or just old fragmented memories.

"I know I saw her. I know I did," Dahlia was saying. So insistent, like she thought he didn't believe her when he couldn't even work up the concentration to believe her or not.

"I thought you shot at her, but…" Dahlia trailed off, he thought. Or maybe he tuned her out.

Then he felt her fingers on his cheek, sort of like before. When he'd kissed her. He *had* kissed her. That had happened. All this was real. *She* was real.

"Grant, what's wrong?"

She looked so concerned, and he knew he had to get it together. They could still be in danger. Just like the highway. They wanted her. And Grant didn't think they particularly cared what happened to him in the process of that. His only saving grace was they didn't seem to be big on the use of guns.

He sucked in one more careful breath and let it out, hoping she'd keep her fingers right there on his face, which helped him do all that grounding he was supposed to do when he had an *episode*.

"You think you saw Rose in that building down there?" he said, hoping his voice sounded as calm to her as it did to him. Not matching what was rioting around inside of him at all.

"I *know* I saw her. At first, I thought I was hallucinating or something, but she moved. From the window to the door. And she was wearing this sweater that I gave her for her birthday a few years ago. It's got all these crazy flowers on it. I found it in a thrift shop, and I knew it was perfect for her."

"Okay. Okay." He tried to give her a reassuring smile. "She was in that building. And there was a man up on that ridge." And he hadn't shot him, because damn if Grant could hit a target these days.

He should have sent Dahlia here with Palmer or Jack or even Anna. Why did he think he could protect her when, very clearly, he couldn't? Couldn't save anyone. Not his parents. Not his sergeant.

Not going to make it, Hudson. Tell the wife I tried.

It had been the worst moment of his life, and this seemed to echo it in all the ways he couldn't allow.

"You have to let me go find her," Dahlia said, her hand still on his face, but she tried to tug her arm out of his grasp.

"It could be a trap," Grant said, not letting her go. She'd take off, and then what? They had to…think this through. Calmly. Rationally. Which meant he had to find his equilibrium. Now.

Her expression turned, and he recognized desperation when he saw it. The need to *do* outweighing common sense. Been there. Done that.

"She could need help," Dahlia insisted, and she sounded so desperate. He could hardly keep holding her here. He didn't want to hurt her. And as much as his instincts shouted at him to get her out of here, were his instincts even any good anymore? Sure, he could shoot at a perceived threat, but he couldn't hit it. He could fight off men and still get stabbed in the process.

Now is not the time for some kind of identity crisis. It wasn't his own voice. He wasn't sure if it sounded more like his father or Sergeant Lincoln, or maybe some imaginary mixture of them both. Regardless of where the thought came from or who it sounded like, he needed to hold on to it.

"We need to get out of here. It isn't safe."

"I can't leave her behind," Dahlia said stubbornly. "Grant, I *know* I saw her. She's alive. She's *here*."

There were tears in her eyes, and if he had to blame his weakness on something, he supposed it was that. On wanting to give Dahlia…the world. "All right. We'll check it out. But you stay behind me. You follow orders. Got it?"

She nodded emphatically.

He should have let her go, moved away from her hand on his face. He should have confronted all the danger around them and come up with a plan. Instead, he pulled her up to standing and pressed his mouth to her forehead. For her comfort. For his.

He just…needed to.

"Promise me. No self-sacrifice," he said, holding her there against him as she leaned into him.

She hesitated, but after a moment, she nodded.

"Out loud, Dahlia."

She let out a hefty sigh and pulled back a little. "Fine. I promise. Can we go find her now?"

It was Grant's turn to sigh. Most of the old visions and voices were gone now. He felt more in charge of the moment and himself. Not that he was particularly sturdy with it.

He turned, keeping his body as a kind of shield between anywhere someone might be and Dahlia. He studied the area. It was too open. Too many places for someone to hide.

He wanted to try to talk her out of it, but if he put himself in her shoes, he knew there'd be no words. If he'd sworn he'd seen his parents down there, wouldn't he do everything no matter the danger to get to them?

"Follow me. Don't look down at the store, watch behind us. Let me know if you see anything, and I mean *anything* that doesn't look right, feel right, whatever. We are basically sitting ducks walking down this street." Once they crossed, they'd be hidden from the ridge, but Grant didn't think whoever had been up there was up there still. And he didn't think they were gone.

"Okay," Dahlia agreed.

Grant turned to the dog. "Willie. Follow." The dog wagged his tail in recognition of the order.

Grant fought down all the bad feelings, all the doubts. It was dangerous. Chances were high it was a trap. But, no, they could hardly just walk away from a potential sighting of her sister.

Dahlia was sure, and he knew what being desperate could do to a person, but…he just believed her. Couldn't help himself. She was sure, and so he'd be sure with her. *For* her.

He started forward, gun drawn, Dahlia far too close at his heels. He fought off the memories of old wars long gone as they moved down the street, as close to cover as he could manage. When they reached the last building, he leaned against the outer wall before crossing in front of the broken window.

"Stay here," he whispered to Dahlia while making the hand signal for stay at Willie. He could tell Dahlia didn't *want* to stay, but he gave her a stern look. "I mean it."

She swallowed but then nodded. Willie stood at the ready right next to her, and Grant had to trust the dog would sound an alarm if something was about to happen to her while he searched the building.

Grant eased into the doorway, gun first, careful to attempt to find cover. But there was none to find, and worse.

It was definitely a trap.

DAHLIA STOOD WITH her back to the building, Willie panting in front of her. But it felt like he was protecting her, somehow. However a dog could.

And all she could do was stand here and think…

Rose. She *had* seen her. She kept replaying the moment in her mind. It was the same sweater. Rose's blond hair. Even the way she'd moved from the window to the door had been *Rose*.

Alive.

Dahlia wanted to cry, but her heart was beating so hard against her chest, and the silence made fear freeze any tears.

Too quiet. Too…much. And Grant moving into that building, alone and off-kilter because *she* wanted him to. She wasn't certain he believed her about seeing Rose, but he knew she needed to know. He *cared* about her well-being, about what she wanted.

It was hard to fathom, but when she focused on that, some of the shaky terror settled. She looked around the abandoned town. To her eye, there was absolutely no sign of anyone. Willie sat at her feet, clearly on watch, but not growling or tensed and ready. Just watchful.

Grant disappeared fully inside, and there wasn't a sound. She wasn't sure how he moved that quietly, but he did. She held her breath.

But nothing happened. He didn't return. There were no sounds. Eventually she had to let out her breath even though she'd been hoping to hold it until he returned so she could hear everything that happened.

Willie began to growl, low in his throat. His tail didn't wag. It was straight up. Ears perked, everything about him was like a dog ready to attack, but he didn't leave her side.

Which felt worse somehow, because to her, it meant the danger had to be coming from inside the building. Grant had told her to stay put, but what if…

"Willie," she whispered. She tried to think of any

of the commands she'd heard Grant and Cash and the others use on the dogs. There was stay and still and… "Free," she whispered. Cash had said that once when he'd been training a few dogs, and when he'd said free, they'd all relaxed and scattered.

Maybe Willie would know her "free" meant to go wherever he needed to go. God, she hoped so.

Willie immediately headed for the door Grant had disappeared into. But just as he reached the opening, Grant's sharp order pierced the air. "Willie. *Go*."

The dog seemed as confused as Dahlia felt, because it hesitated there in the doorway.

"Come here, sweetheart," a feminine voice said from inside the building. Willie growled, but Dahlia couldn't heed the warning.

"Rose." She hurried for the opening and then stopped dead in her tracks. It was Rose. Right there. In the sweater Dahlia had given her. But Dahlia couldn't rush forward and envelop her sister in a hug. Cry in relief and joy.

Because Rose was pointing a gun at Grant's head.

"You're here," Rose said, smiling widely at Dahlia. But she didn't sound like herself. Or maybe it was just the gun pointed at Grant. "At last."

"Rose, what are you doing?"

Rose let out a long breath, but she didn't drop the gun. "I have been *waiting*. Just waiting and waiting." Her smile never faltered, but this was not…

It was Rose, but something was wrong. Very, very wrong. "Rose, are you okay?"

"I'm wonderful. I've found the truth, Dahlia. And now you can too." The smile dimmed a little as her eyes moved to Grant. Who stood stock still, stoic and silent.

Dahlia couldn't imagine what she was thinking, but she didn't like the way Rose was studying him at all.

"Can you put down the gun? He...he's my friend. Please, put down the gun."

Rose pressed her lips together. "He'd have to put his gun down first."

"I'm not pointing it at you," Grant replied. And it was true. The gun in his hand was pointed at the ground. "I don't want to hurt you."

Rose scoffed. "I'm the one with the gun pointed at your head. How could you hurt me?"

"Please, Rose." Dahlia took a halting step forward but stopped because Rose seemed to tighten her grip on the gun. "He helped me find you. Aren't you... Why do you have a gun? It's okay. We can go home now."

"Home? I'm never going home."

Dahlia sucked in a breath. This was all wrong, but she didn't know why. She wanted to cry. Rose was alive. Here and *alive*, and Dahlia wanted nothing else to matter.

But Rose needed to stop pointing that gun at Grant. "I don't understand."

"You haven't found the truth yet," Rose said, and it was almost like the sister she knew. The kind voice but just a *thread* of bossiness. Even though Dahlia was older, she'd always been more timid and introverted. Rose had been the bigger personality, so as they'd gotten older, Rose had taken to telling Dahlia what to do.

Why did everything in the past few weeks seem to come back to her never doing what she wanted? Never standing up for herself? Always bending to make someone else happy or at peace?

It made her angry, and this was definitely the wrong

time to be angry since *guns* were being pointed at people she cared about. Dahlia couldn't really believe Rose would kill Grant. Both because Rose wasn't a killer and because Grant, even in the more submissive position, somehow...*seemed* in control.

"Grant, you could—"

He looked at her for the first time since she'd entered, and his eyes were flat and cold. "No."

Dahlia didn't know what to do with either of these people. "What if you *both* put your guns down?"

"No," they said in unison. Willie even growled like he was also saying no.

"What are you going to do? Just point guns at each other all day? This is ridiculous. Rose, you're safe now. We don't have to go home, but we can get you out of here and to help."

"Help? Dahlia, I've found truth. I've found peace, and once you join us, everything will be perfect. I promise. Come with me. Leave *him* behind."

"Rose." Dahlia couldn't understand what was happening. Rose was part of the cult? Brainwashed or... something?

"I have to take you back," Rose continued. "There's no other choice."

Dahlia could tell Grant wanted to speak, but he didn't. She supposed he understood like Dahlia did that Rose wasn't going to listen to either one of them, but Dahlia had the better chance of getting through.

"You're safe now, Rose."

"And so are you." Rose turned her oddly black gaze to Grant. "I'll let you go, for Dahlia, if you leave. Right now. Don't come back." She looked around him. "You can leave the dog. We'll take good care of him. Won't we, sweetheart?"

Willie still growled.

"His name's Willie," Dahlia managed. She didn't dare look at Grant. "Come here, Willie." She crouched a little and patted her legs, and Willie trotted over. She screwed up the courage to look at Grant.

He had not moved. Not for the door. Not away at all. His expression was impassive, but she saw the flash of emotions in his eyes. Anger and frustration. She tried to beg him with her eyes. *Just leave. I'll get through to her.*

He shook his head infinitesimally, and he was just so…set on something. Determined and honorable somehow. She wanted to reach out and soothe him or beg him or *something*. Because Rose was here, but she wasn't herself, and Dahlia just knew they had to save her somehow.

Grant turned his attention to Rose, everything about him cooling into stoic blankness. But his words were fierce and made Dahlia's heart tremble. "I won't leave Dahlia here with you."

CHAPTER SEVENTEEN

GRANT KNEW DAHLIA wanted him to, and maybe it would have been smart. To go get backup. But he knew someone else was out there. He also knew Dahlia's sister was on something—whether by choice or by force—she was under the influence of some kind of drug.

He couldn't, even for a moment, leave Dahlia alone with her.

They had different coloring, but when staring at both women, it was easy to see they were sisters. The same build, the same mouth, the same too-skinny frame, likely borne of the past year more than anything natural.

But Rose was still his enemy. Until Dahlia was safe.

"I won't leave, but I'll go with you," he said. It was hard. He was not a born actor, but for Dahlia, he'd try. "My maternal grandfather was an elder in the Order of Truth."

Rose looked at him suspiciously. He didn't dare look at Dahlia. He hadn't mentioned it, and he doubted very much Mary or Anna had brought it up. Even with Anna's fascination with the cult, no one was too proud to be the descendent of a Truth elder, especially in Sunrise. It was why his parents had never thought the cult was much of a joke, why his family had always been uncomfortable with Truth and Eugene Green.

His mother had done a lot to make up for being born

into the Islay family. Everyone had told him, both before and after his parents' disappearance that it was good she'd married a Hudson—one of the good, upstanding families. That maybe, just maybe, she wasn't tainted by her relations.

But some had wondered, when both his mother and father had disappeared without a trace, if it had been that Islay blood catching up with them.

"My grandmother left the Order when my mom was a child," Grant went on. "And my mother didn't want us to be a part of it, but I've always thought…" Hell, what kind of nonsense was he supposed to spout to get closer? "The truth sounded more like home than the outside world."

Rose's eyes were narrowed as she stared him down. She didn't believe him. He didn't expect her to right away, but he could be patient.

Because he damn well wasn't letting Dahlia just *go* with the woman. Clearly, Rose wasn't well. And no wonder. She'd been a prisoner of the Truth, likely brainwashed and drugged, for a year.

And if she'd chosen it? Well, he'd cross that bridge with Dahlia when they came to it.

"No one escapes the Order alive," she replied.

"They did after the federal raid."

Rose's mouth firmed. "Put down the gun," she said.

"Grant." He wasn't sure what Dahlia wanted from him now, to lay it down or hold on to it. To stay or to go, but he'd made his decision. They'd get into that cult together and burn it down from the inside.

And he'd keep Dahlia safe. If he had to die to do it.

So, very carefully, he crouched and put his gun on the ground. He could hear Dahlia suck in a breath.

They were at Rose's mercy now.

"Can't you put yours down now?" Dahlia asked, and Grant could tell she was trying to be gentle, but nerves assaulted her.

Grant wasn't feeling too free and easy either. One purposeful pull of the trigger, or even a mistake, and he'd be dead.

"You could easily overpower me," Rose said to him.

Grant straightened and held his hands up in a gesture of surrender while also slowly and casually angling his body so the gun wasn't aimed quite so squarely at his head.

"I could, but I'm not going to. I don't hurt women." *Unlike your little cult*, he thought with some bitterness. Because the violence against women and sacrifice of women had been a *big* part of the cult's identity back in the sixties and seventies. They'd railed against the women's movement and had taken out every last frustration on women. It was the human sacrificing and the arms stockpiling that had brought the Feds in, but it had still created decades of trauma for the women involved.

Including his mother.

Grant took a careful breath. He couldn't afford to get angry.

Rose bit her lower lip, looking so much like Dahlia that sympathy waved through him against his will. Maybe he couldn't be angry, but he also couldn't be swayed by her just yet. It was dangerous.

But he also knew, because Sunrise made sure everyone knew, just what the Order of Truth could do to a person against their will. Particularly a woman. So, it was his job to keep her safe too.

"Rose."

Rose looked over at Dahlia. She frowned a little and brought her free hand to her head. "We need to find Samuel." She didn't lower her gun, but she moved it a pinch, so it didn't feel quite so much like a headshot was imminent.

"What happens when you take us to the cult?" Dahlia asked. One of her hands rested on Willie's head like he was the source of all her calm.

"Dahlia, you don't know how lucky you are." Rose took a step toward her, and Grant had to physically hold himself back from stepping between them. It didn't seem like Rose would hurt Dahlia just for the hell of it, but...

The cult would.

The gun wasn't pointed at Grant anymore as Rose approached Dahlia, but it didn't make him feel any more at ease. Rose stood in front of her sister, gun pointed at the ground.

"Once Samuel gets here, we'll take you to the Lord." Rose reached out and touched Dahlia's hair reverently. "You're the Chosen One."

"I don't... What if I don't want to be?" Dahlia asked. She hesitated, then reached up and took her sister's hand. She drew it away from her hair but then held on.

Rose's expression flickered. "You're *chosen*," she repeated. "The *one*. I thought I could be for a while." She tried to smile, but it faltered. She was also starting to twitch a little. Almost like whatever high she'd been on was starting to wear off.

Grant really wanted to get that gun out of her hand.

He took a step toward her, watching to see if she'd pay attention, but she kept talking to Dahlia as he crept along.

"I can't remember..." Rose shook her head. "It doesn't matter. It's just important that you're here and chosen, so you will be. You'll ascend. You're so lucky."

None of that sounded *lucky*, and Grant would be damned if he let Dahlia be anything in this cult. He was *this* close to being able to get the gun out of Rose's hand when he heard someone's approach. Though it was clearly careful and quiet, Willie sensed it too, growling low in his throat without leaving Dahlia's side.

Grant took a step away from Rose, not sure what they'd be greeted with when whoever it was made an appearance. But he didn't want to look like he was a danger to anyone, and he'd rather position himself between the doorway and Dahlia so she wasn't a target.

She was *clearly* the target.

When the man finally appeared, almost as quiet as a ghost, Grant didn't bother to hide a scowl. "You."

One of the men from the road stood there, and when he recognized Grant, he smirked. He didn't have a gun and didn't reach for one, but a knife was holstered on his hip—much like the one that had stabbed Grant.

"You were only supposed to get the Chosen One, child."

All women in the cult were called child, regardless of age. Grant didn't know how anyone stomached it. But the shakes Rose was beginning to have explained something. She was definitely coming off some kind of drug.

And it didn't quite make sense to him, how a woman would be so elevated as to be chosen in this cult who had, as far as he knew, always treated women as second-class citizens.

"He's a descendent," Rose said.

This Samuel studied Rose, likely seeing the same things Grant did, regarding her shakes.

"Child, did you eat your breakfast this morning?"

"I was too excited to eat."

His frown deepened, then he turned to Grant. "What kind of descendent?"

Grant didn't want to tell him. He didn't want to be a part of this. He remembered, too clearly, how much any mention of the cult had bothered his mother.

But there was also Dahlia, too much a target of this horror. So he had to swallow his aversion and do whatever it took to save her. "Islay."

Samuel's eyes widened. "An *elder*? I don't believe you."

"Spirit Islay was my grandfather."

"That makes you the son of traitors."

Grant shrugged, and he fought for his next words to come out sounding as gross as they were. "I can't control what the women in my family did."

Samuel nodded thoughtfully. "You'll be tested, but we can use the numbers if you pass. Rose, search him."

Rose shuffled over to him. She took the phone and keys out of his pocket, then his wallet. She rifled through, took the cash and shoved it in a pocket of her dress.

She did not get the knife in his boot. Grant had a bad feeling he was going to need it.

"He's clear," she offered to Samuel.

Samuel nodded. "All right. Let's go before someone comes looking for them. Throw their things in their truck."

Rose scurried off to do just that. Grant watched Samuel. He could overpower the man, but he wasn't sure where it would lead them. And Rose still had her gun, so when she came back…

No, there were too many risks. Still, he inched closer to Dahlia and Willie. Once close enough, he took Dahlia's hand in his. Samuel was paying no mind to that, so Grant gave her hand a reassuring squeeze.

She leaned into him a little bit as they stood there faced with a man who was part of some cult that thought Dahlia was chosen for the color of her hair.

"It'll be all right," he murmured. One way or another, he'd make sure of it.

EVERYTHING WAS SO SURREAL, but Dahlia found holding Grant's hand gave her a certain amount of grounding. Maybe none of this made sense, and maybe her being chosen or not, they were clearly in a lot of danger, but they were in it together. And Grant had gotten her out of danger before.

Of course, he'd gotten stabbed in the process.

She glanced uneasily at the gun Rose still held in her hand when she reentered the store.

"Tie them together," the man named Samuel ordered Rose.

Rose moved to hand Samuel the gun but then seemed to think better of it and looked around for someplace to put it.

Dahlia exchanged a glance with Grant. For whatever reason, it seemed some people in their group wouldn't or maybe even couldn't touch guns. It was something to file away.

Rose took the cord Samuel handed her and moved over to Grant and Dahlia. She noted their joined hands with a little frown—not of disapproval exactly but of consideration. Rose looked up at Dahlia, but Dahlia couldn't read her sister's expression. When she'd always been able to.

Was it the year of no contact, of thinking she was dead? Or was it whatever this cult had done to Rose? Or worse, was it that Dahlia had never really known her sister at all?

Dahlia let out a shaky breath. There had to be some way to get through to Rose. But it likely wasn't going to be in front of the beady-eyed man standing in the doorway.

Rose wrapped the cord around Dahlia and Grant's wrists, allowing them to still hold hands. She shook as she tied, but the bonds were still strong, and allowed a bit of lead that she handed to Samuel.

So they were like dogs on a leash.

Samuel gave the lead a tug. "Follow along. The Lord will have to decide if you're telling the truth, Blood of Islay. Chosen One, there will be a grand celebration in your honor."

Dahlia couldn't find a way not to react to the words *Chosen One*. It made her shudder and feel sick to her stomach. She'd never wanted to be chosen by much of anyone, but she *really* didn't want to be chosen by monsters.

Samuel pulled the lead, and she and Grant were jerked forward. Out of the building and then down the middle of Main Street, as if they were being paraded through the town, except there was no one there to cheer.

Willie trailed after them. Rose had given him a little water back in the building, so Dahlia felt like he would at least be treated well. God, she hoped so.

She dared to look up at Grant in the fading sunlight. He appeared as stoic as ever, but she worried about his stab wound. She worried about everything he'd said back in the building.

Had he been telling the truth? Or was he trying to trick Rose? Dahlia had the sneaking suspicion everything he'd said had been true, and it was that truth that had made him dismissive and uncomfortable about every mention of Truth from the beginning until this moment.

It explained Anna's interest, Mary's concern. It explained *everything*.

He hadn't wanted to say any of it, but he had so he could stay with her. So he could keep her safe. He'd sacrificed those truths he didn't want to deal with for her.

So she had to find a way to keep him safe too.

They walked and walked, it seemed like in circles. Until the sun fell, the air cooled and she found herself shivering under a vast, amazing array of stars. When Dahlia braved a look at Rose, she was following along, hugging herself and looking sickly in the silvery moonlight.

Dahlia wanted to say something, reach out, *do* something, but Samuel kept dragging them along, and it was clear whether it was out of force or brainwashing or her own choice, Rose had aligned herself with a cult.

Desperate people do desperate things. She'd said that herself, without ever thinking her sister would be the desperate one.

They climbed hills that felt like mountains. Dahlia's mouth was dry as dust, and her head pounded. She'd kill for a drink of water. She looked over at Grant, but with night getting darker and darker with every passing moment, she could only make out the shadow of him in the moonlight.

She worried about his stab wound. She worried about what would happen when they got wherever they were being led. She worried about everything.

Finally, after what could have only been hours, she started to see flickers of firelight and smell the smoke on the cold air. She was trying desperately to keep her teeth from chattering, but the air got colder and colder.

They got closer and closer, until Dahlia could make out a camp. Lots of little very temporary looking tents set up in a kind of circle around a large RV. Over to the west, a large bonfire was crackling, and many men were sitting around it eating and chatting. To the east, a group of women stood around a kind of cauldron with a much smaller fire. It looked like they were eating as well and cleaning up the remnants of making a meal.

Dahlia's stomach rumbled. Odd to be hungry *now* when emotions had made her incapable of feeling hungry for so long.

But Rose was alive. Maybe Rose wasn't herself. Maybe she was in danger. But she was alive. There was hope.

Or so Dahlia thought. A lot of that hope began to fade when a man approached them. He was dressed in a white robe, and she knew at once he was the man from the security footage. Bald, but a carbon copy of a younger Eugene Green.

"Samuel. My child." He pressed his palms together in front of him, but even in the firelight, Dahlia could see his eyes lock on her. "You've brought me all I desire."

CHAPTER EIGHTEEN

GRANT CALLED UPON every last cell of control not to react. He wanted to fly forward and tackle the robed man to the ground. Stop him from ever laying eyes on Dahlia again.

But he didn't. Couldn't. Though some of the cult members clearly didn't carry guns, some did, and he had to find a way to get Dahlia and Rose out of this unharmed.

And bring *all* these people to justice.

The man's eyes turned to him, and his smile turned into a sneer. "Why have you brought *this*?"

"Lord of Truth, this man claims he's of the elder's blood," Samuel said reverently. He handed the lead on the rope to the other man. "Claims blood Islay."

"Islay? Islay are traitors."

"He says the women were traitors," Samuel replied, head bowed.

This leader, his *Lord of Truth*, nodded as if that made sense, just as Samuel had.

"My Lord," Samuel continued. "The child did not eat her breakfast this morning."

"This is a serious infraction, child," the man said to Rose.

"I'm sorry," Rose said, and her voice shook—part of

it the comedown on whatever drug she clearly missed at breakfast and part fear. "I'll atone at once."

She was the main reason he was in this mess, but he couldn't stop the tide of sympathy. Clearly she'd gotten in over her head, even if she'd chosen the cult.

Except Dahlia was the Chosen One somehow. Whatever *that* meant. Even the man before them, this Lord of Truth, looked at her like all the answers in all the world existed in her.

Grant wanted that to be a reason to believe she'd be safe, that she'd have some power in the situation, but he knew too much, had seen too much. His own grandmother and mother had escaped this.

There was no safety in this cult for anyone, but especially for a woman.

As if to prove it, Samuel took Rose off deeper into the camp, and Grant couldn't be sure if it was to help her or hurt her. Dahlia watched her sister go with worry, and Grant could only squeeze Dahlia's hand, a silent promise they would figure this out.

Somehow.

"I will show you to your tent, Chosen One. Blood of Islay, we will have to convene a meeting to decide what to do with you. Come this way."

Before Grant even opened his mouth to protest, Dahlia was doing it for him.

"No," she said firmly, her grasp on his hand tightening even though their wrists were still tied together. "He has to stay with me."

"Chosen One—"

"If I am chosen and promised and all those other things your men shouted at me when they stopped us on the road a few weeks back, then you…you have to listen to me and do as I say…in this."

She faltered over only a few words. If Grant could have groaned without the man hearing him, he would have. This was hardly the best way to go about it. The man who fancied himself some kind of lord narrowed his eyes, and Grant began to open his mouth, yet again, to stand up for Dahlia. Defend her somehow.

But she did it herself before he could.

"You need me," she said firmly to the man. "You need me to be happy. Until the time."

Time… She seemed so sure, but Grant didn't have a clue what she was talking about.

"Perhaps, but we must test him. We cannot allow just anyone onto our sacred ground."

"You can if the Chosen One wills it."

The man's eyebrows raised. "You've studied us, Chosen One. I'm impressed."

Grant wished what he felt was impressed, but it was only dread and fear that they were getting deeper and deeper into something he couldn't control or escape from safely with Dahlia.

Not just her. Her and Rose, because he knew Dahlia wouldn't leave without her sister. He knew he couldn't ask her to. Rose was a victim here, even if she'd made some dubious choices in how she'd ended up in this mess.

"I presume you wish to share a tent then?"

"Yes," Dahlia said, chin angled upward. Almost regally. She reminded him a little of Mary when she was doling out orders, then figured that's who she was trying to emulate in the moment. If it had been any other situation, he might have smiled.

He'd once had to learn how to be tough too, or tough in a different way than he'd been used to. After his parents had left, he'd had to help Jack run the house. Be the ones the younger kids looked up to. He'd had to never show fury or impatience or any of those other emotions that had been roiling inside of him at sixteen.

So, he'd learned how to be the adult in the situation long before he'd been ready. He'd learned how to be a leader no matter how terrifying that had been.

It wasn't easy, but Dahlia had found some of that leadership, that bravery, despite all the things tumbling around inside of her. He was proud of her.

"All right. Do you know when the time is, my Chosen One?" the Lord asked.

Dahlia swallowed, and though her expression appeared not to change, he felt her hand tremble in his. "No, not exactly."

The man smiled, sending a cold chill down Grant's spine. "Good. It's best when the anticipation is high."

"Pete," the man shouted and clapped his hand. Another skinny man scrambled over. He clearly had a gun tucked into the back of his pants. He didn't wear a robe, and Grant was beginning to think that meant something. The robed men didn't carry weapons. Maybe they were too holy?

"Show them to the Chosen One's tent. Keep them tied until they're inside."

Pete nodded. "Yes, my Lord." Then he was given the lead of the rope and pulled them farther into the center of the camp.

Behind the RV, a large tent was set up—much nicer and bigger than the others. It had its own little fire in front being tended by a woman who didn't look up as the man named Pete led them into the large tent.

He then silently untied the cords from their hands. He bowed to Dahlia, then left.

The tent had a large cot with many blankets, lanterns and decorations. A cooler of food and drinks. Like… the glamping catalogs Mary had shown him one time that had made Jack's lip curl.

But this was a cult. It was beyond creepy. Beyond strange, and Grant knew…there was something he was missing. He turned to face Dahlia. *She* knew more than she wanted him to.

The flap of the tent closed, but Grant was under no illusion they were alone. It was just canvas, and the shadows outside were clear enough. There was a guard posted at the flap door—not robed, so he likely had access to a gun. There was the woman at the fire, who was definitely within hearing distance and was no doubt watching the tent.

"We should probably take turns sleeping," Dahlia offered into the quiet warmth of the tent. She was shivering now.

He couldn't stand it, so he wrapped his arms around her and pulled her close, though it caused a twinge where he'd been stitched up. She leaned into him, the tenseness of her shoulders slowly relaxing as she breathed carefully.

"Explain all this to me," he said, still holding her close.

Her shoulders tensed once again. "Grant…"

"No. No placating. No beating around the bush." He rubbed a hand up and down her back, hoping to warm her or stop her shaking. "Explain it to me. The Chosen One. The time."

She looked so pained, so twisted up, he wished he could comfort her. But he needed the truth first.

"They're going to sacrifice me."

DAHLIA HADN'T TOLD GRANT, or anyone, everything she'd learned in her research of the cult. Maybe she'd even denied it to herself a little bit, but here in the middle of all this...bizarre behavior, she knew it was true.

She would be sacrificed. There was a ritual though, one the cult had to follow to the letter. It hadn't been fully documented in the books, but enough that she knew she was safe until...well, until they decided she wasn't.

But by not telling anyone, she had gotten here. She had found out Rose was alive, and now they just had to save her. And themselves.

"Like hell they are," Grant said with more vehemence than she'd expected. His grip tightened, and she supposed she should feel scared by the threat of violence in his tone, but mostly she felt safe. Protected. Here in the shelter of his arms, she felt like they could really handle this.

But he pulled her away gently with enough of a pull that she had to look at him. Look at the anger and... *hurt* in his eyes.

"Is there anything else you've been keeping to yourself?"

"I didn't know..."

He raised his eyebrows, and the lie died in her throat. It wasn't fair to lie to him when all he'd ever done was try to help. "Yes, I read about the Chosen One and the ritual sacrifice. And, yes, I understood because of how they viewed women and blood…red hair that they might want me for that."

"And you didn't think to *mention* it?"

"I couldn't. I *couldn't*. I knew you'd try to lock me away in some safe room and handle it all yourself. If I had told you, I wouldn't know Rose was alive. We wouldn't be here with the opportunity to stop this. To get Rose *home*."

"Fine. You got what you want. Are you happy?"

It hurt. Because it wasn't just his usual straightforward demeanor. That was betrayal in his tone, lashing out to hurt *her*. But he didn't drop his hands from her shoulders. He didn't release her and step away, so she held on to that.

"No," she said, working to swallow down the tears that threatened. "None of this makes me happy, Grant."

He closed his eyes as if in pain. "I'm sorry," he murmured, then pulled her close again. "Damn it, Dahlia. I *would* have locked you away. This is too dangerous. It's too much of a risk." He blew out a breath that ruffled her hair. She rubbed her palms up and down his back, both assurance and…well, it was a very nice back.

"You really don't know how long it'll be?" he asked, still holding her to him.

"No, that was one of the details that was pretty vague. Only the Lord of Truth knows, I think. Or decides? But they have to keep me happy until that time. Maybe I could ask them to let Rose go?"

He pulled her back again, and this time his hands moved up her shoulders to frame her face. "Dahlia, she'd have to want to go."

Dahlia closed her eyes against the stab of pain the

truth caused. "I know. But…maybe if they told her she could. Maybe she's just afraid. Maybe…"

"She's being drugged," Grant said. "The whole breakfast thing… Too weird to just be breakfast."

"Do you think they're all drugged?"

"It's possible. There was nothing about that in the books you read?"

"No, but they don't speak of the women usually. They're just the servants, more or less, for the men and the truth. The only exception is the Greens, or in this case, the Green bloodline. And only if you're born with red hair." Dahlia didn't know how to feel about that. How Rose must feel about it, drugged or not. A twist of fate, and their situations could be reversed.

"We should get some rest," Grant said, lowering his voice to a whisper, bringing his mouth close to her ear. "They'll have us watched at night. But tomorrow morning, you could say you want a tour. I'll be by your side. We'll figure out where Rose is and map a route out of here."

She had to swallow to focus on the words and not the sensations of his big calloused hands on her face, his breath against her ear. "Do you know where we are?" she asked, attempting her own whisper.

It wasn't about sensations. It was about anyone out there not hearing them.

"I have a general idea. The good news is that even if they covered our tracks, my family isn't going to let us disappear into thin air. They know what we were looking into. They have Kory Smithfield. Anna had some leads."

Dahlia nodded. "You get up earlier than I do. You're injured. You should sleep first."

He frowned at this, but she wasn't about to give up. "They'll likely come wake us up at dawn. Would you rather be the one awake and watching then or the one asleep?"

His frown turned to a scowl.

"It's practical," she insisted, because it *was*. And because if she laid down now, she wouldn't sleep. She'd think about what it felt like in his arms. She'd think about Rose drugged. She'd think about being sacrificed.

That was *quite* the warped combo.

"Can I trust you to wake me up in an hour or two?"

"Of course."

He raised an eyebrow, a clear sign the *of course* was over the top. Which was fair. But she wanted him to truly rest, so she lifted her hand and fitted it over his cheek. "I promise to wake you up. I know I have kept things from you at times, but I don't make promises I don't plan to keep."

He sighed. "It's the 'plan to' that worries me."

She leaned up and gave him a quick friendly peck on the lips. "Good night, Grant."

He grunted, and after a few moments of holding her in place and studying her, he let go and went and lay down on the cot. He fell asleep quickly, and Dahlia set to looking around the tent for something she could use to rebandage his side tomorrow.

She could, of course, demand first aid from one of the cult members, but she wasn't sure she trusted them—not to help him, not to bring suitable bandages.

When that didn't yield anything, she studied the food options, then thought about Rose's discussion about breakfast.

No, she couldn't trust the food or water either.

A noise had her turning to look at Grant. He was asleep—eyes closed, chest rising and falling, but he muttered something, then turned his head violently to one side as if in pain. She took a step forward as he began to thrash. The groan of pain startled her so much she jumped.

But then she hurried to his side. "Grant. Grant. You're having a dream." Wasn't there something about not waking people up? Or was that sleepwalking? She didn't know. She knew he wouldn't want her to see him like this, but worse, he wouldn't want anyone outside to hear him moaning and muttering.

She nudged his shoulder. "Grant, wake up. It's okay. You're…" Well, he wasn't okay, was he? He was the prisoner of a cult.

He grabbed her suddenly. She bit back a scream, because he simply maneuvered her behind him, like he was shielding her from something. "Stay down," he ordered, but she was pretty sure he was still asleep. Or trapped in some kind of dream anyway.

Dahlia didn't know what to do but wrap her arms around him from where she was wedged behind him and the cot's frame. She pressed her cheek to his back. "Grant, it's okay. Wake up. I'm right here."

Something changed. His breathing was ragged, but she could tell he'd woken up. He kept himself tense. There was no more muttering, ordering or thrashing. He held himself still—too still.

"I'm…sorry," he said, sounding ragged and, worse, mortified.

"Don't be sorry." She stayed exactly where she was. Hugging him, cheek pressed to his back. "You have… PTSD?"

"No. Not like… I have dreams sometimes. Flash-backs. But they deemed me A-OK and all that. It's just…normal, I guess."

"Of course it is." She hugged him tighter. "You saw terrible things. That doesn't just leave you."

He sucked in a breath and let it slowly out. "Did I hurt you?"

"Don't be silly," she said. "You tried to protect me."

He nodded. "Yeah, doing a real bang-up job," he muttered. But she could tell he was trying to deflect from the dream.

"Grant. What did you dream about?"

He stiffened in her arms and tried to move, but she held tight. Eventually, he put his hand over hers locked at his chest.

"My superior officer was shot. I tried to get him out under heavy fire. Not regulation, but I did it. Or almost. He had a wife and two kids at home. I had no one. But he died, and I survived."

It broke her heart to hear him say it, to know he'd felt it. When she'd seen him with his family. "You had brothers and sisters and a niece who need you very badly."

"You don't understand, Dahlia." This time he pulled her hands off him. He didn't get off the cot like she expected him to though. He turned to face her. Serious. Tired. "They did just fine without me."

"You underestimate yourself. The Hudson machine does not work if you're not one of the cogs in it."

He almost smiled. "Cogs, huh?"

"It's true. You're a unit. You don't function without each other. I'm sure it comes from losing your parents, but I bet if you asked your siblings—any one of them, even Jack—how things ran without you, they'd say not as smoothly, as balanced as *with* you. You're the counterweight. Without you, Jack's too hard, and Cash is too isolated, and Palmer is too—" she struggled for a word "—wild, I suppose. Same with Anna."

"What about Mary?"

Dahlia considered. "Well, probably too internal." She could relate.

"I don't know about all that."

"I think you do. I think you needed it pointed out to you, but I think now that you see it, you can't unsee it." She studied his face and knew it was true. But she also knew... "You haven't told them, have you?"

"I'm sure they know I've had a nightmare or two."

"But you don't talk to anyone about it."

"I just talked to you."

She didn't know much about PTSD. She knew Grant though. Somehow, she understood him. In these few weeks of watching him—with his family, with the dogs, with her. She knew who he was.

She reached out for him, putting her hands on his cheeks, making sure he had to look her in the eye. "It's your turn to promise me something."

"What?" he replied, clearly trying for unmoved, stoic and failing.

"Just talk to someone. It can be a sibling, a friend. It could probably even be a dog."

He was silent for a long stretch of moments. "What about you?"

Her heart melted. Right here in the middle of this mess she just...fell for him. Hook, line and sinker. "It could always be me."

After another long silence, he nodded. Then he got

up off the cot and gestured to it. "It's your turn to get some sleep, Dahlia. Dawn will come soon enough."

Since he was right, and they had a cult to outmaneuver tomorrow, she nodded and did as she was told. After all, she knew Grant, and a nod from him was as good as a promise. And he was not a man who went back on promises.

So, she laid down and slept. And when she dreamed, she only dreamed of sunshine and him.

CHAPTER NINETEEN

GRANT COULD LET the embarrassment eat him alive, or he could focus on the task at hand. He couldn't do any recon in this tent, but leaving Dahlia sleeping and vulnerable was out of the question.

He looked at his stitches. He'd popped one or two, but they'd stopped bleeding and had scabbed over. He couldn't find anything sterile to use as a bandage, so he'd just have to hope he'd done enough and they'd be out of this soon enough that it wouldn't matter.

His family hadn't known where he and Dahlia had been going, and that's what a person got for sneaking and lying, he supposed. But still, Grant had no doubt they'd started a search by dinnertime, and they'd know to look into Truth. Then, once they found his truck with all his and Dahlia's things in it, they'd be able to track them here.

It would take time though, especially over the dark nighttime hours. They were well and truly out in the middle of nowhere at this camp. Oh, the Samuel guy had tried to trick him with the circles and endless walking up and down hills, but Grant knew this stretch of Wyoming better than anyone, aside from his own family. He might not know the exact map pinpoint, but he knew well enough where they were and how to head back to civilization.

What he didn't know was how to convince Rose to come with them. He could outsmart a cult. Between what he knew and what Dahlia knew, and his own skills, Grant had no doubt he could get out of here.

But Dahlia wouldn't leave her sister, so Grant couldn't either.

Grant looked at Dahlia curled up on the cot. She slept peacefully, which was a relief. They'd need their strength and their wits about them. He hated that she was here surrounded by these people who wanted to *sacrifice* her, but they had a bit of a reprieve tonight.

Maybe if she could convince her sister not to eat the breakfast they were so intent on tomorrow, they could convince her to leave once backup showed up.

The problem was, even drugged, Rose shouldn't be okay with Dahlia being *sacrificed*. Even brainwashed, the idea of her sister being killed should be reason enough not to have brought Dahlia here.

Grant didn't like it, but of course he didn't like any of this. So he had to find a way to get them both out of here before any rituals started.

He heard the shuffle of people outside, saw shadows moving, and then the tent opened. Grant didn't pretend not to be awake and watching. He hoped they got the message that he'd protect Dahlia at all costs.

"Good morning," the man who'd brought them here last night boomed, making Dahlia jerk awake and sit up in the cot wide-eyed.

Grant scowled. "Thanks for the wake-up call, Pete."

Pete bowed at the waist. Hell, this place was weird as could be. "You are most welcome, Blood of Islay."

Grant exchanged a look with Dahlia. She was frowning like he was, but she looked sleep tousled and still a little out of it.

"Come. It's time for breakfast, Chosen One."

Dahlia rubbed her eyes then got off the cot. "It's a bit early to eat, isn't it?"

"We eat with the sun. We worship a new day and the opportunity to find truth in the lies." He led them out of the tent. The fire from last night had died, and there didn't seem to be anyone around tending it anymore.

"Where's Willie? Where's my dog?" Dahlia asked, looking around as they walked.

"The children are taking very good care of him."

Dahlia exchanged a glance with Grant. Worry and confusion. Grant could only shrug his shoulders. They hadn't seemed intent on hurting the dog, so he had to hope that might work in their favor.

Pete led them past the RV and smaller tents to a long table. The women all sat at it with the men standing around. There were bowls in front of each woman with some kind of oatmeal mixture. Rose sat at the end of one bench, and Willie was on the ground next to her. His tail began to wag when he saw Dahlia.

"This is your seat, Chosen One," Pete said, pointing to a chair at the head of the table next to Rose.

All the women bowed and murmured chants of "Chosen One." Grant had to fight the urge to pick her up and walk her right the hell out of here—sister and any objections be damned.

But she wanted her sister, and he wanted to take these people down. So he stood where he was and bit his tongue.

"Blood of Islay." He was handed a stick of some kind

of jerky. "Your breakfast, brother." Grant studied the jerky, then the women and the men.

He didn't know if it was more or less disturbing the men clearly weren't drugged since it appeared all the women were.

The men all stood around the women, watching as if to make sure every last drop was eaten. Grant wondered if this was an everyday occurrence or if it was happening today because Rose had skipped her meal yesterday, so there were extra precautions in place. He glanced at the man next to him, who'd handed him the jerky.

"Do we always eat standing up?" he asked, attempting to be casual.

The man looked around. "We must protect our children."

Grant tried not to make a face at that. It was just so disturbing. Not one of these women appeared to be under eighteen. He supposed the only saving grace was he hadn't seen any evidence of *actual* children.

The man—the "Lord"—from yesterday stepped forward, taking a place at the opposite end of the table Dahlia sat at. He looked at the women and their bowls of oatmeal. "Children, I am your Lord of Truth. And here, in each bowl, is the truth. Eat so that you too may see a glimmer of the truth I feed you."

Dahlia looked over her shoulder at him, eyes wide, clearly worried that she was going to eat.

Over his dead body.

So, Grant would have to create a diversion.

DAHLIA TRIED NOT to panic, but she was not going to eat this laced oatmeal. She looked back at Grant, who stood there looking stoic somehow. But she knew he wasn't.

She wished she had his ability to turn off panic or anger or whatever feeling he was hiding, but she felt like every emotion chased across her face. Refusal and fear and panic.

Grant gave her a little nod, not a *go ahead* nod, she knew. But more something like *I'll take care of it.*

The Lord of Truth blathered on about the importance of eating every bite, of all the truth you could find with a clean bowl.

It was *insanity*. Dahlia tried not to get hung up on how anyone could fall for this nonsense. *Desperate people do desperate things.*

Had Rose been desperate? Had all these women?

Willie barked, causing Dahlia to jerk in surprise. The sudden movement upended her bowl, but before anyone could move to do anything about it, Willie hopped up next to her *on* the table. Then he began to run up and down it, yipping happily while women jumped up in an effort to grab their bowls or stop the dog.

But he ran, bounced, barked. He didn't growl. He acted like he was playing some kind of entertaining game, and every woman's shriek and every man's order to stop was only part of the game.

Dahlia looked at Grant. He was focused on the dog and made a little noise, almost a whistle and a hand motion. Then Willie dismounted the table, barked like crazy and ran away from camp.

Some of the men took off after the dog. Some of the men were ordering the women to clean up or eat what had spilled. In the chaos, Dahlia leaned over to her sister.

"There are drugs in there," Dahlia said, feeling a

little desperate to shake some sense into Rose. "You should avoid eating it at all costs."

"It helps," Rose said. "It is for our own good. It's the truth."

"No, it's for theirs." Dahlia looked around the table. "Try to remember what you felt like before you came here," Dahlia said—not just to her sister but to all of them who could hear her desperate whisper. Maybe they'd grown up in this horror, but maybe they were like Rose and had been kidnapped into it.

Even if Rose had somehow come to believe in it—which Dahlia found hard to accept of her vibrant, passionate sister—Rose wouldn't have joined this cult without a word, leaving everyone behind to worry about her. Dahlia couldn't believe that.

"Avoid what they give you. Just for a day or two. See how you feel. I promise you. It might be bad at first, but you'll be clearer. You'll find the *real* truth. Not their truth."

"Blasphemy," a woman hissed.

But Dahlia ignored her. She kept her gaze on Rose. Imploring. "Please. Just avoid it as best you can. Let your mind clear."

Rose held her gaze, almost like she was considering what her sister was telling her. Then she smiled, but it was a creepy smile, like the Lord of Truth. "Dahlia, you should try our way. The real truth. It's…transcendent."

Dahlia swallowed, hating what she was about to say, but if she had to play the Order of Truth's game to get her sister out of here, then so be it. "I'm the Chosen One, Rose. Wouldn't I know best?"

Rose blinked at that, then looked down at her spilled oatmeal. When she looked back up at Dahlia, it was with an expression Dahlia remembered from their childhood: stubborn rebellion. She took her spoon and began to scoop up every spilled drop of oatmeal. From the table to her mouth, defiantly eating every last bit.

Dahlia was speechless. She was literally rendered immobile by her sister's behavior.

But then Rose ate Dahlia's too. Dahlia wanted to believe it was some kind of self-sacrifice. She was desperate to believe it. But Rose looked at her defiantly as if to say, *See, I'm right. You're wrong.*

"Rose," Dahlia said, wanting to cry. "Why?"

"You don't understand. You can't understand." She was starting to look angry. Certainly not scared or even relieved Dahlia was here. She just looked *mad.* "You're the Chosen One and you don't even understand," Rose said, sounding a bit like a petulant child.

"I understand. Being chosen means they're going to *kill* me," Dahlia replied in a whisper. Most of the men were making sure the women ate their oatmeal off the table or had gone off to find the dog, but they could start paying attention to *her* at any minute.

"Yes," Rose said. As if it were a good thing. A *right* thing. That they wanted her dead eventually in some ritual sacrifice.

Dahlia could only gape at Rose, who smiled.

"And aren't you lucky?"

CHAPTER TWENTY

ONCE THE BREAKFAST ruckus died down and was cleaned up, Grant and Dahlia were escorted back to their tent. Grant was relieved. Standing around the group of people was just...too much. The thought of his mother growing up in this nightmare was painful and the threat of Dahlia being *sacrificed* too much to bear.

There were murmurs about hunting down the dog, but Grant was convinced Willie had gotten a good enough head start. Willie would go find Cash or someone and lead them back.

He would have sent him last night if he'd gotten the chance, but this was perfect. It had allowed Dahlia to avoid eating the drugged oatmeal. Grant didn't know what diversion he'd manage for lunch, but they'd cross that bridge when they came to it.

Before Pete left them, Dahlia spoke. "I want to see my sister. In here. Alone."

Pete blinked, looked at Grant almost like he was looking for permission, then back at Dahlia. "I don't know..."

"I want to see my sister. Do as you're told by the Chosen One, or ask your Lord of Truth. I don't care, but I want her brought to me. Here."

Grant had never heard her speak so forcefully. What happened at breakfast was clearly bothering her, and he wanted to comfort her in some way, but he didn't know how. This was a mess of a situation.

Pete scuttled out of the tent, and Grant figured it would be a while before he returned. He didn't seem very...confident. He'd likely go talk to the lord guy first.

Dahlia was pacing, eyebrows furrowed, tension and upset radiating from her. He couldn't let her keep stewing, so he stood in her path. When she stopped abruptly and looked up at him, he held his arms to the sides.

She closed her eyes, her expression crumpling, and she fell into him. He wrapped his arms around her and held her close. She took a deep breath, and her shoulders relaxed. "Grant, she ate both of our bowls," Dahlia said, voice scratchy.

"She was saving you." He wasn't sure it was true, but he hoped it was for Dahlia's sake.

But she shook her head. "I wish I believed that were true." She looked up at him without releasing her grip or making him release his hold on her. A few tears had fallen over. "She wasn't saving me or doing anything selfless. At least, she didn't act like she was. It was like she was...defying me because I told her they were drugged. Or trying to prove something, like she wants to be here? I don't know, but she thinks I'm *lucky* for being the sacrifice. Grant, I'm afraid I just can't reach her."

Grant brushed some of Dahlia's hair out of her face. "We'll keep trying," he promised.

She let her forehead rest against his chest as she took another ragged breath. "I can't leave this place without her."

"I know." He rubbed her back and then...told her something he swore he'd never tell anyone. "My mother once, and only once, told us about escaping the Order. How hard it was, how many tries it took. How many times her mother would be on the verge of giving up. The only thing that kept my grandmother going was not wanting this life for her daughter."

Dahlia looked up at him. Her eyes had filled again, in sympathy as much as worry over her own sister. So he made her a vow he wouldn't break. "We'll keep trying until we get her out. I promise you that."

A few more tears fell, but she didn't sob or cry. She just squeezed her eyes shut, and the tears fell over. "I don't know how I'll ever repay—"

He took her by the chin. "Dahlia. Stop thinking of this as an exchange. I'm here not just because you hired me—in fact, if that was why, we never would have been taken by that Samuel guy. We wouldn't have been in Truth. We'd have listened to Jack and turned it all over to law enforcement weeks ago. I'm here because I care about you."

She opened her eyes. Met his gaze. For a moment, she simply looked at him. When she spoke, it was with the kind of gravity that humbled him. "I care about you too, Grant."

But anything else they might have said or done was interrupted by the flap being lifted and Rose entering the tent.

She studied them standing in each other's arms. Even with tears on Dahlia's face, there was something cool in Rose's expression that Grant didn't trust. So he didn't let Dahlia go. Didn't step away. He wanted to...protect her somehow.

Because Dahlia was probably right, and there was no reaching Rose—at least here, drugged and in the cult.

Dahlia knew her sister, and Grant knew how this cult in particular could mess with a person and warp them.

But he also knew Dahlia would never just let Rose stay here, whether Rose wanted to leave or not. Dahlia hadn't given up on Rose when she thought she was dead. Why would she give up on her sister alive and standing right here?

Besides, Grant had vowed to get her out, so he'd find a way.

DAHLIA FELT... God, she was so tired of thinking about how she felt. The swings of emotion were such a pendulum, and in the midst of it all, she was in this strange place, and her sister...was a stranger.

"You wanted to see me?" Rose said. She sounded sweet and happy, but there was something about the way she looked at Grant that made Dahlia uncomfortable.

"I wanted to make sure you were okay. Since you ate my meal this morning, you must have ingested twice the amount of drugs meant for any one person."

Rose smiled wide, but her pupils were so dilated her eyes were nearly black. "It was oatmeal, Dahlia. Sustenance. The great gift of truth from the great Lord of Truth. You only have to accept his truth to be free."

Dahlia wanted to press her face into Grant's chest again and just...push all this fanatical talk away. She'd been prepared to deal with Rose being dead. Or even kidnapped. But somehow, being *part* of this cult, saying these things and seeming to believe them...

Dahlia just didn't know what to *do*. How did you get through to someone drugged and brainwashed?

But much like the past thirteen months, she knew

she couldn't give up. "Rose, can you tell me how you ended up here?"

"The truth brought me," she said, still smiling.

"I think Dahlia meant something a little bit more concrete," Grant offered. "You disappeared in Texas."

"No, I found the Lord of Truth in Texas," Rose corrected. Dahlia wouldn't call the look she sent Grant *mean* exactly, but it wasn't nice. "We didn't know you were the Chosen One then."

"How did you find that out?" Grant asked, earning another pointed look from Rose.

"Does it matter?"

"It does to me," Dahlia said earnestly.

Rose sighed heavily. She stood in one place, but her eyes darted around, and she occasionally shook a hand this way or that, like she was filled with an energy she couldn't quite control or decide what to do with.

"The Lord didn't like that you were looking for me, of course. I told him no one would care if I disappeared, and you proved me wrong, sister." It was accusation more than anything good. Like Dahlia *should* have forgotten her sister, assumed she was dead and moved on.

"I had to find out what happened to you," Dahlia replied, trying to keep the hurt out of her voice. Rose wasn't herself. She was *drugged*. Dahlia couldn't take anything at face value or be hurt by Rose's words. "How could I let it go? You *disappeared* into thin air. I thought I was searching for your murderer, Rose." She swallowed down the frustration, reminding herself Rose was alive, and that was what was important. "I'll never give up on bringing you home." It was a promise Dahlia had to keep.

Rose shook her head vehemently. "*This* is my home.

The Order is my home. I have a place here. A role. Not like *home*. Constantly arguing with our small-minded, simpleton parents."

"Rose…" Dahlia didn't have the words. She knew her parents and Rose had a strained relationship, but this felt bigger. Here in the midst of all this insanity.

"People care about me and for me here," Rose continued. "The Lord took special care of me. I'm a Green. I'm special."

"We *aren't* Greens."

"We are! We have the blood!" She stamped her foot like a child, though Rose's temper had always retreated to childishness if given the chance. "And I was important until *you* came along." Her fingers curled into fists. "I had to bring you. The Lord saw you and then wanted *you*. But you should have stayed in Minnesota. You should have forgotten about me, and then maybe *I* would have been chosen."

Dahlia didn't know how to comprehend this. Being chosen meant being sacrificed. Being special meant ending up *dead* in the Order of Truth. Well, if you were a woman.

Why couldn't Rose see that?

Dahlia looked helplessly at Grant. His expression was one of sympathy. He understood what this group could do to a person's mind, and he didn't judge.

But he also didn't know how to fix it. Change it. Did anyone?

"Don't I mean anything to you, Rose?" Dahlia asked, trying to keep her voice from shaking. "You're my sister. I love you."

"You're the Chosen One," Rose replied, her smile wild again. Her eyes darting everywhere. "This is the truth. You will meet the Lord in the sky. You will be free. And your ashes will lead us to a deeper truth." Rose moved forward with every word, reaching out much like the men had done by the highway.

But there was something far more menacing in Rose's eyes. Like she might reach out and try to choke the life out of Dahlia.

Grant stepped forward, blocking Dahlia and stopping Rose's forward progress.

Dahlia was shaken to her core. Her sister...wanted her dead.

Your sister who's been traumatized, drugged and brainwashed for a year. She tried to repeat that to herself over and over again, but she still felt dumbstruck, scared, betrayed.

"You could let us escape," Grant said to Rose. "Dahlia could disappear. Then you could be important again."

Dahlia tried to protest. How could he... How could Grant, of all people... How could he think she'd leave Rose here when he'd promised to help? Surely Grant understood that even with the threats, the anger, Dahlia would never leave without her sister.

Outside of the Order, she could find Rose help. She could have her *actual* sister back. She was sure of it. She had to believe it, hold on to that possibility. Just like no matter how hard she'd tried, she'd always held on to the possibility that Rose was alive.

And Rose *was* alive. There had to be a positive ending to this mess.

Rose seemed to consider Grant's proposition, and when Dahlia opened her mouth to find the air to argue, Grant gave her a firm shake of the head.

"Grant—"

He shook his head again. "I made a promise," he said softly. "I intend to keep it."

He'd promised to get Rose out of here. So...this was some sort of trick or plot or something, and she had to go along with it.

"I also made a promise," Rose said loftily. "To bring my Lord the Chosen One. To find the truth through your glorious sacrifice, Dahlia." Rose smiled once more.

Dahlia didn't know how to reconcile the fact that Rose looked almost exactly the same as she had the last time Dahlia had seen her, but there was...nothing on the inside that was the same.

In the silence that followed, Dahlia heard the faint yip of a dog. Willie? Oh, she hoped not. Even though everyone had been kind to the dog, she had a bad feeling this morning's breakfast shenanigans would earn him some kind of punishment.

"Grant?"

His expression was unreadable. But she knew he'd heard it too. Still, he turned to Rose. "Think about letting us go. Or coming with us when we leave."

"You won't be going anywhere, friends," Rose said sweetly. "Except to the Lord in the sky." She wafted out of the tent.

Dahlia collapsed onto the cot. Her legs couldn't keep her up any longer. She buried her face in her hands, trying to think. She only looked up when she felt Grant's hand on her knee.

He was crouched in front of her at eye level, clearly worried. But before she could say anything, he spoke in a low whisper. "Help is here."

"What?"

"That bark? Willie's alerting. Cash or Palmer or *someone* from my family is here, Dahlia. We have to get out. Now."

Before Dahlia could protest or explain that despite everything, she couldn't leave without her sister, she heard people shouting. Grant ran for the tent flap, so she followed.

When they got out, people were running in the opposite direction. No one was paying much attention to them. But Dahlia heard Willie again. From behind.

She turned with Grant, and there across the open field was Willie. Just standing there. He let out another little yip, and Dahlia saw a flash of light.

Grant grabbed her. "Did you see that light?"

"Yes."

"It's Anna. Run for her. Right now. Don't stop. Don't look back. Just run to right where you saw her, no matter what you hear, no matter what happens. You run."

Her fingers curled into his sweatshirt. "What are you going to do?" she demanded, her heart beating overtime. He wasn't going with her, and she couldn't leave Rose *or* him.

He pried her fingers out of the fabric of his shirt. "I'm going to bring you your sister."

CHAPTER TWENTY-ONE

GRANT RAN. HE DIDN'T have a gun, but he had the knife in his boot. The biggest challenge he faced was the fact he didn't know where Rose would be. Most of the people running around were too busy shouting orders or following them to pay him much mind.

He hoped it would stay that way. The men were all congregating around a kind of hole in the ground. Grant still ran, but when he looked back at the men, he realized what they were doing.

Pulling guns out of some sort of underground stockpile. *Hell.*

It didn't bode well for him, but he had to find Rose. He went around all the tents, even circled back and searched the RV, but he could not find any of the women, and the longer that went on, the more concerned he became.

He decided to return to where the men had been pulling weapons out of the ground in hopes they'd lead him to the women, but now they were gone too.

Damn cults.

He stilled and listened. Even though it was eerily quiet, at some point, he'd have to hear something to go on.

Old flashbacks threatened. Sand and blood and Sergeant Lincoln. Shouting and gunshots and explosions.

But he kept his eyes focused on the here and now. The grass beneath his feet. The sound of the tents flapping gently in the wind. In his mind, he retraced their path here yesterday. Up and down a few hills he'd thought were meant to distract, but maybe...

He headed east, the way they'd come. As he closed in on a hill, he heard it. The faint murmurs of people. So he climbed the hill carefully and silently.

Once close enough to the rise to peek over, he saw all of them in the distance, the men and women, but... the whole scene made his blood chill.

The women were all on their knees, men lined up behind them. With guns. There was another line of men behind them, all in robes that billowed in the wind. They didn't hold guns or any weapons.

They all faced north, and Grant realized even though he couldn't see them, law enforcement was somewhere over the second rise.

Anna had come in from the south in order to get him and Dahlia out before law enforcement moved forward.

It was too much like that federal raid. Hostages. Stockpiles of arms and insanity. Too many people were going to end up hurt or even dead, and still...as he searched the faces of the women on their knees, he didn't see Rose.

Where the hell was she? Had she escaped?

He wished he could believe that, but after everything that had happened in their tent earlier, he couldn't.

If law enforcement was over that hill, these people were set up like the first wave to stop them. The first sacrifice. But there would be a second.

If Dahlia was still here, they'd want her.

Had they gone after her?

His heart felt as though it fully stopped at the idea. But he couldn't let that stop *him*. He turned and moved down the hill, focusing on silence. On stealth.

Not on the panic-inducing thought someone might have gotten to Dahlia and his sister.

But as he moved back through the camp, he heard lowered voices and had to slow. Had to use the tents as cover to creep closer and closer. Until he was at the place where the bonfire yesterday had been—a big stone circle.

But there was no fire lit today. At least yet. Because in the center of the stones was a big wooden pole. And the so-called Lord of Truth was tying Rose to it.

But the thing that made him fully stop in his tracks was the sheer volume of explosives littered around the both of them.

Hell.

As if sensing him, the Lord of Truth stopped and looked around. Grant was hidden by a tent, but as he studied the area, he realized it was just the three of them, and while the lord guy had explosives, he didn't seem to have a gun on him. The Lord was in robes. He was too holy to carry a gun.

Grant hoped.

So Grant did the only thing he could since his end goal was to get Rose out of this. For Dahlia. He pulled the knife out of his boot and stepped forward.

The man tightened the knot he was tying around Rose and the pole but glared at Grant. "I don't know what you think you're going to stop. Violence isn't the answer."

"Says the man tying a woman to a pole surrounded by explosives."

"A sacrifice is good and right. It will bring us the truth, the balance. And a way forward until we are once again reunited with the Chosen One."

"You'll never get your hands on her."

The man shook his head and stepped away from Rose. But that didn't make Grant feel any better, because he didn't think it would take much to set those explosives off. Enough explosives to take all three of them out.

"You brought this evil on us, Blood of Islay."

"Yeah, me. So let Rose…let the child go."

There was a moment in which the man seemed to actually consider it, and Grant used that moment of consideration to inch closer and closer.

The man's gaze turned to the explosives. To Rose. "She's not the Chosen One."

"No, she isn't," Grant agreed. Another step. One or two more, and he could tackle the guy without using the knife. "You should let her go."

"But sacrifice brings truth. We need truth to survive. You've brought the outside world upon us, Blood of Islay, and—"

Grant lunged. The man was so impressed with his own little speech that he didn't seem to see it coming. But he still fought like hell even once Grant got him to the ground.

But he wasn't an adept fighter. His attempts at punches were flailing and weak, the robe tangling his arms so that he couldn't get a good punch in. Grant had him pinned to the ground immobile in less than a minute. All the while, the man kept screaming about truth and sacrifice.

"I built this from the ashes! I am the original Lord's

descendent. The true leader. I am the truth! There was nothing, and then I breathed the flame of truth back into it all!"

"You should have let it die." Grant pulled his fist back and focused on a spot that would ideally knock the man out for the time being. He used his full force for the blow, and the man went limp.

Grant blew out a relieved breath, but when he looked over at Rose, he swore and jumped into action.

DAHLIA HAD MADE it to Anna with Willie leading the way, and now they huddled behind a hill and waited.

Just waited.

It was driving Dahlia insane.

"How can you let him just…be out there risking his life?" she finally demanded when Anna looked as if she were having a grand old time relaxing.

Anna looked over at her and uncharacteristically seemed to consider her words. "Do you think Grant would just…be cool with us running in to help?"

Dahlia didn't say anything. She couldn't, because of course not.

"And given the choice, would he want to send someone else into all that in his place?"

Again, Dahlia didn't answer. It was pointless. She didn't know why she was arguing, she just… "I can't stand waiting around feeling purposeless."

"I get it. Trust me, more than you could ever understand. But we rush in there, we mess up the plan and what they're doing. So we have to be careful and bide our time." Anna studied her for a long perceptive moment. "Grant's my brother. I love him more than anything. When you love someone, you need to let them be who they are. Even when it hurts. I couldn't stop him from going off to war. I can't stop him from being the hero. No one can. It's who he is."

It's who he is. Dahlia knew that. It made her heart feel too vulnerable amid an already too emotional twenty-four hours, let alone *year.* Because she just… *loved* who he was. The hero complex mixed with insecurity. The way war had marked him because he *cared*, and the way he didn't run away from any of that. The way he was with his family. The fact he couldn't soften the truth to save his life, but sometimes he wanted to, tried to.

"You might want to get used to it if you plan on sticking around," Anna added.

Before Dahlia could think of anything to say to that, a loud boom echoed through the air. The explosion shook the ground even though it seemed to come from far away.

Anna swore and took off at a run, Willie not far behind her. Dahlia stood frozen for a moment or two, but then she ran as hard as she could behind them. Toward where smoke plumed and shouts seemed to sound everywhere.

She kept sight of Willie even as Anna ran much faster than her and disappeared into the camp, but Willie, bless that dog, waited until she caught up and then took off again, leading her closer and closer to the smoke.

She could hear gunshots, but they were farther off. Was Grant involved in that? Most of the cult didn't have guns…unless like the cult from before, they'd stockpiled them somewhere.

All her thoughts stopped the moment she ran into

the smoke and flickering flames of the aftermath of the explosion.

Grant was holding a kicking and screaming Rose, and Anna was trying to jump into the fray. There was shouting and shooting coming from farther off—all of it deafening—but it didn't seem to connect with whatever had happened here.

Dahlia watched as Rose fought off two people who'd done nothing but help and been nothing but kind. At her wit's end with all of it, she stepped forward.

"Stop it!" Dahlia screamed at the top of her lungs. She'd never once screamed like that in her entire life.

Rose stilled, surprisingly, and once she did, Grant took one arm and Anna the other. They were all bleeding now. All breathing hard.

"What on earth are you doing?" Dahlia demanded.

"I was going to be the sacrifice," Rose yelled right back. There were tracks of tears down her sooty cheeks. "I was going to be *chosen*. But he stopped it!" She jerked the arm Grant held, but they'd really immobilized her at this point, so she could only yank and yell in response.

Dahlia looked up at Grant. His face was also covered in black grime. He was bleeding from his lip, his nose and his temple. One of his sleeves was burned. And still he stood there stoic—the hero once again.

All the while, gunshots kept sounding in the distance. Shouting. But no more explosions, thank God.

So Dahlia focused on her sister. She stepped forward, close enough they were eye to eye. Dahlia reached out and touched her sister's cheek. "*I'm* choosing you, Rose. And life. For you."

Rose inhaled shakily, but she neither mounted an argument nor looked particularly happy.

"What do we do now?" Dahlia asked of the Hudson siblings.

"Jack's got a whole team," Anna said. "Deputies from a couple counties, some Feds, coming in from the north. Took us some time last night to track you down, but not too long. We've got an escape route to the south so we don't get caught in the..." Anna trailed off, looking first at Rose, then at Dahlia and then never finished.

Dahlia looked at her sister. Rose was staring off in the distance, her expression mutinous. But then it slowly changed, curving into a smile. Dahlia didn't trust that smile. She turned and looked at where Rose was looking while Anna was busy convincing Grant not to run toward the thick of things.

When Dahlia saw what Rose was smiling at, her heart stopped. A man standing on a hill with the perfect view of the four of them.

Holding a gun.

"Get down!" Dahlia yelled, going on instinct and tackling her sister to the ground.

CHAPTER TWENTY-TWO

IT HAPPENED QUICKLY. Dahlia yelled and dove for Rose at the same time Grant had been turning, because something had rippled up his spine. An old wartime sixth sense he'd been trying to ignore.

But Dahlia had seen it first, reacted first, and because Grant had been ignoring his instincts, he grabbed Anna just a second too late.

The gunshot went off, and his sister jerked and let out a yelp.

Grant didn't freeze. He was too well trained to freeze, but as he jumped into action to make sure they were all behind the RV and out of the shooter's target, as he checked to make sure Anna was okay, the *inside* of him froze. Even as he ordered Dahlia to keep an eye on Rose, even as Anna slapped him away and told him she was fine, he was nothing but ice.

"I'm okay," Anna said, giving him another shove with her good arm. She swore a few times, decidedly *not* proving her point. She was *bleeding*. Shot. His baby sister.

But she looked him in the eye. Fully conscious and dead serious. "It isn't bad, Grant. Look." She held up her arm. The bullet had ripped through her sleeve, and the wound bled, but he'd seen worse.

On *soldiers*. Not his baby sister.

"Your arm is burned to hell from that explosion, so don't give me any grief," Anna said.

He sucked in a breath, forcing those old war memories and deaths into the compartment they belonged in. The pain in his arm and everywhere else just seemed like old, faded memories, but Anna's comment made him understand they were real.

This was real. He was injured. And far too much was at stake. Dahlia was struggling with Rose. Trying to talk sense into her.

He didn't bother to tell Dahlia she was wasting her breath. It didn't matter. Dahlia had to do it. He understood that.

And he had to deal with the shooter. The anxiety about shooting he'd had ever since he'd been home tried to crop up. Anna was an okay shot, but she had a *wound* on her shooting arm. His burns were on his left hand.

And there was no way out if they didn't take down that shooter. And since *the gunman* kept shooting, popping one bullet against the RV after the next, Grant couldn't wait him out, hope for reinforcements and let another person get hurt.

"Give me your gun," Grant said to Anna.

She handed it over without a word. He'd done his level best to keep his shooting issues to himself, so she still thought of him as someone who could do this.

Which meant he had to.

"Don't hurt yourself, but see what you can do to help," he muttered at Anna, jutting his chin toward Rose and Dahlia's physical tussle.

"I've got four brothers. Easy peasy." She grinned at him, but she was pale and in pain and...

This had to end.

Grant took a deep breath, felt the weight of the gun and tried to block out everything else. Rose's shouts, Dahlia and Anna's earnest instructions for her to be quiet. The sound of gunfire farther off where maybe his brothers were getting themselves into a situation that—

No. Nothing else. Just taking out the gunman currently threatening him. So Anna didn't get hurt any more, and Dahlia and Rose remained as unscathed as possible.

It was up to him.

But not…*only* up to him. What he'd lost or forgotten in the military, what Dahlia had reminded him of when he'd told her about his nightmare, being honest the way his military therapist had warned him he needed to be—he was part of a family. A team. A *cog* in something bigger than himself.

Everything didn't fall on his shoulders. If it did, he'd still be in one of those tents somewhere trying to come up with a way to sneak Rose out of here against her will. He had a family, backup.

So, he only needed to take care of this one thing. And he *was* good at shooting. He *was* good at accomplishing things when he didn't let everything else crowd around and feel like only his responsibility.

He moved around the RV, calculating angles and where the shooter might be. That old calmness settled over him. When the shooter popped up the next time to fire toward the RV, Grant shot first.

He watched the man drop the gun and then tumble down the hill. He'd hit exactly where he'd meant to.

He let out a shaky breath he hadn't realized he'd been holding. He'd done it. Just like old times.

When he looked back at the women, Anna was right behind him, Dahlia having Rose somewhat subdued.

"Nice shot," Anna offered. "But you're sweating a little," she added with a grin that only trembled a *little* at the edges.

"Better than bleeding," he muttered. "Come on. Let's get the hell out of here."

GRANT AND ANNA led them away from the camp to the south so they could avoid the standoff to the north. Dahlia had to pull her sister, but Rose had stopped mounting arguments.

Granted, it probably had something to do with Anna's threat if she said one more damn word about the truth and sacrificing, Anna was going to knock her teeth out.

Yes, that hadn't been the kindest way of doing things, but it had certainly worked.

They walked for what seemed like forever, Rose walking slower and slower, her head bowing lower and lower as if each step added a weight to her back. Dahlia kept her arm firmly in Rose's but knew she couldn't reach her sister.

No one spoke, but they finally reached a small area where there were a few people milling about. There was a police cruiser and a truck. Mary rushed forward when they came into view.

"Take Anna to the hospital," Grant instructed, grabbing Anna's arm and nudging her toward Mary.

"I'm *fine*," Anna insisted. "He's the one with burns on his arm."

Mary exchanged a look with Grant over Anna's head. "Everyone else is okay?"

"Everyone here," Grant said. "Give us a few."

Mary nodded, offered Dahlia a kind smile and then took Anna toward the truck while a uniformed deputy walked over to them.

"Hey, Grant," the deputy said to him. "Ma'am," she added, nodding toward Dahlia. But when she spoke, it was to Grant. "Jack's handling up north, but he wanted me to tell you it's pretty much done. Collecting weapons, getting everyone transported. Arguing with the Feds, of course. The women will be taken to a psych eval, the men taken into whatever agencies have room. They'll sort it all out from there."

Grant nodded, then gestured at Rose. "She'll need to go with them. This is Rose Easton. The missing person Hudson Sibling Solutions has been working on."

The deputy nodded. "I can transport her myself, but I'm going to have to cuff her."

Grant looked back at Dahlia apologetically, but she understood. Much as she hated it.

"It's okay."

The deputy stepped forward, handcuffs outstretched. Rose didn't look at her, didn't mount a fight, but once the handcuffs were in place, she looked at Dahlia.

"You'll never stop the truth, Dahlia," she said. "Never."

Dahlia wanted to collapse right there, but Grant slid his arm around her shoulders as she watched her sister be lead away. "I know it seems dire," he murmured gently. "But she'll get the help she needs, and she'll be... more the woman you remember."

More. Not totally. Because no matter what help would do, Rose had been fundamentally changed in there. Just as Dahlia had been fundamentally changed trying to find her sister.

When she turned into Grant's chest, she didn't cry. But she let his gentle hold keep her upright, keep her from thinking in worst-case scenarios. He'd become… her rock. When she'd never once had one of those.

It turned out having someone to lean on was really a good thing. Because she knew, since he'd told her about his nightmare, he'd lean on her when he needed to.

But this was over, more or less, and he wasn't hers to lean on anymore. She closed her eyes and held on then for the last few moments of whatever this had been.

THE NEXT FEW days passed in such a blur. Dahlia didn't remember half of it. There were questions and cleanup and the Hudsons being absolute godsends.

They'd told her about cult detox programs, scholarships to pay for it. They'd driven her everywhere, taken care of everything and never once made her feel like even a second of a burden.

She supposed it was because they'd been raised with an understanding of cults. They'd never found their missing people, but they found answers for others and had learned how to tie up all those loose ends.

Rose was still antagonistic toward Dahlia, but she was settled in a facility not far outside of Sunrise. Dahlia knew that she couldn't keep sponging off the Hudsons, but the thought of going home, of being so far from Rose, and the people who'd become her friends…

It was too much. She didn't *want* to go home. She wanted to stay put.

She just didn't know how on earth she was going to make that happen.

Opportunity came from a surprising place. Dahlia was driving her car down Main after a visit with Rose when she saw Freya on the sidewalk frantically waving at her. Dahlia pulled her car to a stop and rolled down her passenger window as Freya jogged over.

"Freya. Hi. Is everything okay?"

"Hi." Freya smiled. "Sorry to flag you down, but I wasn't sure how to get in touch in a way that I didn't have to—well, anyway." She looked up and around the street, then leaned farther into Dahlia's passenger window. "I'm leaving town."

"Oh. Well." Dahlia didn't really know what to do with this information. "I hope for good reasons?"

"Yes! I got this job at a museum in Denver, and it's a great opportunity, and I've never been anywhere and—well, *anyway*," she said again. "My job is up for grabs. It doesn't pay much, but you seemed so taken with the library I thought I'd let you know. If you're interested, I can put in a good word for you with the library association who decides on hiring. I mean, they'd need a résumé and references and all that." Freya waved it away like it was nothing.

And it was…nothing. Dahlia knew she was qualified for a small-town library position. And it would… give her the means to stay close to Rose while she completed the detox program.

And Grant.

In the days since everything had gone down, he was always there. Making sure she ate, helping her with logistics for Rose's care and dealing with all the legalities for both of them. Bandaged up from wounds he'd gotten helping *her*. Helping *Rose*.

But he'd also been…careful. And brought up her leaving often. Not because he wanted her to go, she didn't think, more like he was preparing for the eventuality.

But this was an opportunity not to have that eventuality. She smiled at Freya. "I would love if you'd put in a good word for me."

"Here." Freya handed a little card across the way. "My email and cell. Send me all your stuff. I'll get it sorted."

Dahlia looked at the card, then up at Freya. "Can I ask...why?"

Freya grinned at her. "You said the exact right thing about the library that day, and I wouldn't want to give the job to someone who didn't understand. Besides, I've been making gooey eyes at Grant almost our whole lives and I've never once seen him look at *anyone* the way he looks at you."

Dahlia felt herself blushing. "Well..."

"Just send it ASAP. You'll be a shoo-in." She stepped back from the car and offered Dahlia a little wave.

On a deep breath, Dahlia pulled away from the curb and drove to the Hudson Ranch. When she pulled up to the house, Grant was waiting for her like he always was.

Willie yipped happily and sat next to her car, tail wagging wildly while she got out. She petted him, murmuring happy greetings to him before moving on to Grant.

"You look happy," he greeted. "It went well?"

"Not really," Dahlia replied, taking the seat next to him on the porch swing. He'd made this a kind of...routine. She would get back from a visit with Rose and he and Willie would be waiting. She could talk or just sit.

He really was such a *good* man. And no matter how she told herself, or maybe it was her mother's voice in her head, that she shouldn't make decisions based on any one person…he'd saved her. And Rose. He *cared*.

He was a good man, and she was in love with him. She didn't want to go back to Minnesota, where her life had been gray and boring. She wanted to stay *here*. With Grant.

She didn't want life to be quite as exciting as it had been the past few weeks, but she wanted a life with people who made her feel like the best version of herself.

"There was no change," Dahlia said, trying to accept the bolt of pain and believe it would ease. "She still hates me and went on about truth and sacrifices."

Grant wound his arm around her shoulder. "No matter what she says, she doesn't hate you."

She didn't reply that her sister wanting her dead for any kind of truth wasn't *love*, but she understood what he meant. Rose had been psychologically traumatized and needed time. She needed healing.

She'd give Rose time and herself a life.

"I can't keep staying here, Grant. It isn't right to use your family this way." She lifted her head from his shoulder. "And don't argue with me. It is *using*."

He gave her a tight smile. "All right." He studied her face, and none of that tenseness left his expression. "But whenever you come to visit Rose, you have a place to stay. With friends." He gave her shoulder a squeeze.

And Dahlia realized she'd explained it all wrong, so she laughed.

Which caused him to frown.

"Grant, I can't leave her here." She took a deep breath and used all that bravery she'd found over the past fourteen months. She reached out and touched his cheek. "And I don't *want* to leave you."

He blew out a shaky breath, leaning his forehead to hers. "Thank *God*," he said, making her laugh. He wanted her here. Thank God, indeed.

"Freya is moving to Denver and told me she'd help get me the librarian job."

Grant pulled back a little in surprise. "Freya? Librarian job...here?"

Dahlia nodded. "She said I'd be a shoo-in. It would be a job, so I'd have income. I could find a place of my own in Sunrise. Be close enough to visit Rose and—well, to have a life. Before Rose disappeared, I wasn't really living. I was just existing. Then Rose disappeared and I was only surviving. Now I want a *life*. Here. With friends and Rose and...you."

"Good. Because that's what I want too."

She leaned forward and pressed her mouth to his, not letting herself be afraid or guilty for reveling in the *good* for once.

"I love you, Dahlia," he murmured against her mouth.

It was her turn to let out a shaky "Thank God." She looked into those steady brown eyes and smiled. "I love you too."

So, they sat on the porch talking about the future, the sound of Willie's tail thumping a happy soundtrack to the beginning of a new life.

For both of them.

* * * * *